# THE DIARY OF A YOUNG GIRL

by
Anne Frank

**MAPLE PRESS**

THE DIARY OF A YOUNG GIRL by Anne Frank

Printed in 2018

**MAPLE PRESS PRIVATE LIMITED**
**sales office** A 63, Sector 58, Noida 201 301, U.P., India
**phone** +91 120 455 3581, 455 3583
**email** info@maplepress.co.in
**website** www.maplepress.co.in, www.maplelibrary.com

ISBN: 978-93-50332-10-8

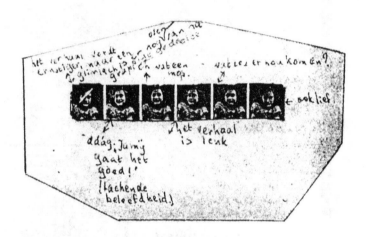

Captions of photos read from left to right:

*Things are getting more serious, but there's still a smile left over from the funny bits*
*Hello. "Yes I'm fine!" (smiling politely.)*
*Oh, what a joke.*
*That's a funny story.*
*Whatever next?*
*Nice one, as well.*

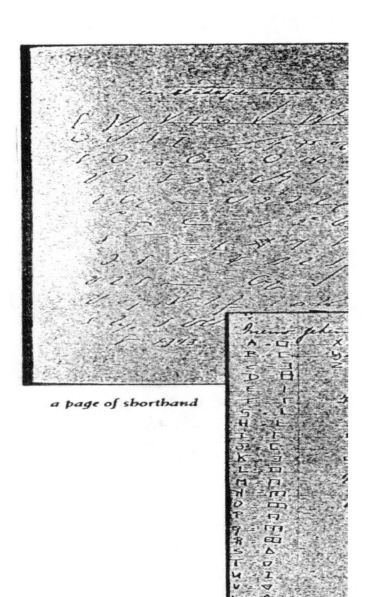

*a page of shorthand*

New secret code!

Anne at the Montessori School she attended in Amsterdam (now the Anne Frank School) until 1940, when Jewish children were ordered to attend separate schools.

*Ik zal hoop ik aan jou alles toevertrouwen, zoals ik het nog aan niemand gekund heb, en ik hoop dat je een grote steun voor me zult zijn.*
*Anne Frank. 12 Juni 1942.*

I hope I shall be able to confide in you completely, as I have never been able to do in anyone before, and I hope that you will be a great support and comfort to me.

# Sunday, 14 June, 1942

On Friday. June 12th, I woke up at six o'clock and no **wonder**[1]; it was my birthday. But of course I was not allowed to get up at that hour, so I had to control my **curiosity**[2] until a **quarter**[3] to seven. Then I could bear it no longer and went to the dining room, where I received a warm welcome from Moortje (the cat).

Soon after seven I went to Mummy and Daddy and then to the sitting room to **undo**[4] my presents. The first to greet me was *you*, possibly the nicest of all. Then on the table there were a bunch of roses, a plant, and some **peonies**[5], and more arrived during the day.

I got masses of things from Mummy and Daddy, and was thoroughly spoiled by various friends. Among other things I was given Camera Obscura, a party game, lots of sweets, chocolates, a puzzle, a **brooch**[6]. Totes and *Legends of the Netherlands* by Joseph Cohen, *Daisy's Mountain Holiday* (a **terrific**[7] book), and some money. Now I can buy The *Myths of* Greece and flame-grand!

Then Lies called for me and we went to school. During recess I treated everyone to sweet biscuits, and then we had to go back to our lessons.

Now I must stop. Bye-bye, we're going to be great pals!

---

1. Wonder – surprise
2. Curiosity – keenness to know
3. Quarter – one fourth of an hour; 15 minutes
4. Undo – to Open
5. Peonies – having large pink, red, white, or yellow flowers
6. Brooch – an ornament
7. Terrific – swesome

# Monday, 15 June, 1942

I had my birthday party on Sunday afternoon. We showed a film *The Lighthouse Keeper* with Rin-Tin-Tin, which my school friends **thoroughly**[8] enjoyed. We had a lovely time. There were lots of girls and boys. Mummy always wants to know whom I'm going to marry. Little does she guess that it's Peter Wessel; one day I managed, without **blushing**[9] or **flickering**[10] an eyelid to get that idea right out of her mind. For years Lies Goosens and Sanne Houtman have been my best friends. Since then, I've got to know Jopie de Waal at the Jewish Secondary School. We are together a lot and she is now my best girl friend. Lies is more friendly with another girl, and Sanne goes to a different school, where she has made new friends.

# Saturday, 20 June, 1942

I haven't written for a few days, because I wanted first of all to think about my diary. It's an **odd**[11] idea for someone like me to keep a diary; not only because I have never done so before, but because it seems to me that neither I-nor for that matter anyone else-will be interested in the **unbosomings**[12] of a thirteen-year-old schoolgirl. Still, what does that matter? I want to write, but more than that, I want to bring ou all kinds of things that lie buried deep in my heart.

There is a saying that "paper is more patient than man"; it came back to me on one of my slightly **melancholy**[13] days, while I sat chin in hand, feeling too bored and limp even to make up my mind whether to go out or stay at home. Yes, there is no doubt that paper is patient and as I don't intend to show this cardboard-covered notebook, bearing the proud name of "diary," to anyone, unless I find a real friend, boy or girl, probably nobody cares. And now I come to the root of the matter, the reason for my starting a diary: it is that I have no such real friend.

---

8. Thoroughly – complete
9. Blushing – to become red in the face
10. Flickering – shining unsteadily
11. Odd – unusual
12. Unbosoming – to confide
13. Melancholy – sadness

Let me put it more clearly, since no one will believe that a girl of thirteen feels herself quite alone in the world, nor is it so. I have darling parents and a sister of sixteen. I know about thirty people whom one might call friends-I have **strings**[14] of boy friends, **anxious**[15] to catch a **glimpse**[16] of me and who, failing that, peep at me through mirrors in class. I have relations, aunts and uncles, who are darlings too, a good home, no—I don't seem to lack anything. But it's the same with all my friends, just fun and joking, nothing more. I can never bring myself to talk of anything outside the common round. We don't seem to be able to get any closer, that is the root of the trouble. Perhaps I lack **confidence**[17], but anyway, there it is, a **stubborn**[18] fact and I don't seem to be able to do anything about it.

Hence, this diary. In order to **enhance**[19] in my mind's eye the picture of the friend for whom I have waited so long, I don't want to set down a series of **bald**[20] facts in a diary like most people do, but I want this diary itself to be my friend, and I shall call my friend Kitty. No one will grasp what I'm talking about if I begin ray letters to Kitty just out of the blue, so, **albeit**[21] unwillingly, I will start by **sketching**[22] in brief the story of my life.

My father was thirtysix when he married my mother, who was then twentyfive. My sister Margot was born in 1926 in Frankfort-On-Main, I followed on June 12,1929, and, as we are Jewish, we **emigrated**[23] to Holland in 1933, where my father was appointed Managing Director of Travies N.V. This firm is in close relationship with the firm of Kolen & Co. in the same building, of which my father is a partner.

The rest of our family, however, felt the full **impact**[24] of Hitler's anti-Jewish laws, so life was filled with anxiety. In 1938 after the pogroms, my two uncles (my mother's brothers) escaped to the U.S.A.

---

14. Strings – a line or series    15. Anxious – eagerly or earnestly desirous
16. Glimpse – a quick look    17. Confidence – trust or faith in a person or thing
18. Stubborn – unreasonably 19. Enhance – to make greater
20. Bald – undisguised    21. Albeit – even though
22. Sketching – making an outline    23. Emigrated – regien to settle in another
24. Impact – impression

My old grandmother came to us, she was then seventythree. After May 1940 good times rapidly fled: first the war, then the **capitulation**[25], followed by the arrival of the Germans, which is when the sufferings of us Jews really began. Anti-Jewish **decrees**[26] followed each other in quick succession. Jews must wear a yellow star*, Jews must hand in their bicycles, Jews are banned from **trams**[27] and are forbidden to drive. Jews are only allowed to do their shopping between three and five o'clock and then only in shops which bear the **placard**[28] "Jewish shop." Jews must be indoors by eight o'clock and cannot even sit in their own gardens after that hour. Jews are forbidden to visit theaters, cinemas, and other places of entertainment. Jews may not take part in public sports. Swimming baths, tennis courts, hockey fields, and other sports grounds are all prohibited to them. Jews may not visit Christians. Jews must go to Jewish schools, and many more restrictions of a similar kind.

So we could not do this and were **forbidden**[29] to do that. But life went on in spite of it all. Jopie used to say to me, "You're scared to do anything, because it may be forbidden." Our freedom was strictly limited. Yet things were still **bearable**[30].

Granny died in January 1942 no one will ever know how much she is present in my thoughts and how much I love her still.

In 1934 I went to school at the Montessori Kindergarten and continued there. It was at the end of the school year, I was in form 6B, when I had to say good-bye to Mrs. K. We both wept, it was very sad. In 1941 I went, with my sister Margot, to the Jewish Secondary School, she into the fourth form and I into the first.

So far everything is all right with the four of us and here I come to the present day.

---

* To distinguish them from others, all Jews were forced by the Germans to wear, prominently displayed, a yellow six-pointed star.

---

25. Capitulation – giving up
26. Decrees – an authoritative order having the force of law
27. Trams – a streetcar        28. Placard – a name plate on a door
29. Forbidden – not permitted by order or law        30. Bearable – tolerable

# Saturday, 20 June, 1942

Dear Kitty,

I'll start straight away. It is so peaceful at the moment. Mummy and Daddy are out and Margot has gone to play ping-pong with some friends.

I've been playing ping-pong a lot myself lately. We pingpongers are very **partial**[31] to an ice cream, especially in summer, when one gets warm at the game, so we usually finish up with a visit to the nearest icecream shop, Delphi or Oasis, where Jews are allowed. We've given up **scrounging**[32] for extra pocket money. Oasis is usually full and among our large circle of friends we always manage to find some kindhearted gentleman or boy friend, who presents us with more ice cream than we could **devour**[33] in a week.

I expect you will be rather surprised at the fact that I should talk of boy friends at my age. Alas, one simply can't seem to avoid it at our school. As soon as a boy asks if he may bicycle home with me and we get into conversation, nine out of ten times I can be sure that he will fall head over heels in love immediately and simply won't allow me out of his sight. After a while it cools down of course, especially as I take little notice of **ardent**[34] looks and pedal **blithely**[35] on.

If it gets so far that they begin about "asking Father" I **swerve**[36] slightly on my bicycle, my **satchel**[37] falls, the young man is bound to get off and hand it to me, by which time I have introduced a new topic of conversation.

These are the most innocent types; you get some who blow kisses or try to get hold of your arm, but then they are definitely knocking at the wrong door. I get off my bicycle and refuse to go further in their company, or I **pretend**[38] to be insulted and tell them in no **uncertain**[39] terms to clear off.

There, the foundation of our friendship is laid, till tomorrow!

Yours, Anne

---

31. Partial – unfair, inequitable  32. Scrounging – borrowing
33. Devour – consume  34. Ardent – sincere  35. Blithely – carefree
36. Swerve – to turn aside  37. Satchel – a small bag
38. Pretend – to give a false appearance of  39. Uncertain – not determined

# Sunday, 21 June, 1942

Dear Kitty,

Our whole class B, is **trembling**[40], the reason is that the teachers'
meeting is to be held soon. There is much **speculation**[41] as to who
will move up and who will stay put. Miep de Jong and I are highly
**amused**[42] at Wim and Jacques, the two boys behind us. They won't
have a **florin**[43] left for the holidays, it will all be gone on betting.
"You'll move up," "Shan't," "Shall," from morning till night. Even
Miep **pleads**[44] for silence and my angry outbursts don't calm them.

According to me, a quarter of the class should stay where they are;
there are some absolute cuckoos, but teachers are the greatest **freaks**[45]
on earth, so perhaps they will be **freakish**[46] in the *right* way for once.

I'm not afraid about my girl friends and myself, we'll **squeeze**[47]
through somehow, though I'm not too certain about my math. Still
we can but wait patiently. Till then, we cheer each other along.

I get along quite well with all my teachers, nine in all, seven masters
and two mistresses. Mr. Keptor, the old math master, was very
annoyed with me for a long time because I **chatter**[48] so much. So I
had to write a composition with "A Chatterbox" as the subject. A
chatterbox! Whatever could one write? However, deciding I would
puzzle that out later, I wrote it in my notebook, and tried to keep
quiet.

That evening, when I'd finished my other homework, my eyes fell
on the title in my notebook. I **pondered**[49], while chewing the end
of my fountain pen, that anyone can **scribble**[50] some nonsense in

---

40. Trembling – to feel fear          41. Speculation – opinion
42. Florin – a British coin worth two shillings
43. Amused – pleasing                 44. Pleads – humbly request
45. Freaks – something unusual        46. Freakish – markedly unusual
47. Squeeze – as in affection         48. Chatter – to talk rapidly
49. Pondered – reflect deeply on a subject
50. Scribble – careless hurried writing

large letters with the words well spaced but the difficulty was to prove beyond doubt the necessity of talking. I thought and thought and then, suddenly having an idea, filled my three allotted sides and felt completely satisfied. My arguments were that talking is a feminine characteristic and that I would do my best to keep it under control, but I should never be cured, for my mother talked as much as I, probably more, and what can one do about **inherited**[51] qualities? Mr. Keptor had to laugh at my arguments, but when I continued to hold forth in the next lesson, another composition followed. This time it was "Incurable Chatterbox" I handed this in and Keptor made no complaints for two whole lessons. But in the third lesson it was too much for him again. "Anne, as punishment for talking, will do a composition entitled 'Quack, quack, quack, says Mrs. Natterbeak.'" Shouts of laughter from the class. I had to laugh too, although I felt that my **inventiveness**[52] on this subject was **exhausted**[53]. I had to think of something else, something entirely original. I was in luck, as my friend Sanne writes good poetry and offered to help by doing the whole composition in verse. I jumped for joy. Keptor wanted to make a fool of me with this absurd theme, I would get my own back and make him the laughingstock of the whole class. The poem was finished and was perfect. It was about a mother duck and a father swan who had three baby ducklings. The baby ducklings were bitten to death by Father because they chattered too much. Luckily Keptor saw the joke, he read the poem loudly to the class, with comments, and also to various other classes.

Since then I am allowed to talk, never get extra work, in fact Keptor always jokes about it.

Yours, Anne

---

51. Inherited – occurring among members of a family
52. Inventiveness – skillful at inventing
53. Exhausted – to wear out completely

# Wednesday, 24 June, 1942

Dear Kitty,

It is boiling hot, we are all positively melting, and in this heat I have to walk everywhere. Now I can fully appreciate how nice a tram is, but that is a forbidden luxury for Jews- shank's mare is good enough for us, I had to visit the dentist in the Jan Luykenstraat in the lunch hour yesterday. It is a long way from our school in the Stadstimmertuinen; I nearly fell asleep in school that afternoon. Luckily, the dentist's assistant was very kind and gave me a drink-she's a good sort.

We are allowed on the ferry and that is about all. There is a little boat from the Josef Israelskade, the man there took us at once when we asked him. It is not the Dutch people's fault that we are having such a miserable time.

I do wish I didn't have to go to school, as my bicycle was stolen in the Easter holidays and Daddy has given Mummy's to a Christian family for safekeeping. But thank goodness, the holidays are nearly here, one more week and the **agony**[54] is over. Something amusing happened yesterday, I was passing the bicycle sheds when someone called out to me. I looked around and there was the nicelooking boy I met on the previous evening, at my girl friend Eva's home. He came **shyly**[55] towards me and introduced himself as Harry Goldberg. I was rather surprised and wondered what he wanted, but I didn't have to wait long. He asked if I would allow him to accompany me to school. "As you're going my way in any case, I will," I replied and so we went together. Harry is sixteen and can tell all kinds of **amusing**[56] stories. He was waiting for me again this morning and I expect he will from now on.

Yours, Anne

---

54. Agony – mental pain          55. Shyly – reserved
56. Amusing – entertaining

# Tuesday, 30 June, 1942

Dear Kitty,

I've not had a moment to write to you until today. I was with friends all day on Thursday. On Friday we had visitors, and so it went on until today. Harry and I have got to know each other well in a week, and he has told me a lot about his life; he came to Holland alone, and is living with his grandparents. His parents are in Belgium.

Harry had a girl friend called Fanny, I know her too, a very soft, dull creature. Now that he has met me, he realizes that he was just daydreaming in Fanny's presence. I seem to act as a **stimulant**[57] to keep him awake. You see we all have our uses, and **queer**[58] ones too at times!

Jopie slept here on Saturday night, but she went to Lies on Sunday and I was bored stiff. Harry was to have come in the evening, but he rang up at 6 p.m. I went to the telephone, he said, "Harry Goldberg here, please may I speak to Anne?"

"Yes, Harry, Anne speaking."

"Hello, Anne, how are you?"

"Very well, thank you."

"I'm terribly sorry I can't come this evening, but I ' would like to just speak to you; is it all right if I come 'in ten minutes?"

"Yes, that's fine, good-bye!"

"Good-bye, I'll be with you soon."

Receiver down.

I quickly changed into another frock and **smartened**[59] up my hair a bit. Then I stood **nervously**[60] at the window watching for him. At last I saw *him* coming. It was a wonder I didn't dash down at once; instead I waited patiently until he rang. Then I went down and he positively burst in when I opened the door. "Anne, my grandmother thinks you are too young to go out regularly with me, and that

---

57. Stimulant – energizer
58. Queer – unconventional, strange
59. Smartened – stylishness
60. Nervously – having a feeling of unease

I should go to the Leurs, but perhaps you know that I am not going out with Fanny any more!"

"No, why is that, have you quarreled?"

"No, not at all. I told Fanny that we didn't get on well together, so it was better for us not to go out together any more, but she was always welcome in our home, and I hope I should be in hers. You see, I thought Fanny had been going out with another boy and treated her accordingly. But that was quite untrue. And now my uncle says I should **apologize**[61] to Fanny, but of course I didn't want to do that so I finished the whole affair. That was just one of the many reasons. My grandmother would rather I went with Fanny than you, but I shan't; old people have such terribly oldfashioned ideas at times, but I just can't fall into line. I need my grandparents, but in a sense they need me too. From now on I shall be free on Wednesday evenings. Officially I go to wood-carving lessons to please my grandparents, in actual fact I go to a meeting of the Zionist Movement. I'm not supposed to, because my grandparents are very much against the Zionists. I'm by no means a **fanatic**[62], but I have a leaning that way and find it interesting. But lately it has become such a mess there that I'm going to quit, so next Wednesday will be my last time. Then I shall be able to see you on Wednesday evening, Saturday afternoon. Sunday afternoon, and perhaps more."

"But your grandparents are against it, you can't do it behind their backs!"

"Love finds a way."

Then we passed the bookshop on the corner, and there stood Peter Wessel with two other boys; he said "Hello"– it's the first time he has spoken to me for ages, I was really pleased.

Harry and I walked on and on and the end of it all was that I should meet him at five minutes to seven in the front of his house next evening.

Yours, Anne

---

61. Apologize – regretful acknowledgment of a fault
62. Fanatic – unreasoned enthusiasm

## Think and Ink...

➢ How grand was Anne's birthday celebrated?

➢ What glimpse do we get about Anne from her own description?

➢ How important is writing a diary? In what ways is it different from sharing feelings with a friend?

➢ Do you think that the life of Jews under Hitler's rule was miserable? What information from Anne prove you this?

➢ Though small, Anne's maturity in thoughts and deeds are apparent – comment on this with reference to Anne's attitude torwards boys.

➢ How friendly was Anne's nature even with her teachers?

➢ Anne had accepted her life as a Jew with all its miseries. How is this proved?

➢ What made her accept Harry Goldberg as her friend whole heartedly?

➢ Describe Harry's character as you find from Anne's details.

### Text-Based Questions

• What was Anne curious about? Why?

• What gifts did she get her birthday?

• Who are Anne's friends?

• Why did not she write for a few days?

• Why did she want to write a diary?

• Describe Anne's father as you find in the text.

- Why was the life of Anne's family members a cause for concern?

- How was the political situation during the time?

- How was Anne attached to her Granny?

- How was her education disturbed with the new situation?

- What was Anne's pastime during summer?

- How did she react to boys' approach?

- What interesting incident happened with Anne on the day of the teachers' meeting?

- How did Anne impress her Mr. Keptor? What concession was she given?

- What was the forbidden luxury for the Jews? How were they affected due to that?

- How did she befriend Harry?

- Who was Fanny?

- How was Anne a 'queer' use for Harry?

- What was Harry's idea about Anne?

# Friday, 3 July, 1942

Dear Kitty,

Harry visited us yesterday to meet my parents. I had bought a cream cake, sweets, tea, and fancy biscuits, quite a spread, but neither Harry nor I felt like sitting **stiffly**[1] side by side **indefinitely**[2], so we went for a walk, and it was already ten past eight when he brought me home. Daddy was very **cross**[3], and thought it was very wrong of me because it is dangerous for Jews to be out after eight o'clock, and I had to promise to be in ten to eight in future.

Tomorrow I've been invited to his house. My girl friend Jopie teases me the whole time about Harry. I'm honestly not in love, oh, no, I can surely have boy friends—no one thinks anything of that—but one boy friend, or **beau**[4], as Mother calls him, seems to be quite different.

Harry went to see Eva one evening and she told me that she asked him, "Who do you like best, Fanny or Anne?" He said, "It's nothing to do with you!" But when he left (they hadn't **chatted**[5] together any more the whole evening), "Now listen, it's Anne, so long, and don't tell a soul." And like a flash he was gone.

It's easy to see that Harry is in love with me, rather fun for a change. Margot would say, "Harry is a decent lad." I agree, but he is more than that. Mummy is full of praise: a good-looking boy, a well-behaved, nice boy. I'm glad that the whole family approve of him. He likes them too, but he thinks my girl friends are very childish, and he's quite right.

Yours, Anne

---

1. Stiffly – tightly
2. Indefinite – undecided
3. Cross – annoyed
4. Beau – the boyfriend of a woman or girl.
5. Chatted – light conversation

# Sunday Morning, 5 July, 1942

Dear Kitty,

Our examination results were announced in the Jewish Theater last Friday. I couldn't have hoped for better. My report is not at all bad, I had one *vix satis,* a five for algebra, two sixes, and the rest were all sevens or eights. They were certainly pleased at home, although over the question of marks my parents are quite different from most. They don't care a bit whether my reports are good or bad as long as I'm well and happy, and not too **cheeky**[6], then the rest will come by itself. I am just the opposite. I don't want to be a bad pupil; I should really have stayed in the seventh form in the Montessori School, but was accepted for the Jewish Secondary. When all the Jewish children had to go to Jewish schools, the headmaster took Lies and me conditionally after a bit of **persuasion**[7]. He **relied**[8] on us to do our best and I don't want to let him down. My sister Margot has her report too, brilliant as usual. She would move up with *cum laude* if that existed at school, she is so brainy. Daddy has been at home a lot lately, as there is nothing for him to do at business; it must be rotten to feel so **superfluous**[9]. Mr. Koophuis has taken over Travies and Mr. Kraler the firm Kolen. & Co. When we walked across our little square together a few days ago, Daddy began to talk of us going into hiding. I asked him why on earth he was beginning to talk of that already. "Yes, Anne," he said, "you know that we have been taking food, clothes, furniture to other people for more than a year now. We don't want our belongings to be seized by the Germans, but we certainly don't want to fall into their **clutches**[10] ourselves. So we shall disappear of our own accord and not wait until they come and fetch us."

"But, Daddy, when would it be?" He spoke so seriously that I grew very **anxious**[11].

---

| | |
|---|---|
| 6. Cheeky – offensively bold | 7. Persuasion – influence |
| 8. Relied – dependent for support | 9. Superfluous – not required |
| 10. Clutches – seizes | 11. Anxious – uneasy |

"Don't you worry about it, we shall arrange everything. Make the most of your **carefree**[12] young life while you can." That was all. Oh, may the fulfilment of these **somber**[13] words remain far distant yet!

Yours, Anne

## Wednesday, 8 July, 1942

Dear Kitty,

Years seem to have passed between Sunday and now. So much has happened, it is just as if the whole world had turned upside down. But I am still alive. Kitty, and that is the main thing. Daddy says.

Yes, I'm still alive, indeed, but don't ask where or how. You wouldn't understand a word, so I will begin by telling you what happened on Sunday afternoon.

At three o'clock (Harry had just gone, but was coming back later) someone rang the front doorbell. I was lying **lazily**[14] reading a book on the **veranda**[15] in the sunshine, so I didn't hear it. A bit later, Margot appeared at the kitchen door looking very excited. "The S.S. have sent a call-up notice for Daddy," she whispered. "Mummy has gone to see Mr. Van Daan already." (Van Daan is a friend who works with Daddy in the business.) It was a great shock to me, a call-up; everyone knows what that means. I picture **concentration**[16] camps and lonely cells— should we allow him to be **doomed**[17] to this? "Of course he won't go," declared Margot, while we waited together. "Mummy has gone to the Van Daans to discuss whether we should move into our hiding place tomorrow. The Van Daans are going with us, so we shall be seven in all." Silence. We couldn't talk any more, thinking about Daddy, who, little knowing what was going on, was visiting some old people in the Joodse Invalide; waiting for Mummy, the heat and suspense, all made us very **overawed**[18] and silent.

---

12. Carefree – free of worries     13. Somber – Serious
14. Lazily – disposed to idleness     15. Veranda – a porch or balcony
16. Concentration – intense mental application
17. Doomed–a decision or judgment  18. Overawed–overcome by a feeling of awe

Suddenly the bell rang again. "That is Harry" I said. "Don't open the door." Margot held me back, but it was not necessary as we heard Mummy and Mr. Van Daan downstairs, talking to Harry, then they came in and closed the door behind them. Each time the bell went, Margot or I had to **creep**[19] softly down to see if it was Daddy, not opening the door to anyone else.

Margot and I were sent out of the room. Van Daan wanted to talk to Mummy alone. When we were alone together in our bedroom, Margot told me that the call-up was not for Daddy, but for her. I was more frightened than ever and began to cry. Margot is sixteen; would they really take girls of that age away alone? But thank goodness she won't go. Mummy said so herself; that must be what Daddy meant when he talked about us going into hiding.

Into hiding-where would we go, in a town or the country, in a house or a cottage, when, how, where . ... ?

These were questions I was not allowed to ask, but I couldn't get them out of my mind. Margot and I began to pack some of our most **vital**[20] belongings into a school satchel. The first thing I put in was this diary, then hair curlers, handkerchiefs, schoolbooks, a comb, old letters; I put in the **craziest**[21] things with the idea that we were going into hiding. But I'm not sorry, memories mean more to me than dresses.

At five o'clock Daddy finally arrived, and we phoned Mr. Koophuis to ask if he could come around in the evening. Van Daan went and **fetched**[22] Miep. Miep has been in the business with Daddy since 1933 and has become a close friend, likewise her brandnew husband, Henk. Miep came and took some shoes, dresses, coats, underwear, and stockings away in her bag, promising to return in the evening. Then silence fell on the house; not one of us felt like eating anything, it was still hot and everything was very strange. We let our large,

---

19. Creep – to move stealthily or cautiously    20. Vital – of great importance
21. Craziest – affected with madness    22. Fetched – brought

upstairs room to a certain Mr. Goudsmit, a divorced man in his thirties, who appeared to have nothing to do on this particular evening; we simply could not get rid of him without being rude, he hung about until ten o'clock. At eleven o'clock Miep and Henk Van Santen arrived. Once again, shoes, stockings, books, and underclothes disappeared into Miep's bag and Henk's deep pockets, and at eleven-thirty they too disappeared. I was dog tired and although I knew that it would be my last night in my own bed, I fell asleep immediately and didn't wake up until Mummy called me at five-thirty the next morning. Luckily it was not so hot as Sunday, warm rain fell steadily all day. We put on heaps of clothes as if we were going to the North Pole, the sole reason being to take clothes with us. No Jew in our situation would have dreamed of going out with a suitcase full of clothing. I had on two vests, three pairs of pants, a dress, on top of that a skirt, jacket, summer coat, two pairs of stockings, laceup shoes, woolly cap, scarf, and still more; I was nearly **stifled**[23] before we started, but no one **inquired**[24] about that.

Margot filled her satchel with schoolbooks, fetched her bicycle, and rode off behind Miep into the unknown, as far as I was concerned. You see I still didn't know where our secret hiding place was to be. At seven-thirty the door closed behind us. Moortje, my little cat, was the only creature to whom I said farewell. She would have a good home with the neighbors. This was all written in a letter addressed to Mr. Goudsmit.

There was one pound of meat in the kitchen for the cat, breakfast things lying on the table, stripped beds, all giving the **impression**[25] that we had left **helter-skelter**[26]. But we didn't care about impressions, we only wanted to get away, only escape and arrive safely, nothing else. Continued tomorrow.

Yours, Anne

---

23. Stifled – feel breathless
24. Inquired – ask a question
25. Impression – an effect
26. Helter-skelter – haphazard

# Thursday, 9 July, 1942

Dear Kitty,

So we walked in the pouring rain. Daddy, Mummy, and I, each with a school satchel and shopping bag filled to the **brim**[27] with all kinds of things thrown together anyhow.

We got sympathetic looks from people on their way to, work. You could see by their faces how sorry they were they couldn't offer us a lift; the **gaudy**[28] yellow star spoke for itself.

Only when we were on the road did Mummy and Daddy begin to tell me bits and pieces about the plan. For months as many of our goods and **chattels**[29] and necessities of life as possible had been sent away and they were sufficiently ready for us to have gone into hiding of our own accord on July 16. The plan had had to be speeded up ten days because of the call-up, so our quarters would not be so well organized, but we had to make the best of it. The hiding place itself would be in the building where Daddy has his office. It will be hard for outsiders to understand, but I shall explain that later on. Daddy didn't have many people working for him: Mr. Kraler, Koophuis, Miep, and Elli Vossen, a twenty-three-year old typist who all knew of our arrival. Mr. Vossen, Ellis father, and two boys worked in the **warehouse**[30]; they had not been told.

I will describe the building: there is a large warehouse on the ground floor which is used as a store. The front door to the house is next to the warehouse door, and inside the front door is a second doorway which leads to a staircase (A) . There is another door at the top of the stairs, with a **frosted**[31] glass window in it, which has "Office" written in black letters across it. That is the large main office, very big, very light, and very full. Elli, Miep, and Mr. Koophuis work there in the

---

27.  Brim – full capacity                    28.  Gaudy – bright
29.  Chattels – personal property
30.  Warehouse – a place where goods are stored prior to their use
31.  Frosted – rusticated

daytime. A small dark room containing the safe, a wardrobe, and a large cupboard leads to a small somewhat dark second office. Mr. Kraler and Mr. Van Daan used to sit here, now it is only Mr. Kraler. One can reach Kralers office from the passage, but only via a glass door which can be opened from the inside, but not easily from the outside.

*This is a photograph of me as I wish I looked all the time. Then I might still have a chance of getting to Holywood. But at present, I'm afraid, I usually look quite different.*

Anne Frank
10 Oct. 1942
Sunday

From Kraler's office a long passage goes past the coal store, up four steps and leads to the showroom of the whole building: the private office. Dark, **dignified** [32] furniture, linoleum and carpets on the floor, radio, smart lamp, everything first class. Next door there is

32. Dignified – stately in appearance

a roomy kitchen with a hotwater **faucet**[33] and a gas stove. Next door the W.C that is the first floor.

A wooden staircase leads from the downstairs passage to the next floor (B). There is a small landing at the top. There is a door at each end of the landing, the left one leading to a storeroom at the front of the house and to the attics. One of those really steep Dutch staircases runs from the side to the other door opening on to the street (C).

The righthand door leads to our "Secret Annexe". No one would ever guess that there would be so many rooms hidden behind that plain gray door. There's a little step in front of the door and then you are inside.

There is a steep staircase immediately opposite the entrance (E). On the left a tiny passage brings you into a room which was to become the Frank family's bed-sitting-room, next door a smaller room, study and bedroom for the two young ladies of the family. On the right a little room without windows containing the washbasin and a small W.C. compartment, with another door leading to Margot's and my room. If you go up the next flight of stairs and open the door, you are simply **amazed**[34] that there could be such a big light room in such an old house by the canal. There is a gas stove in this room (thanks to the fact that it was used as a laboratory) and a sink. This is now the kitchen for the Van Daan couple, besides being general living room, dining room, and **scullery**[35].

A tiny little **corridor**[36] room will become Peter Van Daan's apartment. Then, just as on the lower landing, there is a large attic. So there you are, I've introduced you to the whole of our beautiful "Secret Annexe."

Yours, Anne

---

33. Faucet – a device for regulating the flow of a liquid
34. Amazed – to affect with great wonder
35. Scullery – a small room adjoining a kitchen
36. Corridor – gallery

Front and rear views of 263 Prinsengracht, the office building where the Franks and Van Daans hid for twenty-five months.

# Friday, 10 July, 1942

Dear Kitty,

I expect I have thoroughly bored you with my **longwinded**[37] descriptions of our **dwelling**[38]. But still I think you should know where we've landed.

But to continue my story-you see, I've not finished yet- when we arrived at the Prinsengracht, Miep took us quickly upstairs and into the "Secret Annexe." She closed the door behind us and we were alone. Margot was already waiting for us, having come much faster on her bicycle. Our living room and all the other rooms were **chockfull**[39] of rubbish, **indescribably**[40] so. All the cardboard boxes which had been sent to the office in the previous months lay piled on the floor and the beds. The little room was filled to the ceiling with bedclothes. We had to start clearing up immediately, if we wished to sleep in **decent**[41] beds that night. Mummy and Margot were not in a fit state to take part; they were tired and lay down on their beds, they were miserable, and lots more besides. But the two "clearers-up" of the family—Daddy and myself—wanted to start at once.

The whole day long we unpacked boxes, filled cupboards, hammered and tidied, until we were dead beat. We sank into clean beds that night. We hadn't had a bit of anything warm the whole day, but we didn't care. Mummy and Margot were too tired and keyed up to eat, and Daddy and I were too busy.

On Tuesday morning we went on where we left off the day before. Elli and Miep collected our rations for us. Daddy improved the poor blackout, we scrubbed the kitchen floor, and were on the go the whole day long again. I hardly had time to think about the great

---

37. Longwinded – tiresomely long
38. Dwelling – a place to live in
39. Chockfull – as full as possible
40. Indescribably – impossible to describe
41. Decent – good

change in my life until Wednesday. Then I had a chance, for the first time since our arrival, to tell you all about it, and at the same time to *realize* myself what had actually happened to me and what was still going to happen.

Yours, Anne

# Saturday, 11 July, 1942

Dear Kitty,

Daddy, Mummy, and Margot can't get used to the sound of the Westertoren clock yet, which tells us the time every quarter of an hour. I can. I loved it from the start, and especially in the night it's like a faithful friend. I expect you will be interested to hear what it feels like to "disappear"; well, all I can say is that I don't know myself yet. I don't think I shall ever feel really at home in this house, but that does not mean that I **loathe**[42] it here, it is more like being on vacation in a very peculiar boarding-house. Rather a mad idea, perhaps, but that is how it strikes me. The "Secret Annexe" is an **ideal**[43] hiding place. Although it leans to one side and is **damp**[44], you'd never find such a comfortable hiding place anywhere in Amsterdam, no, perhaps not even in the whole of Holland. Our little room looked very bare at first with nothing on the walls, but thanks to Daddy who had brought my filmstar collection and picture postcards on **beforehand**[45], and with the aid of paste pot and brush, I have transformed the walls into one **gigantic**[46] picture. This makes it look much more cheerful, and, when the Van Daans come, we'll get some wood from the **attic**[47], and make a few little cupboards for the walls and other odds and ends to make it look more lively.

Margot and Mummy are a little bit better now. Mummy felt well enough to cook some soup for the first time yesterday, but then

---

42. Loathe – disgust for
43. Ideal – highly satisfactory
44. Damp – slightly wet
45. Beforehand – early
46. Gigantic – very large
47. Attic – a space or room within the roof of a house

The entrance to the "Secret Annexe" with the bookshelf in place and with the bookshelf swung open, revealing the hidden staircase.

forgot all about it, while she was downstairs talking, so the peas were burned to a **cinder**[48] and refused to leave the pan. Mr. Koophuis has brought me a book called *Young People's Annual*. The four of us went to the private office yesterday evening and turned on the radio. I was so terribly frightened that someone might hear it that I simply begged Daddy to come upstairs with me. Mummy understood how I felt and came too. We are very nervous in other ways, too, that the neighbors might hear us or see something going on. We made curtains straight away on the first day. Really one can hardly call them curtains, they are just light, loose strips of material, all different shapes, quality, and pattern. which Daddy and I sewed together in a most unprofessional way. These works of art are fixed in position with drawing pins, not to come down until we **emerge**[49] from here.

There are some large business **premises**[50] on the right of us, and on the left a furniture workshop; there is no one there after working hours but even so, sounds could travel through the walls. We have forbidden Margotto cough at night, although she has a bad cold, and make her **swallow**[51] large doses of codeine. I am looking for Tuesday when the Van Daans arrive; it will be much more fun and not so quiet. It is the silence that frightens me so in the evenings and at night. I wish like anything that one of our protectors could sleep here at night. I can't tell you how **oppressive**[52] it is *never* to be able to go outdoors, also I'm very afraid that we shall be discovered and be shot. That is not exactly a pleasant **prospect**[53]. We have to whisper and tread lightly during the day, otherwise the people in the warehouse might hear us.

Someone is calling me.

Yours, Anne

---

48. Cinder – partly burned substance
49. Emerge – to come into view, develop
50. Premises – a building
51. Swallow – to pass through the mouth and throat into the stomach
52. Oppressive – burdensome
53. Prospect – something expected

## Think and Ink...

➢ What do you think is Anne's ideas about falling in love, and Harry's interest in her?

➢ What does Anne's reaction to her father's proposal to disappear indicate? Give reasons.

➢ What thoughts fill the mind of Anne as the family prepared themselves to go into hiding?

➢ What impressions does the situation create in your mind?

➢ Do you think Anne is happy with their new hiding place? Justify.

➢ How was life thrown out of gear for Anne?

### Text-Based Questions

• How did Anne treat Harry?

• Why was Anne's father angry?

• What was Anne's opinion about Harry?

• How is Anne different from her parents as far as her education is concerned?

• How did the headmaster favour Anne and Lies?

• Why did Anne's father decide to go on hiding?

• Why was the family anxious?

• What frightened Anne?

• What things did she pack?

- How was the day for the family?

- What preparations did the family make to move into the hiding?

- How did the family plan well before going into hiding?

- Describe the building where the family went into hiding.

- How was the situation after they shifted to the 'secret Annexe'?

- How did Anne come to terms with reality really?

- What does Anne call a faithful friend?

- Why did'nt Anne feel really at home in the house?

- Why did Anne call it a comfortable hiding place?

- How did Anne make the place cheerful?

- How was the family afraid of its neighbors? What did they do to protect themselves?

# Friday, 14 August, 1942

Dear Kitty,

I have **deserted**[1] you for a whole month, but honestly, there is so little news here that I can't find amusing things to tell you every day. The Van Daans arrived on July 13. We thought they were coming on the fourteenth, but between the thirteenth and sixteenth of July the Germans called up people right and left which created more and more **unrest**[2], so they played for safety, better a day too early than a day too late. At nine-thirty in the morning (we were still having breakfast) Peter arrived, the Van Daan's son, not sixteen yet, a rather soft, shy, **gawky**[3] youth; can't expect much from his company. He brought his cat (Mouschi) with him. Mr. and Mrs. Van Daan arrived half an hour later, and to our great amusement she had a large pottie in her hat box. "I don't feel at home anywhere without my chamber," she declared, so it was the first thing to find its permanent resting place under her **divan**[4]. Mr. Van Daan did not bring his, but carried a folding tea table under his arm.

From the day they arrived we all had meals **cozily**[5] together and after three days it was just as if we were one large family. Naturally the Van Daans were able to tell us a lot about the extra week they had spent in the **inhabited**[6] world. Among other things we were very interested to hear what had happened to our house and to Mr. Goudsmit. Mr. Van Daan told us:

"Mr. Goudsmit phoned at nine o'clock on Monday morning and asked if I could come around. I went immediately and found G. in a state of great **agitation**[7]. He let me read a letter that the Franks had

---

| | |
|---|---|
| 1. Deserted – abandoned | 2. Unrest – uneasy |
| 3. Gawky – not elegant | 4. Divan – a long backless sofa |
| 5. Cozily – warmly | 6. Inhabited – lived in |
| 7. Agitation – extreme emotional disturbance | |

left behind and wanted to take the cat to the neighbors as indicated in the letter, which pleased me. Mr. G. was afraid that the house would be searched so we went through all the rooms, tidied up a bit, and cleared away the breakfast things. Suddenly I discovered a writing pad on Mrs. Franks desk with an address in Maastricht written on it. Although I knew that this was done on purpose, I **pretended**[8] to be very surprised and shocked and urged Mr. G. to tear up this **unfortunate**[9] little piece of paper without delay.

I went on pretending that I knew nothing of your disappearance all the time, but after seeing the paper, I got a brain wave. 'Mr. Goudsrait'–I said–It suddenly **dawns**[10] on me what this address may refer to. Now it all comes back to me, a highranking officer was in the office about six months ago, he appeared to be very friendly with Mr. Frank and offered to help him, should the need arise. He was stationed in Maastricht. I think he must have kept his word and somehow or other managed to get them into Belgium and then on to Switzerland. I should tell this to any friends who may **inquire**[11]. Don't, of course, mention Maastricht.

"With these words I left the house. Most of your friends know already, because I've been told myself several times by different people."

We were highly amused at the story and, when Mr. Van Daan gave us further details, laughed still more at the way people can let their imagination run away with them. One family had seen the pair of us pass on bicycles very early in the morning and another lady knew quite definitely that we were **fetched**[12] by a military car in the middle of the night.

Yours, Anne

---

8. Pretended – supposed
9. Unfortunate – regrettable
10. Dawns – understood
11. Inquire – investigate
12. Fetched – brought

# Friday, 21 August, 1942

Dear Kitty,

The entrance to our hiding place has now been properly concealed[13]. Mr. Kraler thought it would be better to put a cupboard in front of our door (because a lot of houses are being searched for hidden bicycles), but of course it had to be a movable cupboard that can open like a door.

Mr. Vossen made the whole thing. We had already let him into the secret and he can't do enough to help. If we want to go downstairs, we have to first bend down and then jump, because the step has gone. The first three days we were all going about with masses of lumps[14] on our foreheads, because we all knocked ourselves against the low doorway. Now we have nailed a cloth filled with wood wool against the top of the door. Let's see if that helps!

I'm not working much at present; I'm giving myself holidays until September. Then Daddy is going to give me lessons; it's shocking how much I've forgotten already. There is little change in our life here. Mr. Van Daan and I usually manage to upset each other, its just the opposite with Margot whom he likes very much. Mummy sometimes treats me just like a baby, which I can't bear. Otherwise things are going better. I still don't like Peter any more, he is so boring; he flops lazily on his bed half the time, does a bit of carpentry, and then goes back for another snooze[15]. What a fool!

It is lovely weather and in spite of everything we make the most we can of it by lying on a camp bed in the attic, where the sun shines through an open window.

Yours, Anne

---

13. Concealed – hidden
14. Lumps – irregularly shaped masses
15. Snooze – a brief light sleep

## Think and Ink...

➤ How did Mr. Van Daan protect Anne's family?

➤ Do you think the family somehow got settled in their new place? How?

➤ Peter exhibits one of the common tendency of children comment.

## Text-Based Questions

• Why did Anne desert the readers?

• What did the Germans do?

• Who arrived at their place?

• What did Van Daans say about the inhabited word?

• What did Mr. Goudsmit find in their house?

• What did Mr. Van find on the writing desk?

• What did he tell Mr. Goudsmit about Mr. Frank?

• What were the views of Anne's neighbors about her family's whereabouts?

• Why and how was the hiding place concealed?

• What did Anne's family do to prevent themselves from knocking against the doorway why?

• How was life for Anne in the new place?

• Why didn't she like Peter?

• What was Anne's opinion about quarreling?

- What picture does Anne present about Peter?

- What were the causes for unpleasantness between Anne's mother and Mr. Van Daan?

- What was the little interruption the family had in their monotonous life?

- Why was Peter's curiosity aroused? What did he do?

- What reason did Anne's mother give for allowing Margot to read the book, and not Peter?

- How did Peter get hold of it? How was he caught hold of?

- How did Peter react? What was his punishment?

- Why does Anne call Mrs. Van Daan 'Unbearable'?

- What did Mr. Koophuis bring Anne?

- How did the children continue their studies?

- How was the family prepared for winter?

- Why did Anne refuse to show the book to Mrs. Van Daan?

# Wednesday, 2 September, 1942

Dear Kitty,

Mr. and Mrs. Van Daan have had a terrific quarrel. I've never seen anything quite like it before. Mummy and Daddy would never dream of shouting at each other. The cause was so **trivial**[1] that the whole thing was a pure waste of breath. But, still, everyone to his own liking.

Naturally it is very unpleasant for Peter, who has to stand by. No one takes him seriously, he is so frightfully **touchy**[2] and lazy. Yesterday he was badly upset because he found that his tongue was blue instead of red; this unusual phenomenon of nature disappeared just as quickly as it had come. Today he is going about with a **scarf**[3] on, as he has a stiff neck, in addition "M'lord" complains of lumbago. Pains around the heart, kidneys, and lungs are not unusual either, he is a real hypochondria (that's the word for such people, isn't it?)! It is not all honey between Mummy and Mrs. Van Daan. there is plenty of cause for unpleasantness. To give a small example, I will tell you that Mrs. Van Daan has taken all three of her sheets out of the common linen cupboard. She takes it for granted that Mummy's sheets will do for all of us. It will be a nasty surprise for her when she finds that Mummy has followed her good example.

Also, she is thoroughly **piqued**[4] that her dinner service and not ours is in use. She is always trying to find out where we have actually put our plates, they are closer than she thinks, they are in a cardboard box behind a lot of junk in the attic. Our plates are **ungettable**[5] at as long as we are here, and a good thing too. I always have bad luck, I **smashed**[6] one of Mrs. Van Daan's soup plates into a thousand pieces yesterday. "Oh!" she cried angrily. "Couldn't you be careful for once—that's the last one I've got." Mr. Van Daan is all sugar to me

---

1. Trivial – ordinary                    2. Touchy – oversensitive
3. Scarf – a long piece of cloth worn about the head
4. Piqued – a feeling of wounded pride        5. Ungettable – inaccessible
6. Smashed – to break (something) into pieces suddenly

nowadays. Long may it last. Mummy gave me another frightful sermon this morning; I can't bear them. Our ideas are completely opposite. Daddy is a darling, although he can sometimes be angry with me for five minutes on end. Last week we had a little interruption in our **monotonous**[7] life, it was over a book about women-and Peter. First I must tell you that Margot and Peter are allowed to read nearly all the books that Mr. Koophuis lends us, but the **grownups**[8] held back this particular book on the subject of women. Peter's curiosity was **aroused**[9] at once. What was it the two of them were not allowed to read in this book? He got hold of the book on the sly, while his mother was downstairs talking, and disappeared with his booty to the attic. All went well for a few days. His mother knew what he was doing, but didn't tell tales, until Father found out. He was very angry, took the book away, and thought that that would finish the whole business. However, he had not allowed for his son's curiosity, which **waxed**[10] rather than waned because of his father's attitude. Peter, determined to finish it, thought of a way to get hold of this **enthralling**[11] book. In the meantime, Mrs. Van Daan had asked Mummy what she thought about it all. Mummy thought this particular book was not suitable for Margot, but she saw no harm in letting her read most books.

"There is a great difference, Mrs. Van Daan," said Mummy, "between Margot and Peter. In the first place Margot is a girl and girls are always more grownup than boys, secondly, Margot has read quite a lot of serious books, and does not go in search of things that are **forbidden**[12] her, and thirdly, Margot is far more developed and intelligent, shown by the fact of her being in the fourth form at school." Mrs. Van Daan agreed, but still thought it was wrong in principle to let children read books which were written for grownups.

---

7. Monotonous – dull and tedious     8. Grownups – adults
9. Aroused – to stir up              10. Waxed – increased
11. Enthralling – holding the attention completely
12. Forbidden – to command (someone) not to do something

In the meantime Peter had found a time of the day when no one bothered[13] about him or the book: seventhirty in the evening—then everyone was in the private office listening to the radio. That was when he took his treasure to the attic again. He should have been downstairs again by eightthirty, but because the book was so thrilling he forgot the time and was just coming downstairs as his father came into the room. You can imagine the **consequences!**[14] With a slap and a **snatch**[15], the book lay on the table and Peter was in the attic. That's how matters stood as we sat down to table. Peter stayed upstairs—no one bothered about him, and he had to go to bed without any supper. We went on with the meal, **chattering**[16] **gaily**[17], when suddenly we heard a **piercing**[18] whistle; we all stopped eating and looked with pale changed faces from one to another. Then we heard Peter's voice, calling down the chimney, "I say, I'm not coming down anyway." Mr. Van Daan **sprang**[19] to his feet, his napkin fell to the floor, and **scarlet**[20] in the face he shouted, "I've had enough of this." Daddy took his arm, afraid of what might happen, and the two men went together to the attic. After a good deal of **resistance**[21] and stamping, Peter landed up in his room with the door closed and we went on eating. Mrs. Van Daan wanted to save one slice of bread for the dear boy, but his father stood firm. "If he doesn't **apologize**[22] soon, he will have to sleep in the attic." Loud protests from the rest of us, as we thought missing supper was quite enough punishment. Besides, Peter might catch cold and we couldn't call a doctor.

Peter did not apologize; he was already in the attic. Mr. Van Daan did nothing more about it, but I noticed! the next morning that Peter's bed had been slept in. Peter was back in the attic at seven

---

13. Bothered – concern oneself
14. Consequences – a penalty imposed for wrongdoing
15. Snatch – to capture
16. Chattering – to talk rapidly
17. gaily – happy manner
18. Piercing – painful
19. Sprang – moved suddenly on
20. Scarlet – vivid red
21. Resistance – a force that tends to oppose
22. Apologize – feel sorry openly

o'clock, but Daddy managed with a few friendly words to **persuade**[23] him to come down again. Sour faces and obstinate silences for three days and then everything went **smoothly**[24] once more.

Yours, Anns

# Monday, 21 September, 1942

Dear Kitty,

Today I'm going to tell you our general news.

Mrs. Van Daan is **unbearable**[25]. I get nothing but "blow-ups" from her for my continuous chatter. She is always **pestering**[26] us in some way or other. This is the latest: she doesn't want to wash up the pans if there is a fragment left, instead of putting it into a glass dish, as we've always done until now, she leaves it in the pan to go bad.

After the next meal Margot sometimes has about seven pans to wash up and then Madame says: "Well, well, Margot, you have got a lot to do!"

I'm busy with Daddy working out his family tree: as we go along he tells me little bits about everyone— it's terribly interesting. Mr. Koophuis brings a few special books for me every other week. I'm thrilled with the *Joop ter Heul* series. I've enjoyed the whole of Cissy van Marxveldt very much. And I've read *Sen Zomerzotheid* four times and I still laugh about some of the **ludicrous**[27] situations that arise.

Term time has begun again, I'm working hard at my French and manage to pump in five irregular verbs per day. Peter **sighs**[28] and **groans**[29] over his English. A few schoolbooks have just arrived; we have a good stock of exercise books, pencils, rubbers, and labels, as I brought these with me. I sometimes listen to the Dutch news from

---

23. Persuade – to induce to undertake a course of action
24. Obstinate – difficult to manage      25. Unbearable – unpleasant
26. Pestering – harassing with petty annoyances    27. Ludicrous – laughable
28. Sighs – to exhale audibly in a long deep breath
29. Groans – cries

London, heard Prince Bernhard recently. He said that Princess Juliana is expecting a baby about next January. I think it is lovely; it surprises the others that I should be so keen on the Royal Family.

I was being discussed and they decided that I'm not completely stupid after all, which had the effect of making me work extra hard the next day. I certainly don't want to still be in the first form when I'm fourteen or fifteen.

Also the fact that I'm hardly allowed to read any decent books was mentioned. Mummy is reading *Heeien, Vrouwen* en Knecbten now, which I'm not allowed (Margot is). First I must be more developed, like my talented sister. Then we talk about my **ignorance**[30] of philosophy and psychology, about which I know nothing. Perhaps by next'year I shall be wiser! (I looked up these difficult words quickly in *Koenen*.)

I have just woken up to the disturbing fact that I have one **longsleeved**[31] dress and three **cardigans**[32] for the winter. I've received permission from Daddy to knit a jumper of white sheep's wool; it's not very nice wool, but as long as its warm that's all that matters. We have some clothes deposited with friends, but unfortunately we shall not see them until after the war, that is if they are still there then. I had just written something about Mrs. Van Daan when in she came. Slap! I closed the book. "Hey, Anne, can't I just have a look?"

"I'm afraid not."

"Just the last page then?"

"No, I'm sorry."

Naturally it gave me a **frightful**[33] shock, because there was an **unflattering**[34] description of her on this particular page.

Yours, Anne

---

30. Ignorance – unaware
31. Long-sleeved – a part of a garment that covers all or part of an arm
32. Cardigans – a knitted garment
33. Frightful – terrifying
34. Unflattering – no good aspects

# Friday, 25 September, 1942

Dear Kitty,

Yesterday evening I went upstairs and "visited" the Van Daans. I do so occasionally to have a chat. Sometimes it can be quite fun. Then we have some moth biscuits (the biscuit tin is kept in the wardrobe which is full of moth balls) and drink lemonade. We talked about Peter. I told them how Peter often **strokes**[35] my cheek and that I wished he wouldn't as I don't like being **pawed**[36] by boys.

In a typical way parents have, they asked if I couldn't get fond of Peter, because he certainly liked me very much. I thought "Oh dear!" and said: "Oh, no!" Imagine it!

I did say that I thought Peter rather **awkward**[37], but that it was probably shyness, as many boys who haven't had much to do with girls are like that.

I must say that the Refuge Committee of the "Secret Annexe" (male section) is very **ingenious**[38]. I'll tell you what they've done now to get news of us through to Mr. Van Dijk, Travies' chief representative and a friend who has **surreptitiously**[39] hidden some of our things for us! They typed a letter to a chemist in South Zeeland, who does business with our firm, in such a way that he has to send the enclosed reply back in an addressed envelope. Daddy addressed the envelope to the office. When this envelope arrives from Zeeland, the enclosed letter is taken out, and is replaced by a message in Daddy's handwriting as a sign of life. Like this. Van Dijk won't become suspicious when he reads the note. They specially chose Zeeland because it is so close to Belgium and the letter could have easily been **smuggled**[40] over the border, in addition no one is allowed into Zeeland without a special permit; so if they thought we were there, he couldn't try and look us up.

Yours, Anne

---

35. Strokes – to rub lightly       36. Pawed – to strike
37. Awkward – uncomfortable        38. Ingenious – having great intelligence
39. Surreptitiously – obtained
40. Smuggled –to import or export without paying lawful customs charges or duties

# Sunday, 27 September, 1942

Dear Kitty,

Just had a big bust-up with Mummy for the **umpteenth**[41] time; we simply don't get on together these days and Margot and I don't hit it off any too well either. As a rule we don't go in for such **outbursts**[42] as this in our family. Still, it's by no means always pleasant for me. Margot's and Mummy's natures are completely strange to me. I can understand my friends better than my own mother-too bad!

We often discuss postwar problems, for example, how one ought to address servants.

Mrs. Van Daan had another **tantrum**[43]. She is terribly **moody**[44]. She keeps hiding more of her private belongings. Mummy ought to answer each Van Daan "disappearance" with a Frank "disappearance." How some people do **adore**[45] bringing up other people's children in addition to their own. The Van Daans are that kind. Margot doesn't need it,, she is such a goodygoody, perfection itself, but I seem to have enough mischief in me for the two of us put together. You should hear us at mealtimes, with **reprimands**[46] and cheeky answers flying to and fro. Mummy and Daddy always defend me **stoutly**[47]. I'd have to give up if it weren't for them. Although they do tell me that I mustn't talk so much, that I must be more retiring and not **poke**[48] my nose into everything, still I seem doomed to failure. If Daddy wasn't so patient, I'd be afraid I was going to turn out to be a terrific disappointment to my parents and they are pretty **lenient**[49] with me.

---

41. Umpteenth – relatively large
42. Outbursts – violent display
43. Tantrum – a fit of bad temper
44. Moody – temperament
45. Adore – like very much
46. Reprimands – criticize, warn
47. Stoutly – powerfully
48. Poke – a punch
49. Lenient – inclined not to be harsh

If I take a small helping of some vegetable I **detest**[50] and make up with potatoes, the Van Daans, and Mevrouw in particular, can't get over it, that any child should be so spoiled.

"Come along, Anne, have a few more vegetables," she says straight away.

"No, thank you, Mrs. Van Daan," *I* answer, "I have plenty of potatoes."

"Vegetables are good for you, your mother says so too. Have a few more," she says, pressing them on *me* until Daddy comes to my rescue.

Then we have from Mrs. Van Daan- "You ought to have been in our home, we were properly brought up. It's **absurd**[51] that Anne's so frightfully spoiled. I wouldn't put up with it if Anne were my daughter."

These are always her first and last words "if Anne were my daughter." Thank heavens I'm not!

But to come back to this "upbringing" business. There was a deadly silence after Mrs. Van Daan had finished speaking yesterday. Then Daddy said, "I think Anne is extremely well brought up she has learned one thing anyway, and that is to make no reply to your long **sermons**[52]. As to the vegetables, look at your own plate." Mrs. Van Daan was beaten, well and truly beaten. She had taken a minute helping of vegetables herself. But she is not spoiled! Oh, no, too many vegetables in the evening make her **constipated**[53]. Why on earth doesn't she keep her mouth shut about me, then she wouldn't need to make such **feeble**[54] excuses. Its **gorgeous**[55] the way Mrs. Van Daan **blushes**[56]. I don't, and that is just what she hates.

                                                        Yours, Anne

---

50. Detest – dislike intensely          51. Absurd – ridiculous
52. Sermons – lengthy and tedious speech
53. Constipated – stiff                 54. Feeble – inadequate
55. Gorgeous – dazzlingly beautiful     56. Blushes – feels embarrassed

# Monday, 28 September, 1942

Dear Kitty,

I had to stop yesterday, long, before I'd finished. I just must tell you about another **quarrel**[57], but before I start on that, something else.

Why do grownups quarrel so easily, so much, and over the most **idiotic**[58] things? Up till now I thought that only children **squabbled**[59] and that that wore off as you grew up. of course, there is sometimes a real reason for a quarrel, but this is just plain **bickering**[60]. I suppose I should get used to it. But I can't **nor**[61] do I think I shall, as long as I am the subject of nearly every discussion (they use the word "discussion" instead of quarrel). Nothing, I repeat, nothing about me is right; my general appearance, my character, my manners are discussed from A to Z. I'm expected (by order) to simply **swallow**[62] all the harsh words and shouts in silence and I am not used to this. In fact, I can't! I'm not going to take all these insults lying down. I'll show them that Anne Frank wasn't born yesterday. Then they'll be surprised and perhaps they'll keep their mouths shut when I let them see that I am going to start educating them. Shall I take up that **attitude**[63]? Plain **barbarism**[64]! I'm simply amazed again and again over their **awful**[65] manners and especially ... stupidity (Mrs. Van Daan's), but as soon as I get used to this—and it won't be long— then I'll give them some of their own back, and no half measures. Then they'll change their tune!

Am I really so badmannered, **conceited**[66], headstrong, pushing, stupid, lazy, etc., etc., as they all say? Oh, of course not. I have my faults, just like everyone else, I know that, but they thoroughly exaggerate everything.

---

57. Quarrel – an angry dispute
58. Idiotic – showing foolishness
59. Squabbled – a noisy quarrel
60. Bickering – a petty quarrel
61. Nor – not either
62. Swallow – to take back; retract
63. Attitude – a state of mind or a feeling
64. Barbarism – an act
65. Awful – terrible
66. Conceited – exaggerated opinion of oneself

Kitty, if only you knew how I sometimes boil under so many gibes[67] and jeers[68]. And I don't know how long I shall be able to stifle[69] my rage. I shall just blow up one day.

Still, no more of this, I've bored you long enough with all these quarrels. But I simply must tell you of one highly interesting discussion at table. Somehow or other, we got on to the subject of Pim (Daddy's nickname) extreme modesty. Even the most stupid people have to admit this about Daddy. Suddenly Mrs. Van Daan says, "I too, have an unassuming nature, more so than my husband."

Did you ever! This sentence in itself shows quite clearly how thoroughly forward and pushing she is! Mr. Van Daan thought he ought to give an explanation regarding the reference to himself. "I don't wish to be modest-in my experience it does not pay." Then to me: "Take my advice, Anne, don't be too unassuming[70], it doesn't get you anywhere."

Mummy agreed with this too. But Mrs. Van Daan had to add, as always, her ideas on the subject. Her next remark was addressed to Mummy and Daddy. "You have a strange outlook[71] on life. Fancy saying such a thing to Anne; it was very different when I was young. And I feel sure that it still is, except in your modern home." This was a direct hit at the way Mummy brings up her daughters.

Mrs. Van Daan was scarlet[72] by this time. Mummy calm and cool as a cucumber. People who blush get so hot and excited, it is quite a handicap[73] in such a situation. Mummy, still entirely unruffled[74], but anxious to close the conversation as soon as possible, thought for a second and then said: "I find, too, Mrs. Van Daan, that one gets on better in life if one is not overmodest[75]. My husband, now, and Margot, and Peter are exceptionally modest, whereas your

---

67. Gibes – to make taunting
68. Jeers – to abuse vocally
69. Stifle – cut off
70. Unassuming – modest
71. Outlook – an attitude, A point of view
72. Scarlet – of a strong to vivid red
73. Handicap – something that hampers
74. Unruffled – calm
75. Overmodest – shy especially in a playful

husband, Anne, you, and I, though not exactly the opposite, don't allow ourselves to be completely pushed to one side."

Mrs. Van Daan: "But, Mrs. Frank, I don't understand you; I'm so very modest and **retiring**[76], how can you think of calling me anything else?" Mummy: "I did not say you were exactly forward, but no one could say you had a retiring **disposition**[77]." Mrs. Van Daan: "Let us get this matter cleared up, once and for all. I'd like to know in what way I am pushing? I know one thing, if I didn't look after myself, I'd soon be **starving**[78]."

This absurd remark in **selfdefense**[79] just made Mummy rock with laughter. That irritated Mrs. Van Daan, who added a **string**[80] of GermanDutch, DutchGerman expressions, until she became completely **tongue-tied**[81]; then she rose from her chair and was about to leave the room.

Suddenly her eye fell on me. You should have seen her. Unfortunately, at the very moment that she turned round, I was shaking my head **sorrowfully**[82]—not on purpose, but quite **involuntarily**[83], for I had been following the whole conversation so closely.

Mrs. Van Daan turned round and began to reel off a lot of **harsh**[84] German, common, and ill-mannered, just like a **coarse**[85], red-faced fishwife—it was a **marvelous**[86] sight. If I could draw, I'd have liked to catch her like this; it was a scream, such a stupid, foolish little person!

---

76. Retiring – shy and reserved
77. Disposition – tendency
78. Starving – dying from extreme
79. Self defense – defense of what belongs to oneself
80. String – (here) sequence
81. Tongue-tied – speechless
82. Sorrowfully – expressing sorrow
83. Involuntarily – acting or done without or against one's will
84. Harsh – unpleasant
85. Coarse – of inferior quality
86. Marvelous – causing wonder or astonishment

Anyhow, I've learned one thing now. You only really get to know people when you've had a jolly good **row**[87] with them. Then and then only can you judge their true characters!

Yours, Anne

# Tuesday, 29 Sptember, 1942

Dear Kitty,

**Extraordinary** [88] things can happen to people who go into hiding. Just imagine, as there is no bath, I use a washtub and because there is hot water in the office (by which I always mean the whole of the lower floor) all seven of us take it in turns to make use of this great **luxury**[89].

But because we are all so different and some are more modest than others, each member of the family has found his own place for carrying out the performance. Peter uses the kitchen in spite of its glass door. When he is going to have a bath, he goes to each one of us in turn and tells us that we must not walk past the kitchen for half an hour. He seems to think this is **sufficient**[90]. Mr. Van Daan goes right upstairs; to him it is worth the bother of carrying hot water all that way, so as to have the **seclusion**[91] of his own room. Mrs. Van Daan simply doesn't bathe at all at present; she is waiting to see which is the best place. Daddy has his bath in the private office. Mummy behind a fire guard in the kitchen; Margot and I have chosen the front-office for our scrub. The curtains there are drawn on Saturday afternoons, so we wash ourselves in semi-darkness.

However, I don't like this place any longer, and since last week I've been on the **lookout**[92] for more comfortable quarters. Peter gave me

---

87.  Row – number of things or persons set out in a circle
88.  Extraordinary – beyond what is ordinary or usual
89.  Luxury – something expensive
90.  Sufficient – being as much as is needed
91.  Seclusion – privacy
92.  Lookout – keep watch

an idea and that was to try the large office W.C. *There* I can sit down have the light on, lock the door, pour my own bath water away, and I'm safe from **prying**[93] eyes.

I tried my beautiful bathroom on Sunday for the first time and although it sounds mad, I think it is the best place of all. Last week the plumber was at work downstairs to move the drains and water pipes from the office W.C. to the passage. This change is a **precaution**[94] against frozen pipes, in case we should have a cold winter. The plumber's visit was far from pleasant for us. Not only were we unable to draw water the whole day, but we could not go to the W.C. either. Now it is rather indecent f tell you what we did to overcome this difficulty, however, I'm not such a prude that I can't talk about these things.

The day we arrived here. Daddy and I improvised a pottie for ourselves, not having a better **receptacle**[95], we sacrificed a glass preserving jar for this purpose. During the plumber's visit, natures offerings were deposited in these jars in the sitting room during the day, I don't think this was nearly as bad as having to sit still and not talk the whole day. You can't imagine what a trial that was for "Miss Quack-Quack." I have to whisper on ordinary days, but not being able to speak or move was ten times worse. After being **flattened**[96] by three days of continuous sitting, my bottom was very stiff and painful. Some exercises at bedtime helped.

Yours, Anne

---

93. Prying – offensive inquisitiveness
94. Precaution – one that serves as protection or a guard
95. Receptacle – a container that holds items or matter
96. Flattened – made low

## Think and Ink...

➤ What was Mrs. Vaan's opinion about Anne?

➤ What practical difficulties does Anne throw light on in their new hiding place?

## Text-Based Questions

- Why did Anne visit the Van Daans? What did she do there?
- Why didn't Anne like Peter?
- Why did Anne call the Refuge Committee ingenious?
- What was the tiff between Anne and her mother?
- What was Anne's self-appraisal?
- What was Mrs. Van Daan's opinion about Anne? Why?
- How did Anne's father defend her?
- How did the argument end?
- What was Anne's views regarding Mrs. Van Daan's discussions about her?
- What did Mrs. Van Daan argue with Mrs. Frank?
- How did Anne react to Mrs. Van's disposition?
- What was a luxury for the Frank family?
- Where do the different members wash themselves?
- Which place did Peter suggest to Anne for bathing?
- Why were the people in the house unable to draw water?

# Thursday, I October, 1942

Dear Kitty,

I got a **terrible**[1] shock yesterday. Suddenly at eight o'clock the bell rang loudly. Of course, I thought that someone had come: you'll guess who I mean. But I calmed down a bit when everyone said it must be some **urchins**[2] or perhaps the postman.

The days are becoming very quiet here. Lewin, a small Jewish chemist and **dispenser**[3], works for Mr. Kraler in the kitchen. He knows the whole building well and therefore we are always afraid that he'll take it into his head to have a peep in the old laboratory. We are as quiet as mice. Who, three months ago, would ever have guessed that **quicksilver**[4] Anne would have to sit still for hours— and, what's more, could?

The twenty-ninth was Mrs. Van Daan's birthday. Although it could not be celebrated in a big way, we managed a little party in her honor, with a specially nice meal, and, she received some small presents and flowers. Red **carnations**[5] from her husband, that seems to be a family tradition. To pause for a moment on the subject of Mrs. Van Daan, I must tell you that her attempts to **flirt**[6] with Daddy are a source of continual irritation for me. She **strokes**[7] his face and hair, pulls her skirt right up, and makes socalled witty remarks, trying in this way to attract Pim's attention. Pim, thank goodness, doesn't find her either attractive or funny, so he doesn't play ball. Mummy doesn't behave like that with Mr. Van Daan, I've said that to Mrs. Van Daan's face.

Now and then Peter comes out of his shell and can be quite funny. We have one thing in common, from which everyone usually gets a

---

1. Terrible – dreadful
2. Urchins – mischievous youngster
3. Dispenser – a person or thing that dispenses
4. Quicksilver – rapid or unpredictable in movement or change
5. Carnations – a flower
6. Flirt – to make playfully romantic
7. Strokes – to rub lightly

lot of **amusement**[8]: we both love dressing up. He appeared in one of Mrs. Van Daan's very narrow dresses and I put on his suit. He wore a hat and I a cap. The grownups were doubled up with laughter and we enjoyed ourselves as much as they did. Elli has bought new skirts for Margot and me at Bijenkorf's. The material is rotten, just like sacking, and they cost 24.00 florins and 7.50 florins respectively. What a difference compared with before the war!

Another nice thing I've been keeping up my sleeve. Elli has written to some **secretarial**[9] school or other and ordered a correspondence course in shorthand for Margot, Peter, and me. You wait and see what perfect experts we shall be by next year. In any case it's extremely important to be able to write in a code.

Yours, Anne

## Saturday, 3 October, 1942

Dear Kitty,

There was another **bust-up**[10] yesterday. Mummy **kicked**[11] up a frightful row and told Daddy just what she thought of me.

Then she had an awful fit of tears so, of course, off I went too, and I'd got such an awful headache anyway. Finally I told Daddy that I'm much more fond of him than Mummy, to which he replied that I'd get over that. But I don't believe it. I have to simply force myself to stay calm with her. Daddy wishes that I would sometimes **volunteer**[12] to help Mummy, when she doesn't feel well or has a headache, but I shan't. I am working hard at my French and am now reading *La Belle Nivernaise*.

Yours, Anne

---

8. Amusement – entertains
9. Secretarial – a person employed to handle correspondence
10. Bust-up – a quarrel
11. Kicked – opposed by argument
12. Volunteer – a person who performs

# Friday, 9 October, 1942

Dear Kitty,

I've only got **dismal**[13] and depressing news for you today. Our many Jewish friends are being taken away by the dozen. These people are treated by the Gestapo without a **shred**[14] of decency, being loaded into cattle trucks and sent to Westerbork, the big Jewish camp in Drente. Westerbork sounds terrible: only one washing cubicle for a hundred people and not nearly enough lavatories. There is no separate accommodation. Men, women, and children all sleep together. One hears of frightful **immorality**[15] because of this; and a lot of the women, and even girls, who stay there any length of time are expecting babies.

It is impossible to escape, most of the people in the camp are branded as inmates by their shaven heads and many also by their Jewish appearance.

If it is as bad as this in Holland whatever will it be like in the distant and barbarous regions they are sent to? We assume that most of them are murdered. The English radio speaks of their being **gassed**[16].

Perhaps that is the quickest way to die. I feel terribly upset. I couldn't tear myself away while Miep told these **dreadful**[17] stories and she herself was equally **wound up**[18] for that matter. Just recently for instance, a poor old **crippled**[19] Jewess was sitting on her doorstep; she had been told to wait there by the Gestapo, who had gone to **fetch**[20] a car to take her away. The poor old thing was terrified by the guns that were shooting at English planes overhead, and by the glaring

---

13. Dismal – depression      14. Shred – a small amount
15. Immorality – morally objectionable behavior   16. Gassed – intoxicated
17. Dreadful – extremely unpleasant
18. Wound up – brought to a state of great tension
19. Crippled – a person or animal that is partially disabled
20. Fetch – bring

beams of the **searchlights**[21]. But Miep did not dare take her in, no one would undergo such a risk. The Germans strike without the **slightest**[22] mercy. Elli too is very quiet: her boy friend has got to go to Germany. She is afraid that the airmen who fly over our homes will drop their bombs, often weighing a million kilos, on Dirk's head. Jokes such as "he's not likely to get a .million" and "it only takes one bomb" are in rather bad taste. Dirk is certainly not the only one who has to go: trainloads of boys leave daily. If they stop at a small station **en route**[23], sometimes some of them manage to get out unnoticed and escape, perhaps a few manage it. This, however, is not the end of my bad news. Have you ever heard of hostages? That's the latest thing in **penalties**[24] for **sabotage**[25]. Can you imagine anything so dreadful?

**Prominent**[26] citizens—innocent people—are thrown into prison to await their fate. If the **saboteur**[27] can't be traced, the Gestapo simply put about five hostages against the wall. Announcements of their deaths appear in the papers frequently. These **outrages**[28] are described as "fatal accidents." Nice people, the Germans! To think that I was once one of them too! No, Hitler took away our nationality long ago. In fact. Germans and Jews are the greatest enemies in the world.

Yours, Anne

---

21. Searchlights – a flashlight
22. Slightest – smallest amount
23. En Route – on or along the way
24. Penalties – required as a forfeit for an offense
25. Sabotage – damage
26. Prominent – immediately noticeable
27. Saboteur – deliberately causes wrecks
28. Outrages – an act of extreme violence

# Friday, 16 October, 1942

Dear Kitty,

I'm terribly busy. I've just translated a chapter out of *La Belle Nivemaise* and made notes of new words. Then a perfectly foul math problem and three pages of French grammar. I **flatly**[29] refuse to do these math problems every day. Daddy agrees that they're **vile**[30]. I'm almost better at them than he is, though neither of us are much good and we often have to **fetch**[31] Margot. I'm the **furthest**[32] one of the three of us in shorthand.

Yesterday I finished *The Assault. Us* quite amusing, but doesn't touch Joop fer *Heul* As a matter of fact, I think Cissy van Marxveldt is a firstrate writer. I shall definitely let my children read her books. Mummy, Margot, and I are as **thick**[33] as thieves again. Its really much better. Margot and I got in the same bed together last evening; it was a frightful **squash**[34], but that was just the fun of it. She asked if she could read my diary. I said "Yes—at least, bits of it", and then I asked if I could read hers and she said "Yes." Then we got on to the subject of the future. I asked her what she wanted to be. But she wouldn't say and made a great secret of it. I gathered something about teaching, I'm not sure if I'm right, but I think so. Really, I shouldn't be so curious!

This morning I was lying on Peter's bed, having chased him off at first. He was furious with me, not that I cared very much. He might be a bit more friendly with me for once, after all I did give him an apple yesterday.

I asked Margot if she thought I was very ugly. She said that I was quite attractive and that I had nice eyes. Rather vague, don't you think?

Till next time,

Yours, Anne

---

29. Flatly – directly        30. Vile – disgusting        31. Fetch – bring
32. Furthest – at the greatest distance in time or space
33. Thick – (here) close; intimate        34. Squash – (here) act

Dit is een foto, zoals ik me zou wensen, altijd zo te zijn. Dan had ik nog wel een kans om naar Holywood te komen. Maar tegenwoordig zie ik er jammer genoeg meestal anders uit.

Annefrank.

10 Oct. 1942 Zondag.

This is a photograph of me as I wish I looked all the time. Then I might still have a chance of getting to Holywood. But at present, I'm afraid, I usually look quite different.

Anne Frank
10 Oct. 1942
Sunday

# Tuesday, 20 October, 1942

Dear Kitty,

My hand still shakes, although it's two hours since we had the shock. I should explain that there are five fire **extinguishers**[35] in the house. We knew that someone was coming to fill them, but no, one had **warned**[36] us when the carpenter, or whatever you call him, was coming.

The result was that we weren't making any attempt to keep quiet, until I heard **hammering**[37] outside on the landing opposite our cupboard door. I thought of the carpenter at once and warned Elli, who was having a meal with us, that she shouldn't go downstairs. Daddy and I posted ourselves at the door so as to hear when the man left. After he'd been working for a quarter of an hour, he laid his hammer and tools down on top of our cupboard (as we thought) and knocked at our door. We turned absolutely white. Perhaps he had heard something after all and wanted to **investigate**[38] our secret den. It seemed like it. The knocking, pulling, pushing, and **wrenching**[39] went on. I nearly fainted at the thought that this **utter**[40] stranger might discover our beautiful secret hiding place. And just as I thought my last hour was at hand, I heard Mr. Koophuis say, "Open the door, it's only me." We opened it immediately. The hook that holds the cupboard, which can be undone by people who know the secret, had got **jammed**[41]. That was why no one had been able to warn us about the carpenter. The man had now gone downstairs and Koophuis wanted to fetch Elli, but couldn't open the cupboard again. It was a great relief to me, I can tell you. In my imagination the man

---

35. Extinguishers – mechanical devices
36. Warned – notify
37. Hammering – a tool or device similar in function
38. Investigate – to observe
39. Wrenching – twisting objects
40. Utter – complete, total
41. Jammed – blocked

who I thought was trying to get in had been growing and growing in size until in the end he appeared to be a giant and the greatest **fascist**[42] that ever walked the earth.

Well! Well! Luckily everything was okay this time. Meanwhile we had great fun on Monday. Miep and Henk spent the night here. Margot and I went in Mummy and Daddy's room for the night, so that the Van Santens could have our room. The meal tasted **divine**[43]. There was one small interruption. Daddy's lamp blew a **fuse**[44], and all of a sudden we were sitting in darkness. What was to be done? There was some fuse wire in the house, but the fuse box is right at the very back of the dark storeroom—not such a nice job after dark. Still the men **ventured**[45] forth and after ten minutes we were able to put the candles away again.

I got up early this morning. Henk had to leave at half past eight. After a cozy breakfast Miep went downstairs. It was pouring and she was glad not to have to cycle to the office. Next week Elli is coming to stay for a night.

Yours, Anne

# Thursday, 29 October, 1942

Dear Kitty,

I am awfully worried. Daddy is ill. He has a high temperature and a red rash, it looks like **measles**[46]. Think of it, we can't even call a doctor! Mummy is letting him have a good sweat. Perhaps that will send his temperature down.

This morning Miep told us all that all the furniture has been removed from the Van Daans' home. We haven't told Mrs. Van Daan yet. She's such a bundle of **nerves**[47] already, and we don't feel like

---

42. Fascist – a reactionary or dictatorial person
43. Divine – perfect                         44. Fuse – an electric circuit
45. Ventured – put at risk
46. Measles – an acute form of viral infection 47. Nerves – anxiety

listening to another **moan**[48] over all the lovely china and beautiful chairs that she left at home.

We had to leave almost all our nice things behind so what's the good of **grumbling**[49] about it now?

I'm allowed to read more grownup books lately. I'm now reading *Eva's Youth* by Nico van Suchtelen. I can't see much difference between this and the schoolgirl love stories. It is true there are bits about women selling themselves to unknown men in back streets. They ask a packet of money for it. I'd die of shame if anything like that happened to me. Also it says that Eva has a monthly period. Oh, I'm so longing to have it too, it seems so important. Daddy has brought the plays of Goethe and Schiller from the big cupboard. He is going to read to me every evening. We've started with *Don Carlos*.

Following Daddy's good example. Mummy has **pressed**[50] her prayer book into my hand. For decency's sake I read some of the prayers in German, they are certainly beautiful but they don't convey much to me. Why does she force me to be **pious**[51], just to oblige her?

Tomorrow we are going to light the fire for the first time. I expect we shall be **suffocated**[52] with smoke. The chimney hasn't been **swept**[53] for ages, let's hope the thing **draws**[54].

Yours, Anne

---

48. Moan – displeasure
49. Grumbling –complain in a surly manner
50. Pressed – insistently
51. Pious – morally excellent
52. Suffocated – to block the air passages
53. Swept – brush
54. Draws – uncover something

## Think and Ink...

> ➤ Describe the significance of Anne's remark, 'what a difference compared with before the war'.

> ➤ How did Hitler take away the nationality of the Jews? How did his army make Germans and the Jews, the greatest enemies in the world?

> ➤ Do you think Anne is a bit self conscious? How does her diary entry of 16 October 1942 prove it?

> ➤ What element of surprise do you find in the diary entry of 20 October 1942?

> ➤ Living in a hide out and falling ill is the worst thing that one could face. Comment on this with reference to the diary entry of 29 October 1942.

## Text-Based Questions

- Why was Anne terribly shocked?

- Why were Anne's family members afraid of Lewin?

- How was Mrs. Van Daan's birthday celebrated?

- What was in common with Peter and Anne?

- How did they both amuse others?

- What did Elli arrange for?

- Why couldn't Anne help her mother?

- What was the depressing news Anne shared with Kitty?

- Why was there no escape from their fate for the Jews?

- How were the Jews in Holland murdered?

- How did the boys escape the Germans?

- What was done to prominent citizens?

- Why were the outrages called as 'fatal accidents'?

- How did Anne keep herself busy?

- What does Anne mean when she says, 'as thick as thieves'?

- Why was Peter furious with Anne?

- What shock did the family have?

- How was the family frightened?

- Who was the greatest fascist that Anne describe? Why did she say so?

- What happened when the candles went off?

- What was the saddening thing about the Frank family?

- What did Anne's mother insist on her?

# Saturday, 7 November, 1942

Dear Kitty,

Mummy is frightfully **irritable**[1] and that always seems to **herald**[2] unpleasantness for me. Is it just chance that Daddy and Mummy never **rebuke**[3] Margot and that they always drop on me for everything? Yesterday evening, for instance: Margot was reading a book with lovely drawings in it; she got up and went upstairs, put the book down ready to go on with it later. I wasn't doing anything, so picked up the book and started looking at the pictures. Margot came back, saw "her" book in my hands, **wrinkled**[4] her forehead and asked for the book back. Just because I wanted to look a little further on, Margot got more and more angry. Then Mummy joined in: "Give the book to Margot, she was reading it," she said. Daddy came into the room. He didn't even know what it was all about, but saw the **injured**[5] look on Margot's face and **promptly**[6] dropped on me: "I'd like to see what you'd say if Margot ever started looking at one of your books!" I gave way at once, laid the book down, and left the room–**offended**[7], as they thought. It so happened I was neither offended nor **cross**[8], just **miserable**[9]. It wasn't right of Daddy to judge without knowing what the **squabble**[10] was about. I would have given Margot the book myself, and much more quickly, if Mummy and Daddy hadn't interfered. They took Margot's part at once, as though she were the **victim**[11] of some great **injustice**[12].

Its obvious that Mummy would **stick**[13] up for Margot, she and Margot always do back each other up. I'm so used to that that I'm utterly **indifferent**[14] to both Mummy's **jawing**[15] and Margot's moods.

---

1. Irritable – annoyed  2. Herald – indicate  3. Rebuke – to criticize
4. Wrinkled – a line or crease in the skin
5. Injured – hurt    6. Promptly – immediately
7. Offended – to be displeasing    8. Cross – frustration
9. Miserable – very uncomfortable    10. Squabble – a noisy quarrel
11. Victim – one who is harmed by or made to suffer from an act
12. Injustice – lack of justice    13. Stick Up – support
14. Indifferent – impartial    15. Jawing – converse

I love them, but only because they are Mummy and Margot. With Daddy it's different. If he holds Margot up as an example, approves of what she does, praises and **caresses**[16] her, then something **gnaws**[17] at me inside, because I **adore**[18] Daddy. He is the one I look up to. I don't love anyone in the world but him. He doesn't notice that he treats Margot differently from me. Now Margot is just the prettiest, sweetest, most beautiful girl in the world. But all the same I feel I have some right to be taken seriously too. I have always been the **dunce**[19], the ne'erdowell of the family, I've always had to pay double for my deeds, first with the **scolding**[20] and then again because of the way my feelings are hurt. Now I'm not satisfied with this apparent **favoritism**[21] any more. I want something from Daddy that he is not able to give me.

I'm not **jealous**[22] of Margot, never have been. I don't envy her good looks or her beauty. It is only that I long for Daddy's real love: not only as his child, but for me— Anne, myself.

I **cling**[23] to Daddy because it is only through him that I am able to **retain**[24] the **remnant**[25] of family feeling. Daddy doesn't understand that I need to give **vent**[26] to my feelings over Mummy sometimes. He doesn't want to talk about it. he simply avoids anything which might lead to remarks about Mummy's **failings**[27]. Just the same. Mummy and her failings are something I find harder to bear than anything else. I don't know how to keep it all to myself. I can't always be drawing attention to her **untidiness**[28], her **sarcasm**[29], and her lack of sweetness, neither can I believe that I'm always in the wrong.

---

16. Caresses – to touch
17. Gnaws – become ground down or deteriorate
18. Adore – to like very much      19. Dunce – slow to learn
20. Scolding – reprimanding      21. Favoritism– unfair treatment of a person
22. Jealous – envious      23. Cling – to remain close
24. Retain – to maintain possession of
25. Remnant – something left over  26. Vent – to express
27. Failings – minor faults      28. Untidiness – unorganized
29. Sarcasm – often ironic remark intended to wound

We are **exact**[30] opposites in everything; so naturally we are bound to run up against each other. I don't **pronounce**[31] judgment on Mummy's character, for that is something I can't judge. I only look at her as a mother, and she just doesn't succeed in being that to me, I have to be my own mother. I've drawn myself apart from them all, I am my own **skipper**[32] and later on I shall see where I come to land. And this comes about particularly because I have in my mind's eye an image of what a perfect mother and wife should be, and in her whom I must call "Mother" I find no **trace**[33] of that image.

I am always making **resolutions**[34] not to notice Mummy's bad example. I want to see only the good side of her and to seek in myself what I cannot find in her. But it doesn't work and the worst of it is that neither Daddy nor Mummy understands this gap in my life, and I blame them for it. I wonder if anyone can ever succeed in making their children **absolutely**[35] content.

Sometimes I believe that God wants to try me, both now and later on, I must become good through my own efforts, without examples and without good advice. Then later on I shall be all the stronger. Who besides me will ever read these letters? From whom but myself shall I get comfort? As I need comforting often, I frequently feel weak, and **dissatisfied**[36] with myself, my **shortcomings**[37] are too great. I know this, and every day I try to improve myself, again and again.

My treatment varies so much. One day Anne is so sensible and is allowed to know everything, and the next day I hear that Anne is just a silly little goat who doesn't know anything at all and imagines that she's learned a wonderful lot from books. I'm not a baby or a spoiled darling any more, to be laughed at, whatever she does. I have my

---

30. Exact – precise　　　　　　　　31. Pronounce – speak
32. Skipper – a coach, director, or other leader
33. Trace – a visible mark　　　　　34. Resolutions – firm determination
35. Absolutely content – something contained
36. Dissatisfied – exhibiting a lack of contentment
37. Shortcomings – flaws, drawbacks

own views, plans, and ideas though I can't put them into words yet. Oh, so many things **bubble**[38] up inside me as I lie in bed, having to put up with people I'm fed up with, who always **misinterpret**[39] my intentions. That's why in the end I always come back to my diary. That is where I start and finish, because Kitty is always patient. I'll promise her that I shall **persevere**[40], in spite of everything, and find my own way through it all, and **swallow**[41] my tears. I only wish I could see the results already or occasionally receive **encouragement**[42] from someone who loves me.

Don't **condemn**[43] me, remember rather that sometimes I too can reach the **bursting**[44] point.

Yours, Anne

# Monday, 9 November, 1942

Dear Kitty,

Yesterday was Peter's birthday, he was sixteen. He had some nice presents. Among other things a game of Monopoly, a razor, and a lighter, Not that he smokes much, its really just for show.

The biggest surprise came from Mr. Van Daan when, at one o'clock, he announced that the British had landed in Tunis, Algiers, Casablanca, and Oran. "This is the beginning of the end," everyone was saying, but Churchill, the British Prime Minister, who had **probably**[45] heard the same thing in England, said: "This is not the end. It is not even the beginning of the end. But it is, perhaps, the end of the beginning." Do you see the difference? There is certainly reason for **optimism**[46]. Stalingrad, the Russian town which they've already been **defending**[47] for three months, still hasn't fallen into German hands.

---

38. Bubble – form
39. Misinterpret – explain inaccurately
40. Persevere – persist in
41. Swallow – suppress
42. Encouragement – one that encourages
43. Condemn – to express strong disapproval of
44. Bursting – exploding
45. Probably – most likely
46. Optimism – a tendency to expect the best possible outcome
47. Defending – keep safe from danger

But to return to **affairs**[48] in our secret den, I must tell you something about our food supply. As you know, we have some real **greedy**[49] pigs on the top floor. We get our bread from a nice baker, a friend of Koophuis. We don't get so much as we used to at home, naturally. But it's sufficient. Four ration cards have also been bought illegally. Their price is going up all the time, it has now gone up from twenty-seven florins to thirty-three. And all that for a little slip of printed paper! In order to have something in the house that will keep, apart from our 150 tins of vegetables, we have bought 270 pounds of dried peas and beans. They are not all for us, some are for the office people. They are in sacks which hang on hooks in our little passage (inside the hidden door). Owing to the weight of the contents, a few stitches in the sacks burst open. So we decided it would be better to put our winter store in the attic and Peter was given the job of **dragging**[50] it all up there.

He had managed to get five of the six sacks upstairs **intact**[51], and he was just busy pulling up number six, when the bottom **seam**[52] of the sack split and a shower-no, a positive **hailstorm**[53] of brown beans came pouring down and **rattled**[54] down the stairs. There were about fifty pounds in the sack and the noise was enough to waken the dead. Downstairs they thought the old house with all its contents was coming down on them. (Thank God there were, no strangers in the house.) It gave Peter a moment's **fright**[55]. But he was soon roaring with laughter, especially when he saw me standing at the bottom of the stairs, like a little island in the middle of a sea of beans! I was entirely surrounded up to my **ankles**[56] in beans. Quickly we started to pick them up. But beans are so **slippery**[57] and small that they seemed to roll into all the possible and impossible corners and holes.

---

| | |
|---|---|
| 48. Affairs – matter | 49. Greedy – extremely eager |
| 50. Dragging – pulling hard | 51. Intact – having the hymen unbroken |
| 52. Seam – a thin layer | 53. Hailstorm – a storm with hail |
| 54. Rattled – to move with sounds | |
| 55. Fright – alarm | 56. Ankles – the joint connecting the leg |
| 57. Slippery – tending to slip | |

Now, every time anyone goes downstairs they bend down once or twice, in order to be able to present Mrs. Van Daan with a handful of beans.

I'd almost forgotten to mention that Daddy is quite better again.

Yours, Anne

PS. The news has just come over the radio that Algiers has fallen. Morocco, Casablanca, and Oran have been in British hands for several days. Now we're waiting for Tunis.

## Tuesday, 10 November, 1942

Dear Kitty,

Great news—we want to take in an eighth person Yes, really! We've always thought that there was quite enough room and food for one more. We were only afraid of giving Koophuis and Kraler more trouble. But now that the **appalling**[58] stories we hear about Jews are getting even worse. Daddy got hold of the two people who had to decide, and they thought it was an excellent plan. "It is just as dangerous for seven as for eight," they said, and quite rightly. When this was settled, we ran through our circle of friends, trying to think of a single person who would fit in well with our "family." It wasn't difficult to hit on someone. After Daddy had refused all members of the Van Daan family, we chose a dentist called Albert Dussel, whose wife was fortunate enough to be out of the country when war broke out. He is known to be quiet, and so far as we and Mr. Van Daan can judge from a **superficial**[59] acquaintance, both families think he is a **congenial**[60] person. Miep knows him too, so she will be able to make arrangements for him to join us. If he comes, he will have to sleep in my room instead of Margot, who will use the camp bed.

Yours, Anne

---

58. Appalling – frightful
60. Congenial – sociable

59. Superficial – not concerned with

# Thursday, 12 November, 1942

Dear Kitty,

Dussel was awfully pleased when Miep told him that she had got a hiding place for him. She urged him to come as soon as possible. **Preferably**[61] Saturday. He thought that this was **rather**[62] doubtful, since he had to bring his card **index**[63] up to date first, see to a couple of patients, and settle his accounts. Miep came to us with this news this morning.

We thought it was **unwise**[64] of him to put it off. All these preparations **entail**[65] explanations to a number of people, whom we would rather keep out of it. Miep is going to ask if he can't manage to come on Saturday after all.

Dussel said no, now he is coming on Monday. I must say I think it's pretty **crazy**[66] that he doesn't jump at the **proposal**[67]— whatever it is. If he were to get picked up outside, would he still be able to do his card index, settle his finances, and see to his patients? Why delay then? I think its stupid of Daddy to have given in. No other news

Yours, Anne

# Tuesday, 17 November, 1942

Dear Kitty,

Dussel has arrived. All went well. Miep had told him that he must be at a special place in front of the Post Office at eleven o'clock, where a man would meet him. Dussel was standing at the **rendezvous**[68] dead on time. Mr. Koophuis, who knows Dussel too, went up to him and told him that the said gentleman could not come, but asked whether he would just go to Miep at the office. Koophuis got into a tram and went back to the office; while Dussel

---

61. Preferably – more desirable
62. Rather – preferably
63. Index – an indicator
64. Unwise – foolish
65. Entail – impose
66. Crazy – affected with madness
67. Proposal – the act of proposing
68. Rendezvous– a place where people meet

walked in the same direction. At twenty past eleven Dussel tapped at the office door. Miep helped him off with his coat, so that the yellow star would not be seen, and took him to the private office, where Koophuis engaged him in conversation until the **charwoman**[69] had gone. Then Miep went upstairs with Dussel under the **pretext**[70] that the private office was needed for something, opened the **swinging**[71] cupboard, and stepped inside before the eyes of the **dumbfounded**[72] Dussel.

We all sat around the table upstairs, waiting with coffee and **cognac**[73] to greet the newcomer. Miep showed him into our sitting room first. He recognized our furniture at once, and had not the **remotest**[74] idea that we were there, above his head. When Miep told him he nearly passed out with surprise. But luckily Miep didn't give him much time and took him straight upstairs.

Dussel sank into a chair, speechless, and looked at us all for a while, as if he had to really take it all in first. After a while he **stuttered**[75] "But... aber, *sind* you not in Belgium then? *1st* der *Militar nicht* come, das *Auto,* the escape is sie *nicht* successful?"

We explained everything to him, that we had spread the story about the soldiers and the car on purpose to put people, and especially the Germans, on the wrong track, should they try to find us.

Dussel was again **struck**[76] dumb by such **ingenuity**[77] and, when he had explored further our **superpractical**[78] **exquisite**[79] little "Secret Annexe," he could do nothing but **gaze**[80] about him in **astonishment**[81].

We all had lunch together. Then he had a little nap and joined us for tea, **tidied**[82] up his things a bit (Miep had brought them beforehand), and began to feel more at home. Especially when he

---

69. Charwoman – a woman hired for cleaning    70. Pretext – a specious excuse
71. Swinging – moving rhythmically to and fro  72. Dumbfounded – astonish
73. Cognac – a brandy distilled from white wine  74. Remotest–located far away
75. Stuttered – a disorder of oral speech    76. Struck – stricken to render
77. Ingenuity – cleverness    78. Superpractical – relating to
79. Exquisite – excellent    80. Gaze – to look steadily
81. Astonishment – great surprise    82. Tidied – cleaned

received the following typed "Secret Annexe Rules" (Van Daan product).

PROSPECTUS AND GUIDE TO THE "SECRET ANNEXE"
Special institution as temporary residence for Jews and suchlike.

*Open all the year round.* Beautiful, quiet, free from woodland surroundings, in the heart of Amsterdam. Can be reached by trams 13 and 17, also by car or bicycle. In special cases also on foot, if the Germans prevent the use of transport.

*Board and lodging: Free.*

*Special fat-free diet.*

*Running water* in the bathroom (alas, no bath) and down various inside and outside walls.

*Ample storage room* for all types of goods. *Own radio center*, direct communication with London, New York, Tel Aviv, and numeruos other stations. This appliance is only for residents' use after six o'clock in the evening. No stations are forbidden, on the understanding that German stations are only listened to in special cases, such as classical music and the like.

*Rest hours:* 10 o'clock in the evening until 7:30 in the morning. 10:15 on Sunday. Residents may rest during the day, conditions permitting, as the directors **indicate**[83]. For reasons of public security rest hours must be strictly observed!!

*Holidays* (outside the home): postponed indefinitely.

*Use of language.* Speak softly at all time, by order! All **civilized**[84] languages are permitted, therefore no German!

*Lessons:* One written shorthand lesson per week. English, French, Mathematics, and History at all times.

*Small Pets—Special Department* (permit is necessary): Good treatment available (vermin excepted).

*Mealtimes:* breakfast, every day except Sundays and Bank Holidays, 9 a.m. Sundays and Bank Holidays, 11:30 a.m. approximately.

---

83. Indicate – point out                    84. Civilized – ethical

*Lunch:* (not very big): l:15p.m, to 1:45 p.m. *Dinner:* cold and/or hot: no fixed time (depending on the news broadcast).

*Duties:* Residents must always be ready to help with office work.

*Baths:* The washtub is available for all residents from 9 a.m. on Sundays. The W.C., kitchen, private office or main office, whichever preferred, are available.

*Alcoholic Beverages:* only with doctor's prescription.

END

Yours, Anne

# Thursday, 19 November, 1942

Dear Kitty,

Dussel is a very nice man, just as we had all imagined. Of course he thought it was all right to share my little room.

Quite honestly I'm not so keen that a stranger should use my things, but one must be prepared to make some **sacrifices**[85] for a good cause, so I shall make my little **offering**[86] with a **goodwill**[87]. "If we can save someone, then everything else is of secondary importance," says Daddy, and he's **absolutely**[88] right.

The first day that Dussel was here, he immediately asked me all sorts of questions: When does the charwoman come? When can one use the bathroom? When is one allowed to use the lavatory? You may laugh, but these things are not so simple in a hiding place. During the day we mustn't make any noise that might be heard downstairs and if there is some stranger— such as the charwoman for examples- then we have to be extra careful. I explained all this carefully to Dussel. But one thing amazed me: he is very slow on the **uptake**[89]. He asks everything twice over and still doesn't seem to remember. Perhaps that will wear off in time, and it's only that he's thoroughly upset fey the sudden change.

---

85. Sacrifices – the act of losing
86. Offering – something
87. Goodwill – friendliness
88. Absolutely – definitely
89. Uptake – the act of accepting

Apart from that, all goes well. Dussel has told us a lot about the outside world, which we have missed for so long now. He had very sad news. Countless friends and **acquaintances**[90] have gone to a terrible fate. Evening after evening the green and gray army lorries **trundle**[91] past. The Germans ring at every front door to inquire if there are any Jews living in the house. If there are, then the whole family has to go at once. If they don't find any, they go onto the next house. No one tjas a chance of **evading**[92] them unless one goes into hiding. Often they go around with lists, and only ring when they know they can get a good **haul**[93]. Sometimes they let them off for cash-so much per head. It seems like the slave hunts of olden times. But it's certainly no joke, it's much too **tragic**[94] for that. In the evenings when it's dark, I often see rows of good, innocent people **accompanied**[95] by crying children, walking on and on, in charge of a couple of these chaps, **bullied**[96] and knocked about until they almost drop. No one is spared- old people, babies, expectant mothers, the sick-each and all join in the march of death.

How fortunate we are here, so well cared for and undisturbed. We wouldn't have to worry about all this misery were it not that we are so **anxious**[97] about all those dear to us whom we can no longer help.

I feel **wicked**[98] sleeping in a warm bed, while my dearest friends have been knocked down or have fallen into a **gutter**[99] somewhere out in the cold night. I get frightened when I think of close friends who have now been delivered into the hands of the **crudest**[100] brutes that walk the earth. And all because they are Jews!

Yours, Anne

---

90. Acquaintances – known person
91. Trundle – move
92. Evading – deceiting
93. Haul – cart
94. Tragic – very sad
95. Accompanied – moved along with
96. Bullied – troubled
97. Anxious – uneasy
98. Wicked – highly offensive
99. Gutter – sewage
100. Crudest – in natural state

# Friday, 20 November, 1942

Dear Kitty,

None of us really knows how to take it all. The news about the Jews had not really **penetrated**[101] through to us until now, and we thought it best to remain as cheerful as possible. Every now and then, when Miep lets out something about what has happened to a friend. Mummy and Mrs. Van Daan always begin to cry, so Miep thinks it better not to tell us any more. But Dussel was immediately plied with questions from all sides, and the stories he told us were so **gruesome**[102] and dreadful that one can't get them out of one's mind.

Yet we shall still have our jokes and **tease**[103] each other, when these horrors have **faded**[104] a bit in our minds. It won't do us any good, or help those outside, to go on being as **gloomy**[105] as we are at the moment. And what would be the object of making our "Secret Annexe" into a "Secret Annexe of Gloom"? Must I keep thinking about those other people, whatever I am doing? And if I want to laugh about something, should I stop myself quickly and feel ashamed that I am cheerful? Ought I then to cry the whole day long? No, that I can't do. Besides, in time this gloom will wear off.

Added to this misery there is another, but of a purely personal kind; and it **pales**[106] into **insignificance**[107] beside all the wretchedness I've just told you about. Still, I can't **refrain**[108] from telling you that lately I have begun to feel deserted. I am surrounded by too great a void. I never used to feel like this, my fun and **amusements**[109], and my girl friends, completely filled my thoughts. Now I either think about unhappy things, or about myself. And at

---

101. Penetrated – pushed into

102. Gruesome – frightful

103. Tease – make fun of

104. Faded – lose brightness

105. Gloomy – marked by hopelessness

106. Pales – decrease in relative importance

107. Insignificance – not important

108. Refrain – hold oneself back

109. Amusements – entertainments

long last I have made the discovery that Daddy, although he's such a **darling**[110], still cannot take the place of my entire little world of **bygone**[111] days. But why do I bother you with such foolish things? I'm very ungrateful, Kitty, I know that. But it often makes my head swim if I'm jumped upon too much, and then on top of that have to think about all those other **miseries**[112]!

Yours, Anne

## Saturday, 28 November, 1942

Dear Kitty,

We have used too much electricity, more than our ration. Result: the utmost economy and the prospect of having it cut off. No light for a **fortnight**[113]; a pleasant thought, that, but who knows, perhaps it won't happen after all! Its too dark to read in the afternoons after four or half past. We pass the time in all sorts of crazy ways: asking riddles, physical training in the dark, talking English and French, **criticizing**[114] books. But it all begins to pall in the end. Yesterday evening I discovered something new: to peer through a powerful pair of field glasses into the lighted rooms of the houses at the back. In the daytime we can't allow even as much as a centimeters chink to appear between our curtains, but it can't do any harm after dark. I never knew before that neighbors could be such interesting people. At any rate, ours are. I found one couple having a meal, one family was in the act of taking a home movie, and the dentist opposite was just attending to an old lady, who was awfully scared.

It was always said about Mr. Dussel that he could get on wonderfully with children and that he loved them all. Now he shows himself in his true colors, a **stodgy**[115], oldfashioned disciplinarian, and preacher of long, drawn-out sermons on manners.

---

110. Darling – a dearly beloved person   111.   Bygone – past events to be put aside
112. Miseries – emotional unhappiness   113.   Fortnight – two weeks
114. Criticizing – finding fault with        115. Stodgy – dull

As I have the unusual good fortune to share my bedroom-alas, a small one-with His Lordship, and as I'm generally considered to be the most badly behaved of the three young people, I have a lot to put up with and have to pretend to be deaf in order to escape the old, much repeated **tickingsoff** [116] and warnings. All this wouldn't be too bad, if he wasn't such a frightful **sneak**[117] and he didn't pick on Mummy of all people to sneak to every time. When I've already had a dose from him. Mummy goes over it all again, so I get a **gale**[118] **aft**[119] as well as **fore**[120]. Then, if I'm really lucky, I'm called on to give an account of myself to Mrs. Van Daan and then I get a **veritable**[121] **hurricane**[122]!

Honestly, you needn't think it's easy to be the "badly broughtup" central figure of a **hypercritical**[123] family in hiding. When I lie in bed at night and think over the many sins and shortcomings attributed to me, I get so confused by it all that I either laugh or cry: it depends what sort of mood I am in.

Then I fall asleep with a stupid feeling of wishing to be different from what I am or from what I want to be; perhaps to behave differently from the way I want to behave, or do behave. Oh, heavens above, now I'm getting you in a **muddle**[124] too. Forgive me, but I don't like crossing things out, and in these days of paper shortage we are not allowed to throw paper away. Therefore I can only advise you not to read the last sentence again, and certainly not to try to understand it, because you won't succeed anyhow!

Yours, Anne

---

116. Ticking off–call attention to an item    117. Sneak – move secretly

118. Gale – A breeze               119. Aft – after

120. Fore – before                 121. Veritable – genuine

122. Hurricane – storm         123. Hypercritical–excessively critical

124. Muddle – informal terms for a difficult situation

## Think and Ink...

➤ Anne had reached the bursting point. How did she exhibit it?

➤ Why couldn't Anne accept her mother as 'a mother who can guide' her?

➤ What drawbacks did Anne find in her parents? How did she overcome her disappartments?

➤ What made the family hoard their rations?

➤ How did Anne analyze the political situation?

➤ Comment on the practical points of view expressed by Anne regarding acceptance of Dussel in their hide out.

➤ What surprise did the family have for Dussel's arrival?

➤ How cleverly did the family mislead the Germans?

➤ How was Dussel astonished with the Secret Annexe?

➤ What 'Rules' were given to Dussel?

➤ How does Anne's family show their concerns for Dussel?

➤ How systematic were the rules laid dawn by the family?

➤ How does Anne Portray the scene of Hitler's high handedness with Jews?

➤ What cruel fate befell the Jews?

➤ It is really miserable to lose one's childhood days to fear and terror. How does Anne exhibit this idea?

### Text-Based Questions

• What made Anne feel miserable?

• How close did Anne feel with her father?

• What aspects of him did she hate?

• What were the failings of Anne's mothers?

• Why were Anne and her mummy opposites to each other?

• Why does Anne say that her mother didn't succeed in being a mother to her?

- What shortcomings of her mother made Anne become a 'skipper' of her own self?
- What did Anne blame her parents for?
- How does Anne make a self-analysis.
- What made her write diary?
- What presents did Peter get on his birthday?
- What was the biggest surprise brought by Mr. Van Daan?
- Why did Anne find Churchill's words optimistic?
- What rations did Anne's family pile up in the den?
- What happened when Peter tried to put the sacks in the attic? How did he create a mess?
- What news did the family get about the political situation?
- What made the family accept an eighth person?
- Why did the family decide upon Albert Dussel?
- Why didn't Dussel join them at once?
- Why did Anne feel her father a stupid?
- What did Anne agree with her father?
- How cautious was Dussel? How was he upset by the sudden change?
- What was the tragic fate of the Jews as described by Anne?
- Why did Anne feel wicked to sleep in a warm bed?
- Why did Anne's parents cry?
- What did Anne feel guilty about?
- How wretched did she feel, being in the Secret Annexe?
- What made Anne feel deserted?
- Why was it difficult to read books after half past four?
- How did the children pass their time in darkness?
- How was Mr. Dussel and how did he preach Anne?
- What effects did the criticism of others about her have an Anne?

# Monday, 7 December, 1942

Dear Kitty,

Chanuka and St. Nicholas Day came almost together this year—just one day's difference. We didn't make much fuss about Chanuka: we just gave each other a few little presents and then we had the candles. Because of the shortage of candles we only had them alight for ten minutes, but it is all right as long as you have the song. Mr Van Daan has made a wooden candlestick, so that too was all properly arranged.

Saturday, the evening of St. Nicholas Day, was much more fun. Miep and Elli had made us very **inquisitive**[1] by whispering all the time with Daddy, so naturally we guessed that something was on.

And so it was. At eight o'clock we all filed down the wooden staircase through the passage in pitch-darkness (it made me **shudder**[2] and wish that I was safely upstairs again) into the little dark room. There, as there are no windows, we were able to turn on a light. When that was done. Daddy opened the big cupboard. "Oh! how lovely," we all cried. A large basket decorated with St. Nicholas paper stood in the corner and on top there was a mask of Black Peter.

We quickly took the basket upstairs with us. There was a nice little present for everyone, with a suitable poem attached. I got a doll, whose skirt is a bag for odds and ends Daddy got book ends, and so on. In any case it was a nice idea and as none of us had ever celebrated St. Nicholas, it was a good way of starting.

Yours, Anne

# Thursday, 10 December, 1942

Dear Kitty,

Mr. Van Daan used to be in the meat, sausage, and spice business. It was because of his knowledge of this trade that he was taken on in

---

1. Inquisitive – eager for knowledge  2. Shudder – tremble suddenly and violently

Daddy's business. Now he is showing the **sausagy**[3] side of himself, which, for us, is by no means disagreeable.

We had ordered a lot of meat (under the counter, of course) for preserving in case we should come upon hard times. It was fun to watch, first the way the pieces of meat went through the **mincer**[4], two or three times, then how all the accompanying ingredients were mixed with the minced meat, and then how the **intestine**[5] was filled by means of a **spout**[6], to make the sausages. We fried the sausage meat and ate it with **sauerkraut**[7] for supper that evening, but the Gelderland sausages had to be thoroughly dried first, so we hung them over a stick tied to the ceiling with string. Everyone who came into the room began to laugh when they caught a glimpse of the row of sausages on show. They looked terribly funny!

The room was in a **glorious**[8] mess. Mr. Van Daan was wearing one of his wife's aprons **swathed**[9] round his substantial person (he looked fatter than he is!) and was busy with the meat. Hands **smothered**[10] in blood, red face, and the soiled apron, made him look like a butcher. Mrs. Van Daan was trying to do everything at once, learning Dutch from a book, stirring the soup, watching the meat being done, sighing and complaining about her injured rib.

That's what happens to elderly ladies who do such idiotic exercises fo reduce their large behind.

Dussel had **inflammation**[11] in one eye and was bathing it with **camomile**[12] tea by the fire. Pim, who was sitting on a chair in a beam of sunlight that shone through the window, kept being pushed from one side to the other. In addition, I think his **rheumatism**[13] was bothering him, because he sat rather **hunched**[14] up with a miserable look on his face, watching Mr. Van Daan at work.

---

3. Sausagy – someone who is odd
4. Mincer – a kitchen utensil that cuts
5. Intestine – an internal organ
6. Spout – nose of a kettle
7. Sauerkraut – shredded cabbage
8. Glorious – magnificent
9. Swathed – to wrap
10. Smothered – to cover thickly
11. Inflammation – the act of inflaming
12. Camomile – a herb
13. Rheumatism – a disability
14. Hunched – cramped posture

He looked exactly like some **shriveled up**[15] old man from an old people's home. Peter was doing acrobatics round the room with his cat. Mummy, Margot, and I were peeling potatoes, and of course, all of us were doing everything wrong because we were so busy watching Mr. Van Daan.

Dussel has opened his dental practice. For the fun of it, I must just tell you about his first patient. Mummy was ironing; and Mrs. Van Daan was the first to face the **ordeal**[16]. She went and sat on a chair in the middle of the room. Dussel began to unpack his case in an awfully important way, asked for some eau de cologne as a **disinfectant**[17] and vaseline to take the place of wax.

He looked in Mrs. Van Daan's mouth and found two teeth which, when touched, just made her **crumple**[18] up as if she was going to pass out, uttering **incoherent**[19] cries of pain. After a lengthy examination (in Mrs. Van Daan's case, lasting in actual fact not more than two minutes) Dussel began to **scrape**[20] away at one of the holes. But, no fear—it was out of the question— the patient flung her arms and legs about wildly in all directions until at one point Dussel let go of the **scraper**[21]—that remained stuck in Mrs. Van Daan's tooth.

Then the fat was really in the fire! She cried as far as it was possible with such an instrument in one's mouth), tried to pull the thing out of her mouth, and only succeeded in pushing it further in. Mr. Dussel stood with his hands against his sides calmly watching the little comedy.

The rest of the audience lost all control and roared with laughter. It was **rotten**[22] of us, because I for one am quite sure that I should have screamed even louder. After much turning, kicking, screaming, and calling out, she got the instrument free at last and Mr. Dussel went on with his work, as if nothing had happened.

---

15. Shriveled up – wrinkled
16. Ordeal – painful experience
17. Disinfectant – producing antisepsis
18. Crumple – to fold up
19. Incoherent – lacking cohesion
20. Scrape – to smooth or clean
21. Scraper – a hand tool
22. Rotten – very bad

This he did so quickly that Mrs. Van Daan didn't have time to start any fresh tricks. But he'd never had so much help in all his life before. Two assistants are pretty useful: Van Daan and I performed our duties well. The whole scene looked like a picture from the Middle Ages entitled "A Quack at Work." In the meantime, however, the patient hadn't much patience; she had to keep an eye on "her" soup and "her" meal. One thing is certain, Mrs. Van Daan won't be in such a hurry to allow herself to be treated again!

Yours, Anne

## Sunday, 13 December, 1942

Dear Kitty,

I'm sitting cozily in the main office, looking outside through a slit in the curtain. It is dusk[23] but still just light enough to write to you.

It is a very queer[24] sight, as I watch the people walking by, it looks just as if they are all in a terrible hurry and nearly trip over their own toes. With cyclists, now, one simply can't keep pace with their speed. I can't even see what sort of person is riding on the machine.

The people in this neighborhood[25] don't look very attractive. The children especially are so dirty you wouldn't want to touch them with a barge[26] pole. Real slum kids with running noses. I can hardly understand a word they say.

Yesterday afternoon Margot and I were having a bath here and I said, "Supposing we were to take the children who are walking past, one by one, hoist them up with a fishing rod, give them each a bath, wash and mend their clothes, and then let them go again, then ..." Margot interrupted me, "By tomorrow they would look just as filthy[27] and ragged as before."

But I'm just talking nonsense; besides, there are other things to see-cars, boats, and rain. I like particularly the screech[28] of the trams as they go by.

| | |
|---|---|
| 23. Dusk – enemy | 24. Queer – strange |
| 25. Neighborhood – area around | 26. Barge – a long, large |
| 27. Filthy – disgustingly dirty | 28. Screech – make a high-pitched sound |

There is no more variety in our thoughts than there is for ourselves. They go round and round like a roundabout-from Jews to food and from food to politics. By the way, talking of Jews, I saw two Jews through the curtain yesterday. I could hardly believe my eyes; it was a horrible feeling, just as if I'd **betrayed**[29] them and was now watching them in their misery. There is a houseboat immediately opposite, where a bargeman lives with his family. He has a small **yapping**[30] dog. We only know the little dog by his bark and his tail, which . we can see when he runs round the deck. Ugh! How its started to rain and most of the people are hidden under umbrellas. I see nothing but raincoats and occasionally the back of someone's hat. Really I don't need to see more. I'm gradually getting to know all the women at a **glance**[31], blown out with potatoes, wearing a red or a green coat, **trodden down**[32] heels and with a bag under their arms. Their faces either look grim or kind-depending on their husbands' dispositions.

Yours, Anne

## Tuesday, 22 December, 1942

Dear Kitty,

The "Secret Annexe" has heard the joyful news that each person will receive an extra quarter of a pound of butter for Christmas. It says half a pound in the newspapers, but that's only for the lucky **mortals**[33] who get their ration books from the government, not for Jews who have gone into hiding, who can only afford to buy four illegal ration books, instead of eight.

We are all going to bake something with our butter. I made some biscuits and two cakes this morning. Everyone is very busy upstairs and Mummy has told me I must not go there to work or read, until the household jobs are done.

---

29. Betrayed – cheated
31. Glance – cursory look
33. Mortals – relating to humankind

30. Yapping – barking sharply
32. Trodden down – walked

Mrs. Van Daan is in bed with her **bruised**[34] rib, complains the whole day long, allows herself to be given fresh dressings all the time, and isn't satisfied with anything. I shall be glad when she's on her feet again and **tidies**[35] up her own things, because I must say this for her; she's **exceptionally**[36] **industrious**[37] and tidy, all the while she is healthy in mind and body. She is cheerful too.

Just as if I didn't hear enough "sshssh" during the day, for making too much noise, my gentleman bedroom companion now repeatedly calls out "ssh-ssh" to me at night too. According to him, I am not even allowed to turn over! I refuse to take the slightest notice of him, and shall go "ssh-ssh" back at him the next time.

He makes me furious, on Sundays especially, when he turns the light on early to do his exercises. It seems to take simply hours, while I, poor **tormented**[38] creature, feel the chairs, which are placed at the head of my bed to lengthen it, slide backwards and forwards continually under my sleepy head. When he has ended his muscles. His Lordship begins his toilet. His pants are hanging up, so to and fro he must go to collect them. But he forgets his tie, which is lying on the table. Therefore once more he pushes and bumps past the chairs to get it.

But I won't bore you any longer on the subject of old men. It won't make things any better and all my plans of **revenge**[39] (such as disconnecting the lamp, shutting the door, hiding his clothes) must be **abandoned**[40] in order to keep the peace. Oh, I'm becoming so sensible! One must apply one's reason to everything here, learning to obey, to hold your tongue, to help, to be good, to give in, and I don't know what else. I'm afraid I shall use up all my brains too quickly, and I haven't got so very many. Then I shall not have any left for when the war is over.

Yours, Anne

---

34. Bruised – wounded
35. Tidies – orderly
36. Exceptionally – uncommon
37. Industrious – assiduous in work
38. Tormented – a state of distress,
39. Revenge – avenge
40. Abandoned – forsaken

## Think and Ink...

➤ How did the family try to keep up their good spirits inspite of their misfortunes?

➤ Comment on the comic relief that the family was treated to by Mrs. Van Daan.

➤ Why does Anne remark that there is no more variety in our thoughts than there is for ourselves?

➤ Discuss the annoyances that Mr.Dussel make and how those things indeed help Anne to discipline herself.

### Text-Based Questions

• How did the family celebrate Chanuka and St. Nicholas?

• What did Miep and Elli do?

• How were the kids made happy?

• How did the family preserve meat?

• What was so funny about their house?

• How were the inmates ill? Why were they doing everything wrong?

• How did Dussel examine Mrs. Van Daan's teeth? What little comedy happened then?

• What was the reaction of Mr. Dussel to the little comedy?

• What was the queen right that Anne had?

• How were the children of the neighbourhood?

• What did Anne suggest Margot?

• Why was Anne feeling horrible to see the Jews?

• What things that Anne find around her place?

• What was the Joyful news heard by the inmates of the Secret Annexe?

• What qualities of Mrs. Van Daan did Anne Appreciate?

• What annoyed Anne about Mr. Dussel?

• Why didn't Anne want to take revenge on him?

# Wednesday, 13 January, 1943

Dear Kitty,

Everything has upset me again this morning, so I wasn't able to finish a single thing properly.

It is terrible outside. Day and night more of those poor miserable people are being dragged off, with nothing but a **rucksack**[1] and a little money. On the way they are **deprived**[2] even of these possessions. Families are torn apart, the men, women, and children all being separated. Children coming home from school find that their parents have disappeared. Women return from shopping to find their homes shut up and their families gone.

The Dutch people are anxious too, their sons are being sent to Germany. Everyone is afraid.

And every night hundreds of planes fly over Holland and go to German towns, where the earth is blowed up by their bombs, and every hour hundreds and thousands of people are killed in Russia and Africa. No one is able to keep out of it, the whole globe is waging war and although it is going better for the Allies, the end is not yet in sight. And as for us, we are fortunate. Yes, we are luckier than millions of people. It is quiet and safe here, and we are, so to speak, living on capital. We are even so selfish as to talk about "after the war" **brighten**[3] up at the thought of having new clothes and new shoes, whereas we really ought to save every penny, to help other people, and save what is left from the **wreckage**[4] after the war.

The children here run about in just a thin blouse and clogs, no coat, no hat, no stockings/and no one helps them. Their tummies are empty, they chew an old carrot to stay the pangs, go from their cold homes out into the cold street and, when they get to school, find themselves in an even colder classroom. Yes, it has even got so

---

1. Rucksack – a knapsack
3. Brighten – to make brighter
2. Deprived – removed
4. Wreckage – something wrecked

bad in Holland that **countless**[5] children stop the passers-by and beg for a piece of bread. I could go on for hours about all the suffering the war has brought, but then I would only make myself more dejected. There is nothing we can do but wait as calmly as we can till the misery comes to an end. Jews and Christians wait, the whole earth waits; and there are many who wait for death.

Yours, Anne

## Saturday, 30 January, 1943

Dear Kitty,

I'm boiling with rage, and yet I mustn't show it. I'd like to stamp my feet, scream, give Mummy a good shaking, cry, and I don't know what else, because of the horrible words, **mocking**[6] looks, and **accusations**[7] which are leveled at me repeatedly every day, and find their mark, like **shafts**[8] from a tightly **strung**[9] bow, and which are just as hard to draw from my body.

I would like to shout to Margot, Van Daan, Dussel—and Daddy too— "Leave me in peace, let me sleep one night at least without my pillow being wet with tears, my eyes burning and my head **throbbing**[10]. Let me get away from it all, preferably away from the world!" But I can't do that, they mustn't know my **despair**[11], I can't let them see the **wounds**[12] which they have caused, I couldn't bear their sympathy and their kindhearted jokes, it would only make me want to **scream**[13] all the more. If I talk, everyone thinks I'm showing off; when I'm silent they think I'm **ridiculous**[14]; rude if I answer, **sly**[15] if I get a good idea, lazy if I'm tired, selfish if I eat a mouthful more than I should, stupid, cowardly, **crafty**[16], etc., etc. The whole

---

| | |
|---|---|
| 5. Countless – infinite | 6. Mocking – rude and discourteous |
| 7. Accusations – offence | 8. Shafts – arrow |
| 9. Strung – tying | 10. Throbbing – vibrating |
| 11. Despair – lose all hope | 12. Wounds – an injuries |
| 13. Scream – as from pain | 14. Ridiculous – silly |
| 15. Sly – mentally quick | 16. Crafty – cunning |

day long I hear nothing else but that I am an **insufferable**[17] baby, and although I laugh about it and **pretend**[18] not to take any notice, I *do* mind. I would like to ask God to give me a different nature, so that I didn't put everyone's back up. But that can't be done. I've got the nature that has been given to me and I'm sure it can't be bad. I do my very best to please everybody, far more than they'd ever guess. I try to laugh it all off, because I don't want to let them see my trouble. More than once, after a whole string of undeserved **rebukes**[19], I have **flared**[20] up at Mummy: "I don't care what you say anyhow. Leave me alone: I'm a hopeless case anyway." Naturally, I Was then told I was rude and was **virtually**[21] ignored for two days and then, all at once, it was quite forgotten, and I was treated like everyone else again. It is impossible for me to be all sugar one day and spit **venom**[22] the next. I'd rather choose the golden mean (which is not so golden), keep my thoughts to myself, and try for *once* to be just as **disdainful**[23] to them as they are to me. Oh, if only I could!

Yours, Anne

---

17. Insufferable – intolerable
18. Pretend – act
19. Rebukes – scoldings
20. Flared – out burst
21. Virtually – practically
22. Venom – poison
23. Disdainful – rude and discourteous

## Think and Ink...

➤ What thoughts do the descriptions of the war-torn Holland bring to your mind?

➤ From her description, what idea do you form of Anne? Is she over reacting, or the people around her over react with her?

## Text-Based Questions

• What picture of misery does Anne present about the socio political conditions around her?

• Why did Anne feel fortunate?

• What were the conditions of the children?

• What made Anne boil with rage?

• What remarks of the people around drive Anne to despair?

• What effect did Anne's flaring up have?

• What was the golden mark Anne chose?

# Friday, 5 February,

Dear Kitty,

Although I haven't written anything, about our rows for a long time, there still isn't any change. The **discord**[1], long accepted by us, struck Mr. Dussel as a calamity at first. But he is getting used to it now and tries not to think about it. Margot and Peter aren't a bit what you would call "young," they are both so **staid**[2] and quiet. I show up terribly against them and am always hearing, "You don't find Margot and Peter doing that-why don't you follow their example?" I simply **loathe**[3] it. I might tell you I don't want to be in the least like Margot. She is much too soft and **passive**[4] for my liking, and allows everyone to talk her around, and gives in about everything. I want to be a stronger character! But I keep such ideas to myself: they would only laugh at me, if I came along with this as an explanation of my **attitude**[5]. The atmosphere at table is usually **strained**[6], though luckily the outbursts are sometimes checked by "the soup eaters"! The "soup eaters" are the people from the office who come in and are served with a cup of soup. This afternoon Mr.Van Daan was talking about Margot eating so little again. "I suppose you do it to keep slim," he added, teasing her. Mummy, who always defends Margot, said loudly: "I can't bear your stupid **chatter**[7] any longer." Mr. Van Daan turned **scarlet**[8], looked straight in front of him, and said nothing. We often laugh about things, just recently Mrs. Van Daan came out with some perfect nonsense. She was **recalling**[9] the past, how well she and her father got on together and what a flirt she was. "And do you know," she went on, "if a man gets a bit **aggressive**[10], my father used to say, then you must say to him, 'Mr. So and So, remember I am a lady!' and he will know what

| | |
|---|---|
| 1. Discord – disagreement | 2. Staid – serious |
| 3. Loathe – dislike | 4. Passive – inactive |
| 5. Attitude – a state of mind | 6. Strained – forced |
| 7. Chatter – trivial talk | 8. Scarlet – vivid red |
| 9. Recalling – take back | 10. Aggressive – Intense or harsh |

you mean." We thought that was a good joke and burst out laughing. Peter too, although usually so quiet, sometimes gives cause for mirth[11], He is blessed with a passion for foreign words, although he does not always know their meaning. One afternoon we couldn't go to the lavatory because there were visitors in the office, however. Peter had to pay an urgent call. So he didn't pull the plug. He put a notice up on the lavatory door to warn us, with "S.V.P gas" on it. Of course he meant to put "Beware of gas", but he thought the other looked more genteel[12]. He hadn't got the faintest notion it meant "if you please."

Yours, Anne

## Saturday, 27 February, 1943

Dear Kitty,

Pim is expecting the invasion[13] any day. Churchill has had pneumonia, but is improving slowly. The freedom-loving Gandhi of India is holding his umpteenth[14] fast. Mrs. Van Daan claims to be fatalistic[15]. But who is the most scared when the guns go off? No one else but Petronella.

Henk brought a copy of the bishop's letter to churchgoers for us to read. It was very fine and inspiring[16]. "Do not rest, people of the Netherlands, everyone is fighting with his own weapons to free the country, the people, and their religion." "Give help, be generous, and do not dismay!" is what they cry from the pulpit, just like that. Will it help? It won't help the people of our religion.

You'd never guess what has happened to us now. The owner of these premises has sold the house without informing Kraler and Koophuis. One morning the new owner arrived with an architect to

---

11. Mirth – gladness and gaiety     12. Genteel – refined in manner
13. Invasion – attack     14. Umpteenth – innumerable
15. Fatalistic – acceptance of the belief that all events are predetermined and inevitable
16. Inspiring – stimulating

have a look at the house. Luckily, Mr. Koophuis was present and showed the gentlemen everything except the "Secret Annexe." He professed[17] to have forgotten the key of the communicating door. The new owner didn't question any further. It will be all right as long as he doesn't come back and want to see the "Secret Annexe," because then it won't look too good for us.

Daddy has emptied[18] a card index[19] box for Margot and me, and put cards in it. It is to be a book card system; then we both write down which books we have read, who they are by, etc. I have procured[20] another little notebook for foreign words.

Lately Mummy and I have been getting on better together, but we still *never* confide[21] in each other. Margot is more catty[22] then ever and Daddy has got something he is keeping to himself, but he remains the same darling.

New butter and margarine rationing[23] at table! Each person has their little bit of fat put on their plate. In my opinion the Van Daans don't divide it at all fairly[24]. However, my parents are much too afraid of a row to say anything about it. Pity, I think you should always give people like them tit for tat.

Yours, Anne

---

17. Professed – pretended
19. Index – catalog
21. Confide – reveal
23. Rationing – a fixed portion
18. Emptied – holding
20. Procured – obtain
22. Catty – subtly cruel
24. Fairly – in a fair manner

## Think and Ink...

➢ Do you think Anne's parents are a bit submissive to the Van Daans? Why / why not?

➢ Comment on how the family contributed to the rivalry between Anne and the other two children?

### Text-Based Questions

- Why was Anne pitted against Margot and Peter?

- Who were the soup eaters?

- What was Mrs. Van Daan's perfect nonsense? How was it received by others?

- What were the historical news Anne gives us?

- What did the bishop's letter say? Why was it inspiring?

- What did the new owner do?

- How did Daddy keep the girls occupied?

- Why did Anne feel there should be a tit for tat?

# Wednesday 10 March, 1943

Dear Kitty,

We had a **short circuit**[1] last evening, and on top of that the guns kept **banging**[2] away all the time. I still haven't got over my fear of everything connected with shooting and planes, and I **creep**[3] into Daddy's bed nearly every night for comfort. I know its very childish but you don't know what it is like. The A.A. guns roar so loudly that you can't hear yourself speak. Mrs. Van Daan, the fatalist, was nearly crying, and said in a very **timid**[4] little voice, "Oh, it is so unpleasant! Oh, they are shooting so hard," by which she really means I'm so frightened."

It didn't seem nearly so bad by candlelight as in the dark. I was shivering, just as if I had a temperature, and begged Daddy to light the candle again. He was **relentless**[5], the light remained off. Suddenly there was a burst of machine-gun fire, and that is ten times worse than guns. Mummy jumped out of bed and, to Pirn's **annoyance**[6], lit the candle. When he complained her answer was firm: "After all, Anne's not exactly a **veteran**[7] soldier," and that was the end of it.

Have I already told you about Mrs. Van Daan's other fears? I don't think so. If I am to keep you informed of all that happens in the "Secret Annexe," you must know about this too. One night Mrs. Van Daan thought she heard burglars ir the **attic**[8]; she heard loud footsteps and was so frightened that she woke her husband. Just at that moment the burglars disappeared and the only sounds that Mr. Van Daan could hear were the heartbeats of the frightened **fatalist**[9] herself. "Oh, Putti Mr, Van Daan's nickname], they are sure to have taken the sausages and all our peas and beans. And Peter, I wonder if he is still safely in bed?"

---

1. Short circuit – shortage in electric supply  2. Banging – a sudden loud noise
3. Creep – to move  4. Timid – fearful
5. Relentless – not feeling bad  6. Annoyance – a nuisance
7. Veteran – aged, experienced  8. Attic – a space under the roof
9. Fatalist – relating to fatalism, Acceptance

"They certainly won't have stolen Peter, Listen, don't worry and let me go to sleep." But nothing came of that. Mrs. Van Daan was far too nervous to sleep another **wink**[10]. A few nights after that the whole Van Daan family was woken by **ghostly**[11] sounds. Peter went up to the attic with a torch-and **scamper**[12]-scamper! What do you think it was running away? A swarm of enormous rats! When we knew who the thieves were, we let Mouschi sleep in the attic and the **uninvited**[13] guests didn't come back again; at least not during the night.

Peter went up to the loft a couple of evenings ago to fetch some old newspapers. He had to hold the trap door firmly to get down the steps. He put his hand down without looking... and went tumbling down the ladder from the sudden shock and pain. Without knowing it he had put his hand on a large rat, and it had bitten him hard. By the time he reached us, as white as a sheet and with his knees **knocking**[14], the blood had **soaked**[15] through his pajamas. And no wonder, it's not very pleasant to stroke a large rat; and to get bitten into the bargain is really **dreadful**[16].

Yours, Anne

# Friday, 12 March, 1943

Dear Kitty,

May I introduce someone to you: Mama Frank, champion of youth! Extra butter for the young, the problems of modern youth! Mummy defends youth in everything and after a certain amount of **squabbling**[17] she always gets her way. A bottle of preserved sole has gone bad: gala dinner for Mouschi and Boche; You haven't met Boche yet, although she was here before we went into hiding. She is the

---

10. Wink – a brief period of sleep
11. Ghostly – an apparition
12. Scamper – to run
13. Uninvited – not welcome
14. Knocking – causing to collide
15. Soaked – thoroughly wet
16. Dreadful – terrible
17. Squabbling – a noisy quarrel

warehouse[18] and office cat and keeps down the rats in the storerooms. Her odd political name requires an explanation. For some time the firm had two cats, one for the warehouse and one for the attic. Now it occasionally happened that the two cats met, and the result was always a terrific fight. The **aggressor**[19] was always the warehouse cat, yet it was always the attic cat who managed to win—just like among nations. So the storehouse cat was named the German or "Boche" and the attic cat the English or "Tommy." Tommy was got rid of later, we are all entertained by Boche when we go downstairs.

We have eaten so many kidney beans and haricot beans that I can't bear the sight of them any more. The mei'e thought of them makes me feel quite sick. Bread is no longer served in the evenings now. Daddy has just said that he doesn't feel in a good mood. His eyes look so sad again—poor soul!

I can't drag myself away from a book called *The Knock at the Door* by Ina Boudier-Bakker. The story of the family is exceptionally well written. Apart from that, it is about war, writers, the **emancipation**[20] of women and quite honestly I'm not **awfully**[21] interested. Horrible air raids on Germany. Mr. Van Daan is in a bad mood, the cause— cigarette shortage. Discussions over the question of whether we should, or should not, use our **canned**[22] vegetables ended in our favour.

I can't get into a single pair of shoes any more, except ski boots, which are not much use about the house. A pair of rush sandals costing 6.50 florins lasted me just one week, after which they were out of action. Perhaps Miep will **scrounge**[23] something under the counter. I must cut Daddy's hair. Pim maintains that he will never have another barber after the war, as I do the job so well. If only I didn't **snip**[24] his ear so often!

Yours, Anne

---

18. Warehouse – usually wholesale shop
19. Aggressor – someone who attacks
20. Emancipation – the act
21. Awfully – extremely bad
22. Canned – preserved
23. Scrounge – begging
24. Snip – cut

# Thursday, 18 March, 1943

Dear Kitty,

Turkey is in the war. Great excitement. Waiting in **suspense**[25] for the news.

Yours, Anne

# Friday, 19 March, 1943

Dear Kitty,

An hour later joy was followed by disappointment. Turkey is not in the war yet. It was only a cabinet minister talking about them soon giving up their neutrality. A newspaper in the Dam* was crying, "Turkey on England's side." The newspapers were torn out of his hands. This is how the joyful news reached us too; 500 and 1000-guilder notes have been declared no longer valid. It is a trap for black marketeers and suchlike, but even more for people who have got other kinds of "black" money, and for people in hiding. If you wish to hand in a 1000-guilder note you must be able to declare, and prove, exactly how you got it. They may still be used to pay taxes, but only until next week. Dussel has received an old-fashioned foot-operated dentist's drill, I expect he'll soon give me a thorough check-over. The "Fuhrer aller Germanen" has been talking to wounded soldiers. Listening in to it was pitiful. Question and answer went something like this:

"My name is Heinrich Scheppel."

"Wounded where?"

"Near Stalingrad."

"What kind of wound?"

"Two feet frozen off and a broken joint in the left arm." This is exactly what the frightful puppet show on the radio was like. The

---

* A square in front of the Royal Palace.

25.  Suspense – something not known

wounded seemed to be proud of their wounds- the more the better. One of them felt so moved at being able to shake hands with the Fuhrer (that is, if he still had a hand!) that he could hardly get the words out of his mouth.

Yours, Anne

# Thursday, 25 March, 1943

Dear Kitty,

Yesterday Mummy, Daddy, Margot, and I were sitting pleasantly together when suddenly Peter came in and whispered something in Daddy's ear. I heard something about "a barrel fallen over in the warehouse" and "someone **fumbling**[26] about at the door." Margot had heard it too, but when Daddy and Peter went off immediately, she tried to calm me down a bit, because I was naturally as white as a sheet and very **jittery**[27].

The three of us waited in suspense. A minute or two later Mrs. Van Daan came upstairs; she'd been listening to the wireless in the private office. She told us that Pim had asked her to turn off the wireless and go softly upstairs. But you know what that's like, if you want to be extra quiet, then each step of the old stairs **creaks**[28] twice as loudly. Five minutes later Pim and Peter appeared again, white to the roots of their hair, and told us their experience.

They had hidden themselves under the stairs and waited, with no result at first. But suddenly, yes, I must tell you, they heard two loud bumps, just as if two doors were banged here in the house. Pim was upstairs in one leap, peter warned Dussel first, who finally landed upstairs with lot of fuss and noise. Then we all went up in **stockinged**[29] feet to the Van Daans on the next floor. Mr. Van Daan had a bad cold and had already gone to bed, so we all drew up closely around his bed and whispered our suspicions to him.

---

26. Fumbling – mishandling 27. Jittery – feeling nervous unease
28. Creaks – noise      29. Stockinged – with stockings

Each time Mr. Van Daan coughed loudly, Mrs. Van Daan and I were so scared that we thought we were going to have a fit. That went on until one of us got the bright idea of giving him some codeine, which soothed the cough at once. Again we waited and waited, but we heard no more and finally we all came to the conclusion that the thieves had taken to their heels when they heard footsteps in the house, which was otherwise so silent.

Now it was unfortunate that the wireless downstairs was still turned to England, and that the chairs were neatly arranged round it. If the door had been forced, and the air-raid wardens had noticed and warned the police, then the result might have been very unpleasant. So Mr. Van Daan got up and put on his coat and hat and followed Daddy cautiously downstairs. Peter took up the rear, armed with a large hammer in case of emergencies. The ladies upstairs (including Margot and me) waited in suspense, until the gentlemen reappeared five minutes later and told us that all was quiet in the house.

We arranged that we would not draw any water or pull the plug in the lavatory. But as the excitement had affected most of our **tummies**[30], you can imagine what the atmosphere was like when we had each paid a visit in succession.

When something like that happens, heaps of other things seem to come at the same time, as now. Number One was that the clock at the Westertoren, which I always find so **reassuring**[31], did not strike! Number Two was that, Mr. Vossen having left earlier than usual the previous evening, we didn't know definitely whether Elli had been able to get hold of the key, and had perhaps forgotten to shut the door. It was still evening and we were still in a state of uncertainty, although we certainly did feel a bit reassured by the fact that from about eight o'clock, when the burglar had alarmed the house, until half past ten we had not heard a sound. On further **reflection**[32] it also seemed very unlikely to us that a thief would have forced open a

---

30. Tummies – the human stomach        31. Reassuring – to assure again
32. Reflection – thought

door so early in the evening, while there were still people about in the street. Moreover, one of us got the idea that it was possible that the caretaker of the warehouse next door was still at work since, in the excitement, and with the thin walls, one can easily make a mistake, and what's more, one's imagination can play a big part at such critical moments.

So we all went to bed; but none of us could get to sleep. Daddy as well as Mummy and Mr. Dussel were awake, and without much **exaggeration**[33] I can say that I hardly slept a wink. This morning the men went downstairs to see whether the outside door was still shut, and everything turned out to be quite safe. We gave everyone a detailed description of the **nerve-racking**[34] event. They all made fun of it, but it is easy to laugh at such things afterwards. Elli was the only one who took us seriously.

Yours, Anne

## Saturday, 27 March, 1943

Dear Kitty,

We have finished our shorthand course, now we are beginning to practice speed. Aren't we getting clever? I must tell you more about my time-killing subjects (I call them such, because we have got nothing else to do but make the days go by as quickly as possible, so that the end of our time here comes more quickly); I'm mad on Mythology and especially the Gods of Greece and Rome. They think here that it is just a passing craze, they've never heard of an **adolescent**[35] kid of my age being interested in Mythology. Well, then, I shall be the first!

Mr. Van Daan has a cold, or rather he has a little **tickle**[36] in his throat. He makes a tremendous fuss about it. **Gargling**[37] with

---

33. Exaggeration – overstate    34. Nerve-racking event – irritating to the nerves
35. Adolescent – immature    36. Tickle – odd feel
37. Gargling – to rinse

camomile tea, painting his throat with **tincture**[38] of myrrh, rubbing eucalyptus all over his chest, nose, teeth, and tongue and then getting into an evil mood on top of it all.

Rauter, one of the German big shots, has made a speech. "All Jews must be out of the Germanoccupied countries before July 1. Between April 1 and May 1 the province of .Utrecht must be cleaned out [as if the Jews were cockroaches]. Between May 1 and June 1 the provinces of North and South Holland," These wretched people are sent to **filthy**[39] slaughterhouses like a herd of sick, **neglected**[40] cattle. But I won't talk about it, I only get **nightmares**[41] from such thoughts.

One good little piece of news is that the German department of the Labor Exchange has been set on fire by **saboteurs**[42]. A few days after, the Registrar's Office went the same way. Men in German police uniforms **gagged**[43] the guards and managed to destroy important papers.

Yours, Anne

---

38. Tincture – a medicine
39. Filthy – dirty
40. Neglected – not attended to
41. Nightmares – deeply distressing dream
42. Saboteurs – those who deliberately causes wrecks
43. Gagged – tied

## Think and Ink...

> ➤ Was the nerve-racking event described by Anne, simply and imagination, or real? Justify your claim.

### Text-Based Questions

- What effects did the gunshots have on Anne?
- How did the inmates react to the gunshots?
- What happened are night? What did they find in the attic?
- How was Peter bitten by a rat?
- How did Boche get her name?
- How sickly were the inmates with their food?
- How were the black marketers trapped?
- What conversation went between "Fuhrer aller Germanen" and the wounded soldiers?
- What did Anne overhear of Peter?
- How did the family react to the entry of thieves?
- What did Anne's Daddy and Mr. Van Daan do?
- What other coincidences happened?
- What time-killing tasks did Anne and others indulge in?
- How did Mr. Van Daan treat his cold?
- What did Rauter announce and how did Anne react to his remarks?
- What was the good news for Anne about the German department?
- What was the misfortune that Mr. Koophuis and Mr. Vossen had?
- Why was Anne's daddy anxious ?
- How did Anne, her daddy, and Margot overhear the discussions?

# Thursday, 1 April, 1943

Dear Kitty,

I'm really not April-fooling (see the date), but the opposite; today I can easily quote the saying: "Misfortunes never come singly." To begin with, Mr. Koophuis, the one who always cheers us up, has had **hemorrhage**[1] of the stomach and has got to stay in bed for at least three weeks. Secondly, Elli has flu. Thirdly, Mr. Vossen is going to the hospital next week. He has probably got an abdominal ulcer. And fourthly, some important business conferences, the main points of which Daddy had discussed in detail with Mr. Koophuis, were due to be held, but now there isn't time to explain everything thoroughly to Mr. Kraler.

The gentlemen who had been expected duly arrived; even before they came Daddy was **trembling**[2] with anxiety as to how the talks would go. "If only I coald be there, if only I was downstairs," he cried. "Why don't you go and lie with one ear pressed against the floor, then you'll be able to hear everything." Daddy's face cleared, and at half past ten yesterday morning Margot and Pim (two ears are better than one!) took up their positions on the floor. The talks were not finished in the morning, but by the afternoon Daddy was not in a fit state to continue the listening campaign. He was half **paralyzed**[3] from remaining in so unusual and uncomfortable a position. I took his place at half past two, as soon as we heard voices in the passage. Margot kept me company. The talk at times was so longwinded and boring that quite suddenly I fell asleep on the cold hard **linoleum**[4] floor. Margot did not dare to touch me for fear they might hear us, and talking was out of the question. I slept for a good half hour and then woke up with a shock, having forgotten every word of the important discussions. Luckily Margot had paid more attention.

Yours, Anne

---

1. Hemorrhage – profuse bleeding
3. Paralyzed – unable to move
2. Trembling – shake in anxiety
4. Linoleum – durable

# Friday, 2 April, 1943

Dear Kitty,

Oh dear: I've got another terrible black mark against my name. I was lying in bed yesterday evening waiting for Daddy to come and say my prayers with me, and wish me good night, when Mummy came into my room, sat on my bed, and asked very nicely, "Anne, Daddy can't come yet, shall I say your prayers with you tonight?" "No, Mummy," I answered.

Mummy got up, paused by my bed for a moment, and walked slowly towards the door. Suddenly she turned around, and with a **distorted**[5] look on her face said, "I don't want to be cross, love cannot be forced." There were tears in her eyes as she left the room.

I lay still in bed, feeling at once that I had been **horrible**[6] to push her away so rudely. But I knew too that I couldn't have answered differently. It simply wouldn't work. I felt sorry for Mummy, very, very sorry, because I had seen for the first time in my life that she minds my **coldness**[7]. I saw the look of sorrow on her face when she spoke of love not being forced. It is hard to speak the truth, and yet it is the truth: she herself has pushed me away, her **tactless**[8] remarks and her **crude**[9] jokes, which I don't find at all funny, have now made me **insensitive**[10] to any love from her side. Just as I **shrink**[11] at her hard words, so did her heart when she realized that the love between us was gone. She cried half the night and hardly slept at all. Daddy doesn't look at me and if he does for a second, then I read in his eyes the words: "How can you be so unkind, how can you bring yourself to cause your mother such sorrow?"

---

5. Distorted – misshape
7. Coldness – unfriendly attitude
9. Crude – raw
11. Shrink – small

6. Horrible – dreadful
8. Tactless – bluntly inconsiderate
10. Insensitive – numb

They expect me to apologize; but this is something I can't apologize for because I spoke the truth and Mummy will have to know it sooner or later anyway. I seem, and indeed am, indifferent both to Mummy's tears and Daddy's looks, because for the first time they are both aware of something which I have always felt. I can only feel sorry for Mummy, who has now had to discover that I have adopted her own attitude. For myself, I remain silent and **aloof**[12]; and I shall not shrink from the truth any longer, because the longer it is put off, the more difficult it will be for them when they do hear it.

Yours, Anne

## Tuesday 27 April, 1943

Dear Kitty,

Such **quarrels**[13] that the whole house thunders! Mummy and I, the Van Daans and Daddy, Mummy and Mrs. Van Daan, everyone is angry with everyone else. Nice atmosphere, isn't it? Anne's usual list of failings has been brought out again and fully **ventilated**[14].

Mr. Vossen is already in the Binnengasthuis hospital. Mr. Koophuis is up again, the hemorrhage having slopped sooner than usual. He told us that the Registrars Office received additional damage from the Fire Service who, instead of just **quenching**[15] the flames, **soaked**[16] the whole place with water. I'm glad!

The Carlton Hotel is **smashed**[17] to bits. Two British planes loaded with **incendiary**[18] bombs fell right on top of the "Offiziersheim."[1] The whole Vijzelstraat-Singel comer is burned down. The air raids

---

12. Aloof – apart
14. Ventilated – as for airing
16. Soaked – to make thoroughly wet
18. Incendiary – rousing, provoking

13. Quarrels – argument
15. Quenching – to put out
17. Smashed – shattered

on German towns are growing in strength every day. We don't have a single quiet night. I've got dark rings under my eyes from lack of sleep. Our food is miserable. Dry bread and coffee substitute for breakfast. Dinner: spinach or lettuce for a fortnight on end. Potatoes twenty centimeters long and tasting sweet and rotten. Whoever wants to follow a slimming course should stay in the "Secret Annexe"! They complain bitterly upstairs, but we don't regard it as such a tragedy. All the men who fought in 1940 or were **mobilized** [19] have been called up to work for "der Fuhrer" as prisoners of war. Suppose they're doing that as a **precaution** [20] against **invasion** [21].

Yours, Anne

---

19. Mobilized – made to move
20. Precaution – preventive measure
21. Invasion – attack

## Think and Ink...

➤ Do you Justify Anne's attitude towards her mother? Why / why not?

➤ How miserable was life for those at the Secret Annexe?

## Text-Based Questions

• What did Anne's Mummy suggest her? What reply did she get from Anne?

• Why was Anne insensitive towards her mother love?

• Why did not Anne apologise?

• How hostile was the atmosphere at the Secret Annexe?

• What was Anne glad about?

• Why did Anne remark that whoever wants to follow a slimming course should stay in the Secret Annexure?

# Saturday, 1 May, 1943

Dear Kitty,

If I just think of how we live here, I usually come *to* the conclusion that it is a **paradise**[1] compared with how other Jews who are not in hiding must be living. Even so, later on, when everything is normal again, I shall be amazed to think that we, who were so **spick and span**[2] at home, should have sunk to such a low level. By this I mean that our manners have **declined**[3]. For instance, ever since we have been here, we have had one oilcloth on our table which, owing to so much use, is not one of the cleanest. Admittedly I often try to clean it with a dirty dishcloth, which is more hole than cloth. The table doesn't do us much credit either, in spite of hard **scrubbing**[4]. The Van Daans have been sleeping on the same **flannelette**[5] sheet the whole winter, one can't wash it here because the soap powder we get on the ration isn't sufficient, and besides it's not good enough. Daddy goes about in **frayed**[6] trousers and his tie is beginning to show signs *of* wear too. Mummy's **corsets**[7] have split today and are too old to be repaired, while Margot goes about in a brassiere two sizes too small for her.

Mummy and Margot have managed the whole winter with three vests between them, and mine are so small that they don't even reach my tummy.

Certainly, these are all things which can be overcome. Still, I sometimes realize with a shock: "How are we, now going about in wornout things, from my pants down to Daddy's shaving brush, ever going to get back to our prewar standards?"

---

1. Paradise – heaven
2. Spick and Span–Immaculately clean
3. Declined – polite refusal
4. Scrubbing – rubbing
5. Flannelette – a soft cotton fabric with a nap.
6. Frayed – worned out away
7. Corsets – a close-fitting undergarment

They were **banging**[8] away so much last night that four times I gathered all my belongings together. Today I have packed a suitcase with the most necessary things for an escape. But Mummy quite rightly says: "Where will you escape to?" The whole of Holland is being punished for the strikes which have been going on in many parts of the country. Therefore a state of **siege**[9] has been declared and everyone gets one butter coupon less. What naughty little children!

Yours, Anne

# Tuesday, 18 May, 1943

Dear Kitty,

I **witnessed**[10] a **terrific**[11] air battle between German and British planes. Unfortunately a couple of the Allies had to jump from burning machines. Our milkman, who lives in Halfweg, saw four Canadians sitting by the roadside, one of them spoke fluent Dutch. He asked the milkman to give him a light for his cigarette, and told him that the crew had consisted of six men. The pilot was burned to death, and their fifth man had hidden himself somewhere. The German police came and **fetched**[12] the four perfectly fit men. I wonder how they managed to have such clear brains after that terrifying parachute trip.

Although it is fairly warm, we have to light our fires every other day, in order to burn vegetable peelings and refuse. We can't put anything in the garbage pails, because we must always think of the warehouse boy. How easily one could be **betrayed**[13] by being a little careless!

All students who wish either to get their degrees this year, or continue their studies, are compelled to sign that they are in sympathy with the Germans and approve of the New Order. Eighty per cent

---

8. Banging – a sudden loud noise
9. Siege – blockading of a city
10. Witnessed – observed
11. Terrific – astounding
12. Fetched – bring back
13. Betrayed – be disloyal to

have refused to go against their **consciences**[14]. Naturally they had to bear the consequences. All the students who do not sign have to go to a labour camp in Germany. What will be left of the youth of the country if they have all got to do hard labour in Germany? Mummy shut the window last night because of all the **banging**[15]: I was in Pirn's bed. Suddenly Mrs. Van Daan jumped out of bed above us, just as if Mouschi had bitten her. A loud clap followed immediately. It sounded just as if an **incendiary**[16] bomb had fallen beside my bed. I **shrieked**[17] out, "Light, light!" Pim turned on the lamp, I expected nothing less than to see the room **ablaze**[18] within a few minutes. Nothing happened. We all hurried upstairs to see what was going on. Mr. and Mrs, Van Daan had seen a red **glow**[19] through the open window. He thought that there was a fire in the neighborhood and she thought that our house had caught fire. When the clap came Mrs Van Daan was already on her feet with her knees knocking. But nothing more happened and we all **crept**[20] back into our beds.

Before a quarter of an hour had passed the shooting started up again. Mrs. Van Daan sat bolt upright at once and then went downstairs to Mr. Dussels room, **seeking**[21] there the rest which she could not find with her **spouse**[22]. Dussel received her with the words, "Come into my bed, my child!" which sent us off into uncontrollable laughter. The gunfire troubled us no longer, our fear was **banished**[23]!

Yours, Anne

---

14. Consciences – consciousness
16. Incendiary – inflammatory
18. Ablaze – being on fire
20. Crept – move silently
22. Spouse – husband

15. Banging – explosive noise
17. Shrieked – often frantic cry
19. Glow – to shine brightly
21. Seeking – search for
23. Banished – moved out

## Think and Ink...

➢ How sickening it would be to wear wornout clothes for days together?

➢ What idea do you gather about the siege in Holland?

➢ Comment on how the reveres situation was relieved by the comedy of Mr. Dussel.

## Text-Based Questions

- How was their oil maintained?

- Why could not they go for new clothes?

- What was the situation in Holland?

- What happened after the air battle between German and British planes?

- How did Anne show her concern for the warehouse boy?

- What condition was imposed b the Germans?

- How and why was Mrs. Van Daan frightened?

# Sunday, 13 June, 1943

Dear Kitty,

My birthday poem from Daddy is too good to keep from you. As Pim usually writes verses in German, Margot **volunteered**[1] to translate it. Judge for yourself whether Margot didn't do it brilliantly. After the usual summary of the events of the year, this is how it ran:

*Though youngest here, you are no longer small. But life is very hard, since one and all Aspire to be your teacher, thus and thus: "We have experience, take a tip from us." "We know) because we did it long ago." "Elders are always better, you must know." At least that's been the rule since life began! Our personal* **faults**[2] *are much too small to scan. This makes it easier to* **criticize**[3]. *The faults of others, which seem double size. Please bear with us, your parents, for we try to judge you fairly and with sympathy. Correction sometimes take against your will.*

*Though it's like* **swallowing**[4] *a bitter pill. Which must be done if were to keep the peace. While time goes by till all this suffering* **cease**[5]. *You read and study nearly all the day. Who might have lived in such a different way. You're never bored and bring us all fresh air. Your only moan is this: "What can I wear? I have no knickers, all my clothes are small. My vest might be a loincloth, that is all. To put on shoes would mean to cut off toes. Oh dear, I'm worried by so many woes".* There was also a bit about food that Margot could not translate into rhyme, so I shall leave it out. Don't you think my birthday poem is good? I have been thoroughly spoiled in other ways and received a lot of lovely things. Among other things a fat book on my pet subject-the mythology of Greece and Rome. I can't complain of a **shortage**[6] of sweets either—everyone has broken into their last reserves. As the Benjamin of the family in hiding, I am really more honored than I deserve.

Yours, Anne

---

| | |
|---|---|
| 1. Volunteered – a person who performs | 2. Faults – a mistake |
| 3. Criticize – to find fault with | 4. Swallowing – consume |
| 5. Cease – terminate | 6. Shortage – insufficiency |

# Tuesday, 15 June, 1943

Dear Kitty,

Lots of things have happened, but I often think that all my uninteresting **chatter**[7] bores you very much and that you are glad not to receive too many letters. So I shall give you the news in brief.

Mr. Vossen has not been operated on for his **duodenal**[8] ulcer. When he was on the operating table and they had opened him up, the doctors saw that he had cancer, which was far too advanced to operate. So they stitched him up again, kept him in bed for three weeks and gave him good food, and finally sent him home again. I do pity him terribly and think it is **rotten**[9] that we can't go out, otherwise I should certainly visit him frequently to cheer him up. It is a **disaster**[10] for us that good old Vossen won't be able to keep us in touch with all that goes on, and all he hears in the warehouse. He was our best helper and security adviser; we miss him very much indeed.

It will be our turn to hand in our radio next month. Koophuis has a **clandestine**[11] baby set it home that he will let us have to take the place of our big Phillips. It certainly is a shame to have to hand in our lovely set, but in a house where people are hiding, one daren't, under any circumstances, take **wanton**[12] risks and so draw the attention of the authorities. We shall have the little radio upstairs. On top of hidden Jews, clandestine money and clandestine buying, we can add a clandestine radio. Everyone is trying to get hold of an old set and to hand that in instead of their "source of courage." It is really true that as the news from outside gets worse, so the radio with its **miraculous**[13] voice helps us to keep up our **morale**[14] and to say again, "Chins up, stick it out, better times will come!"

Yours, Anne

---

7. Chatter – to talk rapidly
8. Duodenal – a peptic ulcer
9. Rotten – embarrassed
10. Disaster – misfortune
11. Clandestine – secret
12. Wanton – immoral
13. Miraculous – unbelievable
14. Morale – confidence

## Think and Ink...

➤ Why did Anne's Daddy find it necessary to pour his real feelings towards her? How was the poem appreciated by Anne?

### Text-Based Questions

- What gift did Anne get from her Daddy?
- What confession did Anne's father make to her?
- What happened to Mr. Vossen?
- Why should the family turn to radio?
- How did the news through radio helped the family keep up their morale?

# Sunday, 11 July, 1943

Dear Kitty,

To return to the "**upbringing**[1]" theme for the **umpteenth**[2] time, I must tell you that I really am trying to be helpful, friendly, and good, and to do everything I can so that the rain of **rebukes**[3] dies down to a light summer **drizzle**[4]. It is mighty difficult to be on such model behavior with people you can't bear, especially when you don't mean a word of it. But I do really see that I get on better by **shamming**[5] a bit, instead of my old habit of telling everyone exactly what I think (although no one ever asked my opinion or attached the slightest importance to it).

I often lose my **cue**[6] and simply can't swallow my rage at some **injustice**[7], so that for four long weeks we hear nothing but an **everlasting**[8] chatter about the **cheekiest**[9] and most shameless girl on earth. Don't you think that sometimes I've cause for complaint? It's a good thing I'm not a **grouser**[10], because then I might get sour and **badtempered**[11].

I have decided to let my shorthand go a bit, firstly to give me more time for my other subjects and secondly because of my eyes. I'm so miserable and wretched as I've become very shortsighted and ought to have had glasses for a long time already (phew, what an owl I shall look!} but you know, of course, in hiding one cannot. Yesterday everyone talked of nothing but Anne's eyes, because Mummy had suggested sending me to the **oculist**[12] with Mrs. Koophuis. I shook in my shoes somewhat at this announcement, for it is no small thing to do. Go out of doors, imagine it, in the street—doesn't bear thinking

---

1. Upbringing – to nourish
2. Umpteenth – innemerable
3. Rebukes – to check
4. Drizzle – to rain gently
5. Shamming – something false
6. Cue – suggestion
7. Injustice – a specific unjust
8. Everlasting – eternal
9. Cheekiest – impertinently bold
10. Grouser – a temporary pile
11. Bad-tempered – irritable
12. Oculist – an optometrist

about! I was **petrified** [13] at first, then glad. But it doesn't go as easily as that, because all the people who would have to approve such a step could not reach an agreement quickly. All the difficulties and risks had first to be carefully weighed, although Miep would have gone with me straight away.

In the meantime I got out my gray coat from the cup-board, but it was so small that it looked as if it belonged to my younger sister.

I am really curious to know what will come of it all, but I don't think the plan will come off because the British have landed in Sicily now and Daddy is once again hoping for a "quick finish."

Elli gives Margot and me a lot of office work; it makes us both feel quite important and is a great help to her. Anyone can file away correspondence and write in the sales book, but we take special pains.

Miep is just like a pack **mule** [14], she fetches and carries so much. Almost every day she manages to get hold of some vegetables for us and brings everything in shopping bags on her bicycle. We always long for Saturdays when our books come. Just like little children receiving a present.

Ordinary people simply don't know what books mean to us, shut up here. Reading, learning, and the radio are our amusements.

Yours, Anne

## Tuesday, 13 July, 1943

Dear Kitty,

Yesterday afternoon, with Daddy's permission, I asked Dussel whether he would please be so good (being really very polite) as to allow me to use the little table in our room twice a week in the afternoons, from four o'clock till half past five. I sit there every day from half past two till four, while Dussel sleeps, but otherwise the room plus table are out of **bounds** [15]. Inside, in our common room,

---

13. Petrified – paralyze with terror      14. Mule – a horse breed
15. Bounds – limits

there is much too much going on, it is impossible to work there, and besides. Daddy likes to sit at the writing table and work too sometimes.

So it was quite a **reasonable**[16] request, and the question was put very **politely**[17]. Now honestly what do you think the very learned Dussel replied: "No." Just plain "No!" I was **indignant**[18] and refused to be put off like that, so I asked him the reason for his "No." But I was sent away with a **flea**[19] in my ear. This was the **barrage**[20] which followed:

"I have to work too, and if I can't work in the afternoons, then there is no time left for me at all. I must finish my task, otherwise I've started it all for nothing. Anyway, you don't work seriously at anything. Your mythology, now just what kind of work is that; knitting and reading are not work either. I am at the table and shall stay there." My reply was:

"Mr. Dussel, I do work seriously and there is nowhere else for me to work in the afternoons. I beg of you to kindly reconsider my request!"

With these words the offended Anne turned her back on the very learned doctor, ignoring him completely. I was **seething**[21] with rage, and thought Dussel **frightfully**[22] rude (which he certainly was) and myself very friendly. In the evening when I could get hold of Pim, I told him how it had gone off and discussed what I should do next, because I was not going to give in, and **preferred**[23] to clear it up myself. Pim told me how I ought to **tackle**[24] the problem, but warned me that it would be better to leave it till the next day, as I was so het up. I let this advice go to the winds, and waited for Dussel after the dishes were done. Pim sat in the room next to us, which had a calming

---

16. Reasonable – fair
17. Politely – elegantly
18. Indignant – angry
19. Flea – mite, louse
20. Barrage – an artificial obstruction
21. Seething – violently excited
22. Frightfully – terrifying
23. Preferred – to give priority
24. Tackle – deal with

influence on me. I began: "Mr. Dussel, I don't suppose you see any point in discussing the matter any more, but I must ask you to do so." Dussel then remarked with his sweetest smile: "I am always, and at all times, prepared to discuss this matter, but it has already been settled."

I went on talking, though continually **interrupted**[25] by Dussel. "When you first came here we arranged that this room should be for both of us. if we were to divide it fairly, you would have the morning and I all the afternoon! But I don't even ask that much, and I think that my two afternoons are really perfectly reasonable." At this Dussel jumped up a? if someone had **stuck**[26] a needle into him. "You can't talk about your rights here at all. And where am I to go, then? I shall ask Mr. Van Daan whether he will build a little **compartment**[27] in the attic, then I can go and sit there. I simply can't work anywhere. With you one always gets trouble. If your sister Margot, who after all has more reason to ask such a thing, would have come to me with the same questions, I should not think of refusing, but you . . ." Then followed the business about the mythology and the knitting, and Anne was insulted again. However, she did not show it and let Dussel finish speaking: "But you, one simply can't talk to you. You are so **outrageously**[28] selfish, as long as you can get what you want, you don't mind pushing everyone else to one side, I've never seen such a child. But after all, I suppose I shall be **obliged**[29] to give you your own way, because otherwise I shall be told later on that Anne Frank failed her exam because Mr. Dussel would not give up the table for her."

It went on and on and finally it was such a **torrent**[30] I could hardly keep pace with it. At one moment I thought, "In a minute I'll give him such a **smack**[31] in the face that he'll fly up to the ceiling together

---

25. Interrupted – to break the continuity
26. Stuck – especially
27. Compartment – section
28. Outrageously – in a very offensive manner
29. Obliged – grateful
30. Torrent – disturbed
31. Smack – to kiss noisily

with his lies' but the next moment I said to myself, "Keep calm! Such a fellow isn't worth getting worked up about."

After giving final **vent**[32] to his fury. Master Dussel left the room with an expression of mixed **wrath**[33] and **triumph**[34], his coat stuffed with food. I **dashed**[35] to Daddy and told him all that he had not already heard of the story. Pim decided to talk to Dussel the same evening, which he did. They talked for over half an hour. The theme of the conversation was something like this: first of all they talked about whether Anne should sit at the table, yes or no. Daddy said that he and Dussel had already discussed the subject once before, when he had professed to agree with Dussel, in order not to put him in the wrong in front of the young. But Daddy had not thought it fair then. Dussel thought that I should *not* speak as if he was an intruder who tried to **monopolize**[36] everything, but Daddy stuck up for me firmly over that, because he had heard for himself that I had not **breathed**[37] a word of such a thing.

To and fro it went. Daddy **defending**[38] my selfishness and my "**trifling**[39]" work, Dussel **grumbling**[40] continually.

Finally, Dussel had to give in after all, and I had the opportunity of working undisturbed until five o'clock for two afternoons a week. Dussel looked down his nose very much, didn't speak to me for two days and still had to go and sit at the table from five till half past-frightfully childish.

A person of fiftyfour who is still so pedantic and **smallminded**[41] must be so by nature, and will never improve,

Yours, Anne

---

32. Vent – an outlet
33. Wrath – often vindictive anger
34. Triumph – victory or conquest
35. Dashed – rushed
36. Monopolize – rule over singly
37. Breathed – voiceless
38. Defending – supporting
39. Trifling – insignificant, petty
40. Grumbling – complaining
41. Small-minded – narrow-minded

# Friday, 16 July, 1943

Dear Kitty,

Burglars again, but real this time! This morning Peter went to the warehouse at seven o'clock as usual, and at once noticed that both the warehouse door and the door opening on to the street were ajar. He told Pim, who tuned the radio in the private office to Germany and locked the door. Then they went upstairs together.

The **standing**[42] orders for such times were observed as usual: no taps to be turned on, therefore, no washing, silence, everything to be finished by eight o'clock and no lavatory. We were all very glad that we had slept so well and not heard anything. Not until half past eleven did we learn from Mr. Koophuis that the burglars had pushed in the outer door with a **crowbar**[43] and had forced the warehouse door, However, they did not find much to steal, so they tried their luck upstairs. They stole two cashboxes containing forty florins, postal orders and checkbooks and then, worst of all, all the coupons for 150 kilos of sugar.

Mr. Koophuis thinks that they belonged to the same gang as the ones who tried all three doors six weeks ago. They were unsuccessful then.

It has caused rather a stir in the building, but the "Secret Annexe" can't seem to go on without sensations like this. We were very glad that the typewriters and money in our wardrobe, where they are brought upstairs every evening, were safe.

Yours, Anne

# Monday, 19 July, 1943

Dear Kitty,

North Amsterdam was very heavily bombed on Sunday. The destruction seems to be terrible. Whole streets lie in ruins, and it will take a long time before all the people are dug out. Up till now there

---

42. Standing – fixed or lasting          43. Crowbar – a straight bar of iron

are two hundred dead and countless wounded; the hospitals are crammed[44]. You hear of children lost in the smoldering[45] ruins, looking for their parents.

I shudder when I recall the dull droning[46] rumble[47] in the distance, which for us marked the approaching destruction[48].

Yours, Anne

## Friday, 23 July, 1943

Dear Kitty,

Just for fun I'm going to tell you each person's first wish, when we are allowed to go outside again. Margot and Mr. Van Daan long more than anything for a hot bath filled to overflowing[49] and want to stay in it for half an hour. Mrs. Van Daan wants most to go and eat cream cakes immediately. Dussel thinks of nothing but seeing Lotje, his wife; Mummy of her cup of *coffee;* Daddy is going to visit Mr. Vossen first; Peter the town and a cinema, while I should find it so blissful[50], I shouldn't know where to start! But most of all, I long for a home of our own, to be able to move freely and to have some help with my work again at last, in other words-school.

Elli has offered to get us some fruit. It-costs next to nothings—grapes f.5.00 per kilo, gooseberries f.0.70 per pound, *one* peach f .0.50, one kilo melon f. 1.50* Then you see in the newspapers every evening in bold letters, "Play fair and keep prices down!"

Yours, Anne

---

\* Equivalent prices, in order, would be approximately $1.40, twentyone cents, fourteen cents, and fortytwo cents.

---

44. Crammed – squeeze into an insufficient space
45. Smoldering – showing scarcely suppressed anger
46. Droning – noise of a bee
47.  Rumble – move
48. Destruction – the act of destroying
49. Overflowing – to be filled beyond capacity
50. Blissful – extreme happiness

# Monday, 26 July, 1943

Dear Kitty,

Nothing but **tumult**[51] and **uproar**[52] yesterday, we are still very het up about it all. You might really ask, does a day go by without some excitement?

We had the first warning **siren**[53] while we were at breakfast, but we don't give a **hoot**[54] about that, it only means that the planes are crossing the coast.

After breakfast I went and lay down for an hour as I had a bad headache, then I went downstairs. It was about two o'clock. Margot had finished her office work at half past two: she had not packed her things together when the sirens began to wail, so upstairs I went again with her. It was high time, for we had not been upstairs five minutes when they began shooting hard, so much so that we went and stood in the passage. And yes, the house rumbled and shook, and down carne the bombs.

I clasped my "escape bag" close to me, more because I wanted to have something to hold than with an idea of escaping, because there's nowhere we can go. If ever we come to the extremity of fleeing from here, (he street would be just as dangerous as an air raid. This one **subsided**[55] after half an hour, but the activity in the house increased. Peter came down from his lookout post in the attic, Dussel was in the main office, Mrs. Van Daan felt safe in the private office, Mr. Van Daan had been watching from the loft, and we on the little landing **dispersed**[56] ourselves too: I went upstairs to see rising above the **harbor**[57] the columns of smoke Mr. Van Daan had told us about. Before long you could smell burning, and outside it looked as if a thick **mist**[58] hung everywhere. Although such a big fire is not a

---

51. Tumult – a disorderly commotion
52. Uproar – unpleasant shouls
53. Siren – often wailing sound as a signal
54. Hoot – to shout down
55. Subsided – settle down
56. Dispersed – distribute widely
57. Harbor – to provide a place
58. Mist – to cover or be covered with fog

pleasant sight, luckily for us it was all over, and we went about our respective tasks. That evening at dinner: another air-raid alarm! It was a nice meal, but my hunger vanished, simply at the sound of the alarm. Nothing happened and three quarters of an hour later it was all clear. The dishes were **stacked**[59] ready to be done: air-raid warning, ack-ack fire, an awful lot of planes. "Oh, dear me, twice in one day, that's too much," we all thought, but that didn't help at all, once again the bombs rained down, the other side this time, on *Schiphol, according to the British. The planes dived and climbed, we heard the **hum**[60] of their engines and it was very **gruesome**[61]. Each moment I thought: "Ones falling now. Here it comes."

I can assure you that when I went to bed at nine o'clock I couldn't hold my legs still. I woke up at the stroke of twelve: planes. Dussel was undressing. I didn't let that put me off, and at the first shot, I leaped out of bed, wide awake. Two hours with Daddy and still they kept coming. Then they ceased firing and I was able to go to bed. I fell asleep at half past two.

Seven o'clock. I sat up in bed with a start. Mr. Van Daan was with Daddy. Burglars was my first thought. I heard Mr. Van Daan say "everything." I thought that everything had-been stolen. But no, this time it was wonderful news, such as we have not heard for months, perhaps in all the war years. "Mussolini has resigned, the King of Italy has taken over the government." We jumped for joy. After the terrible day yesterday, at last something good again and— hope. Hope for it to end, hope for *peace.*

Kraler called in and told us that Fokkers has been badly damaged. Meanwhile we had another airraid alarm with planes overhead and one more warning siren. I'm just about **choked**[62] with alarms, very tired and don't feel a bit like work. But now the suspense over Italy will awaken the hope that it will soon end, perhaps even this year.

Yours, Anne

---

* Amsterdam Airport.

---

| | |
|---|---|
| 59. Stacked – arranged in a stack | 60. Hum – buzz |
| 61. Gruesome – frightful and shocking | 62. Choked – to block up |

# Thursday, 29 July, 1943

Dear Kitty,

Mrs. Van Daan, Dussel, and I were doing the dishes and I was extraordinarily quiet, which hardly ever happens, so they would have been sure to notice.

In order to avoid questions I quickly sought a fairly **neutral**[63] topic, and thought that the book *Henry from the Other Side* would meet the need. But I had made a mistake. If Mrs. Van Daan doesn't **pounce**[64] on me, then Mr. Dussel does. This was what it came to: Mr. Dussel had specially **recommended**[65] us this book as being excellent. Margot and I thought it was anything but excellent. The boy's character was certainly well drawn, but the rest— I had better gloss over that. I said something to that effect while we were washing the dishes, but that brought me a packet of trouble.

"How can you understand the psychology of a man! Of a child is not so difficult (!). You are much too young for a book like that; why, even a man of twenty would not be able to grasp it." (Why did he so especially recommend this book to Margot and me?) Now Dussel and Mrs. Van Daan continued together: "You know much too much about things that are unsuitable for you, you've been brought up all wrong. Later on, when you are older, you won't enjoy anything, then you'll say: 'I read that in books twenty years ago. "You had better make haste, if you want to get a husband or fall in love— or everything is sure to be a disappointment to you. You are already **proficient**[66] in the theory, it's only the practice that you still lack!"

I suppose it's their idea of a good upbringing to always try to set me against my parents, because that is what they often do. And to tell a girl of my age nothing about "grownup" subjects is an equally

---

63. Neutral – not supporting
64. Pounce – seize something swiftly and eagerly
65. Recommended – advised
66. Proficient – expert

fine method! I see the results of that kind of upbringing **frequently**[67] and all too clearly.

I could have slapped both their faces at that moment as they stood there making a fool of me. I was beside myself with rage and I'm just counting the days until I'm rid of "those" *people.*

Mrs. Van Daan is a nice one! She sets a fine example . . . she certainly sets one—a bad one. She is well known as being very pushing, selfish, cunning, calculating, and is never content. I can also add **vanity**[68] and **coquetry**[69] to the list. There is no question about it, she is an unspeakably disagreeable person. I could write whole chapters about Madame, and who knows, perhaps I will someday. Anyone can put on a fine coat of **varnish**[70] outside. Mrs. Van Daan is friendly to strangers and especially men, so it is easy to make a mistake when you have only known her for a short time. Mummy thinks she is too stupid to waste words over, Margot too unimportant. Pim too ugly (literally and figuratively), and I, after long observation— for I was never **prejudiced**[71] from the start— have come to the conclusion that she is all three and a lot more! She has so many bad qualities, why should I even begin about one of them?

PS.—Will the reader take into consideration that when this story was written the writer had not cooled down from her fury!

Yours, Anne

---

67. Frequently – often
68. Vanity – pride
69. Coquetry – flirtation
70. Varnish – give a smooth and glossy finish to
71. Prejudiced – biased

### Think and Ink...

➤ What opinion do you form about Mr. Dusssel after this incident?

➤ How did Anne bring alive the was scene to her friend kitty?

➤ How did Anne assess Mrs. Van Daan? What made Anne furies about the lady?

### Text-Based Questions

- What change had come upon Anne when she listened to others' criticism about her?

- What did Anne's Mummy suggest for Anne's short-sight? Why could not Anne approve of it?

- How did the inmates amuse themselves?

- What did Anne ask from Dussel? Why?

- How did Dussel respond to her request?

- Why did not Anne listen to her father's advice?

- How was the issue settled, and by whom?

- How did the burglars strike again?

- What standing orders were observed by the inmates?

- What happened at north Amsterdam? What did it portend?

- What was each person's first wish as Anne found?

- How was the atmosphere during and after bombardment?

- What news came to Anne the next morning?

- What argument followed when Anne tried to read the book *Henry from the Other Side*?

- Why did Anne criticize Mrs. Van Daan's and Dussel's idea of upbringing a child?

# Tuesday, 3 August, 1943

Dear Kitty,

Political news excellent. In Italy the Fascist party has been banned. The people are fighting the Fascists in many places— even the army is actually taking part in the battle. Can a country like that wage war against England?

We've just had a third air raid, I clenched[1] my teeth together to make myself feel courageous. Mrs. Van Daan, who has always said, "A terrible end is better than no end at all," is the greatest coward of us all now. She was shaking like a leaf this morning and even burst into tears. When her husband, with whom she has just made it up after a week's squabbling[2], comforted her, the expression on her face alone almost made me feel sentimental.

Mouschi has proved that keeping cats has disadvantages as well as advantages. The whole house is full of fleas[3], and the plague gets worse every day. Mr. Koophuis has scattered yellow powder in every nook and corner, but the fleas don't seem to mind a bit. It's making us all quite nervous, one keeps imagining an itch on one's arms, legs and various parts of the body, which is why quite a lot of us are doing gymnastics, so as to be able to look at the back of our necks or legs while standing up. Now we're being paid back for not being more supple—we're too stiff to even turn our heads properly. We gave up real gymnastics long ago.

Yours, Anne

# Wednesday, 4 August, 1943

Dear Kitty,

Now that we have been in the "Secret Annexe" for over a year, you know something of our lives, but some of it is quite indescribable[5].

---

1. Clenched – to close tightly          2. Squabbling – a noisy quarrel
3. Fleas – wingless                     4. Supple – soft, adaptable
5. Indescribable – impossible to describe

There is so much to tell, everything is so different from ordinary times and from ordinary people's lives. But still, to give you a closer look into our lives, now and again I **intend**[6] to give you a description of an ordinary day. Today I'm beginning with the evening and night.

*Nine o'clock in the evening.* The bustle of going to bed in the "Secret Annexe" begins and it is always really quite a business. Chairs are shoved about, beds are pulled down, blankets unfolded, nothing remains where it is during the day. I sleep on the little divan, which is not more than one and a half meters long. So chairs have to be used to lengthen it. A quilt, sheets, pillows, blankets, are all **fetched**[7] from Dussel's bed where they remain during the day. One hears terrible creaking in the next room: Margot's concertina-bed being pulled out. Again, divan, blankets, and pillows, everything is done to make the wooden slats a bit more comfortable. It sounds like thunder above, but it is only Mrs. Van Daan's bed. This is shifted to the window, you see, in order to give Her Majesty in the pink red jacket fresh air to tickle her dainty nostrils!

After Peters finished, 1 step into the washing **cubicle**[8], where I give myself a thorough wash and general toilet; it occasionally happens (only in the hot weeks or months) that there is a tiny flea floating in the water. Then teeth cleaning, hair curling, manicure, and my cottonwool pads with hydrogen peroxide (to bleach black mustache hairs)—all this in under half an hour.

Half past nine. Quickly into dressing gown, soap in one hand, pottie, hairpins, pants, curlers, and cotton wool in the other, I hurry out of the bathroom, but usually I'm called back once for the various hairs which decorate the washbasin in graceful curves, but which are not approved of by the next person.

Ten o'clock. Put up the blackout. Good night! For at least a quarter of an hour there is creaking of beds and a **sighing**[9] and of broken springs, then all is quiet, at least that is if our neighbors upstairs don't quarrel in bed.

---

6. Intend – plan
7. Fetched – brought
8. Cubicle – a small compartment
9. Sighing – relief

*Half past 'eleven.* The bathroom door creaks. A narrow strip of light falls into the room. A squeak of shoes, a large coat, even larger than the man inside it—Dussel returns from his night work in Kraler's office. **Shuffling**[10] on the floor for ten minutes, crackle of paper (that is the food which has to be **stowed**[11] away), and a bed is made. Then the form disappears again and one only hears suspicious noises from the lavatory from time to time.

*Three o'clock.* I have to get up for a little job in the metal pot under my bed, which is on a rubber mat for safety's sake in case of leakage. When this has to take place, I always hold my breath, as it **clatters**[12] into the tin like a brook from a mountain. Then the pot is returned to its place and the figure in the white nightgown, which evokes the same cry from Margot every evening: "Oh, that indecent nightdress!" steps back into bed.

Then a certain person lies awake for about a quarter of an hour, listening to the sounds of the night. Firstly, to whether there might not be a burglar downstairs, then to the various beds, above, next door, and in my room, *from* which one is usually able to make out how the various members of the household are sleeping, or how they pass the night in wakefulness.

The latter is certainly not pleasant, especially when it concerns a member of the family by the name of Dussel. First, I hear a sound like a fish **gasping**[13] for breath, this is repeated nine or ten times, then with much **ado**[14] and interchanged with little smacking sounds, the lips are moistened, followed by a lengthy twisting and turning in bed and rearranging of pillows. Five minutes' perfect *peace* and then the same sequence of events **unfolds**[15] itself at least three times more, after the doctor has **soothed**[16] himself to sleep again for a little while. It can also happen that we get a bit of shooting in the night, varying

---

10.  Shuffling – to sliding (the feet) along the floor
11.  Stowed – secretly packed                  12.  Clatters – make a rattling sound
13.  Gasping – breathe convulsively             14.  Ado – trouble
15.  Unfolds – reveales                          16.  Soothed – relieved

between one o'clock and four. I never really realize it, until from habit I am already standing at my bedside. Sometimes I'm so busy dreaming that I'm thinking about French irregular verbs or a quarrel upstairs. It is some time before I begin to realize that guns are firing and that I am still in the room. But it usually happens as described above. I quickly grab a pillow and handkerchief, put on my dressing gown and slippers, and scamper to Daddy, like Margot wrote in this birthday poem:

> *The first shot sounds at dead of night*
> > *Hush, look! A door creaks open wide,*
> *A little girl glides into sight.*
> > *Clasping a pillow to her side.*

Once landed in the big bed, the worst is over, except if the firing gets Very bad.

*Quarter to seven.* Trrrrr—the alarm clock that raises its voice at any hour of the day (if one asks for it and sometimes when one doesn't). Crack—ping—Mrs. Van Daan has turned it off. Creak— Mr. Van Daan gets up. Puts on water and then full speed to the bathroom.

*Quarter past seven.* The door creaks again. Dussel can go to the bathroom. Once alone, I take down the blackout— and a new day in the "Secret Annexe" has begun.

Yours, Anne

# Thursday, 5 August, 1943

Dear Kitty,

Today I am going *to* take lunchtime.

*It is half past twelve.* The whole mixed crowd breathes again. The warehouse boys have gone home now. Above one can hear the noise of Mrs. Van Daan's vacuum cleaner on her beautiful, and only, carpet. Margot goes with a few books under her arm for her Dutch lesson "for children who make no progress," because that's Dussel's attitude. Pim goes into a corner with his inseparable Dickens to try and find peace somewhere. Mummy hurries upstairs to help the **industrious**[17] housewife, and I go to the bathroom to tidy it up a bit, and myself at the same time.

*Quarter to one.* The place is filling up. First Mr. Van Santen, then Koophuis or Kraler, Elli and sometimes Miep as well.

One *o'clock.* We' re all sitting listening to the B.B.C., seated around the baby wireless, these are the only times when the members of the "Secret Annexe" do not interrupt each other, because now someone is speaking whom even Mr. Van Daan can't interrupt.

*Quarter* past one. The great **shareout**[18]. Everyone from below gets a cup of soup and if there is ever a **pudding**[19], some of that as well. Mr. Van Santen is happy and goes to sit on the divan or lean against the writing table. Newspaper, cup, and usually the cat, beside him. If one of the three is missing he's sure to protest. Koophuis tells us the latest news from town, he is certainly an excellent source of information. Kraler comes helter-skelter upstairs—a short, firm Knock on the door and in he comes rubbing his hands, according to his mood, in a good temper and talkative, or bad tempered and quiet.

*Quarter to two.* Everyone rises from the table and goes about his own business. Margot and Mummy do the dishes. Mr. and Mrs. Van Daan to their divan. Peter up to the attic. Daddy to the divan downstairs. Dussel to his bed and Anne to her work. Then follows the most peaceful hour, everyone is asleep, no one is disturbed. Dussel dreams of lovely food— the expression on his face gives this away, but I don't look long because the time goes so fast and at four o'clock the **pedantic**[20] doctor is standing, clock in hand, because I'm one minute late in clearing the table for him.

Yours, Anne

---

17. Industrious – diligent       18. Share-out – something distributed
19. Pudding – a sweet dessert     20. Pedantic – dull, obscure

# Monday, 9 August, 1943

Dear Kitty,

To continue the "Secret Annexe" daily timetable. I shall now describe the evening meal:

Mr *Van Daan* begins. He is first to be served, takes a lot of everything if it is what he likes. Usually talks at the same time, always gives his opinion as the only one worth listening to, and once he has spoken it is **irrevocable**[21]. Because if anyone *darts to* question it, then he **flares**[22] up at once. Oh, he can spit like a cat-I'd rather not argue, I can tell you-if you've once tried you don't try again. He has the best opinion, he knows the most about everything. All right then, he has got brains, but "self-satisfaction" has reached a high grade with this gentleman.

*Madame.* Really, I should remain silent. Some days, especially if there is a bad mood coming on, you can't look at her face. On closer examination, she is the guilty one in all the arguments. Not the subject! Oh, no, everyone prefers to remain aloof over that, but one could perhaps call her the "kindler." Stirring up trouble, that's fun. Mrs. Frank against Anne; Margot against Daddy doesn't go quite so easily.

But now at table, Mrs. Van Daan doesn't go short, although she thinks so at times. The tiniest potatoes, the sweetest mouthful, the best of everything; picking over is her system. The others will get their turn, as long as 1 have the best. Then talking. Whether anyone is interested, whether they are listening or not, that doesn't seem to matter. I suppose she thinks: "Everyone is interested in what Mrs. Van Daan says." Coquettish smiles, behaving as if one knew everything, giving everyone a bit of advice and encouragement, that's sure to make a good impression. But if you look longer, then the good soon wears off.

One, she is industrious, two, gay, three, a coquette— and, occasionally, pretty. This is Petronella Van Daan.

---

21.  Irrevocable – unalterable               22.  Flares – erupts

*The third table companion.* One doesn't hear much from him. Young Mr. Van Daan is very quiet and doesn't draw much attention to himself. As for appetite: a Danaidean vessel, which is never full and after the heartiest meal declares quite calmly that he could have eaten double.

*Number four—Margot.* Eats like a little mouse and doesn't talk at all. The only things that go down are vegetables and fruit. "Spoiled" is the Van Daans' judgment; "not enough fresh air and games," our opinion.

*Beside her—Mummy.* Good appetite, very talkative. Mo one has the impression, as Mrs. Van Daan: this is the housewife. What is the difference? Well, Mrs. Van Daan does the cooking, and Mummy washes up and polishes.

*Number six and seven. I* won't say much about Daddy and me. The former is the most **unassuming**[23] of all at table. He looks first to see if everyone else has something. He needs nothing himself, for the best things are for the children. He is the perfect example, and sitting beside him, the "Secret Annexes" "bundle of nerves."

*Dr. Dussel.* Helps himself, never looks up, eats and doesn't talk. And if one must talk, then for heaven's sake let it be about food. You don't quarrel about it, you only brag. **Enormous**[24] helpings go down and the word "No" is never heard, never when the food is good, and not often when it's bad. Trousers wrapping his chest, red coat, black bedroom slippers, and horn-rimmed spectacles. That is how one sees him at the little table, always working, **alternated**[25] only by his afternoon nap, food, and—his favorite spot—the lavatory. Three, four, five times a day someone stands impatiently in front of the door and **wriggles**[26], **hopping**[27] from one foot to the other, hardly able to contain himself. Does it disturb him? Not a bit! From quarter past seven till half past, from half past twelve till one o'clock, from

---

23. Unassuming – exhibiting no pretensions    24. Enormous – extent

25. Alternated – to occur in a successive manner    26. Wriggles – moves aboute

27. Hopping – moving quickly

two till quarter past, from four till quarter past, from six till quarter past, and from half past eleven until twelve. One can make a note of it— these are the regular "sitting times." He won't come off or pay any heed to an imploring voice at the door, giving warning of approaching disaster!

*Number nine* isn't a member of the "Secret Annexe" family, but rather a companion in the house and at table. Elli has a healthy appetite. Leaves nothing on her plate and is not picky-and-choosy. She is easy to please and that is just what gives us pleasure. Cheerful and good tempered, willing and good natured, these are her characteristics.

Yours, Anne

## Tuesday, 10 August, 1943

Dear Kitty,

New idea. I talk more to myself than to the others at mealtimes, which is to be recommended for two reasons. Firstly, because everyone is happy if I don't chatter the whole time, and secondly, I needn't get annoyed about other people's opinions. I don't think my opinions are stupid and the "others do; so it is better to keep them to myself. I do just the same if I have to eat something that I simply can't stand. I put my plate in front of me, pretend that it is something delicious, look at it as little as possible, and before I know where I am, it is gone. When I get up in the morning, also a very unpleasant process, I jump out of bed thinking to myself: "You'll be back in a second," go to the window, take down the **blackout**[28], **sniff**[29] at the crack of the window until I feel a bit of fresh air, and I'm awake. The bed is turned down as quickly as possible and then the temptation is removed. Do you know what Mummy calls this sort of thing? "The Art of Living"— that's an odd expression. For the last week we've all been in a bit of a **muddle**[30] about time, because our dear and beloved

---

28. Blackout – a cutoff of electrical power
29. Sniff – inhale forcibly through the nose
30. Muddle – make turbid or muddy.

Westertoren clock bell has apparently been taken away for war purposes, so that neither by day nor night do we ever know the exact time. I still have some hope that they will think up a substitute (tin, copper or some such thing) to remind the ᵇ neighborhood of the clock.

Whether I'm upstairs or down, or wherever I am, my feet are the admiration of all, **glittering**[31] in a pair of (for these days) exceptionally fine shoes. Miep managed to get hold of them second-hand for 27.50 florins, wine colored suede leather with fairly high **wedge**[32] heels. I feel as if I'm on stilts and look much taller than I am. Dussel has indirectly **endangered**[33] our lives. He actually let Miep bring a **forbidden**[34] book for him, one which, **abuses**[35] Mussolini and Hitler. On the way she happened to be run into by an S.S. car. She lost her temper, shouted, "Miserable **wretches**[36]," and rode on. It is better not to think of what might have happened if she had had to go to their headquarters.

Yours, Anne

# Wednesday, 18 August, 1943

Dear Kitty,

The title for this piece is: "The **community**[37] task of the day: potato **peeling**[38]!"

One person fetches the newspapers, another the knives (keeping the best for himself, of course), a third potatoes, and the fourth a pan of water.

---

31. Glittering – sparkling brilliantly
32. Wedge – the bottom of a shoe
33. Endangered – to expose to harm
34. Forbidden – not permitted by order or law
35. Abuses – insult verbally
36. Wretches – terrible people
37. Community – a group of people living in the same locality and under the same government
38. Peeling – removing the skin

Mr. Dussel begins, does not always **scrape**[39] well, but scrapes **incessantly**[40], glancing right and left. Does everyone do it the way he does? No! "Anne, look here, I take the knife in my hand like this, scrape from the top downwards! No, not like that-like this!"

"I get on better like *this,* Mr. Dussel," I remark timidly.

"But still this is the best way. But *du kannst* take *dies* from me. Naturally I don't care a bit, *aber du* must know for yourself." We scrape on. I look slyly once in my neighbor's direction. He shakes his head thoughtfully once more (over me, I suppose) but is silent.

I scrape on again. Now I look to the other side, where Daddy is sitting; for him scraping potatoes is not just a little odd job, but a piece of precision work. When he reads, he has a deep wrinkle at the back of his head, but if he helps prepare potatoes, beans, or any other vegetables, then it seems as if nothing else penetrates. Then he has on his "potato face," and he would never hand over an imperfectly scraped potato; it's out of the question when he makes that face!

I work on again and then just look up for a second; I know it already. Mrs. Van Daan is trying to attract Dussel's attention. First she looks in his direction and Dussel appears not to notice anything. Then she winks an eye; Dussel works on. Then she laughs, Dussel doesn't look up. Then Mummy laughs too; Dussel takes no notice. Mrs. Van Daan has not achieved anything, so she has to think of something else. A pause and then: "Putti, do put on an apron! Tomorrow I shall have to get all the spots out of your suit!"

I'm not getting myself dirty!"

Another moment's silence.

"Putti, why don't you sit down?"

"I'm comfortable standing up and prefer it!" Pause.

"Putti, look, *du spatst schon!* ("You are making a mess!")

---

39.  Scrape – smooth by rubbing with a sharp object
40.  Incessantly – continuing without interruption

"Yes, Mammy, I'm being careful."

Mrs. Van Daan searches for another subject. "I say, Putti, why aren't there any English air raids now?"

"Because the weather is bad, Kerli."

"But it was lovely yesterday, and they didn't fly then either."

"Let's not talk, about it."

"Why, surely one can talk about it, or give one's opinion?"

"No."

"Why ever not?"

"Do be quiet, mammi' chen."

"Mr. Frank always answers his wife, doesn't he?"

Mr. Van Daan **wrestles**[41] with himself. This is his tender spot, it's something he can't take and Mrs. Van Daan begins again: "The invasion seems as if it will never come!"

Mr Van Daan goes white; when Mrs. Van Daan sees this, she turns red, but goes on again: "The British do nothing!" The bomb explodes!

"And now hold your tongue, *donnerwetter-noch-einmal!*"

Mummy can hardly hold back her laughter. I look straight in front of me.

This sort of thing happens nearly every day unless they have just had a very bad quarrel, because then they both keep their mouths shut.

I have to go up to the attic to fetch some potatoes. Peter is busy there **debusing**[42] the cat. He looks up, the cat notices— pop—he has disappeared through the open window into the **gutter**[43]. Peter **swears**[44]. I laugh and disappear.

Yours, Anne

41. Wrestles – struggles
42. Debusing – unloading
43. Gutter – a channel for sewage at the edge of a street
44. Swears – pledges

# Friday 20 August, 1943

Dear Kitty,

The men in the warehouse go home sharp at half past five and then we are free.

*Half past five.* Elli comes to give us our evening freedom. Immediately we begin to make some **headway**[45] with our work. First, I go upstairs with Elli, where she usually begins by having a bit from our second course.

Before Elli is seated, Mrs. Van Daan begins thinking of things she wants. It soon comes out: "Oh, Elli, I have only one little wish. . .." Elli winks at me; whoever comes upstairs, Mrs. Van Daan never misses a single opportunity of letting them know what she wants. That must be one of the reasons why none of them like coming upstairs.

*Quarter to six.* Elli departs. I go two floors down to have a look around. First to the kitchen, then to the private office, after that the **coalhole**[46], to open the trap door for Mouschi. After a long tour of inspection I land up in Kraler's room. Van Daan is looking in all the drawers and **portfolios**[47] to find the days post. Peter is fetching the warehouse key and Boche, Pim is **hauling**[48] the typewriters upstairs; Margot is looking for a quiet spot to do her office work; Mrs, Van Daan puts a kettle on the gas ring; Mummy is coming downstairs with a pan of potatoes; each one knows his own job.

Peter soon returns from the **warehouse**[49]. The first question is bread. This is always put in the kitchen cupboard by the Ladies, but it is not there. Forgotten?

Peter offers to look in the main office. He **crouches**[50] in front of the door to make himself as small as possible and crawls towards the steel lockers on hands and knees, so as not to be seen from outside, gets the bread, which had been put there, and disappears; at least, he wants to disappear, but before he quite realizes what has happened, Mouschi has jumped over him and gone and sat right under the writing table.

---

45. Headway – Forward movement      46. Coalhole – a bin for holding coal
47. Portfolios – A portable case for holding material
48. Hauling – dragging                49. Warehouse – a storehouse
50. Crouches – bends

Peter looks all-around—aha, he sees him there, he crawls into the office again and pulls the animal by its tail. Mouschi spits. Peter sighs. What has he achieved? Now Mouschi is sitting right up by the window cleaning himself, very pleased to have escaped Peter. Now Peter is holding a piece of bread under the cats nose as a last decoy. Mouschi will not be **tempted**[51] and the door closes. I stood and watched it all through the crack of the door. We work on. Rat, tat, tat. three taps means a meal!

Yours, Anne

## Monday, 23 August, 1943

Dear Kitty,

Continuation of the "Secret Annexe" daily timetable. As the clock strikes half past eight in the morning, Margot and Mummy are jittery: "Ssh... Daddy, quiet. Otto, ssh . Pim." "It is half past eight, come back here, you can't run any more water, walk quietly!" These are the various cries to Daddy in the bathroom. As the clock strikes half past eight, he has to be in the living room. Not a drop of water, no lavatory, no walking about, everything quiet. As long as none of the office staff are there, everything can be heard in the warehouse. The door is opened upstairs at twenty minutes past eight and shortly after there are three taps on the floor: Anne's porridge. I climb upstairs and fetch my "puppydog" plate. Down in my roon, again, everything goes at terrific speed: do my hair, put away my noisy tin pottie, bed in place. Hush, the clock strikes! Upstairs Mrs. Van Daan has changed her shoes and is shuffling about in bedroom slippers. Mr. Van Daan, too, all is quiet.

Now we have a little bit of real family life I want to read or work, Margot as well, also Daddy and Mummy, Daddy is sitting (with Dickens and the dictionary, naturally) on the edge of tne **sagging**[52], squeaky bed, where there aren't even any decent mattresses:

---

51.  Tempted – inviting
52.  Sagging – hanging down

*two* **bolsters** [53] on top of each other will also serve the purpose, then he thinks: "Mustn't have them, then I'll manage without!"

Once he is reading he doesn't look up, or about him, laughs every now ana then, takes awful trouble to get Mummy interested in a little story. Answer: "I haven't got time now." Looks disappointed for just a second, then reads on again; a little later, when he comes to something extra amusing, he tries it again: "You must read this. Mummy!" Mummy sits on the "Opklap"* bed, reads, sews, knits, or works, whatever she feels like. She suddenly thinks of something. Just says it quickly: "Anne, do you know ... Margot, just jot down ... I" After a while peace returns once more.

Margot closes her book with a clap. Daddy raises his eyebrows into a funny curve, his reading **wrinkle** [54] deepens again, and he is lost in his book once more. Mummy begins to chatter with Margot, I become curious and listen too! Pim is drawn into the discussion... nine o'clock! Breakfast!

Yours, Anne

---

\* Dutch type of bed, which folds against the wall to look like a bookcase with curtains hanging before it.

---

53. Bolsters – cushions     54. Wrinkle – folding

## Think and Ink...

➤ Anne gives minute-to-minute description of the happening during the right? How signification were these descriptions?

➤ What idea does Anne give us as she describes the attitude of each of the members at the dining table?

➤ Why do you think Anne appreciates her father as the perfect example?

### Text-Based Questions

• What favorable news did they get about the political situation?

• How did Mrs. Van Daan react to the third air said?

• How was the family affected by the fleas and plague?

• What frustration did Anne have due to her situation?

• How did the afternoon pass for the family?

• What comments did Anne make about each of the inmates during meal time?

• What did Anne do on getting up in the morning?

• How did Dussel endanger their lives?

• How did the potato peeling process go about?

• What did Mrs. Van Daan do to attract Dussels attention? How did her efforts end up?

• What daily routines does Anne describe from half past five till nine o' clock?

# Friday, 10 September, 1943

Dear Kitty,

Every time I write to you something special seems to have happened, but they are more often **unpleasant**[1] than pleasant things. However, now there is something wonderful going on. Last Wednesday evening, 8 September, we sat around listening to the seven o'clock news and the first thing we heard was: "Here follows the best news of the whole war. Italy has **capitulated**[2]!" Italy's unconditional surrender! The Dutch program from England began at quarter past eight. "Listeners, an hour ago, I had just finished writing the **chronicle**[3] of the day when the wonderful news of Italy's capitulation came in. I can tell you that I have never deposited my notes in the waste-paper basket with such joy!" "God Save the King," the American national anthem, and the "Internationale" were played. As always, the Dutch program was **uplifting**[4], but not too **optimistic**[5].

Still we have troubles, too; it's about Mr. Koophuis. As you know, we are all very fond of him, he is always cheerful and amazingly brave, although he is never well, has a lot of pain, and is not allowed to eat much or do much walking. "When Mr. Koophuis enters, the sun begins to shine," Mummy said just recently, and she is quite right. Now he has had to go into the hospital for a very unpleasant abdominal operation and will have to stay there for at least four weeks. You really ought to have seen how he said goodby to us just as usual—he might have simply been going out to do a bit of shopping.

Yours, Anne

# Thursday, 16 September, 1943

Dear Kitty,

Relations between us here are getting worse all the time. At mealtimes, no one dares to open their mouths (except to allow a

---

1. Unpleasant – not pleasing
2. Capitulated – come to terms
3. Chronicle – history
4. Uplifting – improving
5. Optimistic – being positive

mouthful of food to slip in) because whatever is said you either annoy someone or it is misunderstood. I **swallow**[6] Valerian pills every day against **worry**[7] and **depression**[8], but it doesn't prevent me from being even more miserable the next day. A good hearty laugh would help more than ten Valerian pills, but we've almost forgotten how to laugh. I feel afraid sometimes that from having to be so serious I'll grow a long face and my mouth will **droop**[9] at the corners. The others don't get any better either, everyone looks with fear and **misgivings**[10] towards that great terror, winter. Another thing that does not cheer us up is the fact that the warehouseman, V.M., is becoming suspicious about the "Secret Annexe." We really wouldn't mind what V.M. thought of the situation if he wasn't so exceptionally **inquisitive**[11], difficult to **fob off**[12], and, moreover, not to be trusted. One day Kraler wanted to be extra careful, put on his coat at ten minutes to one, and went to the chemist round the corner. He was back in less than five minutes, and **sneaked**[13] like a thief up the steep stairs that lead straight to us. At a quarter past one he wanted to go again, but Elli came to warn him that V.M. was in the office. He did a right-about turn and sat with us until half past one. Then he took off his shoes and went in stockinged feet to the front attic door, went downstairs step by step, and, after balancing there for a quarter of an hour to avoid creaking, he landed safely in the office, having entered from the outside. Elli had been freed of V.M. in the meantime, and came up to us to fetch Kraler, but he had already been gone a long time; he was still on the staircase with his shoes off. Whatever would the people in the street have thought if they had seen the Manager putting on his shoes outside? Gosh! the Manager in his socks!

Yours, Anne

---

6. Swallow – to pass through the mouth and throat into the stomach.

7. Worry – feel uneasy          8. Depression – a state of mind

9. Droop – hang downward       10. Misgivings – distrust

11. Inquisitive – inclined to investigate    12. Fob off – to dispose

13. Sneaked – move in a quietly

# Wednesday, 29 September, 1943

Dear Kitty,

It is Mrs. Van Daan's birthday. We gave her a pot of jam, as well as coupons for cheese, meat, and bread.

From her husband, Dussel, and our protectors she received things to eat and flowers. Such are the times we live in!

Elli had a fit of nerves this week; she had been sent out so often, time and again she had been asked to go and fetch something quickly, which meant yet another **errand**[14] or made her *feel* that she had done something wrong. If you just think that she still has to finish her office work downstairs, that Koophuis is ill, Miep at home with a cold, and that she herself has a **sprained**[15] ankle, love worries, and a **grumbling**[16] father, then its no wonder she's at her wit's end. We comforted her and said that if she puts her foot down once or twice and says she has no time, then the shopping lists will automatically get shorter.

There is something wrong with Mr. Van Daan again, I can see it coming on already! Daddy is very angry for some reason or other. Oh, what kind of explosion is hanging over us now? If only I wasn't mixed up so much with all these rows! If I could only get away! They'll drive us crazy before long!

Yours, Anne

---

14. Errand – a mission
15. Sprained – a painful wrenching
16. Grumbling – mutter discontentedly

## Think and Ink...

➤ Do you agree that whatever is said during meal times result in trouble? Why / Why not?

➤ What do you think of Anne's condition when we read of her swallowing Valerian pills for curing depression?

➤ Was it possible for anyone to keep calm under such a situation as we find in Holland then?

➤ How serious was the situation of Germans attaching the Jews, resulting in depression even for children?

### Text-Based Questions

• What wonderful thing happened on the 8th of September?

• What was the condition of Mr. Koophuis?

# Sunday, 17 October, 1943

Dear Kitty,

Koophuis is back again, thank goodness! He still looks rather pale but in spite of this sets out cheerfully to sell clothes for Van Daan. It is an unpleasant fact that the Van Daans have run right out of money. Mrs. Van Daan won't part with a thing from her pile of coats, dresses, and shoes. Mr. Van Dann's suit isn't easily disposed[1] of, because he wants too much for it. The end of the story is not yet in sight. Mrs. Van Daan will certainly have to part with her fur coat. They've had a terrific row upstairs about it, and now the reconciliation[2] period of "oh, darling Putti" and "precious Kerli" has set in.

I am dazed[3] by all the abusive exchanges that have taken place in this virtuous[4] house during the past month. Daddy goes about with his lips tightly pursed; when anyone speaks to him, he looks up startled[5], as if he is afraid he will have to patch up[6] some tricky relationship again. Mummy has red patches on her cheeks from excitement. Margot complains of headaches. Dussel can't sleep. Mrs. Van Daan grouses the whole day and I'm going completely crazy! Quite honestly, I sometimes forget who we are quarreling with and with whom we've made it up.

The only way to take one's mind off it all is to study, and I do a lot of that.

Yours, Anne

---

1. Disposed – arrange
2. Reconciliation – reestablishing cordial relations
3. Dazed – to stun
4. Virtuous – righteous
5. Startled – frightened
6. Patch up – to settle

# Friday. 29 October, 1943

Dear Kitty,

There have been **resounding**[7] rows again between Mr. and Mrs. Van Daan. It came about like this: as I have already told you, the Van Daans are at the end of their money. One day, some time ago now, Koophuis spoke about a furrier with whom he was on good terms, this gave Van Daan the idea of selling his wife's fur coat. It's a fur coat made from rabbit skins, and she has worn it seventeen years. He got 325 florins for it— an enormous sum. However, Mrs. Van Daan wanted to keep the money to buy new clothes after the war, and it took some doing before Mr. Van Daan made it clear to her that the money was urgently needed for the household.

The yells and screams, **stamping**[8] and abuse-you can't possibly imagine it! It was frightening. My family stood at the bottom of the stairs, holding their breath, ready if necessary to drag them apart! All this shouting and weeping and **nervous**[9] tension are so **unsettling**[10] and such a strain, that in *the* evening I drop into my bed crying, thanking heaven that I sometimes have half an hour to myself.

Mr. Koophuis is away again; his stomach gives him no peace. He doesn't even know whether it has stopped bleeding yet. For the first time, he was very down when he told us that he didn't feel well and was going home.

All goes well with me on the whole, except that I have no appetite. I keep being told: "You don't look at all well." I must say that they are doing their very best to keep me up to the mark. Crape sugar, codliver oil, yeast tablets, and calcium have all been lined up.

---

7. Resounding – clear and emphatic
8. Stamping – putting down the foot hard
9. Nervous – ansxious
10. Unsettling – disturbing

My nerves often get the better of me: it is especially on Sundays that I feel **rotten**[11]. The atmosphere is so **oppressive**[12], and sleepy and as heavy as lead. You don't hear a single bird singing outside, and a **deadly**[13] close silence hangs everywhere, catching hold of me as if it will drag me down deep into an **underworld**[14].

At such times Daddy, Mummy, and Margot leave me cold. I **wander**[15] from one room to another, downstairs and up again, feeling like a **songbird**[16] whose wings have been **clipped**[17] and who is **hurling**[18] himself in utter darkness against the bars of his cage. "Go outside, laugh, and take a breath of fresh air," a voice cries within me, but I don't even feel a response any more; I go and lie on the divan and sleep, to make the time pass more quickly, and the stillness and the terrible fear, because there is no way of killing them.

Yours, Anne

---

11. Rotten – decayed
12. Oppressive – burdensome
13. Deadly – extreme
14. Underworld – gangland a region
15. Wander – move about aimlessly
16. Songbird – a bird
17. Clipped – to cut
18. Hurling – throwing

## Think and Ink...

➢ Why had so much of abusive exchanges taken place in the house during recent times?

➢ Comment on why Anne felt rotten on Sundays.

➢ Do you think her attitude is right? Why?

➢ How was life nightmarish for Anne, given her circumstances?

➢ Imagine what your would have done under such a circumstance of prolonged misery?

➢ What disparity was Anne thrown into as she found her fountain pen burnt? Why?

➢ As days pass by life become hopeless for the inmates of the secret Anne's Comment on the with reference to Anne's diary entry for 17 November 1943.

### Text-Based Questions

• What did Kraler do? Why was he stopped by kill?

• How was Mrs. Van Daan's birthday celebrated?

• Why was Elli at her wit's end?

• What was the unpleasant fact about the Van Daans?

• Why could not Mrs. Van Daan spare her fur coat?

• Why was there a nervous tension up stairs?

• Why did Anne lose her appetite?

• Why did she feel the atmosphere oppressive on Sundays?

# Wednesday, 3 November, 1943

Dear Kitty,

In order to give us something to do, which is also educational. Daddy applied for a **prospectus**[1] from the Teachers' Institute in Leiden. Margot nosed through the thick book at least three times without finding anything to her liking or to suit her purse. Daddy was quicker, and wants a letter written to the Institute asking for a trial lesson in "Elementary Latin."

To give me something new to begin as well. Daddy asked Koophuis for a children's Bible so that I could find out something about the New Testament at last.

"Do you want to give Anne a Bible for Chanuka?" asked Margot, somewhat perturbed. "Yes-er, I think St. Nicholas Day is a better occasion," answered Daddy, "Jesus just doesn't go with Chanuka."*

Yours, Anne

# Monday Evening, 8 November, 1943

Dear Kitty,

If you were to read my pile of letters one after another, you would certainly be struck by the many different moods in which they are written. It annoys me that I am so dependent on the atmosphere here, but I'm certainly not the only one-we all find it the same. If I read a book that impresses me, I have to take myself firmly in hand, before I mix with other people, otherwise they would think my mind rather queer. At the moment, as you've probably noticed, I'm going through a spell of being depressed. I really couldn't tell you why it is, but I believe it's just because I'm a coward, and that's what I keep bumping up against.

* See entry for 7 December, 1942.

1. Prospectus – a catalog listing the courses offered by a college

This evening, while Elli was still here, there was a long, loud, penetrating ring at the door. I turned white at once, got a tummy-ache and heart **palpitations**[2], all from fear. At night, when I'm in bed, I see myself alone in a **dungeon**[3], without Mummy and Daddy. Sometimes I wander by the roadside, or our "Secret Annexe" is on fire, or they come and take us away at night. I see everything as if it is actually taking,place, and this gives me the feeling that it may all happen to me very soon. Miep often says she envies us for possessing such **tranquillity**[4] here. That may be true, but she is not thinking about all our fears. I simply can't imagine that the world will ever be normal for us again. I do talk about "after the war," but then it is only a castle in the air, something that will never really happen. If I think back to our old house, my girl friends, the fun at school, it is just as if another person lived it all, not me.

I see the eight of us with our "Secret Annexe" as if we were a little piece of blue heaven, surrounded by heavy black rain clouds. The round, clearly defined spot where we stand is still safe, but the clouds gather more closely about us and the circle which separates us from the approaching danger closes more and more tightly. Now we are so surrounded by danger and darkness that we bump against each other, as we search desperately for a means of escape. We all look down below, where people are fighting each other, we look above, where it is quiet and beautiful, and meanwhile we are cut off by the great dark mass, which will not let us go upwards, but which stands before us as an **impenetrable**[5] wall, it tries to crush us, but cannot do so yet. I can only cry and **implore**[6]: "Oh, if only the black circle could **recede**[7] and open the way for us!"

Yours, Anne

2. Palpitations – rapid beating
3. Dungeon – dark place
4. Tranquility – peace
5. Impenetrable – impossible to penetrate
6. Implore – entreat
7. Recede – move away

# Thursday, 11 November, 1943

Dear Kitty,

I have a good title for this chapter.

ODE TO MY FOUNTAIN PEN IN MEMORIAM

My fountain pen has always been one of my most priceless possessions, I value it highly, especially for its thick nib, for I can only really write neatly with a thick nib. My fountain pen has had a very long and" interesting pen-life, which I will briefly tell you about.

When I was nine, my fountain pen arrived in a packet (wrapped in cotton wool) as "sample without value" all the way from Aachen, where my Grandmother, the kind donor, used to live, I was in bed with flu, while February winds howled round the house. The glorious fountain pen had a red leather case and was at once shown around to all my friends. I, Anne Frank, the proud owner of a fountain pen! When I was ten I was allowed to take the pen to school and the mistress went so far as to permit me to write with it.

When I was eleven, however, my treasure had to be put away again, because the mistress in the sixth form only allowed us to use school pens and inkpots.

When I was twelve and went to the Jewish Lyceum,* my fountain pen received a new case in honor of the great occasion, it could take a pencil as well, and as it closed with a zipper looked much more impressive.

At thirteen the fountain pen came with us to the "Secret Annexe," where it has raced through countless diaries and compositions for me.

Now I am fourteen, we have spent our last year together.

It was on a Friday afternoon after five o'clock. I had come out of my room and wanted to go and sit at the table to write, when I was roughly pushed on one side and had to make room for Margot and

---

* A type of secondary school specializing in the classics, common in most continental countries

Daddy, who wanted to practice their "Latin." The fountain pen remained on the table unused while, with a sigh, its owner contented herself with a tiny little corner of the table and started rubbing beans. "Bean rubbing" is making moldy beans decent again. I swept the floor at a quarter to six and threw the dirt, together with the bad beans, into a newspaper and into the stove. A terrific flame leaped out and I thought it was grand that the fire should burn up so well when it was practically out. All was quiet again, the "Latinites" had finished, and I went and sat at the table to clear up my writing things, but look as I might, my fountain pen was nowhere to be seen. I looked again, Margot looked, but there was not a trace of the thing. "Perhaps it fell into the stove together with the beans," Margot suggested. "Oh, no, of course not!" I answered. When my fountain pen didn't turn up that evening, however, we all took it that it had been burned, all the more as celluloid[8] is terribly inflammable.

And so it was, our unhappy fears were confirmed; when Daddy did the stove the following morning the clip used for fastening was found among the ashes.

Not a trace of the gold nib was found. "Must have melted and stuck to some stone or other," Daddy thought.

I have one consolation[9], although a slender[10] one: my fountain pen has been cremated[11], just what I want later!

Yours, Anne

## Wednesday, 17 November, 1943

Dear Kitty,

Shattering[12] things are happening. Diphtheria[13] reigns in Elli's home, so she is not allowed to come into contact with us for six weeks. It makes it very awkward[14] over food and shopping, not to

---

8. Celluloid – highly flammable        9. Consolation – relieve
10. Slender – long and thin            11. Cremated – to burn up
12. Shattering – ruin of               13. Diphtheria – an infectious disease
14. Awkward – causing inconvenience

mention missing her **companionship**[15]. Koophuis is still in bed and has had nothing but **porridge**[16] and milk for three weeks. Kraler is **frantically**[17] busy.

The Latin lessons Margot sends in are corrected by a teacher and returned, Margot writing in Ell's name. The teacher is very nice, and **witty**[18], too. I expect he is glad to have such a clever pupil.

Dussel is very put out, none of us knows why. It began by his keeping his mouth closed upstairs, he didn't utter a word to either Mr. or Mrs. Van Daan. Everyone was struck by it, and when it lasted a couple of days. Mummy took the opportunity of warning him about Mrs. Van Daan, who, if he went on like this, could make things very disagreeable for him.

Dussel said that Mr. Van Daan started the silence, so he was not going to be the one to break it.

Now I must tell you that yesterday was the sixteenth of November the day he had been exactly one year in the "Secret Annexe." Mummy received a plant in honor of the occasion, but Mrs. Van Daan, who for weeks **beforehand**[19] had made no bones about the fact that she thought Dussel should treat us to something, received nothing.

Instead of expressing, for the first time, his thanks for our **unselfishness**[20] in taking him in, he didn't say a word. And when I asked him, on the morning of the sixteenth, whether I should congratulate or **condole**[21], he answered that it didn't matter to him. Mummy, who wanted to act as **peacemaker**[22], didn't get one step further, and finally the situation remained as it was.

*'Der Man hat einen grossen Geist , Und ist so klein von Taten!'*

Yours, Anne

---

15. Companionship – fellowship
16. Porridge – another meal in water or milk
17. Frantically – in a wild manner    18. Witty – funny
19. Beforehand – in anticipation    20. Unselfishness – acting generously
21. Condole – to express sympathy
22. Peacemaker – someone who tries to bring peace

# Saturday, 27 November, 1943

Dear Kitty,

Yesterday evening, before I fell asleep, suddenly appear before my eyes but Lies!

I saw her in front of me, clothed in rags, her face thin and worn. Her eyes were very big and she looked so sadly and **reproachfully**[23] at me that I could read in her eyes: "Oh Anne, why have you **deserted**[24] me? Help, oh, help me, rescue me from this hell.'"

And I cannot help her, I can only look on, how others suffer and die, and can only pray to God to send her back to us.

I just saw Lies, no one else, and now I understand. I **misjudged**[25] her and was too young to understand her difficulties. She was attached to a new girl friend, and to her it seemed as though I wanted to take her away. What the poor girl must have felt like, I know, I know the feeling so well myself!

Sometimes, in a **flash**[26], I saw something of her life, but a moment later I was selfishly absorbed again in my own pleasures and problems. It was **horrid**[27] of me to treat her as I did, and now she looked at me, oh so helplessly, with her pale face and **imploring**[28] eyes. If only I could help her!

Oh, God, that I should have all I could wish for and that she should be **seized**[29] by such a terrible fate. I am not more **virtuous**[30] than she, she, too, wanted to do whst was right, why should I be chosen to live and she probably to die? What was the difference between us? Why are we so far from each other now?

---

23. Reproachfully – expressing reproach
24. Deserted – left alone
25. Misjudged – to judge wrongly
26. Flash – brief
27. Horrid – dreadful
28. Imploring – urgent request to
29. Seized – take hold of
30. Virtuous – possessing

Quite honestly, I haven't thought about her for months, yes, almost for a year. Not completely forgotten her, but still I had never thought about her like this, until I saw her before me in all her misery.

Oh Lies, I hope that, if you live until the end of the war, you will come back to us and that I shall be able to take you in and do something to make up for the wrong I did you.

But when I am able to help her again, then she will not need my help so badly as now. I wonder if she ever thinks of me, if so, what would she feel?

Good Lord, **defend**[31] her, so that at least she is not alone. Oh, if only you could tell her that I think lovingly of her and with sympathy, perhaps that would give her greater **endurance**[32].

I must not go on thinking about it, because I don't get any further. I only keep seeing her great big eyes, and cannot free myself from them, I wonder if Lies has real faith in herself, and not only what has been thrust upon her?

I don't even know, I never took the trouble to ask her!

Lies, Lies, if only I could take you away, if only I could let you share all the things I enjoy. It is too late now, I can't help, or repair the wrong I have done. But I shall never forget her again, and I shall always pray for her.

Yours, Anne

---

31. Defend – keep safe from danger
32. Endurance – patience

## Think and Ink...

➤ One year after Dussel had come, as Anne says, should he be condoled or congratulated?

➤ Comment on the helpless situation Anne had been in and her feeling of guilt for her helplessness.

## Text-Based Questions

- What did Anne's father to make her learn?
- What shattering things were happening?
- How did Margot learn Latin?
- What happened to Dussel?
- Who came in Anne's dreams? Why?

# Monday, 6 December, 1943

Dear Kitty,

When St. Nicholas' Day approached, none of us could help thinking of the **prettily**[1] decorated basket we had last year and I, especially, thought it would be very dull to do nothing at all this year. I thought a long time about it, until I invented something, something funny.

I consulted Pim, and a week ago we started composing a little poem for each person.

On Sunday evening at a quarter to eight we appeared upstairs with the Jarge laundry basket between us, decorated with little figures, and bows of pink and blue carbon copy paper. The basket was covered with a large piece of brown paper, on which a letter was pinned. Everyone was rather astonished at the size of the surprise package. I took the letter from the paper and read:

*"Santa Claus has come once more.*
*Though not quite as fie came before;*
*We can't celebrate his day*
*In last years fine and pleasant way.*
*For then our hopes were high and bright.*
*All the optimists seemed right,*
*None supposing that this year*
*We would welcome Santa here.*
*Still we'll make his spirit live,*
*And since we've nothing left to give.*
*We've thought of something else to do*
*Each please look inside his shoe. "*

As each owner took his shoe from the basket there was a **resounding**[2] peal of laughter. A little paper package lay in each shoe with the address of the shoe's owner on it.

Yours, Anne

---

1. Prettily – pleasing          2. Resounding – echoing

# Wednesday, 22 December, 1943

Dear Kitty,

A bad attack of flu has prevented me from writing to you until today. It's wretched to be ill here. When I wanted to cough-one, two, three-1 crawled under the blankets and tried to **stifle**[3] the noise. Usually the only result was that the **tickle**[4] wouldn't go away at all, and milk and honey, sugar or **lozenges**[5] had to be brought into operation. It makes me dizzy to think of all the cures that were tried on me. Sweating, compresses, wet cloths on my chest, dry cloths on my chest, hot drinks, gargling, throat painting, lying still, cushion for extra warmth, hot water bottles, lemon squashes, and, in addition, the thermometer every two hours!

Can anyone really get better like this? The worst moment of all was certainly when Mr. Dussel thought he'd play doctor, and came and lay on my naked chest with his greasy head, in order to listen to the sounds within. Not only did his hair tickle unbearably, but I was embarrassed, in spite of the fact that he once, thirty years ago, studied medicine and has the title of Doctor. Why should the fellow come and lie on my heart? He's not my lover, after all! For that matter, he wouldn't hear whether its healthy or unhealthy inside me anyway, his ears need **syringing**[6] first, as he's becoming alarmingly hard of hearing.

But that is enough about illness. I'm as fit as a fiddle again, one centimeter taller, two pounds heavier, pale, and with a real appetite for learning.

There is not much news to tell you. We are all getting on well together for a change. There's no quarreling—we haven't had such peace in the home for at least half a year. Elli is still parted from us.

We received extra oil for Christmas, sweets and syrup the "chief present" is a brooch, made out of a two-and-a-half-cent piece, and

---

3. Stifle – suppress
4. Tickle – itching
5. Lozenges – a medicated lozenge used to soothe the throat
6. Syringing – cleansing

shining beautifully. Anyway, lovely, but **indescribable**[7]. Mr. Dussel gave Mummy and Mrs. Van Daan a lovely cake which he had asked Miep to bake for him. With all her work, she has to do that as well.' I have also something for Miep and Elli. For at least two months I have saved the sugar from my porridge, you see, and with Mr. Koophuiss help I will have it made into **fondants**[8].

It is drizzly weather, the stove smells, the food lies heavily on everybody's tummy, causing **thunderous**[9] noises on all sides.' The war at a standstill, **morale**[10] rotten.

Yours, Anne

# Friday, 24 December, 1943

Dear Kitty,

I have previously written about how much we are-affected by atmospheres here, and I think that in my own case this trouble is getting much worse lately.

*"Himmelhoch jaucbzend undzum lode betrubt"*\* certainly fits here. I am *"Himmelhoch jaucbzend"* if I only think how lucky we are here compared with other Jewish children, and "zum Tode *betrubt"* comes over me when, as happened today, for example, Mrs. Koophuis comes and tells us about her daughter Cony's hockey club, canoe trips, theatrical performances, and friends. I don't think I'm jealous of Corry, but I couldn't help feeling a great longing to have lots of fun myself for once, and to laugh until my tummy **ached**[11]. Especially at this time of the year with all the holidays for Christmas and the New Year, and we are stuck here like **outcasts**[12]. Still, I really ought not to write this, because it seems **ungrateful**[13] and I've certainly been

---

\* A famous line from Goethe: "on top of the world, or in the depths of despair."

---

7.  Indescribable – impossible to describe
8.  Fondants – a candy
9.  Thunderous – loud enough to cause (temporary) hearing loss
10. Morale – confidence          11. Ached – pained
12. Outcasts – rejected          13. Ungrateful – unrewarding or unpleasant

**exaggerating**[14]. But still, whatever you think of me, I can't keep everything to myself, so I'll remind you of my opening words— "Paper is patient."

When someone comes in from outside, with the wind in their clothes and the cold on their faces, then I could bury my head in the blankets to stop myself thinking: "When will we be granted the privilege of smelling fresh air?" And because I must not bury my head in the blankets, but the reverse— I must keep my head high and be brave, the thoughts will come, not once, but oh, countless times. Believe me, if you have been shut up for a year and a half, it can get too much for you some days. In spite of all justice and thankfulness, you can't crush your feelings. Cycling, dancing, whistling, looking out into the world, feeling young, to know that I'm free- that's what I long for, still, I mustn't show it, because I sometimes think if all eight of us began to pity ourselves, or went about with **discontented**[15] faces, where would it lead us? I sometimes ask myself, "Would anyone, either Jew or non-Jew, understand this about me, that I am simply a young girl badly in need of some **rollicking**[16] fun?" I don't know, and I couldn't talk about it to anyone, because then I know I should cry. Crying can bring such relief.

In spite of all my theories, and however much trouble I take, each day I miss having a real mother who understands me. That is why with everything I do and write I think of the "Mumsie" that I want to be for my children later on. The "Mumsie" who doesn't take everything that is said in general conversation so seriously, but who does take what I say seriously. I have noticed, though I *can't* explain how, that the word "Mumsie" tells you everything. Do you know what I've found? To give me the feeling of calling Mummy something which sounds like "Mumsie" I often call her "Mum", then from that comes "Mums": the incomplete "Mumsie," as it were, whom I would so love to honor with the extra "ie" and yet who does not realize it.

14. Exaggerating – overstate
15. Discontented – restlessly unhappy
16. Rollicking – carefree and high-spirited

It's a good thing, because it would only make her unhappy. That's enough about that, writing has made my "zum tode *betrubt*" go off a bit.

Yours, Anne

# Saturday, 25 December, 1943

Dear Kitty,

During these days, now that Christmas is here, I find myself thinking all the time about Pim, and what he told me about the love of his youth. Last year I didn't understand the meaning of his words as well as I do now. If he'd only talk about it again, perhaps I would be able to show him that I understand.

I believe that Pim talked about it because he who "knows the secrets of so many other hearts" had to express his own feelings for once; because otherwise Pim never says a word about himself, and I don't think Margot has any idea of all Pim has had to go through. Poor Pim, he can't make me think that he has forgotten everything. He will never forget this. He has become very **tolerant**[17]. I hope that I shall grow a bit like him, without having to go through all that.

Yours, Anne

# Monday, 27 December, 1943

Dear Kitty,

On Friday evening for the first time in my life I received something for Christmas. Koophuis, Kraler and the girls had prepared a lovely surprise again. Miep has made a lovely Christmas cake, on which was written "Peace 1944." Elli had provided a pound of sweet biscuits of **prewar**[18] quality. For Peter, Margot, and me a bottle of yoghourt, and a bottle of beer for each of the grownups. Everything was so nicely done up, and there were pictures stuck on the different packages. Otherwise Christmas passed by quickly for us.

Yours, Anne

---

17. Tolerant – broad-minded          18. Prewar – before the war

# Wednesday, 29 December, 1943

Dear Kitty,

I was very unhappy again last evening. Granny and Lies came into my mind. Granny, oh, darling Granny, how little we understood of what she suffered, or how sweet she was. And besides all this, she knew a terrible secret which she carefully kept to herself the whole time. How faithful and good Granny always was, she would never have Jet one of us down. Whatever it was, however naughty I had been. Granny always **stuck up**[19] for me.

Granny, did you love me or didn't you understand me either? I don't know. No one ever talked about themselves to Granny. How lonely Granny must have been, how lonely in spite of us! A person can be lonely even if he is loved by many people, because he is still not the "One and Only" to anyone.

And Lies, is she still alive? What is she doing? Oh, God, protect her and bring her back to us. Lies, I see in you all the time what my lot might have been, I keep seeing myself in your place. Why then should I often be unhappy over what happens here? Shouldn't I always be glad, contented, and happy, except when I think about her and her companions in distress? I am selfish and **cowardly**[20]. Why do I always dream and think of the most terrible things—my fear makes me want to scream out loud sometimes. Because still in spite of everything, I have not enough faith in God. He has given me so much—which I certainly do not deserve—and I still do so much that is wrong every day. If you think of your fellow creatures, then you only want to cry, you could really cry the whole day long. The only thing to do is to pray that God will perform a **miracle**[21] and save some of them. And I hope that I am doing that enough!

Yours, Anne

---

19. Stuck up – caught or fixed      20. Cowardly – lacking courage
21. Miracle – wonderful event

## Think and Ink...

➤ How did Anne and Pim keep up their good spirit on St. Nicholas day to make other happy?

➤ What made Anne comment that morale was rotten?

➤ Anne was a representative of all the Jews who suffered in the hands of Germans. How did she express her feeling and her desperation for being an outcast?

➤ What were the aims and dreams of Anne as she expresses in her diary entry of 24 December 1943?

➤ The diary entry for Sunday January 1944 is a self realization on the part of Anne. How different are her thoughts in this entry?

## Text-Based Questions

• Why were not the inmates enthusiastic to celebrate st. Nicholas day?

• How did Anne under go the attack of flu?

• How was Christmas celebrated?

• What were Anne's longings?

• Why did Anne remember Pim? What were her feelings towards him?

• What does Anne mean when she says biscuits of pre-war quality?

• What gifts were given to Anne for Christmas?

• How was she attached to her Granny?

• What thoughts troubled Anne?

• Why did Anne feel herself selfish and cowardly?

• What did Anne prey God for?

• How, according to Anne, should a mother be? How did her mother fall short of these qualities?

• What happened when Anne had been to the dentist with her mother and Margot?

• What changes did Anne experience in herself. why?

# Sunday, 2 January, 1944

Dear Kitty,

This morning when I had nothing to do I turned over some of the pages of my diary and several times I came across letters dealing with the subject "Mummy" in such a **hotheaded**[1] way that I was quite shocked, and asked myself: "Anne, is it really you who mentioned hate? Oh, Anne, how could you." I remained sitting with the open page in my hand, and thought about it and how it came about that I should have been so **brimful**[2] of rage and really so filled with such a thing as hate that I had to **confide**[3] it all in you, I have been trying to understand the Anne of a year ago and to excuse her, because my **conscience**[4] isn't clear as long as I leave you with these **accusations**[5], without being able fo explain, on looking back, how it happened.

I suffer now-and-suffered then-from moods which kept my head under water (so to speak) and only allowed me to see the things **subjectively**[6] without enabling me to consider quietly the words of the other side, and to answer them as the words of one whom I, with my hotheaded **temperament**[7], had offended or made unhappy.

I hid myself within myself, I only considered myself and quietly wrote down all my joys, sorrows, and contempt in my diary. This diary is of great value to me, because it has become a book of **memoirs**[8] in many places, but on a good many pages I could certainly put "past and done with."

I used to be furious with Mummy, and still am sometimes. It's true that she doesn't understand me, but I don't understand her either. She did love me very much and she was tender, but as she landed in so many unpleasant situations through me, and was nervous and

---

1. Hotheaded – easily angered       2. Brimful – full to overflowing
3. Confide – to tell (something) in confidence
4. Conscience – the awareness of a moral
5. Accusations – allegations        6. Subjectively – in a subjective way
7. Temperament – behaviour          8. Memoirs – a biography

irritable because of other worries and difficulties, it is certainly understandable that she snapped at me.

I took it much too seriously, I was offended, and was rude and **aggravating**[9] to Mummy, which, in turn, made her unhappy. So it was really a matter of unpleasantness and misery **rebounding**[10] all the time. It wasn't nice for either of us, but it is passing.

I just didn't want to see all this, and pitied myself very much, but that, too, is understandable. Those violent **outbursts**[11] on paper were only giving vent to anger which in a normal life could have been worked off by stamping my feet a couple of times in a locked room, or calling Mummy names behind her back.

The period when I caused Mummy to shed tears is over. I have grown wiser and Mummy's nerves are not so much on edge. I usually keep my mouth shut if I get annoyed, and so does she, so we appear to get on much better together. I can't really love Mummy in a dependent childlike way— I just don't have that feeling. I **soothe**[12] my conscience now with the thought that it is better for hard words to be on paper than that Mummy should carry them in her heart.

Yours, Anne

## Wednesday, 5 January, 1944

Dear Kitty,

I have two things to confess to you today, which will take a long time. But I must tell someone and you are the best one to tell, as I know that, come what may, you always keep a secret.

The first is about Mummy. You know that I've **grumbled**[13] a lot about Mummy, yet still tried to be nice to her again. Now it is suddenly clear to me what she lacks. Mummy herself has told us that she looked upon us more as her friends than her daughters. Now that is all very fine, but still, a friend can't take a mother's place.

9. Aggravating – more troublesome        10. Rebounding – resound
11. Outbursts – violent display            12. Soothe – relieve
13. Grumbled – complained

I need my mother as an example which I can follow, I want to be able to respect her. I have the feeling that Margot thinks differently about these things and would never be able to understand what I've just told you. And Daddy avoids all arguments about Mummy.

I imagine a mother as a woman who, in the first place, shows great tact[14], especially towards her children when they reach our age, and who does not laugh at me if I cry about something—not pain, but other things—like "Mum" does.

One thing, which perhaps may seem rather **fatuous**[15], I have never forgiven her. It was on a day that I had to go to the dentist. Mummy and Margot were going to come with me, and agreed that I should take my bicycle. When we had finished at the dentist, and were outside again, Margot and Mummy told me that they were going into the town to look at something or buy something—I don't remember exactly what. I wanted to go, too, but was not allowed to, as I had my bicycle with me. Tears of rage **sprang**[16] into my eyes, and Mummy and Margot began laughing at me. Then I, became so furious that I stuck my tongue out at them in the street just as an old woman happened to pass, by, who looked very shocked! I rode home on my bicycle, and I know I cried for a long time, It is **queer**[17] that the wound that Mummy made then still burns, when I think of how angry I was that afternoon.

The second is something that is very difficult to tell you, because it is about myself.

Yesterday I read an article about **blushing**[18] by Sis Heyster. This article might have been addressed to me personally. Although I don't blush very easily, the other things in it certainly all fit me. She writes roughly something like this-that a girl in the years of **puberty**[19] becomes quiet within and begins to think about the wonders that are happening to her body.

---

| | |
|---|---|
| 14. Tact – skill | 15. Fatuous – excellent (self satisfied way) |
| 16. Sprang – come forth suddenly | 17. Queer – strange |
| 18. Blushing – embarrassment | 19. Puberty – adulthood |

I experience that, too, and that is why I get the feeling lately of being embarrassed about Margot, Mummy, and Daddy. Funnily enough, Margot, who is much more **shy**[20] than I am, isn't at all **embarrassed**[21].

I think what is happening to me is so wonderful, and not only what can be seen on my body, but all that is taking place inside. I never discuss myself or any of these things with anybody, that is why I have to talk to myself about them.

Each time I have a period-and that has only been three times— I have the feeling that in spite of all the pain, unpleasantness, and **nastiness**[22], I have a sweet secret, and that is why, although it is nothing but a nuisance to me in a way, I always long for the time that I shall feel that secret within me again.

Sis Heyster also writes that girls of this age don't feel quite certain of themselves, and discover that they themselves are individuals with ideas, thoughts, and habits. After I came here, when I was just fourteen, I began to think about myself sooner than most girls, and to know that I am a "person." Sometimes, when I lie in bed at night, I have a terrible desire to feel my breasts and to listen to the quiet rhythmic beat of my heart.

I already had these kinds of feelings **subconsciously**[23] before I came here, because I remember that once when I slept with a girl friend I had a strong desire to kiss her, and that I did do so. I could not help being terribly **inquisitive**[24] over her body, for she had always kept it hidden from me. I asked her whether, as a proof of our friendship, we should feel one another's breasts, but she refused. I go into **ecstasies**[25] every time I see the naked figure of a woman, such as Venus, for example. It strikes me as so wonderful and exquisite that I have difficulty in stopping the tears rolling down my cheeks. If only I had a girl friend!

Yours, Anne

---

20. Shy – lacking self-confidence　21. Embarrassed – disconcert
22. Nastiness – disgustingly dirty　23. Subconsciously – imperfectly conscious
24. Inquisitive – inquiring　25. Ecstasies – intense joy

# Thursday, 6 January, 1944

Dear Kitty,

My longing to talk to someone became so **intense**[26] that somehow or other I took it into my head to choose Peter.

Sometimes if I've been upstairs into Peters room during the day, it always struck me as very **snug**[27], but because Peter is so **retiring**[28] and would never turn anyone out who became a nuisance, I never dared stay long, because I was afraid he might think me a bore. I tried to think of an excuse to stay in his room and get him talking, without it being too noticeable, and my chance came yesterday. Peter has a mania for crossword puzzles at the moment and hardly does anything else. I helped him with them and we soon sat opposite each other at his little table, he on the chair and me on the divan.

It gave me a queer feeling each time I looked into his deep blue eyes, and he sat there with that mysterious laugh playing round his lips. I was able to read his inward thoughts. I could see on his face that look of 'helplessness and uncertainty how to behave, and, at the same time, a trace of his sense of manhood. I noticed his shy manner and it made me feel very gentle; I couldn't refrain from meeting those dark eyes again and again, and with my whole heart I almost **beseeched**[29] him: oh, tell me, what is going on inside you, oh, can't you look beyond this ridiculous **chatter**[30]?

But the evening passed and nothing happened, except that I told him about blushing—naturally not what I have written, but just so that he would become more sure of himself as he grew older.

When I lay in bed and thought over the whole situation, I found it far from encouraging, and the idea that I should beg for Peter's **patronage**[31] was simply **repellent**[32]. One can do a lot to satisfy ones longings, which certainly sticks out in my case, for I have made up my mind to go and sit with Peter more often and to get him talking somehow or other.

| | | |
|---|---|---|
| 26. Intense – deep | 27. Snug – cozy | 28. Retiring – (here) modest |
| 29. Beseeched – implored | 30. Chatter – to talk rapidly | |
| 31. Patronage – support | 32. Repellent – able to repel, revolt | |

Whatever you do, don't think I'm in love with Peter- not a bit of it! If the Van Daans had had a daughter instead of a son, I should have tried to make friends with her too.

I woke at about five to seven this morning and knew at once, quite positively, what I had dreamed. I sat on a chair and opposite me sat Peter... Wessel. We were looking together at a book of drawings by Mary Bos. The dream was so **vivid**[33] that I can still partly remember the drawings. But that was not all—the dream went on. Suddenly Peter's eyes met mine and I looked into those fine, velvet brown eyes for a long time. Then Peter said very softly, If I had only known, I would have come to you long before!" I turned around **brusquely**[34] because the emotion was too much for me. And after that I felt a soft, and oh, such a cool kind cheek against mine and it felt so good, so good....

I awoke at this point, while I could still feel his cheek against mine and felt his brown eyes looking deep into my heart, so deep, that there he read how much I had loved him and how much I still love him. Tears sprang into my eyes once more, and I was very sad that I had lost him again, but at the same time glad because it made me feel quite certain that Peter was still the chosen one.

It is strange that I should often see such vivid images in my dreams here. First I saw Grandma* so clearly one night that I could even **distinguish**[35] her thick, soft, wrinkled velvety skin. Then Granny appeared as a guardian angel, then followed Lies, who seems to be a symbol to me of the sufferings of all my girl friends and all Jews. When I pray for her, I pray for all Jews and all those in need. And now Peter, my darling Peter- never before have I had such a clear picture of him in my mind. I don't need a photo of him, I can see him before my eyes, and oh, so well!

Yours, Anne

---

\* Grandma is grandmother on father's side, Grany on mother's side.

---

33. Vivid – bright, brilliant     34. Brusquely – discourteously blunt
35. Distinguish – differentiate, recognize

# Friday, 7 January, 1944

Dear Kitty,

What a silly ass I am! I am quite forgetting that I have never told you the history of myself and all my boy friends.

When I was quite small-I was even still at a kindergarten—I became attached to Karel Samson. He had lost his father, and he and his mother lived with an aunt. One of Karel's cousins, Robby, was a slender, goodlooking dark boy, who aroused more admiration than the little, humorous fellow, Karel. But looks did not count with me and I was very fond of Karel for years.

We used to be together a lot for quite a long time, but for the rest, my love was unreturned.

Then Peter crossed my path, and in my childish way I really fell in love. He liked me very much, too, and we were **inseparable**[36] for one whole summer. I can still remember us walking hand in hand through the streets together, he in a white cotton suit and me in a short summer dress. At the end of the summer holidays he went into the first form of the high school and I into the sixth form of the lower school. He used to meet me from school and, **vice versa**[37], I would meet him. Peter was a very goodlooking boy, tall, handsome, and slim, with an earnest, calm, intelligent face. He had dark hair, and wonderful brown eyes, ruddy cheeks, and a pointed nose, I. was mad about his laugh, above all, when he looked so **mischievous**[38] and naughty! I went to the country for the holidays, when I returned. Peter had in the meantime moved, and a much older boy lived in the same house. He **apparently**[39] drew Peter's attention to the fact that I was a childish little **imp**[40], and Peter gave me up. I adored him so that I didn't want to face the truth. I tried to hold on to him until it dawned on me that if I went on running after him I should soon get the name of being boy-mad. The years passed. Peter went around

---

36. Inseparable – very closely associated
37. Vice Versa – conversely
38. Mischievous – teasing way
39. Apparently – visibly
40. Imp – a mischievous child

with girls of his own age and didn't even think of saying "Hello" *to* me any more, but I couldn't forget him.

I went to the Jewish Secondary School. Lots of boys in our class were keen on me-I thought it was fun, felt honored, but was otherwise quite untouched. Then later on, Harry was mad about me, but, as I've already told you, I never fell in love again.

There is a saying "Time heals all wounds," and so it was with me. I imagined that I had forgotten Peter and that I didn't like him a bit any more. The memory of him, however, lived so strongly in my subconscious mind that I admitted to myself sometimes I was jealous of the other girls, and that was why I didn't like him any more. This morning I knew that nothing has changed; on the contrary, as I grew older and more mature my love grew with me. I can quite understand now that Peter thought me childish, and *yet* it still hurt that he had so completely forgotten me. His face was shown so clearly to me, and now I know that no one else could remain with me like he does.

I am completely upset by the dream. When Daddy kissed me this morning, I could have cried out: "Oh, if only you were Peter!" I think of him all the time and I keep repeating to myself the whole day, "Oh, Peter, darling, darling Peter. . .!"

Who can help me now? I must live on and pray to God that He will let Peter cross my path when I come out of here, and that when he reads the love in my eyes he will say, "Oh, Anne, if I had only known, I would have come to you long before!"

I saw my face in the mirror and it looks quite different. My eyes look so dear and deep, my cheeks are pink— which they haven't been for weeks—my mouth is much softer, I look as if I am happy, and yet there is something so sad in my expression and my smile slips away from my lips as soon as it has come. I'm not happy, because I might know that Peter's thoughts are not with me, and yet I still feel his wonderful eyes upon me and his cool soft cheek against mine.

Oh, Peter, Peter, how will I ever free myself of your image? Wouldn't any other in your place be a miserable substitute? I love you, and with such a great love that it can't grow in my heart any more but has to leap out into the open and suddenly manifest itself in such a devastating way!

A week ago, even yesterday, if anyone had asked me, "Which of your friends do you consider would be the most suitable to marry?" I would have answered, "I don't know", but now I would cry, "Peter, because I love him with all my heart and soul. I give myself completely!" But one thing, he may touch my face, but no more.

Once, when we spoke about sex. Daddy told me that I couldn't possibly understand the longing yet; I always knew that I did understand it and now I understand it fully. Nothing is so beloved to me now as he, my Peter.

Yours, Anne

# Wednesday, 12 January, 1944

Dear Kitty,

Elli has been back a fortnight. Miep and Henk were away from their work for two days—they both had **tummy**[41] upsets. 1 have a craze for dancing and **ballet**[42] at the moment, and practice dance steps every evening **diligently**[43]. I have made a supermodern dance frock from a light blue petticoat edged with lace belonging *to* Mansa. A ribbon is threaded through round the top and ties in a bow in the center, and a pink corded ribbon completes the creation. I tried in vain to convert my gym shoes into real ballet shoes. My stiff limbs are well on the way to becoming supple again like they used to be. One terrific exercise is to *sit* on the floor, hold a heel in each hand, and then lift both legs up in the air. I have to have a cushion under me, otherwise my poor little behind has a rough time.

Everyone here is reading the book *Cloudless Morn*. Mummy thought it exceptionally good; there are a lot of youth problems in it. I thought to myself rather ironically: "Take a bit more trouble with your own young people first!"

---

41. Tummy – stomach　42. Ballet – a dance form　**43.** Diligently – carfully

I believe Mummy thinks there could be no *better* relationship between parents and their children, and that no one could take a greater interest in their children's lives than she. But quite definitely she only looks at Margot, who I don't think ever had such problems and thoughts as I do. Still, I wouldn't dream of pointing out to Mummy that, in the case of her daughters, it isn't at all as she imagines, because she would be **utterly**[44] amazed and wouldn't know how to change anyway. I want to save her the unhappiness it would cause her, especially as I know that for me everything would remain the same anyway.

Mummy certainly feels that Margot loves her much more than I do, but she thinks that this just goes in phases! Margot has grown so sweet; she seems quite different from what she used to be, isn't nearly so catty these days and is becoming a real friend. Nor does she any longer regard me as a little kid who counts for nothing.

I have an odd way of sometimes, as it were, being able to see myself through someone else's eyes. Then I view the affairs of a certain "Anne" at my ease, and browse through the pages of her life as if she were a stranger. Before we came here, when I didn't think about things as much as I do now, I used at times to have the feeling that I didn't belong to Mansa, Pim, and Margot, and that I would always be a bit of an outsider.

Sometimes I used to **pretend**[45] I was an orphan, until I **reproached**[46] and **punished**[47] myself, telling myself it was all my own fault that I played this self-pitying role, when I was really so fortunate. Then came the time that I used to force myself to be friendly. Every morning, as soon as someone came downstairs I hoped that it would be Mummy who would say good morning to me I greeted her warmly, because I really longed for her to look lovingly at me. Then she made some, remark or other that seemed unfriendly, and I would go off to school again feeling **thoroughly**[48]

---

44. Utterly – completely    45. Pretend – act
46. Reproached – disgrace   47. Punished – to subject to a penalty for an offense
48. Thoroughly – absolute

disheartened[49]. On the way home I would make excuses for her because she had so many worries, arrive home very cheerful, chatter nineteen to the dozen, until I began repeating myself, and left the room wearing a **pensive**[50] expression, my satchel under my arm. Sometimes I decided to remain cross, but when I came home from school I always had so much news that my **resolutions**[51] were gone with the wind and Mummy, whatever she might be doing, had to lend an ear to all my adventures. Then the time came once more when I didn't listen for footsteps on the staircase any longer, and at night my pillow was wet with tears.

Everything grew much worse at that point, *enfin* you know all about it.

Now God has sent me a helper— Peter... I just clasp my pendant, kiss it, and think to myself, "What do I care about the lot of them! Peter belongs to me and no one knows anything about it." This way I can get over all the snubs I receive. Who would ever think that so much can go on in the soul of a young girl?

Yours, Anne

## Saturday, 15 January, 1944

Dear Kitty,

There is no point in telling you every time the exact details of our rows and arguments. Let it **suffice**[52] to tell you that we have divided up a great many things, such as butter and meat, and that we fry our own potatoes. For some time now we've been eating wholemeal bread between meals as an extra, because by four o'clock in the afternoon we are longing for cur supper so much that we hardly know how to control our rumbling tummies.

Mummy's birthday is rapidly approaching. She got some extra sugar from Kraler, which made the Van Daans jealous as Mrs. Van Daan had not been favored in this way for her birthday. But what's

---

49. Disheartened – dispirit
50. Pensive – thoughtful
51. Resolutions – firmness or determination
52. Suffice – be sufficient

the use of annoying each other with yet more unkind words, tears, and angry outbursts. You can be sure of one thing. Kitty, that we are even more fed up with them than ever! Mummy has expressed the wish— one which cannot come true just now-not to see the Van Daans for a fortnight.

I keep asking myself, whether one would have trouble in the long run, whoever one shared a house with. Or did we strike it extra unlucky? Are most people so selfish and stingy then? I think it's all to the good to have learned a bit about human beings, but now I think I've learned enough. The war goes on just the same, whether or not we choose to quarrel, or long for freedom and fresh air, and so we should try to make the best of our stay here. Now I'm preaching, but I also believe that if I stay here for very long I shall grow into a dried-up old beanstalk[53]. And I did so want to grow into a real young woman!

Yours, Anne

## Saturday, 22 January, 1944

Dear Kitty,

I wonder whether you can tell me why it is that people always try so hard to hide their real feelings? How is it that I always behave quite differently from what I should in other people's company?

Why do we trust one another so little? I know there must be a reason, but still I sometimes think it's horrible that you find you can never really confide[54] in people, even in those who are nearest to you.

It seems as if I've grown up a lot since my dream the other night. I'm much more of an "independent being." You'll certainly be amazed when I tell you that even my attitude towards the Van Daans has changed. I suddenly see all the arguments and the rest of it in a different light, and am not as prejudiced[55] as I was.

---

53. Beanstalk – the stem of a bean plant     54. Confide – entrust
55. Prejudiced – being biased

How can I have changed so much? Yes, you see it suddenly struck me that if Mummy had been different, a real Mumsie, the relationship might have been quite, quite different. It's true that Mrs. Van Daan is by no means a nice person, but still I do think that half the quarrels could be avoided if it weren't for the fact that when the conversation gets tricky Mummy is a bit difficult too.

Mrs. Van Daan has one good side, and that is that you can talk to her. Despite all her selfishness, **stinginess**[56], and **underhandedness**[57], you can make her give in easily, as long as you don't **irritate**[58] her and get on the wrong side of her. This way doesn't work every time, but if you have patience you can try again and see how far you get.

All the problems of our "upbringing" of our being spoiled, the food-it could have been quite different if we'd remain perfectly open and friendly, and not always only on the lookout for something to seize on. I know exactly what you'll say, Kitty, "But, Anne, do these words really come from your lips? From you, who have had to listen to so many harsh words from the people upstairs, from you, the girl who has suffered so many injustices?" And yet they come from me.

I want to start afresh and try to get to the bottom of it all, not be like the saying "the young always follow a bad example." I want to examine the whole matter carefully myself and find out what is true and what is exaggerated. Then if I myself am disappointed in them, I can adopt the same line as Mummy and Daddy; if not, I shall try first of all to make them alter their ideas and if I don't succeed I shall stick to my own opinions and judgment. I shall **seize**[59] every opportunity to discuss openly all our points of argument with Mrs. Van Daan and not be afraid of **declaring**[60] myself **neutral**[61], even at the cost of being called a "know-all." It is not that I shall be going against my own family, but from today there will be no more unkind gossip on my part.

---

56.  Stinginess – being miserly   57.  Underhandedness – dishonest and sneaky
58.  Irritate – annoy          59.  Seize – take forcibly
60.  Declaring – to make known formally   61.  Neutral – not aligned with

Until now I was immovable.' I always thought the Van Daans were in the wrong, but we too are partly to blame. We have certainly been right over the subject matter, but handling of others from intelligent people (which we consider ourselves to be one expects more **insight**[62]. I hope that I have acquired a bit of insight and will use it well when the occasion arises.

Yours, Anne

# Monday, 24 January, 1944

Dear Kitty,

Something has happened to me, or rather, I can hardly describe it as an event, except that I think it is pretty crazy. Whenever anyone used to speak of sexual problems at home or at school, it was something either mysterious or revolting. Words which had any bearing on the subject were whispered, and often if someone didn't understand he was laughed at. It struck me as very odd and I thought, "Why are people so secretive and tiresome when they talk about these things?" But as I didn't think that I could change things, I kept my mouth shut as much as possible, or sometimes asked girl friends for information. When I had learned quite a lot and had also spoken about it with my parents, Mummy said one day, "Anne, let me give you some good advice; never speak about this subject to boys and don't reply if they begin about it." I remember exactly what my answer was: I said, "No, of course not! The very idea!" And there it remained.

When we first came here. Daddy often told me about things that I would really have **preferred**[63] to hear trom Mummy, and I found out the rest from books and things I picked up from conversations. Peter Van Daan was never as tiresome over this as the boys at school— once or twice at first perhaps—but he never tried to get me talking.

Mrs. Van Daan told us that she had never talked about these things to Peter, and for all she knew neither had her husband. Apparently she didn't even know how much he knew.

---

62. Insight – deep study      63. Preferred – to give priority

Yesterday, when Margot, Peter, and I were peeling potatoes, somehow the conversation turned to Boche. "We still don't know what sex Boche is, do we?" I asked.

"Yes, certainly," Peter answered. "He's a tom."

I began to laugh. "A tomcat that's expecting, that's marvelous!"

Peter and Margot laughed too over this silly mistake. You see, two months ago. Peter had stated that Boche would soon be-having a family, her tummy was growing visibly. However, the fatness appeared to come from the many stolen bones, because the children didn't seem to grow fast, let alone make their appearance!

Peter just had to defend himself. "No", he said. "You can go with me yourself to look at him. Once when I was playing around with him, I noticed quite clearly that he's a tom."

I couldn't control my curiosity, and went with him to the warehouse. Boche, however, was not receiving visitors, and was nowhere to be seen. We waited for a while, began to get cold, and went upstairs again. Later in the afternoon I heard Peter go downstairs for the second time. I **mustered**[64] up all my courage to walk through the silent house alone, and reached the warehouse. Boche stood on the packing table playing with Peter, who had just put him on the scales to weigh him.

"Hello, do you want to see him?" He didn't make any lengthy preparations, but picked up the animal, turned him over on to his back, **deftly**[65] held his head and paws together, and the lesson began. "These are the male organs, these are just a few stray hairs, and that is his bottom." The cat did another half turn and was standing on his white socks once more.

If any other boy had shown me "the male organs," I would never have looked at him again. But Peter went on talking quite normally on what is otherwise such a painful subject, without meaning anything unpleasant, and finally put me sufficiently at my ease for me to be normal too. We played with Boche, amused ourselves,

64. Mustered – gathered                    65. Deftly – quick and skillful

chattered together, and then **sauntered**[66] through the large warehouse towards the door, "Usually, when I want to know something, I find it in some book or other, don't you?" I asked.

"Why on earth? I just ask upstairs. My father knows more than me and has had more experience in such things."

We were already on the stairs, so I kept my mouth shut after that.

"Things may alter," as Brer Rabbit said. Yes. Really I shouldn't have discussed these things in such a normal way with a girl. I know too definitely that Mummy didn't mean it that way when she warned me not to discuss the subject with boys. I wasn't quite my usual pelf for the rest of the day though, in spite of everything. When I thought over our talk, it still seemed rather odd. But at least I'm wiser about one thing, that there really are young people—and of the opposite sex too—who can discuss these things naturally without making fun of them.

I wonder if Peter really does ask his parents much. Would he honestly behave with them as he did with me yesterday? Ah, what would I know about it!

Yours, Anne

## Thursday, 27 January, 1944

Dear Kitty,

Lately I have developed a great love for family trees and **genealogical**[67] tables of the royal families, and have come to the conclusion that, once you begin, you want to delve still deeper into the past, and can keep on making fresh and interesting discoveries. Although—I am extraordinarily industrious over my lessons, and can already follow the English Home Service quite well on the wireless, I still devote many Sundays to sorting and looking over my large collection of film stars, which is quite a respectable size by now.

---

66.  Sauntered – to walk in a casual manner
67.  Genealogical – a record or table of the descent of a person, family

I am awfully pleased whenever Mr. Kraler brings the *Cinema and Theater* with him on Mondays. Although this little gift is often called a waste of money by the less worldly members of the household, they are amazed each time at how accurately I can state who is in a certain film, even after a year. Elli, who, on her days off, often goes to the movies with her boy friend, tells me the titles of the new films each week; and in one breath I **rattle**[68] off the names of the stars who appear in them, together with what the reviews say. Not so long ago, Mum said that I wouldn't need to go to a cinema later on because I knew the plots, the names of the stars, and the opinions of the reviews all by heart.

If ever I come sailing in with a new hair style, they all look disapprovingly at me, and I can be quite sure that someone will ask which **glamorous**[69] star I'm supposed to be imitating. They only half believe me if I reply that its my own invention.

But to continue about the hair style—it doesn't stay put for more than half an hour, then I'm so tired of the remarks people pass that I quickly hasten to the bathroom and restore my ordinary housegarden-kitchen hair style.

Yours, Anne

## Friday, 28 January, 1944

Dear Kitty,

I asked myself this morning whether you don't sometimes feel rather like a cow who has had to chew over all the old pieces of news again and again, and who finally **yawns**[70] loudly and silently wishes that Anne would occasionally dig up something new.

Alas, I know it's dull for you, but try to put yourself in my place, and imagine how sick I am of the old cows who keep having to be pulled out of the **ditch**[71] again. If the conversation at mealtimes isn't over politics or a delicious meal, then Mummy or Mrs. Van Daan

| | |
|---|---|
| 68. Rattle – to talk rapidly | 69. Glamorous – beautiful and smart |
| 70. Yawns – mouth open wide | 71. Ditch – hollow pit |

trot[72] out one of the old stories of their youth, which we've heard so many times before or Dussel **twaddles**[73] on about his wife's extensive wardrobe, beautiful race horses, leaking rowboats, boys who can swim at the age of four, muscular pains and nervous patients. What it all boils down to is this-that if one of the eight of us opens his mouth, the other seven can finish the story for him! We all know the point of every joke from the start, and the storyteller is alone in laughing at his witticisms. The various milkmen, grocers, and butchers of the two ex-housewives have already grown beards in our minds, so often they have been praised to the skies or pulled to pieces, it is impossible for anything in the conversation here to be fresh or new.

Still, all this would be **bearable**[74] if the grownups didn't have their little way of telling the stories, with which Koophuis, Henk, or Miep **oblige**[75] the company ten times over and adding their own little **frills**[76] and **furbelows**[77], so that I often have to pinch my arm under the table to prevent myself from putting them right. Little children such as Anne must never, under any circumstances, know better than the grownups, however many **blunders**[78] they make, and to whatever extent they allow their imaginations to run away with them.

One favorite subject of Koophuiss and Henks is that of people in hiding and in the underground movement. They know very well that anything to do with other people in hiding interests us **tremendously**[79], and how deeply we can sympathize with the sufferings of people who get taken away, and **rejoice**[80] with the **liberated**[81] prisoner.

We are quite as used to the idea of going into hiding, or "underground," as in bygone days one was used to Daddy's bedroom slippers warming in front of the fire.

---

| | |
|---|---|
| 72. Trot – proceed rapidly | 73. Twaddles – talk foolishly |
| 74. Bearable – tolerable | 75. Oblige – please |
| 76. Frills – feathers about the neck of an animal | 77. Furbelows – a strip of frill |
| 78. Blunders – mistake | 79. Tremendously – greatly |
| 80. Rejoice – be delighted | 81. Liberated – to set free |

There are a great number of organizations, such as "The Free Netherlands" which **forge**[82] identity cards, supply money to people "underground," find hiding places for people, and work for young men in hiding, and it is amazing how much noble, unselfish work these people are doing, risking their own lives to help and save others. Our helpers are a very good example. They have pulled us through up till-now and we hope they will bring us safely to dry land. Otherwise, they will have to share the same fate as the many others who are being searched for. Never have we heard one word of the **burden**[83] which we certainly must be to them, never has one of them complained of all the trouble we give.

They all come upstairs every day, talk to the men about business and politics, to the women about food and wartime difficulties, and about newspapers and books with the children. They put on the brightest possible faces, bring flowers and presents for birthdays and bank holidays, are always ready to help and do all they can. That is something we must never forget; although others may show heroism in the war or against the Germans, our helpers display **heroism**[84] in their cheerfulness and affection.

The wildest tales are going around, but still they are usually founded on fact. For instance, Koophuis told us this week that in Gelderland two football elevens met, and one side consisted **solely**[85] of members of the "underground" and the other was made up of members of the police. New ration books are being handed out in Hilversum. In order that the many people in hiding may also draw rations, the officials have given instructions to those of them in the district to come at a certain time, so that they can collect their documents from a separate little table. Still, they'll have to be careful that such **impudent**[86] tricks do not reach the ears of the Germans.

Yours, Anne

---

82. Forge – counterfeit          83. Burden – overload
84. Heroism – heroic conduct     85. Solely – alone
86. Impudent – disrespectful

## Think and Ink...

➤ What did Anne entertain towards Peter?

➤ What transition do you perceive in Anne's feelings towards Peter first and then later?

➤ What, according to you, is the reason behind the cause of friction between Anne and her mother? Is Anne overreacting? Justify your stand.

## Text-Based Questions

- Why did Anne go to Peter's room?

- How did Peter react?

- What did Anne dream of?

- Who was Anne's childhood boy friends?

- What sort of personality did Peter have?

- How did their friendship stop?

- How was Anne troubled by the memories of Peter?

- What was the new craze in Anne?

- What misunderstandings did Anne's mother have according to Anne?

- How strained was their relationship?

- Why did Anne want Peter in place of her mother?

- What made Anne feel more of an independent being?

- How was one to deal with Mrs. Van Daan? Why?

- How did Anne reexamine herself?

- What was the change we find in her approach towards the criticisms of Van Daans?
- What was the latest subject of interest for Anne?
- How did Anne gain knowledge about cinema and theaters?
- How did people react when Anne put up a new hair style?
- What stories drove Anne to boredom?
- How did Koophuiss and Henks tell their stories?
- What did the free Netherlands do?
- What was the attitude of the helpers?
- What sort of wild tales went around?

# Thursday, 3 February, 1944

Dear Kitty,

Invasion fever in the country is mounting daily. If you were here, on the one hand, you would probably feel the effect of all these preparations just as I do and, on the other, you would laugh at us for making such a fuss-who knows-perhaps for nothing.

All the newspapers are full of the invasion and are driving people mad by saying that "In the event of the English landing in Holland, the Germans will do all they can to defend the country; if necessary they will resort to flooding," With this, maps have been published, on which the parts of Holland that will be under water are marked. As this applies to large parts of Amsterdam, the first question was, what shall we do if the water in the streets rises to one meter? The answers given by different people vary considerably.

"As walking or cycling is out of the question, we shall have to wade through the stagnant water."

"Of course not, one will have to try and swim. We shall all put on our bathing suits and caps and swim under water as much as possible, then no one will see that we are Jews."

"Oh, what nonsense! I'd like to see the ladies swimming, if the rats started biting their logs!" (That was naturally a man: just see who screams the loudest!)

"We shan't be able to get out of the house anyway; the warehouse will definitely collapse *if* there is a flood, it is so wobbly already."

"Listen, folks, all joking apart, we shall try and get a boat."

"Why bother? I know something much better. We each get hold of a wooden packing case from the attic and row with a soup ladle!"

"I shall walk on stilts: I used to be an expert at it in my youth."

"Henk Van Santen won't need to, he's sure to take his wife on his back, then she'll be on stilts."

This gives you a rough idea, doesn't it, Kit?

This chatter is all very amusing, but the truth may be otherwise. A second question about the invasion was bound to arise: what do we do if the Germans evacuate Amsterdam?

"Leave the city too, and disguise ourselves as best we can."

"Don't go, whatever happens, stay put! The only thing to do is remain here! The Germans are quite capable of driving the whole population right into Germany, where they will all die."

"Yes, naturally, we shall stay here, since this is the safest place. We'll try and fetch Koophuis and his family over here to come and live with us. We'll try and get hold of a sack of wood wool, then we can sleep on the floor. Let's ask Miep and Koophuis to start bringing blankets here."

"We'll order some extra corn in addition to our sixty pounds. Let's get Henk to try and obtain more peas and beans; we have about sixty pounds of beans and ten pounds of peas in the house at present. Don't forget that we've got fifty tins of vegetables."

"Mummy, just count up how much we've got of other food, will you?"

"Ten tins of fish, forty tins of milk, ten kilos of milk powder, three bottles of salad oil, four preserving jars of butter, four ditto of meat, two wicker-covered bottles of strawberries, two bottles of raspberries, twenty bottles of tomatoes, ten pounds of rolled oats, eight pounds of rice and that's all.

"Our stocks not too bad, but if you think that we may be having visitors as well and drawing from reserves each week, then it seems more than it actually is. We have sufficient coal and firewood in the house, also candles. Let's all make little moneybags, which could easily be hidden in our clothing, in case we want to take money with us.

"We'll make lists of the most important things to take, should we have to run for it, and pack rucksacks now in readiness. If it gets that far, we'll put two people on watch, one in the front and one in the back loft. I say, what's the use of collecting such stocks of food, if we haven't any water, gas, or electricity?"

"Then we must cook on the stove. Filter and boil our water. We'll clean out some large wicker bottles and store water in them."

I hear nothing but this sort of talk the whole day long, invasion and nothing but invasion, arguments about suffering from hunger, dying, bombs, fire extinguishers, sleeping bags, Jewish vouchers, poisonous gases, etc., etc. None of it is exactly cheering. The gentlemen in the "Secret Annexe" give pretty straightforward warnings, an example is the following conversation with Henk:

"Secret Annexe": "We are afraid that if the Germans withdraw, they will take the whole population with them."

Henk: "That is impossible, they haven't the trains at their disposal."

"S.A.": "Trains? Do you really think they'd put civilians in carriages? Out of the question. They could use 'shank's mare' *(Per pedes apostolorum,* Dussel always says.)

H: "I don't believe a word of it, you look on the black side of everything. What would be their object in driving all the civilians along with them?"

"S.A.": "Didn't you know that Goebbels said, if we have to withdraw, we shall slam the doors of all the occupied countries behind us?"

H: "They have said so much already."

"S.A.": "Do you think the Germans are above doing such a thing or too **humane**[1]? What they think is this: 'If we have got to go down, then everybody in our **clutches**[2] will go down with us.'"

H: "Tell that to the Marines, I just don't believe it!"

"S.A."; "It's always the same song; no one will see danger approaching until it is actually on top of him."

H: "But you know nothing definite; you just simply suppose,"

"S.A.": "We have all been through it ourselves, first in Germany, and then here. And what is going on in Russia?"

---

1.  Humane – compassion, mercy          2.  Clutches – control or power

H.: "You mustn't include the Jews. I don't think anyone knows what is going on in Russia. The English and the Russians are sure to exaggerate things for propaganda purposes, just like the Germans."

"S.A.": "Out of the question, the English have always told the truth over the wireless. And suppose they do exaggerate the news, the facts are bad enough anyway, because you can't deny that many millions of peace-loving people were just simply murdered or gassed in Poland and Russia."

I will spare you further examples of these conversations, I myself keep very quiet and don't take any notice of all the fuss and excitement. I have now reached the stage that I don't care much whether I live or die. The world will still keep on turning without me; what is going to happen, will happen, and anyway it's no good trying to **resist**[3].

I trust to luck and do nothing but work, hoping that all will end well.

Yours, Anne

## Saturday, 12 February, 1944

Dear Kitty,

The sun is shining, the sky is a deep blue, there is a lovely breeze and I'm longing—so longing—for everything. To talk, for freedom, for friends, to be alone. And I do so long ... to cry! I feel as if I'm going to burst, and I know that it would get better with crying; but I can't, I'm restless, I go from one room to the other, breathe through the crack of a closed window, feel my heart beating, as if it is saying, "Can't you satisfy my longings at last?"

I believe that it's spring within me, I feel that spring is **awakening**[4], I feel it in my whole body and soul. It is an effort to behave normally, I feel utterly confused, don't know what to read, what to write, what to do, I only know that I am longing..!

Yours, Anne

---

3.  Resist – stop                    4.  Awakening – arousing, initiating

# Sunday, 13 February, 1944

Dear Kitty,

Since Saturday a lot has changed for me. It came about like this. I longed—and am still longing—but... now something has happened, which has made it a little, just a little, less.

To my great joy—I will be quite honest about it— already this morning I noticed that Peter kept looking at me all the time. Not in the ordinary way, I don't know how, I just can't explain.

I used to think that Peter was in Jove with Margot, but yesterday I suddenly had the feeling that it is not so. I made a special effort not to look at him too much, because whenever I did, he kept on looking too and then-yes, then-it gave me a lovely feeling inside, but which I mustn't feel too often.

I desperately want to be alone. Daddy has noticed that I'm not quite my usual self, but I really can't tell him everything. "Leave me in peace, leave me alone," that's what I'd like to keep crying out all the time. Who knows, the day may come when I'm left alone more than I would wish!

Yours, Anne

# Monday, 14 February, 1944

Dear Kitty,

On Sunday evening everyone except Pim and me was sitting beside the wireless in order to listen to the "Immortal Music of the German Masters." Dussel **fiddled**[5] with the **knobs**[6] continually. This annoyed Peter, and the others too. After **restraining**[7] himself for half an hour. Peter asked somewhat irritably if the twisting and turning might stop. Dussel answered in his most **hoity-toity**[8] manner, "I'm getting it all right." Peter became angry, was rude, Mr. Van Daan took his side, and Dussel had to give in. That was all.

---

5. Fiddled – played
6. Knobs – a rounded handle
7. Restraining – prevent
8. Hoity-toity – silliness

The reason in itself was very unimportant, but Peter seems to have taken it very much to heart. In any case.

when I was **rummaging**[9] about in the bookcase in the attic, he came up to me and began telling me the whole story. I didn't know anything about it, but Peter soon saw that he had found an attentive ear and got fairly into his **stride**[10].

"Yes, and you see," he said, "I don't easily say anything, because I know **beforehand**[11] that I'll only become **tonguetied**[12]. I begin to **stutter**[13], blush, and twist around what I want to say, until I have to break off because I simply can't find the words. That's what happened yesterday, I wanted to say something quite different, but once I had started, I got in a hopeless **muddle**[14] and that's frightful. I used to have a bad habit; I wish I still had it now. If 1 was angry with anyone, rather than argue it out I would get to work on him with my fists. I quite realize that this method doesn't get me anywhere; and that is why I admire you. You are never at a loss for a word, you say exactly what you want to say to people and are never the least bit shy."

"I can tell you, you're making a big mistake," I answered. "I usually say things quite differently from the way I meant to say them, and then I talk too much and far too long, and that's just as bad."

I couldn't help laughing to myself over this last sentence. However, I wanted to let him go on talking about himself, so I kept my amusement to myself, went and sat on a cushion on the floor, put my arms around my bent knees, and looked at him attentively.

I am very glad that there is someone else in the house who can get into the same fits of rage as I get into. I could see it did Peter good to pull Dussel to pieces to his hearts content, without fear of my telling tales. And as for me, I was very pleased, because I sensed a real feeling of fellowship, such as I can only remember having had with my girl friends.

Yours, Anne

---

9. Rummaging – to discover by searching thoroughly  10. Stride–effective pace
11. Beforehand – early          12. Tongue-tied – speechless
13. Shutter – one that shuts    14. Muddle – confusion

# Wednesday, 16 February, 1944

Dear Kitty,

It's Margot's birthday. Peter came at half past twelve to look at the presents and stayed talking much longer than was strictly necessary—a thing he'd have never done otherwise. In the afternoon I went to get some coffee and, after that, potatoes, because I wanted to spoil Margot for just that one day in the year. I went through Peter's room, he took all his papers off the stairs at once and I asked whether I should close the trap door to the attic, "Yes," he replied, "knock when you come back, then I'll open it for you."

I thanked him, went upstairs, and searched at least ten minutes in the large **barrel**[15] for the smallest potatoes. Then my back began to ache and I got cold. Naturally I didn't knock, but opened the trap door myself, but still he came to meet me most **obligingly**[16], and took the pan from me.

"I've looked for a long time, these are the smallest I could find," I said.

"Did you look in the big barrel?"

By this time I was standing at the bottom of the stairs and he looked searchingly in the pan which he was still holding. "Oh, but these are first-rate," he said, and added when I took the pan from him, "I congratulate you!" At the same time he gave me such a gentle warm look which made a tender glow within me. I could really see that he wanted to please me, and because he couldn't make a long **complimentary**[17] speech he spoke with his eyes. I understood him, oh, so well, and was very grateful. It gives me pleasure even now when I recall those words and that look he gave me.

When I went downstairs. Mummy said that I must get some more potatoes, this time for supper. I willingly offered to go upstairs again.

---

15. Barrel – a large cylindrical container
16. Obligingly – accommodatingly
17. Complimentary – flattering

When I came into Peter's room, I **apologized**[18] at having to disturb him again. When I was already on the stairs he got up, and went and stood between the door and the wall, firmly took hold of my arm, and wanted to hold me back by force.

"I'll go," he said. I replied that it really wasn't necessary and that I didn't have to get particularly small ones this time. Then he was convinced and let my arm go. On the way down, he came and opened the trap door and took the pan again. When I reached the door, I asked, "What are you doing?" "French," he replied. I asked if I might glance through the exercises, washed my hands, and went and sat on the divan opposite him.

We soon began talking, after I'd explained some of the French to him. He told me that he wanted to go to the Dutch East Indies and live on a **plantation** [19] later on. He talked about his home life, about the black market, and then he said that he felt so useless. I told him that he certainly had a very strong **inferiority**[20] complex. He talked about the Jews. He would have found it much easier if he'd been a Christian and if he could be one after the war. I asked if he wanted to be **baptized**[21], but that wasn't the case either. Who was to know whether he was a Jew when the war was over? he said.

This gave me rather a **pang**[22], it seems such a pity that there's always just a **tinge**[23] of dishonesty about him. For the rest we chatted very pleasantly about Daddy, and about judging people's characters and all kinds of things, I can't remember exactly what now. It was half past four by the time I left. In the evening he said something else that I thought was nice. We were talking about a picture of a film star that I'd given him once, which has now been hanging in his room for at least a year and a half. He liked it very much and I offered to give him a few more sometime. "No," he replied, "I'd

---

18.  Apologized – regretful acknowledgment of a fault
19.  Plantation – an area under cultivation
20.  Inferiority – low or lower in quality          21.  Baptized – to become christian
22.  Pang – pain                                    23.  Tinge – affect slightly

rather leave it like this. I look at these every day and they have grown to be my friends."

Now I understand more why he always hugs Mouschi. He needs some affection, too, of course.

I'd forgotten something else that he talked about. He said, "I don't know what fear is, except when I think of my own shortcomings. But I'm getting over that too."

Peter has a terrible inferiority complex. For instance, he always thinks that he is so stupid, and we are so clever. It I help him with his French, he thanks me a thousand times. One day I shall turn around and say: "Oh, shut up, you're much better at English and geography!"

Yours, Anne

## Friday, 18 February, 1944

Dear Kitty,

Whenever I go upstairs now I keep on hoping that I shall see "him." Because my life now has an object, and I have something to look forward to, everything has become more pleasant.

At least the object of my feelings is always there, and I needn't be afraid of rivals, except Margot. Don't think I'm in love, because I'm not, but I do have the feeling all the time that something fine can grow up between us, something that gives confidence and friendship. If I get half a chance, I go up to him now. It's not like it used to be when he didn't know how to begin. Its just the opposite-he's still talking when I'm half out of the room.

Mummy doesn't like it much, and always says I'll be a nuisance and that I must leave him in peace. Honestly, doesn't she realize that I've got some **intuition**[24]? She looks at me so queerly every time I go into Peter's little room. If I come downstairs from there, she asks me where I've been. I simply can't bear it, and think it's horrible.

Yours, Anne

---

24. Intuition – a perceptive insight

# Saturday, 19 February, 1944

Dear Kitty,

It is Saturday again and that really speaks for itself. The morning was quiet. I helped a bit upstairs, but I didn't have more than a few **fleeting**[25] words with "him" At half past two, when everyone had gone to their own rooms, either to sleep or to read, I went to the private office, with my blanket and everything, to sit at the desk and read or write. It was not long before it all became too much for me, my head **drooped**[26] on to my arm, and I **sobbed**[27] my heart out. The tears streamed down my cheeks and I felt desperately unhappy. Oh, if only "he" had come to comfort me. It was four o'clock by the time I went upstairs again. I went for some potatoes, with fresh hope in my heart of a meeting, but "while I was still **smartening**[28] up my hair in the bathroom, he went down to see Boche in the warehouse.

Suddenly I felt the tears coming back and I hurried to the lavatory, quickly **grabbing**[29] a pocket mirror as I passed. There I sat then, fully dressed, while the tears made dark spots on the red of my apron, and I felt very wretched.

This is what was going through my mind. Oh, I'll never reach Peter like this. Who knows, perhaps he doesn't like me at all and doesn't need anyone to confide in. Perhaps he only thinks about me in a casual sort of way. I shall have to go on alone once more, without friendship and without Peter. Perhaps soon I'll be without hope, without comfort, or anything to look forward to again. Oh, if I could nestle my head against his shoulder and not feel so hopelessly alone and **deserted**[30]! Who knows, perhaps he doesn't care about me at all and looks at the others in just the same way. Perhaps I only imagined that it was especially for me? Oh, Peter, if only you could see or hear me. If the truth were to prove as bad as that, it would be more than I could bear.

---

| | |
|---|---|
| 25. Fleeting – passing quickly | 26. Drooped – hang downward |
| 27. Sobbed – shed tears because of grief | 28. Smartening – stylishness |
| 29. Grabbing – grasping suddenly | 30. Deserted – abandoned |

However, a little later fresh hope and anticipation seemed to return, even though the tears were still streaming down my cheeks.

Yours, Anne

# Wednesday, 23 February, 1944

Dear Kitty,

It's lovely weather outside and I've quite **perked**[31] up since yesterday. Nearly every morning I go to the attic where Peter works to blow the stuffy air out of my lungs. From my favorite spot on the floor I look up at the blue sky and the bare chestnut tree, on whose branches little raindrops shine, appearing like silver, and at the seagulls and other birds as they **glide**[32] on the wind.

He stood with his head against a thick beam, and I sat down. We breathed the fresh air, looked outside, and both felt that the spell should not be broken by words. We remained like this for a long time, and when he had to go up to the loft to chop wood, I knew that he was a nice fellow. He climbed the ladder, and I followed, then he chopped wood for about a quarter of an hour, during which time we still remained silent. I watched him from where I stood, he was obviously doing his best to show off his strength. But I looked out of the open window too, over a large area of Amsterdam, over all the roofs and on to the horizon, which was such a pale blue that it was hard to see the dividing line. "As long as this exists," I thought, "and I may live to see it, this sunshine, the cloudless skies, while this lasts, I cannot be unhappy."

The best remedy for those who are afraid, lonely, or unhappy is to go outside, somewhere where they can be quite alone with the heavens, nature, and God. Because only then does one feel that all is as it should be and that God wishes to see people happy, amidst the

---

31. Perked – to refresh        32. Glide – to fly without propulsion

simple beauty of Nature. As long as this exists, and it certainly always will, I know that then there will always be comfort for every sorrow, whatever the circumstances may be. And I firmly believe that nature brings solace in all troubles.

Oh, who knows, perhaps it won't be long before I can share this **overwhelming**[33] feeling of **bliss**[34] with someone who feels the way I do about it.

A thought:

We miss so much here, so very much and for so long now: I miss it too, just as you do. I'm not talking of outward things, for we are looked after in that way; no, I mean the inward things. Like you, I long for freedom and fresh air, but 1 believe now that we have **ample**[35] compensation for our **privations**[36]. I realized this quite suddenly when I sat in front of the window this morning. I mean **inward**[37] **compensation**[38].

When 1 looked outside right into the depth of Nature and God, then I was happy, really happy. And Peter, so long as I have that happiness here, the joy in nature, health and a lot more besides, all the while one has that, one can always **recapture**[39] happiness.

Riches can all be lost, but that happiness in your own heart can only be veiled, and it will still bring you happiness again, as long as you live. As long as you can look fearlessly up into the heavens, as long as you know that you are pure within, and that you will still find happiness.

Yours, Anne

---

33. Overwhelming – strong
34. Bliss – ecstasy
35. Ample – sufficient
36. Privations – comforts of life
37. Inward – within
38. Compensation – the act of compensating
39. Recapture – recall

# Sunday, 27 February, 1944

Dear Kitty,

From early in the morning till late at night, I really do hardly anything else but think of Peter. I sleep with his image before my eyes, dream about him and he is still looking at me when I awake.

I have a strong feeling that Peter and I are really not so different as we would appear to be and I will tell you why. We both lack a mother. His is too **superficial**[40], loves **flirting**[41] and doesn't trouble much about what he thinks. Mine does bother about me, but lacks sensitiveness, real motherliness.

Peter and I both **wrestle**[42] with our inner feelings, we are still uncertain and are really too sensitive to be roughly treated. If we are, then my reaction is to "get away from it all." But as that is impossible, I hide my feelings, throw my weight about the place, am noisy and **boisterous**[43], so that everyone wishes that I was out of the way.

He, on the contrary, shuts himself up, hardly talks at all, is quiet, daydreams and in this way carefully conceals his true self.

But how and when will we finally reach each other? I don't know quite how long my common sense will keep this longing under control.

Yours, Anne

# Monday, 28 February, 1944

Dear Kitty,

It is becoming a bad dream—in daytime as well as at night. I see him nearly all the time and can't get at him, I mustn't show anything, must remain gay while I'm really in **despair**[44].

---

40. Superficial – on the surface
41. Flirting – to be playfully romantic
42. Wrestle – struggle
43. Boisterous – tendency to fight
44. Desperately – having lost all hope

Peter Wessel and Peter Van Daan have grown into one Peter, who is beloved and good, and for whom I long desperately.

Mummy is tiresome. Daddy sweet and therefore all the more tiresome, Margot the most tiresome because she expects me to wear a pleasant expression, and all I want is to be left in peace.

Peter didn't come to me in the attic. He went up to the loft instead and did some carpentry. At every creak and every knock some of my courage seemed to **seep**[45] away and I grew more unhappy. In the distance a bell was playing "Pure in body, pure in soul." I'm sentimental—I know. I'm desperate and silly—I know that too. Oh, help me!

Yours, Anne

---

45. Seep – to escape little by little

## Think and Ink...

➢ How did the war atmosphere spark fear among the people of Holland as we find from the questions and arguments that rise in their minds?

➢ What positivity do you find in the arguments of Henk with the gentlemen in the Secret Annexe?

➢ Were the restlessness in Anne because of the changes in her self or a result of her being in hiding for a long time? How?

➢ Why was Anne desperate at the thought of Peter? What did she need from her?

➢ Compare the character of Anne and Peter?

### Text-Based Questions

• What news did the papers carry?

• Why did Anne trust luck? What frustration did she exhibit in her thoughts?

• Why was Anne restless?

• How did she feel when Peter looked at her? Why?

• What happened on the Sunday evening?

• What did Peter share with Anne?

• How was Peter's attitude similar to Anne's, as she found it to be?

• Why did Anne search for potatoes?

• What gave her pleasure about Peter?

• What ideas did Anne and Peter share?

• Why did Anne feel that Peter had inferiority complex?

• What did Anne's mother object to her? Why?

• What saddened Anne?

• Why and how did Anne feel that she can not be unhappy?

• What remedy does Anne suggest those who are afraid lonely and unhappy? How does it work?

• What inward compensation does Anne talk about?

• What was becoming a bad dream?

• Describe the burglary at Anne's house. How was it complicated than the one in July 1928?

# Wednesday, I March, 1944

Dear Kitty,

My own affairs have been pushed into the background by- a burglary. I'm becoming boring with all my burglars, but what can I do, they seem to take such a delight in honoring Kolen & Co. with their visits. This burglary is much more **complicated**[1] than the one in July 1943.

When Mr. Van Daan went to Kraler's office at half past seven, as usual, he saw that the communicating glass doors and the office door were open. Surprised at this, he walked through and was even more amazed to see that the doors of the little dark room were open too, and that there was a terrible mess in the main office.

"There has been a burglar," he thought to himself at once, and to satisfy himself he went straight downstairs to look at the front door, felt the Yale lock, and found everything closed. "Oh, then both Peter and Elli must have been very **slack**[2] this evening," he decided. He remained in Kraler's room for a while, then switched off the lamp, and went upstairs, without worrying much about either the open doors or the untidy office.

This morning Peter knocked at bur door early and came with the not so pleasant news that the front door was wide open. He also told us that the projector and Kraler's new portfolio had both disappeared from the cupboard. Peter was told to close the door. Van Daan told us of his discoveries the previous evening and we were all **awfully**[3] worried.

What must have happened is that the thief had a **skeleton**[4] key, because the lock was quite undamaged. He must have crept into the house quite early and closed the door behind him, hidden himself when disturbed by Mr. Van Daan, and when he **departed**[5] fled with his spoils, leaving the door open in his haste. Who can have our key?

---

1. Complicated – not easy to understand       2. Slack – slow
3. Awfully – terrible 4. Skeleton – a supporting structure 5. Departed – left

Why didn't the thief go to the warehouse? Might it be one of our own warehousemen, and would he perhaps betray us, since he certainly heard Van Daan and perhaps even saw him?

It is all very **creepy**[6], because we don't know whether this same burglar may not take it into his head to visit us again. Or perhaps it gave him a shock to find that there was someone walking about in the house?

Yours, Anne

# Thursday, 2 March, 1944

Dear Kitty,

Margot and I were both up in the attic today, although we were not able to enjoy it together as I had imagined, still I do know that she shares my feelings over most things.

During dish washing Elli began telling Mummy and Mrs. Van Daan that she felt very discouraged at times. And what help do you think they gave her? Do you know what Mummy's advice was? She should try to think of all the other people who are in trouble! What is the good of thinking of misery when one is already miserable oneself?

I said this too and was told, "You keep out of this sort of conversation."

Aren't the grownups **idiotic**[7] and stupid? Just as if Peter, Margot, Elli, and I don't all feel the same about things, and only a mother's love or that of a very, very good friend can help us. These mother's here just don't understand us at all. Perhaps Mrs. Van Daan does a little more than Mummy. Oh, I would have so liked to say something to poor Elli, something that I know from experience would have helped her. But Daddy came between us and pushed me aside.

Aren't they all stupid! We aren't allowed to have any opinions. People can tell you to keep your mouth shut, but it doesn't stop you having your own opinion. Even if people are still very young, they shouldn't be prevented from saying what they think.

---

6. Creepy – slow-moving          7. Idiotic – showing foolishness

Only great love and devotion can help Elli, Margot, Peter, and me, and none of us gets it. And no one, especially the stupid "know-alls" here, can understand us, because we are much more **sensitive**[8] and much more advanced in our thoughts than anyone here would ever imagine in their wildest dreams.

Mummy is grumbling again at the moment-she is obviously jealous because I talk more to Mrs. Van Daan than to her nowadays.

I managed to get hold of Peter this afternoon and we talked for at least three quarters of an hour. Peter had the greatest difficulty in saying anything about himself, it took a long time to draw him out. He told me how often his parents quarrel over politics, cigarettes, and all kinds of things. He was very shy.

Then I talked to him about my parents. He defended Daddy: he thought him a "first-rate chap." Then we talked about "upstairs" and "downstairs" again, he was really rather amazed that we don't always like his parents. "Peter," I said, "you know I'm always honest, so why shouldn't I tell you that we can see their faults too." And among other things I also said, "I would so like to help you. Peter, can't I? You are in such an awkward position and, although you don't say anything, it doesn't mean that you don't care." "Oh, I would always welcome your help." "Perhaps you would do better to go to Daddy, he wouldn't let anything go any further, take it from me, you can easily tell him!"

"Yes, he is a real pal."

"You're very fond of him, aren't you?" Peter nodded and I went on: "And he is of you too!"

He looked up quickly and blushed, it was really moving to see how these few words pleased him.

"Do you think so?" he asked.

"Yes," I said, "you can easily tell by little things that slip out now and then!"

Peter is a firstrate chap, too, just like Daddy.

Yours, Anne

---

8. Sensitive – touchy

# Friday, 3 March, 1944

Dear Kitty,

When I looked into the candle this evening I felt calm and happy. Oma seems to be in the candle and it is Oma too who shelters and protects me and who always makes me feel happy again.

But. . . there is someone else who governs all my moods and that is ... Peter. When I went up to get potatoes today and was still standing on the stepladder with the pan, he at once asked, "What have you been doing since lunch?" I went and sat on the steps and we started talking.

At a quarter past five (an hour later) the potatoes, which had been sitting on the floor in the meantime, finally reached their destinations.

Peter didn't say another word about his parents, we just talked about books and about the past. The boy has such warmth in his eyes, I believe I'm pretty near to being in love with him. He talked about that this evening. I went into his room, after peeling the potatoes, and said that I felt so hot.

"You can tell what the temperature is by Margot and me, if its cold we are white, and if it is hot we are red in the face," I said.

"In love?" he asked.

"Why should I be in love?" My answer was rather silly.

"Why not?" he said, and then we had to go for supper.

Would he have meant anything by that question? I finally managed to ask him today whether he didn't find my chatter a nuisance, he only said: "It's okay, I like it!"

To what extent this answer was just shyness, I am not able to judge.

Kitty, I' m just like someone in love, who can only talk about her darling. And Peter really is a darling. When shall I be able to tell him so? Naturally, only if he thinks I'm a darling too. But I'm quite capable of looking after myself, and he knows that very well. And he likes his tranquillity, so I have no idea how much he likes me. In any case, we are getting to know each other a bit. I wish we dared to tell each other much more already. Who knows, the time may come sooner than I think! I get an understanding look from him about twice a day, I wink back, and we both feel happy. I certainly seem quite mad to be talking about him being happy, and yet I feel pretty sure that he thinks just the same as I do.

Yours, Anne

# Saturday, 4 March, 1944

Dear Kitty,

This is the first Saturday for months and months that hasn't been boring, **dreary**[9], and dull. And Peter is the cause.

This morning I went to the attic to hang up my apron, when Daddy asked whether I'd like to stay and talk some French. I agreed. First we talked French, and I explained something to Peter, then we did some English. Daddy read out loud to us from Dickens and I was in the seventh heaven, because I sat on Daddy's chair very close to Peter.

I went downstairs at eleven o'clock. When I came upstairs again at half past eleven, he was already waiting for me on the stairs. We talked until a quarter to one. If.'as I leave the room, he gets a chance after a meal, for instance, and if no one can hear, he says: "Goodby, Anne, see you soon."

Oh, I am so pleased! I wonder if he is going to fall in love with me after all? Anyway, he is a very nice fellow and no one knows what lovely talks I have with him!

Mrs. Van Daan quite approves when I go and talk to him, but she asked today **teasingly**[10], "Can I really trust you two up there together?"

"Of course," I protested, "really you quite **insult**[11] me!" From morn till night I look forward to seeing Peter.

Yours, Anne

---

9. Dreary – dismal
10. Teasingly – mock playfully
11. Insult – hurt

# Monday, 6 March, 1944

Dear Kitty,

I can tell by Peter's face that he thinks just as much as I do, and when Mrs. Van Daan yesterday evening said **scoffingly**[12]: "The thinker!" I was irritated. Peter **flushed**[13] and looked very embarrassed, and I was about to **explode**[14].

Why can't these people keep their mouths shut?

You can't imagine how horrible it is to stand by and see how lonely he is and yet not be able to do anything. I can so well imagine, just as if I were in his place, how **desperate**[15] he must feel sometimes in quarrels and in love. Poor Peter, he needs love very much!

When he said he didn't need any friends how harsh the words sounded to my ears. Oh, how mistaken he is! I don't believe he meant it a bit.

He **clings**[16] to his solitude, to his affected **indifference**[17] and his grownup ways, but it's just an act, so as never, never to show his real feelings. Poor Peter, how long will he be able to go on playing this role? Surely a terrible outburst must follow as the result of this superhuman effort?

Oh, Peter, if only I could help you, if only you would let me! Together we could drive away your loneliness and mine!

I think a lot, but 1 don't say much. I am happy if I see him as if the sun shines when I'm with him. I was very excited yesterday, while I was washing my hair, I knew that he was sitting in the room next to

---

12. Scoffingly —mockingly
13. Flushed – embarrassment
14. Explode – without control
15. Desperate – having lost all hope
16. Clings – maintains, adheres
17. Indifference – unresponsiveness

ours. I couldn't do anything about it; the more quiet and serious I feel inside, the more noisy I become outwardly.

Who will be the first to discover and break through this **armor**[18]? I'm glad after all that the Van Daans have a son and not a daughter, my **conquest**[19] could never have been so difficult, so beautiful, so good, if 1 had not happened to hit on someone of the opposite sex.

PS: You know that I'm always honest with you, so I must tell you that I actually live from one meeting to the next. I keep hoping to discover that he too is waiting for me all the time and I'm **thrilled**[20] if I notice a small shy advance from his side. I believe he'd like to say a lot just like I would; little does he know that its just his **clumsiness**[21] that attracts me.

Yours, Anne

## Tuesday, 7 March, 1944

Dear Kitty,

If I think now of my life in 1942, it all seems so unreal. It was quite a different Anne who enjoyed that heavenly existence from the Anne who has grown wise within these walls. Yes, it was a heavenly life. Boy friends at every turn, about twenty friends and **acquaintances**[22] of my own age, the darling of nearly all the teachers, spoiled from top to toe by Mummy and Daddy, lots of sweets, enough pocket money, what more could one want?

You will certainly wonder by what means I got around all these people. Peter's word "attractiveness" is not altogether true. All the teachers were entertained by my cute answers, my amusing remarks, my smiling face, and my questioning looks. That is all I was—a terrble flirt, **coquettish**[23] and amusing. I had one or two advantages, which kept me rather in favor. I was industrious, honest, and frank.

---

18. Armor – a defensive covering
19. Conquest – process of conquering
20. Thrilled – excite greatly
21. Clumsiness – awkwardness
22. Acquaintances – a person whom one knows
23. Coquettish – romantic overtures

I would never have dreamed of **cribbing**[24] from anyone else. I shared my sweets generously, and I wasn't **conceited**[25].

Wouldn't I have become rather forward with so much admiration? It was a good thing that in the midst of, at the height of all, this gaiety, I suddenly had to face reality, and it took me at least a year to get used to the fact that there was no more admiration **forthcoming**[26].

How did I appear at school? The one who thought of new jokes and **pranks**[27], always "king of the castle," never in a bad mood, never a **crybaby**[28]. No wonder everyone liked to cycle with me, and I got their attentions.

Now I look back at that Anne as an amusing, but very **superficial**[29] girl, who has nothing to do with the Anne of today. Peter said quite rightly about me: "If ever I saw you, you were always surrounded by two or more boys and a whole troupe of girls. You were always laughing and always the center of everything!"

What is left of this girl? Oh, don't worry, I haven't forgotten how to laugh or to answer back readily. I'm just as good, if not better, at criticizing people, and I can still flirt if... I wish. That's not it though, I'd like that sort of life again for an evening, a few days, or even a week; the life which seems so **carefree**[30] and gay. But at the end of that week, I should be dead beat and would be only too thankful to listen to anyone who began to talk about something sensible. I don't want followers, but friends, admirers who fall not for a **flattering**[31] smile but for what one does and for one's character.

I know quite well that the circle around me would be much smaller. But what does that matter, as long as one still keeps a few sincere friends?

Yet I wasn't entirely happy in 1942 in spite of everything, I often felt deserted, but because I was on the go the whole day long, I didn't

---

24. Cribbing – complaining
25. Conceited – excessively proud
26. Forthcoming – upcoming
27. Pranks – a mischievous trick
28. Crybaby – a child who cries frequently
29. Superficial – artificial
30. Carefree – no worry
31. Flattering – effective

think about it and enjoyed myself as much as I could. Consciously or unconsciously, I tried to drive away the emptiness I felt with jokes and pranks. Now I think seriously about life and what I have to do. One period of my life is over forever. The carefree schooldays are gone, never to return.

I don't even long for them any more, I have outgrown them, I can't just only enjoy myself as my serious side is always there.

I look upon my life up till the New Year, as it were, through a powerful **magnifying**[32] glass. The sunny life at home, then coming here in 1942, the sudden change, the quarrels, the **bickerings**[33]. I couldn't understand it, I was taken by surprise, and the only way I could keep up some bearing was by being **impertinent**[34].

The first half of 1943: my fits of crying, the loneliness, how I slowly began to see all my faults and shortcomings, which are so great and which seemed much greater then. During the day I deliberately talked about anything and everything that was farthest from my thoughts, tried to draw Pim to me but couldn't. Alone I had to face the difficult task of changing myself, to stop the **everlasting**[35] reproaches, which were so oppressive and which reduced me to such terrible **despondency**[36]. Things improved slightly in the second half of the year, I became a young woman and was treated more like a grownup. I started to think, and write stories, and come to the conclusion that the others no longer had the right to throw me about like an india-rubber ball. I wanted to change in accordance with my own desires. But one thing that struck me even more was when I realized that even Daddy would—never become my **confidant**[37] over everything. I didn't want to trust anyone but myself any more.

At the beginning of the New Year: the second great change, my dream.... And with it I discovered my longing, not for a girl friend,

---

| | |
|---|---|
| 32. Magnifying – enlarge | 33. Bickering – bad tempered quarrel |
| 34. Impertinent – irreverent | 35. Everlasting – prolonged |
| 36. Despondency – low sprits | 37. Confidant– person in whom one confides |

but for a boy friend, I also discovered my inward happiness and my **defensive**[38] armor of superficiality and gaiety. In due time I **quieted**[39] down and discovered my boundless desire for all that is beautiful and good.

And in the evening, when I lie in bed and end my prayers with the words, "I thank you, God, for all that is good and dear and beautiful," I am filled with joy. Then I think about "the good" of going into hiding, of my health and with my whole being of the "dearness" of Peter, of that which is still **embryonic**[40] and impressionable and which *were neither of us* dare to name or touch, of that which will come sometime; love, the future, happiness and of "the beauty" which exists in the world, the world, nature, beauty and all, all that is **exquisite**[41] and fine.

I don't think then of all the misery, but of the beauty that still remains. This is one of the things that Mummy and I are so entirely different about. Her counsel when one feels melancholy is: "Think of all the misery in the world and be thankful that you are not sharing in it!" My advice is: "Go outside, to the fields, enjoy nature and the sunshine, go out and try to recapture happiness in yourself and in God. Think of all the beauty that's still left in and around you and be happy.'"

I don't see how Mummy's idea can be right, because then how are you supposed to behave if you go through the misery yourself? Then you are lost. On the contrary, I've found that there is always some beauty left—in nature, sunshine, freedom, in yourself; these can all help you. Look at these things, then you find yourself again, and God, and then you regain your balance.

And whoever is happy will make others happy too. He who has courage and faith will never **perish**[42] in misery!

Yours, Anne

---

38. Defensive– resisting attack     39. Quieted – making no noise
40. Embryonic – rudimentary image     41. Exquisite–very beautiful and delicate
42. Perish – complete ruin, destruction

# Sunday, 12 March, 1944

Dear Kitty,

I can't seem to sit still lately, I run upstairs and down and then back again. I love talking to Peter, but I'm always afraid of being a nuisance. He has told me a bit about the past, about his parents and about himself. It's not half enough though and I ask myself , why it is that I always long for more. He used to think I was unbearable, and I returned the compliment, now I have changed my opinion, has he changed his too?

I think so; still it doesn't necessarily mean that we shall become great friends, although as far as I am concerned it would make the time here much more bearable. But still, I won't get myself upset about it-I see quite a lot of him and there's no need to make you unhappy about it too, Kitty, just because I feel so miserable.

On Saturday afternoon I felt in such a **whirl**[43], after hearing a whole lot of sad news, that I went and lay on my divan for a sleep. I only wanted to sleep to stop myself thinking. I slept till four o'clock, then I had to go into the living room. I found it difficult to answer all Mummy's questions and think of some little excuse to tell Daddy, as an explanation for my long sleep. I resorted to a "headache, which, wasn't a lie, as I had one ... but inside!

Ordinary people, ordinary girls, teenagers like myself, will think I'm a bit **cracked**[44] with all my self-pity. Yes, that's what it is, but I pour out my heart to you, then for the rest of the day I'm as **impudent**[45], gay, and selfconfident as I can be, in order to avoid questions and getting on my own nerves.

Margot is very sweet and would like me to trust her, but still, I can't tell her everything. She's a darling, she's good and pretty, but she lacks the **nonchalance**[46] for conducting deep discussions,

---

43.  Whirl – a rapid  movement round and round       44.  Cracked – broken

45.  Impudent – not showing care for the consequenes of an action

46.  Nonchalance – casually calm, relaxed

she takes me so seriously, much too seriously, and then thinks about her queer little sister for a long time afterwards, looks searchingly at me, at every word I say, and keeps on thinking: "Is this just a joke or does she really mean it?" I think that's because we are together the whole day long, and that if I trusted someone completely, then I shouldn't want them hanging around me all the time.

When shall I finally untangle my thoughts, when shall I find peace and rest within myself again?

Yours, Anne

## Tuesday, 14 March, 1944

Dear Kitty,

Perhaps it would be entertaining for you-though not in the least for me-to hear what we are going to eat today. As the charwoman is at work downstairs. I'm sitting on the Van Daans' table at the moment. I have a handkerchief soaked in some good scent {bought before we came here) over my mouth and held against my nose. You won't gather much from this, so let's "begin at the beginning."

The people from whom we obtained food coupons have been caught, so we just have our five ration cards and no extra coupons, and no fats. As both Miep and Koophuis are ill, Elli hasn't time to do any shopping, so the atmosphere is dreary and dejected, and so is the food. From tomorrow we shall not have a scrap of fat, butter, or margarine left. We can't have fried potatoes to save bread) for breakfast any longer, so we have **porridge**[47] instead, and as Mrs. Van Daan thinks we're starving, we have bought some full cream milk "under the counter." Our supper today consists of a **hash**[48] made from **kale**[49] which has been preserved in a **barrel**[50]. Hence the precautionary measure with the handkerchief! It's incredible how kale can **stink**[51]

---

47.  Porridge–a dish consisting of oatmeal or another cereal boiled wit water or milk
48.  Hash – a dish of diced cooked meat reheated with potatoes
49.  Kale – a variety of cabbage          50.  Barrel – a cylindrical container
51.  Stink – unpleasant smell

when it's a year old! The smell in the room is a mixture of bad plums, strong preservatives, and rotten eggs. Ugh! the mere thought of eating that **muck**[52] makes me feel sick.

Added to this, our potatoes are suffering from such peculiar diseases that out of two buckets *of pommes de terre,* one whole one ends up on the stove. We amuse ourselves by searching for all the different kinds of diseases, and have come to the conclusion that they range from cancer and smallpox to measles! Oh, no, it's no joke to be in hiding during the fourth year of the war. If only the whole rotten business was over!

Quite honestly, I wouldn't care so much about the food, if only it were more pleasant here in other ways. There's the rub: this **tedious**[53] existence is beginning to make us all **touchy**[54].

The following are the views of the five grownups on the present situation:

Mrs. Van Daan: "The job as queen of the kitchen lost its attraction a long time ago. It's dull to sit and do nothing, so I go back to my cooking again. Still, I have to complain that its impossible to cook without any fats, and all these nasty smells make me sick. Nothing but **ingratitude**[55] and rude remarks do I get in return for my services. I am always the black sheep, always the guilty one. Moreover, according to me, very little progress is being made in the war, in the end the Germans will still win. I'm afraid we're going to starve, and if I'm in a bad mood I scold everyone."

Mr. Van Daan: "I must smoke and smoke and smoke, and then the food, the political situation, and Kerli's moods don't seem so bad. Kerli is a darling wife."

But if he hasn't anything to smoke, then nothing is right, and this is what one hears: "I'm getting ill, we don't live well enough, I must have meat. Frightfully stupid person, my Kerli!" After this a terrific quarrel is sure to follow.

---

52. Muck – dirt or mud
53. Tedious – too long slow or dull.
54. Touchy – over sensitive
55. Ingratitude – lack of gratitude

Mrs. Frank: "Food is not very important, but I would love a slice of rye bread now, I feel so terribly hungry. If I were Mrs. Van Daan I would have put a stop to Mr. Van Daan's everlasting smoking a long time ago. But now I must definitely have a cigarette, because my nerves are getting the better of me. The English make a lot of mistakes, but still the war is progressing. I must have a chat and be thankful I'm not in Poland." Mr. Frank: "Everything's all right, I don't require anything. Take it easy, we've ample time. Give me my potatoes and then I will keep my mouth shut. Put some of my rations on one side for Elli. The political situation is very promising, I'm extremely optimistic!"

Mr. Dussel'; "I must get my task for today, everything must be finished on time. Political situation out schtanding and it is 'eempossihle' that we'll be caught.

Yours, Anne

## Wednesday, 15 March, 1944

Dear Kitty,

Phew.' Oh dear, oh dear-released from the **somber**[56] scenes for a moment! Today I hear nothing but "if this or that should happen, then we are going to be in difficulties ... if he or she should become ill, then we'll be completely **isolated**[57], and then if. Enfin I expect you know the rest, at least I **presume**[58] you know the "Secret Annexers" well enough by this time to be able to guess the trend of their conversations.

The reason for all this "if, if" is that Mr. Kraler has been called up to go digging. Elli has a streaming cold and will probably have to stay at home tomorrow. Miep hasn't fully recovered from her flu yet, and Koophuis has had such bad hemorrhage of the stomach that he lost consciousness. What a tale of woe.'

The warehouse people are getting a free day tomorrow, Elli can stay at home, then the door will remain locked and we shall have to

56. Somber-dark or dull 57. Isolated-lonely, single 58. Presume-take for granted

be as quiet as mice, so that the neighbors don't hear us. Henk is coming to visit the **deserted**[59] ones at one o'clock-playing the role of zookeeper, as it were. For the first time in ages he told us something about the great wide world this afternoon. You should have seen the eight of us sitting around him, it looked exactly like a picture of Grandmother telling a story. He talked nineteen to the dozen to his grateful audience about food, of course, and then Miep's doctor, and everything that we asked about. "Doctor," he said, "don't talk to me about the doctor! I rang him up this morning, had his assistant on the phone and asked for a prescription for flu. The reply was that I could come and get the prescription any time between eight and nine in the morning. If you have a very bad attack of flu, the doctor comes to the telephone himself and says 'Put out your tongue, say Aah. I can hear all right that your throat is **inflamed**[60]. I'll write out a prescription for you to order from the chemist. Goodby.' And that's that." A fine practice that, run by telephone only.

But I don't want to criticize the doctors; after all, a person has but two hands, and in these days there's an **abundance**[61] of patients and very few doctors to cope with them. Still, we couldn't help laughing when Henk repeated the telephone conversation to us.

I can just imagine what a doctor's waiting room must look like nowadays. One doesn't look down on panel patients any more, but on the people with minor **ailments**[62], and thinks: "Hi, you, what are you doing here, end of the line, please, urgent cases have priority!"

Yours, Anne

## Thursday, 16 March, 1944

Dear Kitty,

The weather is lovely, superb, I can't describe it. I'm going up to the attic in a minute.

Now I know why I'm so much more restless than Peter. He has his own room where he can work, dream, think, and sleep. I am

---

59. Deserted - abandoned                      60. Inflamed - sour throat
61. Abundance - very large quantity of something    62. Ailments - minor illness

shoved about from one corner to another. I hardly spend any time in my "double" room and yet it's something I long for so much. That is the reason too why I so frequently escape to the attic. There, and with you, I can be myself for a while, just a little while. Still, I don't want to **moan**[63] about myself, on the contrary, I want to be brave. Thank goodness the others can't tell what my inward feelings are, except that I'm growing cooler towards Mummy daily. I'm not so affectionate to Daddy and don't tell Margot a single thing. I'm completely closed up. Above all, I must maintain my outward **reserve**[64], no one must know that war still reigns **incessantly**[65] within. War between **desire**[66] and common sense. The **latter**[67] has won up till now, yet will the former prove to be the stronger of the two? Sometimes I fear that it will and sometimes I long for it to be!

Oh, it is so terribly difficult never to say anything to Peter, but I know that the first to begin must be he, there's so much I want to say and do, I've lived it all in my dreams, it is so hard to find that yet another day has gone by, and none of it comes true! Yes, Kitty, Anne is a crazy child, but I do live in crazy times and under still crazier circumstances.

But, still, the brightest spot of all is that at least I can write down my thoughts and feelings, otherwise I would be absolutely **stifled**[68]! I wonder what Peter thinks about all these things? I keep hoping that I can talk about it to him one day. There must be something he has guessed about me, because he certainly can't love the outer Anne, which is the one he knows so far.

How can he, who loves peace and quiet, have any liking for all my **bustle**[69] and din? Can he possibly be the first and only one to have looked through my **concrete**[70] armor? And will it take him long to get there? Isn't there an old saying that love often springs from pity,

63. Moan – complaint or grumble
64. Reserve – retain
65. Incessantly – continuing without pause.
66. Desire – feeling of wanting something
67. Latter – second mention of two peoples
68. Stifled – suffocated
69. Bustle – activity and movement
70. Concrete – strong substance

or that the two go hand in hand? Is that the case with me too? Because I'm often just as sorry for him as I am for myself.

I really don't honestly know how to begin, and however would he be able to, when he finds talking so much more difficult than I do? If only I could write to him, then at least I would know that he would grasp what I want to say, because its so terribly difficult to put it into words!

                                                        Yours, Anne

## Friday, 17 March, 1944

Dear Kitty,

A sigh of relief has gone through the "Secret Annexe." Kraler has been **exempted**[71] from digging by the Court. Elli has given her nose a talking to and strictly **forbidden**[72] it to be a nuisance to her today. So everything is all right again, except that Margot and I are getting a bit tired of our parents. Don't misunderstand me, I can't get on well with Mummy at the moment, as you know. I still love Daddy just as much, and Margot loves Daddy and Mummy, but when you are as old as we are, you do want to decide just a few things for yourself, you want to be independent sometimes.

If I go upstairs, then I'm asked what I'm going to do, I'm not allowed salt with my food, every evening regularly at a quarter past eight Mummy asks whether I ought not to start undressing, every book I read must be **inspected**[73]. I must admit that they are not at all strict, and I'm allowed to read nearly everything, and yet we are both sick of all the remarks plus all the questioning that go on the whole day long.

Something else, especially about me, that doesn't please them: I don't feel like giving lots of kisses any more and I think fancy nicknames are terribly affected. In short, I'd really like to be rid of them for a while. Margot said last evening, "I think it's awfully

---

71.  Exempted - freed from liability          72.  Forbidden - banned
73.  Inspected - checked

annoying[74], the way they ask if you've got a headache, or whether you don't feel well, if you happen to give a sigh and put your hand to your head!"

It is a great blow to us both, suddenly to realize how little remains of the confidence and harmony that we used to have at home. And it's largely due to the fact that we're all "skew-wiff" here. By this I mean that we are treated as children over outward things, and we are much older than most girls of our age inwardly.

Although I'm only fourteen, I know quite well what I want, I know who is right and who is wrong, I have my opinions, my own ideas and principles, and although it may sound pretty mad from an adolescent, I feel more of a person than a child, I feel quite independent of anyone.

I know that I can discuss things and argue better than Mummy, I know I'm not so **prejudiced**[75], I don't exaggerate so much, I am more **precise**[76] and **adroit**[77] and because of this— you may laugh— I feel superior to her over a great many things. If I love anyone, above all I must have admiration for them, admiration and respect. Everything would be all right if only I had Peter, for I do admire him in many ways. He is such a nice, goodlooking boy!

Yours, Anne

## Sunday, 19 March, 1944

Dear Kitty,

Yesterday was a great day for me. I had decided to talk things out with Peter. Just as we were going to sit down to supper I whispered to him, "Are you going to do shorthand this evening. Peter?" "No," was his reply. "Then I'd just like to talk to you later!" He agreed. After the dishes were done, I stood by the window in his parents' room awhile for the look of things, but it wasn't long before I went to Peter. He was standing on the left side of the open window, I went and stood on the right side, and we talked. It was much easier to talk

---

74. Annoying – irritating
76. Precise – exact
75. Prejudiced – pre conceived opinion
77. Adroit – clever or skillful

beside the open window in semidarkness than in bright light, and I believe Peter felt the same.

We told each other so much, so very very much, that I can't repeat it all, but it was lovely the most wonderful evening I have ever had in the "Secret Annexe." I will just tell you briefly the various things we talked about. First we talked about the quarrels and how I regard them-quite differently now, and then about the estrangement between us and our parents.

I told Peter about Mummy and Daddy, and Margot, and about myself.

At one moment he asked, "I suppose you always give each other a good night kiss, don't you?"

"One, dozens, why, don't you?"

"No, I have hardly ever kissed anyone."

"Not even on your birthday?"

"Yes, I have then."

We talked about how we neither of us **confide**[78] in our parents, and how his parents would have loved to have his confidence, but that he didn't wish it. How I cry my heart out in bed, and he goes up into the loft and **swears**[79]. How Margot and I really only know each other well for a little while, but that, even so, we don't tell each other everything, because we are always together. Over every imaginable thing-oh, he was just as I thought!

Then we talked about 1942, how different we were then. We just don't recognize ourselves as the same people any more. How we simply couldn't bear each other in the beginning. He thought I was much too **talkative**[80] and **unruly**[81], and I soon came to the conclusion that I'd no time for him. I couldn't understand why he didn't flirt with me, but now I'm glad. He also mentioned how much he isolated himself from us all. I said that there was not much difference between my noise and his silence. That I love peace and quiet too, and have nothing for myself alone, except my diary. How glad he is that my

---

78. Confide – disclose  　　79. Swears – promise solemnly or on oath
80. Talkative – fond of talking  　81. Unruly – disorderly and disruptive

parents have children here, and that I'm glad he is here. That I understand his reserve now and his relationship with his parents, and how I would love to be able to help him.

"You always do help me," he said. "How?" I asked, very surprised. "By your cheerfulness." That was certainly the loveliest thing he said. It was wonderful, he must have grown to love me as a friend, and that is enough for the time being. I am so grateful and happy, I just can't find the words. I must **apologize**[82], Kitty, that my style is not up to **standard**[83] today.

I have just written down what came into my head. I have the feeling now that Peter and I share a secret. If he looks at me with those eyes that laugh and wink, then it's just as if a little light goes on inside me. I hope it will remain like this and that we may have many, many more **glorious**[84] times together!

Yours, Anne

## Monday, 20 March, 1944

Dear Kitty,

This morning Peter asked me if I would come again one evening, and said that I really didn't disturb him, and if there's room for one there's room for two. I said that I couldn't come every evening, because they wouldn't like it downstairs, but he thought that I needn't let that bother me. Then I said that I would love *to* come one Saturday evening and especially asked him to warn me when there was a moon. "Then we'll go downstairs," he answered, "and look at the moon from there."

In the meantime a little shadow has fallen on my happiness. I've thought for a long time that Margot liked Peter quite a lot too. How much she loves him I don't know, but I think it's wretched. I must cause her terrible pain each time I'm with Peter, and the funny part of it is that she hardly shows it.

---

82. Apologize – express regret for something that one has done
83. Standard – a level of quality or attainment
84. Glorious – impressive and pleasant

I know quite well that I'd be desperately jealous, but Margot only says that I needn't pity her.

"I think its so rotten that you should be the odd one out," I added. I'm used to that," she answered, somewhat **bitterly**[85].

I don't dare tell Peter this yet, perhaps later on, but we've got to talk about so many other things first.

I had a little **ticking**[86] off yesterday evening from Mummy, which I certainly deserved. I mustn't **overdo**[87] my **indifference**[88] towards her. So in spite of everything, I must try once again to be friendly and keep my observations to myself.

Even Pim is different lately. He is trying not to treat me as such a child, and it makes him much too cool. See what comes of it!

Enough for now, I'm full to the brim with Peter and can do nothing but look at him!

Evidence of Margot's goodness: I received this today, MARCH 20TH, 1944

*Anne, when I said yesterday that I was not jealous of you I was only fifty per cent honest. It is like this. I'm jealous of neither you nor Peter. I only feel a bit sorry that I haven't found anyone yet and am not likely to, for the time being, with whom I can discuss my thoughts and feelings. But I should not grudge it to you for that reason. One misses enough here anyway, things that other people just take for granted.*

*On the other hand, I know for certain that I would never have got so far with Peter, anyway, because I have the feeling that if I wished to discuss a lot with anyone, I should want to be on rather intimate terms with him. I would want to have the feeling that he understood me through and through without my having to say much. But for that reason it would have to be someone whom I felt was my superior*

---

85. Bitterly – in a resentful manner
86. Ticking – (here) scolding
87. Overdo – exaggerate
88. Indifference – having no interest

*intellectually*[89], *and that is not the case with Peter. But I can imagine it being so with you and Peter.*

*You are not doing me out of anything which is my due, do not* **reproach**[90] *yourself in the least on my account. You and Peter can only gain by the friendship.*

My reply:

*DearMargot,*

*I thought your letter was exceptionally sweet, but I still don't feel quite happy about it and nor do I think thct I shall.*

*At present there is no question of such confidence as you have in mind between Peter and myself, but in the* **twilight**[91] *beside an open window you can say more to each other than in brilliant sunshine. Also it's easier to whisper your feelings than to* **trumpet**[92] *them forth out loud. I believe that you are beginning to feel a kind of sisterly affection for Peter, and that you would love to help him, just as much as I. Perhaps you will still be able to do that sometime, although that is not the kind of confidence we have in mind. I think it must come from both sides, and I believe that's the reason why Daddy and I have never got so far.*

*Let's not talk about it any more, but if you still want anything please write to me about it because I can say what I mean much better on paper.*

*You don't know how much I admire you, and I only hope that I may yet* **acquire**[93] *some of the goodness that you and Daddy have, because now I don't see much difference between you and Daddy in that sense.*

Yours, Anne

---

89.  Intellectually – having a highly developed intellect
90.  Reproach – criticize, scold
91.  Twilight – the soft glowing light from the sky when the sun is below the horizon
92.  Trumpet – a musical instrument
93.  Acquire – obtain

# Wednesday, 22 March, 1944

Dear Kitty,

I received this from Margot this evening:

*Dear Anne,*

*After your letter yesterday I have the unpleasant feeling that you will have **prickings**[94] of conscience when you visit Peter but really there is no reason for this. In my heart of hearts I feel that I have the right to share* mutual *confidence with someone, but I could not hear Peter in that role yet.*

*However, I do feel just as you say, that Peter is a bit like a brother, but—a younger brother, we have put out **feelers**[95] towards each other, the affection of a brother and sister might grow if they touched, perhaps they will later—perhaps never, however, it has certainly* not reached that stage yet.

*Therefore you really needn't pity me. Now that you've found companionship, enjoy it as much as you can.*

In the meantime it is getting more and more wonderful here. I believe, Kitty, that we may have a real great love in the "Secret Annexe." Don't worry. I'm not thinking of marrying him. I don't know what he will be like when he grows up, nor do I know whether we should ever love each other enough to marry. I know now that Peter loves me, but just how I myself don't know yet.

Whether he only wants a great friend, or whether I attract him as a girl or as a sister, I can't yet discover.

When he said that I always helped him over his parents' quarrels, I was awfully glad, it was one step towards making me believe in his friendship, I asked him yesterday what he would do if there were a dozen Annes here who always kept coming to him. His reply was, "If they were all like you, it certainly wouldn't be too bad!"

94. Pricking – feeling
95. Feelers – a tentative proposal intended to ascertain someone's attitude or opinion

He's tremendously **hospitable**[96] towards me and I really believe he likes to see me. Meanwhile he is working **diligently**[97] at his French, even when he's in bed, going on until a quarter past ten. Oh, when I think about Saturday evening and recall it all, word for word, then for the first time I don't feel discontented about myself; I mean that I would still say exactly the same and wouldn't wish to change anything, as is usually the case.

He is so handsome, both when he laughs and when he looks quietly in front of him, he is such a darling and so good. I believe what surprised him most about me was when he discovered that I'm not a bit the superficial worldly Anne that I appear, but just as dreamy a **specimen**[98], with just as many difficulties as he himself.

Yours, Anne

Reply:

*Dear Margot,*

*I think the best thing we can do is simply to wait and see what happens. It can't be very long before Peter and I come to a definite decision, either to go* on *as before or be different. Just which way it will go I don't know myself, and I don't bother to look beyond my own nose. But I shall certainly do one thing, if Peter and I decide to be friends, I shall tell him that you are very fond of him too and would always be prepared to help him should the need arise. The latter may not be what you wish, but I don't care now, I don't know what Peter thinks about you, but I shall ask him then.*

*I'm sure it's not bad—the opposite! You are always welcome to join us in the attic, or wherever we are, you honestly won't disturb us bemuse I feel we have a silent agreement to talk only in the evenings when it's dark.*

*Keep your courage up! Like I do. Although it's not always easy, your time may come sooner than you think.*

Yours, Anne

---

96.  Hospitable – friendly          97.  Diligently – painstakingly
98.  Specimen – sample

# Thursday, 23 March, 1944

Dear Kitty,

Things are running more or less normally again now. Our coupon men are out of prison again, thank goodness!

Miep returned yesterday. Elli is better, although she still has a cough; Koophuis will have to stay at home for a long time still.

A plane crashed near here yesterday, the **occupants**[99] were able to jump out in time by parachute. The machine crashed onto a school, but there were no children there at the time. The result was a small fire and two people killed. The Germans shot at the airmen terribly as they were coming down. The Amsterdammers who saw it nearly exploded with rage and indignation at the **cowardliness**[100] of such a deed. We—I'm speaking of the ladies—nearly jumped out of our skins, I **loathe**[101] the blasted shooting.

I often go upstairs after supper nowadays and take a breath of the fresh evening air. I like it up there, sitting on a chair beside him and looking outside.

Van Daan and Dussel make very feeble remarks when I disappear into his room; "Anne's second home," they call it, or "Is it suitable for young gentlemen to receive young girls in semidarkness?" Peter shows amazing wit in his replies to these socalled humorous **sallies**[102]. For that matter. Mummy too is somewhat curious and would love to ask what we talk about, if she wasn't secretly afraid of being **snubbed**[103]. Peter says it's nothing but **envy**[104] on the part of the grownups, because we are young and we don't pay much attention to their **spitefulness**[105]. Sometimes he comes and gets me from downstairs, but he turns simply **scarlet**[106] in spite of all

---

99. Occupants – persons who occupiy a place at a given time.
100. Cowardliness – lacking courageousness
101. Loathe – feel hatred              102. Sallies – comment
103. Snubbed – to ignore or behave coldly 104. Envy – discontent or resentful
105. Spitefulness – maliciousness        106. Scarlet – a brilliant red color

precautions[107], and can hardly get the words out of his mouth. How thankful I am that I don't **blush**[108], it must be a highly unpleasant sensation. Daddy always says I'm **prudish**[109] and vain but that's not true, I'm just simply vain! I have not often had anyone tell me 1 was pretty. Except a boy at school; who said I looked so attractive when I laughed. Yesterday I received a genuine compliment from Peter, and just for fun I will tell you roughly how the conversation went:

Peter so often used to say, "Do laugh, Anne!" This struck me as odd, and I asked, "Why must I always laugh?"

"Because I like it, you get such **dimples**[110] in your cheeks when you laugh, how do they come, actually?"

"I was bom with them, I've got one in my chin too. That's my only beauty,'"

"Of course not, that's not true."

"Yes, it is, I know quite well that I'm not a beauty, I never have been and never shall be."

"I don't agree at all, I think you're pretty."

"That's not true."

"If I say so, then you can take it from me it is."

Then I naturally said the same of him.

I hear-a lot from all sides about the sudden friendship. We don't take much notice of all this parental chatter, their remarks are so **feeble**[111]. Have the two sets of parents forgotten their own youth? It seems like it, at least they seem to take us seriously, if we make a joke, and laugh at us when we are serious.

Yours, Anne

---

107. Precautions – a measure taken in advance to prevent something undesirable happening
108. Blush – become red in the face through shyness, embarrassment or shame.
109. Prudish – easily offended or shocked by matters
110. Dimples – a small depression in the flesh, either permanent or forming in the cheeks whenone smiles
111. Feeble – lacking physical strength

# Monday, 27 March, 1944

Dear Kitty,

One very big chapter of our history in hiding should really be about politics, but as this subject doesn't interest me personally very much, I've rather let it go. So for once I will **devote**[112] my whole letter to politics today.

It goes without saying that there are very many different opinions on this topic, and its even more logical that it should be a favorite subject for discussion in such critical times, but- it's just simply stupid that there should be so many quarrels over it.

They may speculate, laugh, abuse, and **grumble**[113], let them do what they will, as long as they **stew**[114] in their own juice and don't quarrel, because the **consequences**[115] are usually unpleasant.

The people from outside bring with them a lot of news that is not true, however, up till now our radio hasn't lied to us. Henk, Miep, Koophuis, Elli, and Kraler all show ups and downs in their political moods, Henk least of all.

Political feeling here in the "Secret Annexe" is always about the same. During the countless arguments over invasion, air raids, speeches, etc., etc., one also always hears the countless cries of "impossible," or *"Urn Gottes* Willen, if they are going to start now however long is it going to last." "It's going splendidly, first class, good!" Optimists and pessimists, and, above all, don't let's forget the realists who give their opinions with **untiring**[116] energy and, just as with everything else, each one thinking he is right. It annoys a certain lady that her **spouse**[117] has such unparalleled faith in the British, and

112. Devote – dedicate
113. Grumble – complaint in a bad tempered way
114. Stew – a dish of meat and vegetables cooked slowly in liquid in closed dish or pan.
115. Consequences – results
116. Untiring – continuing at the same rate without loss of vigour
117. Spouse – a husband or wife considered in relation to their partner

a certain gentleman attacks his lady because of her **teasing**[118] and **disparaging**[119] remarks about his beloved nation.

They never seem to tire of it. I have discovered something— the effects are **stupendous**[120], just like pricking someone with a pin and waiting to see how they jump. This is what I do: begin on politics. One question, one word, one sentence, and at once they're off!

Just as if the German Wehrmacht news bulletins and the English B.B.C. were not enough, they have now introduced "Special Air-Raid Announcements." In one word, **magnificent**[121]; but on the other hand often disappointing too. The British are making a non-stop business of their air attacks, with the same **zest**[122] as the Germans make a business of lying. The radio therefore goes on early in the morning and is listened to at all hours of the day, until nine, ten, and often eleven o'clock in the evening.

This is certainly a sign that the grownups have infinite patience, but it also means the power of absorption of their brains is pretty limited, with exceptions, of course—I don't want to hurt anyone's feelings. One or two news bulletins would be ample per day! But the old geese, well— I've said my piece!

Arbeiter-Programm, Radio "Oranje," Frank Phillips or Her Majesty Queen Wilhelmina, they each get their turn, and an ever attentive ear. And if they are not eating or sleeping, then they're sitting around the radio and discussing food, sleep, and politics.

Ugh! It gets so boring, and it's quite a job not to become a dull old stick oneself. Politics can't do much more harm to the parents!

I must mention one shining exception—a speech by our beloved Winston Churchill is quite perfect;

---

118. Teasing – playfully make fun of or attempt to provoke
119. Disparaging – represent as being of little worth.
120. Stupendous – extremely impressive
121. Magnificent – very beautiful or impressive
122. Zest – great enthusiasm and energy

Nine o'clock on Sunday evening. The teapot stands, with the cozy[123] over it, on the table, and the guests come in. Dussel next to the radio on the left, Mr. Van Daan in front of it, with Peter beside him. Mummy next to Mr. Van Daan and Mrs. Van Daan behind him, and Pim at the table, Margot and I beside. I see I haven't described very clearly how we sit. The gentlemen puff away at their pipes, Peter's eyes are **popping**[124] out of his head with the strain of listening. Mummy wearing a long dark **negligee**[125], and Mrs. Van Daan trembling because of the planes, which take no notice of the speech but fly **blithely**[126] on towards Essen, Daddy sipping tea, Margot and 1 united in a sisterly fashion by the sleeping Mouschi, who is **monopolizing**[127] both our knees. Margot's hair is in **curlers**[128], I am wearing a nightdress, which is much too small, too narrow, and too short.

It all looks so **intimate**[129], **snug**[130], peaceful, and this time it is too, yet I await the consequences with horror. They can hardly wait till the end of the speech, stamping their feet, so impatient are they to get down to discussing it. Brr, brr, brr—they egg each other on until the arguments lead to **discord**[131] and quarrels.

Yours, Anne

# Tuesday, 28 March, 1944

Dear Kitty,

I could write a lot more about politics, but I have **heaps**[132] of other things to tell you today. First, Mummy 'has more or less

---

123. Cozy – comfortable warm secure          124. Popping – bulging
125. Negligee – a women's light filmy dressing gown.
126. Blithely – cheerfully of thoughtlessly
127. Monopolizing – hold or obtain a monopoly on
128. Curlers – a player in the game of curling.
129. Intimate – closely acquainted          130. Snug – warm and cozy
131. Discord – lack of agreement of harmony
132. Heaps – a mound or a pile of substance

forbidden[133] me to go upstairs so often, because, according to her, Mrs. Van Daan is jealous. Secondly, Peter has invited Margot to join us upstairs, I don't know whether it's just out of politeness or whether he really means it. Thirdly, 1 went and asked Daddy if he thought I need pay any regard to Mrs. Van Daan's jealousy, and he didn't think so. What next? Mummy is cross, perhaps jealous too. Daddy doesn't grudge[134] us these times together, and thinks it's nice that we get on so well. Margot is fond of Peter too, but feels that two's company and three's a crowd.

Mummy thinks that Peter is in love with me; quite frankly, I only wish he were, then we'd be quits and really be able to get to know each other. She also says that he keeps on looking at me. Now, I suppose that's true, but still I can't help it if he looks at my dimples and we wink at each other occasionally, can 1?

I'm in a very difficult position Mummy is against me and I'm against her. Daddy closes his eyes and tries not to see the silent battle between us. Mummy is sad, because she does really love me, while I'm not in the least bit sad, because I don't think she understands. And Peter-1 don't want to give Peter up, he's such a darling. I admire him so, it can grow into something beautiful between us, why do the "old 'uns" have to poke[135] their noses in all the time? Luckily I'm quite used to hiding my feelings and I manage extremely well not to let them see how mad I am about him. Will he ever say anything? Will I ever feel his cheek against mine, like I felt Peter's cheek in my dream? Oh, Peter and Peter, you are *one* and the same! They don't understand us, won't they ever grasp[136] that we are happy, just sitting together and not saying a word. They don't understand what has driven us together like this. Oh, when will all these difficulties be overcome? And yet it is good to overcome them, because then the end will be all the more wonderful. When he lies with his head on his arm with his eyes closed, then he is still a child, when he plays

---

133. Forbidden – unfriendly          134. Grudge – feeling of resentment
135. Poke – jab or prod with a finger or a sharp object
136. Grasp – seize and hold firmly

with Boche, he is loving, when he carries potatoes or anything heavy, then he is strong, when he goes and watches the shooting, or looks for burglars in the darkness, then he is brave, and when he is so awkward and **clumsy**[137], then he is just a pet.

I like it much better if he explains something to me than when I have to teach him; I would really adore him to be my superior in almost everything.

What do we care about the two mothers? Oh, but if only he would speak!

Yours, Anne

# Wednesday, 29 March, 1944

Dear Kitty,

Bolkestein, an M.P., was speaking on the Dutch News from London, and he said that they ought to make a collection of diaries and letters after the war. Of course, they all made a rush at my diary immediately. Just imagine how interesting it would be if I were to publish a romance of the "Secret Annexe." The title* alone would be enough to make people think it was a detective story.

But, seriously, it would seem quite funny ten years after the war if we Jews were fo tell how we lived and what we ate and talked about here. Although I tell you a lot, still, even so, you only know very little of our lives.

How scared the ladies are during the air raids. For instance, on Sunday, when 350 British planes dropped half a million kilos of bombs on Ijmuiden, how the houses **trembled**[138] like a **wisp**[139] of grass in the wind, and who knows how many **epidemics**[140] now rage. You don't know anything about all these things, and I would

---

* The original little of this Diary was *Het Achterbuis*. There is no exact translation into English, the Nearest being *The Seret Annexe*.

---

137. Clumsy - lacking tact or skills    138. Trembled - shake involuntarily
139. Wisp - a small thin bunch strand or amount of something
140. Epidemics - a widespread occurrence of an infectious disease

need to keep on writing the whole day if I were to tell you everything in detail. People have to line up for vegetables and all kinds of other things, doctors are unable to visit the sick, because if they turn their backs on their cars for a moment, they are stolen, burglaries and thefts **abound**[141], so much so that you wonder what has taken hold of the Dutch for them suddenly to have become such thieves. Little children of eight and eleven years break the windows of people's homes and steal whatever they can lay their hands on. No one **dares**[142] to leave his house unoccupied for five minutes, because if you go, your things go too. Every day there are announcements in the newspapers offering rewards for the return of lost property, typewriters, Persian rugs, electric clocks, cloth, etc., etc. Electric clocks in the streets are **dismantled**[143], public telephones are pulled to pieces—down to the last thread. **Morale**[144] among the population can't be good, the weekly rations are not enough to last for two days except the coffee substitute. The invasion is a long time coming, and the men have to go to Germany. The children are ill or **undernourished**[145], everyone is wearing old clothes and old shoes. A new sole costs 7.50 florins in the black market; moreover, hardly any of the shoemakers will *accept* shoe repairs or, if they do, you have to wait months, during which time the shoes often disappear.

There's one good thing in the midst of it all, which is that as the food gets worse and the measures against the people more severe, so **sabotage**[146] against the authorities steadily increases. The people in the food offices, the police, officials, they all either work with their fellow citizens and help them or they tell tales on them and have them sent to prison. Fortunately, only a small percentage of Dutch people are on the wrong side.

Yours, Anne

---

141. Abound - exists in large numbers or amounts    142.  Dares - have the courage
143. Dismantled - take to pieces
144. Morale - the confidence and feeling of well being of a person or group at a particular time
145. Undernourished - having insufficient food or nutrients
146. Sabotage - deliberately destroy

# Friday, 31 March, 1944

Dear Kitty,

Think of it, it's still pretty cold, but most people hav&-been without coal for about a month—pleasant, eh! In general public feeling over the Russian front is optimistic again, because that is terrific! You know I don't write much about politics, but I must just tell you where they are now; they are right by the Polish border and have reached the Pruth near Rumania. They are close to Odessa. Every evening here they expect an extra **communique**[147] from Stalin.

They fire off so many **salvos**[148] in Moscow to *celebrate* their victories that the city must **rumble**[149] and shake just about every day-whether they think it's fun to pretend that the war is close at hand again or that they know of no other way of expressing their joy, I don't know!

Hungary is occupied by German troops. There are still a million Jews there, so they too will have had it now. The **chatter**[150] about Peter and me has calmed down a bit now. We are very good friends, are together a lot and discuss every imaginable subject. It is awfully nice never to have to keep a check on myself as I would have to with other boys, whenever we get on to **precarious**[151] ground. We were talking, for instance, about blood and via that subject we began talking about menstruation. He thinks we women are pretty tough. Why on earth? My life here has improved, greatly improved. God has not left me alone and will not leave me alone.

Yours, Anne

---

147. Communiqué - dispatch
148. Salvos - a simultaneous discharge of artillery or other guns in a battle
149. Rumble - deep resonant sound
150. Chatter - talk informally about minor matters
151. Precarious - uncertain

Anne alternated between print and cursive writing, tending more toward the latter as she grew older.

Diary entries from September 1942

From Anne's letter to Kitty of March 29, 1944

## Think and Ink...

➤ What generation gap in thoughts is reflected in Anne's opinions about herself her mother and Peter?

➤ What qualities of Peter did Anne actually get attracted?

➤ How had Anne grown wise within the walls?

➤ Does Anne like her present disposition? Why/why not?

➤ How did the transformation come to her?

➤ In what ways did she start enjoying nature?

➤ Do you think nature is the ultimate healer? How has Anne proved it?

➤ 'He who has courage and faith will never perish in misery' – What helped Anne make this revelation?

➤ How did the near starvation condition of the inmates make them desperate? How optimistic did Mr. Frank sound?

➤ What do you gather about the character as they express their views on their condition?

➤ Finally, Anne and Peter talk their heart out. What impression do they form in you about themselves?

➤ Throw light on Margot's character as revealed in her letter to Anne.

➤ What sort of maturity in thought did Margot and Anne exhibit in their personal communication?

➤ Do you think that closed life at the Secret Annexe had contributed for the sisters understanding each other? Justify your standpoint.

➤ How were the optimists and pessimists the secret Annexe analyze the political situation?

➤ How does a diary help in retracing the his historical happenings?

➤ How did the Russians contribute for the war?

## Text-Based Questions

- What made Anne feel that grownups are idiotic and stupid?
- What did Anne tell Peter about?
- Why was not the Saturday boring?
- What was Mrs. Van Daan's reaction??
- What did Mrs. Van Daan call Peter? Why?
- Did Anne enjoy facing a difficult conquest against the Van Daans for their son? How?
- How was Anne in school?
- What was Peter's opinion about her?
- Why did Anne feel that Peter had changed his opinion about her?
- Describe Margot's character as Anne found her to be.
- What was the condition of the family's ration why?
- What was the condition of Koophius?
- What did Henk tell the inmates?
- How were the doctors helpless?
- What was going on within Anne?
- Why was Anne worried about Peter's thoughts about her?
- What westerns rise in Anne's mind about Peter's Opinion of her?
- What attitude of her mother sickens Anne?
- What was a great blow to Margot and Anne?
- Why did Anne feel herself superior to her mother?
- What was the loveliest thing that Peter tell Anne?

- What was Margot's reaction when Peter and Anne were together?

- What did Margot write to Anne, and what was her reply in return?

- Describe the blasted shooting as Anne describes it.

- Which is Anne's second home? What did others think about it?

- Why did not Anne and Peter bother about the elder's comments?

- How did Anne justify her friendship with Peter?

- Why did Anne's mother stop her from going to Peter's room?

- What did Anne think about her mother's attitude stop her?

- The friction between a mother and daughter is universal phenomenon. In Anne's case, how were she and her mother divided over her friendship with Peter? Who do you favour? Why?

- What did Bolkestein say?

- Why did Anne say that it would be funny to know about the Jew's lives after ten years?

- What was the atonality of the lives of Jews during the war?

- What was the one good thing in the war situation?

# Saturday, 1 April, 1944

Dear Kitty,

And yet everything is still so difficult, I expect you can guess what I mean, can't you? I am so longing for a kiss, the kiss that is so long in coming. I wonder if all the time he still regards me as a friend? Am I nothing more?

You know and I know that I am strong, that I can carry most of my **burdens**[1] alone. I have never been used to sharing my troubles with anyone, I have never **clung**[2] to my mother, but now I would so love to lay my head on "his" shoulder just once and remain still.

1 can't, I simply can't ever forget that dream of Peter's cheek, when it was all, all so good! Wouldn't he long for it too? Is it that he is just too shy to **acknowledge**[3] his love? Why does he want me with him so often? Oh, why doesn't he speak?

I'd better stop, I must be quiet, I shall remain strong and with a bit of patience the other will come too, but-and that is the worst of it-it looks just as if I'm running after him, I am always the one who goes upstairs, he doesn't come to me.

But that is just because of the rooms, and he is sure to understand the difficulty.

Oh, yes, and there's more he'll understand.

Yours, Anne

# Monday, 3 April, 1944

Dear Kitty,

Contrary to my usual custom, I will for once write more fully about food because it has become a very difficult and important matter, not only here in the "Secret Annexe" but in the whole of Holland, all Europe, and even beyond.

---

1. Burdens – a heavy load    2. Clung – hold tightly
3. Acknowledge – accept or admit

In the twentyone months that we've spent here we have been through a good many "food cycles"—you'll understand what that means in a minute. When I talk of "food cycles" I mean periods in which one has nothing else to eat but one particular dish or kind of vegetable. We had nothing but **endive**[4] for a long time, day in, day out, endive with sand, endive without sand, stew with endive, boiled or en casserole; then it was spinach, and after that followed kohlrabi, salsify, cucumbers, tomatoes, sauerkraut, etc., etc.

For instance, it's really disagreeable to eat a lot of sauerkraut for lunch and supper every day, but you do it if you're hungry. However, we have the most delightful period of all now, because we don't get any fresh vegetables at all. Our weekly menu for supper consists of kidney beans, pea soup, potatoes with dumplings, potato-chalet and, by the grace of God, occasionally turnip tops or rotten carrots, and then the kidney beans once again. We eat potatoes at every meal, beginning with breakfast, because of the bread shortage. We make our soup from kidney or haricot beans, potatoes. Julienne soup in packets, French beans in packets, kidney beans in packets. Everything contains beans, not to mention the bread!

In the evening we always have potatoes with gravy substitute and—thank goodness we've still got it-beetroot salad. I must still tell you about the dumplings, which we make out of government flour, water, and yeast. They are so sticky and tough, they lie like stones in one's stomach—ah, well!

The great attraction each week is a slice of liver sausage, and jam on dry bread. But we're still alive, and quite often we even enjoy our poor meals.

Yours, Anne

# Tuesday, 4 April, 1944

Dear Kitty,

For a long time I haven't had any idea of what I was working for any more, the end of the war is so terribly far away, so unreal, like a

4.  Endive – an edible Mediterranean plant

fairy tale. If the war isn't over by September, I shan't go to school any more, because I don't want to be two years behind. Peter filled my days— nothing but Peter, dreams and thoughts until Saturday, when I felt so utterly miserable; oh, it was terrible, I was holding back my tears all the while I was with Peter, then laughed with Van Daan over a lemon punch, was cheerful and excited, but the moment I was alone I knew that I would have to cry my heart out. So, clad in my nightdress, I let myself go and slipped down onto the floor.

First I said my long prayer very earnestly, then I cried with my head on my arms, my knees bent up, on the bare floor, completely folded up. One large sob brought me back to earth again, and I quelled my tears because I didn't want them to hear anything in the next room. Then I began trying to talk some courage into myself. I could only say: "I must, I must, I must..." Completely stiff from the unnatural position, I fell against the side of the bed and fought on, until I climbed into bed, again just before half past ten. It was over!

And now it's all over. I must work, so as not to be a fool, to get on, to become a journalist, because that's what I want! I know that I can write, a couple of my stories are good, my descriptions of the "Secret Annexe" are **humorous**[5], there's a lot in my diary that speaks, but-whether I have real talent remains to be seen.

"Eva's Dream" is my best fairy tale, and the queer thing about it is that I don't know where it comes from. Quite a lot of "Cady's Life" is good too, but, on the whole, it's nothing.

I am the best and sharpest critic of my own work. I know myself what is and what is not well written. Anyone who doesn't write doesn't know how wonderful it is. I used to **bemoan**[6] the fact that I couldn't draw at all, but now I am more than happy that I can at least write. And if I haven't any talent for writing books or newspaper articles, well, then I can always write for myself.

I want to get on, I can't imagine that I would have to lead the same sort of life as Mummy and Mrs. Van Daan and all the women who

5. Humorous – funny        6. Bemoan – lament

do their work and are then forgotten. I must have something besides a husband and children, something that I can devote myself to!

I want to go on living even after my death! And therefore I am grateful to God for giving me this gift, this possibility of developing myself and of writing, of expressing all that is in me.

I can shake off everything if I write, my sorrows disappear, my courage is **reborn**[7]. But, and that is the great question, will I ever be able to write anything great, will I ever become a journalist or a writer? I hope so, oh, I hope so very much, for I can **recapture**[8] everything when I write, my thoughts, my ideals and my fantasies.

I haven't done anything more to "Cady's Life" for ages, in my mind I know exactly how to go on, but somehow it doesn't flow from my pen. Perhaps I never shall finish it, it may land up in the wastepaper basket, or the fire ... that's a horrible idea, but then I think to myself, "At the age of fourteen and with so little experience, how can you write about philosophy?"

So I go on again with fresh courage; I think I shall succeed, because I want to write!

Yours, Anne

## Thursday, 6 April, 1944

Dear Kitty,

You asked me what my hobbies and interests'lifere, so 1 want to reply. I warn you, however, that theiWtere heaps of them, so don't get a shock First of all: writing, but that hardly counts as a hobby.

Number two: family trees. I've been searching for family trees of the French, German, Spanish, English, Austrian, Russian, Norwegian, and Dutch royal families in all the newspapers, books, and pamphlets I can find. I've made great progress with a lot of them, as, for a long time already, I've been taking down notes from all the biographies and history books that I read, I even copy out many passages of

---

7.  Reborn – born again                    8.  Recapture – recover

history. My third hobby then is history, on which Daddy has already bought me a lot of books. I can hardly wait for the day that I shall be able to comb through the books in a public library.

Number four is Greek and Roman mythology. I have various books about this too.

Other hobbies are film stars and family photos. Mad on books and reading. Have a great liking for history of art, poets and painters. I may go in for music later on. I have a great **loathing**[9] for algebra, geometry, and figures.

I enjoy all the other school subjects, but history above all!

Yours, Anne

# Tuesday, 11 April 1944

Dear Kitty,

My head **throbs**[10], I honestly don't know where to begin.

On Friday (Good Friday) we played Monopoly, Saturday afternoon too. These days passed *quickly* and uneventfully. On Sunday afternoon, on my invitation, Peter came to my room at half past four, at a quarter past five we went to the front attic, where we remained until six o'clock. There was a beautiful Mozart concert on the radio from six o'clock until a quarter past seven. I enjoyed it all very much, but especially the "Kleine Nachtmusik." I can hardly listen in the room because I'm always so **inwardly**[11] **stirred**[12] when I hear lovely music.

On Sunday evening Peter and I went to the front attic together and, in order to sit comfortably, we took with us a few divan cushions that we were able to lay our hands on. We seated ourselves on one packing case. Both the case and the cushions were very narrow, so we sat absolutely squashed together, leaning against other cases. Mouschi kept us company too, so we weren't unchaperoned.

---

9. Loathing – hatredness
10. Throbs – beat or sound with a strong
11. Inwardly – inside
12. Stirred – moved, touched, affected

Suddenly, at a quarter to nine, Mr. Van Daan whistled and asked if we had one of Dussel's cushions. We both jumped up and went downstairs with cushion, cat, and Van Daan.

A lot of trouble arose out of this cushion, because Dussel was annoyed that we had one of his cushions, one that he used as a pillow. He was afraid that there might be **fleas**[13] in it and made a great commotion about his beloved cushion! Peter and I put two hard brushes in his bed as a revenge. We had a good laugh over this little interlude!

Our fun didn't last long. At half past nine Peter knocked softly on the door and asked Daddy if he would just help him upstairs over a difficult English sentence. "That's a blind," I said to Margot, "anyone could see through that one!" I was right. They were in the act of breaking into the warehouse. Daddy, Van Daan, Dussel, and Peter were downstairs in a flash. Margot, Mummy, Mrs. Van Daan, and I stayed upstairs and waited.

Four frightened women just have to talk, so talk we did, until we heard a **bang**[14] downstairs. After that all was quiet, the clock struck a quarter to ten. The color had **vanished**[15] from our faces, we were still quiet, although we were afraid. Where could the men be? What was that bang? Would they be fighting the burglars? Ten o'clock, footsteps on the stairs: Daddy, white and nervous, entered, followed by Mr. Van Daan. "Lights out, creep upstairs, we expect the police in the house!"

There was no time to be frightened: the lights went out, I quickly grabbed a jacket, and we were upstairs. "What has happened? Tell us quickly!" There was no one to tell us, the men having disappeared downstairs again. Only at ten past ten did they reappear, two kept watch at Peter's open window, the door to the landing was closed, the **swinging**[16] cupboard shut. We hung a jersey round the night light, and after that they told us:

---

13.  Fleas - a small wingless jumping insect  14.   Bang - a sudden sharp loud noise
15.  Vanished - disappear suddenly          16.   Swinging - moving lively

Peter heard two loud bangs on the landing, ran downstairs, and saw there was a large **plank**[17] out of the left half of the door. He dashed upstairs, warned the "Home Guard" of the family, and the four of them proceeded downstairs. When they entered the warehouse, the burglars were in the act of enlarging the hole. Without further thought Van Daan shouted: "Police!"

A few hurried steps outside, and the burglars had fled. In order to avoid the hole being noticed by the police, a plank was put against it, but a good hard kick from outside sent it flying to the ground. The men were perplexed at such **impudence**[18], and both Van Daan and Peter felt murder welling up within them. Van Daan beat on the ground with a chopper, and all was quiet again. Once more they wanted to put the plank in front of the hole. Disturbance! A married couple outside **shone**[19] a torch through the opening, lighting up the whole warehouse. "Hell!" muttered one of the men, and now they switched over from their role of police to that of burglars. The four of them sneaked upstairs. Peter quickly opened the doors and windows of the kitchen and private office, flung the telephone onto the floor, and finally the four of them landed behind the swinging cupboard.

# END OF PART ONE

---

17. Plank - a long thin flat piece of timber
18. Impudence - disrespect
19. Shone - gave out a bright light

The married couple with the torch would probably have warned the police: it was Sunday evening, Easter Sunday, no one at the office on Easter Monday, so none of us could budge until Tuesday morning. Think of it, waiting in such fear for two nights and a day! No one had anything to suggest, so we simply sat there in pitch-darkness, because Mrs. Van Daan in her fright had unintentionally turned the lamp right out; talked in whispers, and at every creak one heard *Shl sh!"

It turned half past ten, eleven, but not a sound; Daddy ar.d Van Daan joined us in turns. Then a quarter past eleven, a bustle and noise downstairs. Everyone's breath was audible, otherwise no one moved. Footsteps in the House, in the private office, kitchen, then ... on our staircase. No one breathed audibly now, footsteps on our staircase, then a rattling of the swinging cupboard. This moment is indescribable. "Now we are lost!" I said, and could see us all being taken away by the Gestapo that very night. Twice they **rattled**[20] at the cupboard, then there was nothing, the footsteps withdrew, we were saved so far. A shiver seemed to pass from one to another, I heard someone's teeth chattering, no one said a word.

There was not another sound in the house, but a light was burning on our landing, right in front of the cupboard. Could that be because it was a secret cupboard? Perhaps the police had forgotten the light? Would someone come back to put it out? Tongues loosened, there was no one in the house any longer, perhaps there was someone on guard outside.

Next we did three things: we went over again what we supposed had happened, we trembled with fear, and we had to go to the lavatory. The buckets were in the attic, so all we had was Peter's tin wastepaper basket. Van Daan went first, then Daddy, but Mummy was too shy to face it. Daddy brought the wastepaper basket into the room, where Margot, Mrs. Van Daan, and 1 gladly made use of it. Finally Mummy decided to do so too. People kept on asking for paper—fortunately I had some in my pocket!

20.  Rattled – make noise

The tin smelled **ghastly**[21], everything went on in a whisper, we were tired, it was twelve o'clock. "Lie down on the floor then and sleep." Margot and I were each given a pillow and one blanket; Margot lying just near the store cupboard and I between the table legs. The smell wasn't quite so bad when one was on the floor, but still Mrs. Van Daan quietly brought some chlorine, a tea towel over the pot serving as a second expedient.

Talk, whispers, fear, stink, **flatulation**[22], and always someone on the pot; then try to go to sleep! However, by half past two I was so tired that I knew no more until half past three. I awoke when Mrs. Van Daan laid her head on my foot.

"For heaven's sake, give me something to put on!" I asked. I was given something, but don't ask what—a pair of woolen knickers over my pajamas, a red jumper, and a black skirt, white oversocks and a pair of sports stockings full of holes. Then Mrs. Van Daan sat in the chair and her husband came and lay on my feet. I lay thinking till half past three, shivering the whole time, which prevented Van Daan from sleeping. I prepared myself for the return of the police, then we'd have to say that we were in hiding; they would either be good Dutch people, then we'd be saved, or N.S.Bers,* then we'd have to bribe them!

"In that case, destroy the radio," sighed Mrs. Van Daan. "Yes, in the stove!" replied her husband. "If they find us, then let them find the radio as well!"

"Then they will find Anne's diary," added Daddy. "Burn it then," suggested the most terrified member of the party. This, and when the police rattled the cupboard door, were my worst moments, "Not my diary; if my diary goes, I go with it!" But luckily Daddy didn't answer.

---

* The Dutch National Social Movement.

---

21.  Ghastly – causing great horror or fear
22.  Flatulation – inflated or pretentious in speech or writing

There is no object in **recounting**[23] all the conversations that I can still remember, so much was said. I comforted Mrs. Van Daan, who was very scared. We talked about escaping and being questioned by the Gestapo, about ringing up, and being brave.

"We must behave like soldiers, Mrs. Van Daan. If all is up now, then let's go for Queen and Country, for freedom, truth, and right, as they always say on the Dutch News from England. The only thing that is really rotten is that we get a lot of other people into trouble too."

Mr. Van Daan changed places again with his wife after an hour, and Daddy came and sat beside me. The men smoked nonstop, now and then there was a deep sigh, then someone went on the pot and everything began all over again.

Four o'clock, five o'clock, half past five. Then I went and sat with Peter by his window and listened, so close together that we could feel each others bodies quivering; we spoke a word or two now and then, and listened attentively. In the room next door they took down the blackout. They wanted to call up Koophuis at seven o'clock and get him to send someone around. Then they wrote down everything they wanted to tell Koophuis over the phone. The risk that the police on guard at the door, or in the warehouse, might hear the telephone was very great, but the danger of the police returning was even greater. The points were these:

Burglars broken in: police have been in the house, as far as the swinging cupboard, but no further.

Burglars apparently disturbed, forced open the door in the warehouse and escaped through the garden.

Main entrance bolted, Kraler must have used the second door when he left. The typewriters and adding machine are safe in the black case in the private office.

Try to warn Henk and fetch the key from Elli, then go and look round the office-on the pretext of feeding the cat.

---

23. Recounting – remembering

Everything went according to plan. Koophuis was phoned, the typewriters which we had upstairs were put in the case. Then we sat around the table again and waited for Henk or the police.

Peter had fallen asleep and Van Daan and I were lying on the floor, when we heard loud footsteps downstairs. I got up quietly: "That's Henk."

"No, no, it's the police," some of the others said. Someone.knocked at the doo; Miep whistled. This was too much for Mrs. Van Daan, she turned as white as a sheet and sank limply into a chair, had the tension lasted one minute longer she would have fainted.

Our room was a perfect picture when Miep and Henk entered, the table alone would have been worth photographing! A copy of Cinema and Theaer, covered with jam and a remedy for diarrhea, opened at a page of dancing girls, two jam pots, two started loaves of bread, a mirror, comb, matches, ash, cigarettes, tobacco, ash tray, books, a pair of pants, a torch, toilet paper, etc., etc., lay jumbled together in **variegated**[24] splendor.

Of course Henk and Miep were greeted with shouts and tears. Henk mended the hole in the door with some planks, and soon went off again to inform the police of the burglary. Miep had also found a letter under the warehouse door from the night watchman Slagter, who had noticed the hole and warned the police, whom he would also visit.

So we had half an hour to tidy ourselves. I've never seen such a change take place in half an hour. Margot and I took the bedclothes downstairs, went to the W.C., washed, and did our teeth and hair. After that I tidied the room a bit and went upstairs again. The table there was already cleared, so we ran off some water and made coffee and tea, boiled the milk, and laid the table for lunch. Daddy and Peter emptied the potties and cleaned them with warm water and chlorine.

At eleven o'clock we sat round the table with Henk, who was back by that time, and slowly things began to be more normal and cozy again. Henk's story was as follows:

---

24.  Variegated – multicolored

Mr. Slagter was asleep, but his wife told Henk that her husband had found the hole in our door when he was doing his tour round the canals, and that he had called a policeman, who had gone through the building with him. He would be coming to see Kraler on Tuesday and would tell him more then. At the police station they knew nothing of the burglary yet, but the policeman had made a note of it at once and would come and look round on Tuesday. On the way back Henk happened to meet our green-grocer at the corner, and told him that the house had been broken into. "I know that," he said quite coolly. "I was passing last evening with my wife and saw the hole in the door. My wife wanted to walk on, but I just had a look in with my torch, then the thieves cleared at once. To be on the safe side, I didn't ring up the police, as with you I didn't think it was the thing to do. I don't know anything, but I guess a lot."

Henk thanked him and went on. The man obviously guesses that we're here, because he always brings the potatoes during the lunch hour. Such a nice man!

It was one by the time Henk had gone and we'd finished doing the dishes. We all went for a sleep. I awoke at a quarter to three and saw that Mr. Dussel had already disappeared. Quite by chance, and with my sleepy eyes, I ran into Peter in the bathroom, he had just come down. We arranged to meet downstairs.

I tidied myself and went down. "Do you still dare to go to the front attic?" he asked. I nodded, fetched my pillow, and we went up to the attic. It was glorious weather, and soon the sirens were **wailing**[25], we stayed where we were. Peter put his arm around my shoulder, and I put mine around his and so we remained, our arms around each other, quietly waiting until Margot came to fetch us for coffee at four o'clock.

We finished our bread, drank lemonade and joked (we were able to again), otherwise everything went normally. In the evening I thanked Peter because he was the bravest of us all.

---

25.　Wailing – a prolonged high pitched cry

None of us has ever been in such danger as that night. God truly protected us, just think of it-the police at our secret cupboard, the light on right in front of it, and still we remained undiscovered.

If the invasion comes, and bombs with it, then it is each man for himself, but in this case the fear was also for our good, innocent protectors. "We are saved, go on saving us!" That is all we can say.

This affair has brought quite a number of changes with it. Mr. Dussel no longer sits downstairs in Kraler's office in the evenings, but in the bathroom instead. Peter goes round-the house for a checkup at half past eight and half past nine. Peter isn't allowed to have his window open at nights any more. No one is allowed *to* pull the plug after half past nine. This evening there's a carpenter coming to make the warehouse doors even stronger."

Now there are **debates**[26] going on all the time in the "Secret Annexe." Kraler reproached us for our carelessness. Henk, too, said that in a case like that we must never go downstairs. We have been pointedly reminded that we are in hiding, that we are Jews in chains, chained to one spot, without any rights, but with a thousand duties. We Jews mustn't show our feelings, must be brave and strong, must accept all inconveniences and not grumble, must do what is within our power and trust in God. Sometime this terrible war will be over. Surely the time will come when we are people again, and not just Jews.

Who has **inflicted**[27] this upon us? Who has made us Jews different from all other people? Who has allowed us to suffer so terribly up till now? It is God that has made us as we are, but it will be God, too, who will raise us up again. If we bear all this suffering and if there are still Jews left, when it is over, then Jews, instead of being **doomed**[28], will be held up as an example. Who knows, it might even be our

---

26. Debates – a formal discussion
27. Inflicted – cause something unpleasant or painful to be suffered by someone else
28. Doomed – destined

religion from which the world and all peoples learn good, and for that reason and that reason only do we have to suffer now. We can never become just Netherlander, or just English, or representatives of any country for that matter, we will always remain Jews, but we want to, too.

Be brave! Let us remain aware of our task and not **grumble**[29], a solution will come, God has never **deserted**[30] our people. Right through the ages there have been Jews, through all the ages they have had to suffer, but it has made them strong too, the weak fall, but the strong will remain and never go under!

During that night I really felt that I had to die, I waited for the police, I was prepared, as the soldier is on the battlefield. I was eager to lay down my life for the country, but now, now I've been saved again, now my first wish after the war is that I may become Dutch! I love the Dutch, I love this country, I love the language and want to work here. And even if I have to write to the Queen myself, I will not give up until I have reached my goal.

I am becoming still more independent of my parents, young as I am, I face life with more courage than Mummy, my feeling for justice is immovable, and truer than hers. I know what I want, I have a goal, an opinion, I have a religion and love. Let me be myself and then I am satisfied. I know that I'm a woman, a woman with inward strength and plenty of courage.

If God lets me live, I shall **attain**[31] more than Mummy ever has done, I shall not remain **insignificant**[32], I shall work in the world and for mankind.'

And now I know that first and foremost I shall require courage and cheerfulness!

Yours, Anne

---

29. Grumble – complaint in a bad tempered way
30. Deserted – abandoned
31. Attain – achieve
32. Insignificant – of less value

# Friday, 14 April, 1944

Dear Kitty,

The atmosphere here is still extremely **strained**[33]. Pim has just about reached boiling point. Mrs. Van Daan is in bed with a cold and **trumpeting**[34] away. Mr. Van Daan grows pale without his fags, Dussel, who is giving up a lot of his comfort, is full of observations, etc.

There is no doubt that our luck's not in at the moment. The lavatory leaks and the washer of the tap has gone, but, thanks to our many connections, we shall soon be able *to get* these things put right.

I am sentimental sometimes, I know that, but there is occasion to be sentimental here at times, when Peter and I are sitting somewhere together on a hard, wooden **crate**[35] in the midst of masses of rubbish and dust, our arms around each others shoulders, and very close, he with one of my curls in his hand, when the birds sing outside and you see the trees changing to green, the sun invites one to be out in the open air, when the sky is so blue, then-oh, then, I wish for so much!

One sees nothing but dissatisfied, **grumpy**[36] faces here, nothing but **sighs**[37] and **suppressed**[38] complaints, it really would seem as if suddenly we were very badly off here. If the truth is told, things are just as bad as you yourself care to make them. There's no one here that sets a good example, everyone should see that he gets the better of his own moods. Every day you hear, "If only it was all over."

My work, my hope, my Jove, my courage, all these things keep my head above water and keep me from **complaining**[39].

---

33. Strained – stressed
34. Trumpeting – an act of playing of a musical instrument
35. Crate – wooden case
36. Grumpy – bad tempered and sulky
37. Sighs – a deep exhalation expressing sadness, tiredness relief
38. Suppressed – forcibly put an end to
39. Complaining – expressing dissatisfaction

I really believe. Kits, that I'm slightly bats today, and yet I don't know why. Everything here is so mixed up, nothings connected any more, and sometimes I very much doubt whether in the future anyone will be interested in all my **tosh**[40].

"The **unbosomings**[41] of an ugly duckling" will be the title of all this nonsense. My diary really won't be much use to Messrs. Bolkestein or Gerbrandy.[1]

Yours, Anne

# Saturday, 15 April, 1944

Dear Kitty,

"Shock upon shock. Will there ever be an end?" We honestly can ask ourselves that question now. Guess what's the latest. Peter forgot to **unbolt**[42] the front door (which is bolted on the inside at night) and the lock of the other door doesn't work. The result was that Kraler and the men could *not get into the* house, so he went to the neighbors, forced open the kitchen window, and entered the building from the back. He is **livid**[43] at us for being so stupid.

I can tell you, its upset Peter frightfully. At one meal, when Mummy said she felt more sorry for Peter than anyone else, he almost started to *cry. We're* all just as much to **blame**[44] as he is, because nearly every day the men ask whether the door's been unbolted and, just today, no one did.

Perhaps I shall be able to console him a bit later on I would so love *to help* him.

Yours, Anne

---

40. Tosh – rubbish, nonsense
41. Unbosoming – disclose one's secrets
42. Unbolt – open by drawing back a bolt
43. Livid – furiously angry
44. Blame – assign responsibility for a fault

# Sunday Morning, Just before Eleven O'clock, 16 April, 1944

Darlingest Kitty,

Remember yesterday's date, for it is a very important day in my life. Surely it is a great day for every girl when she receives her first kiss? Well, then, it is just as important for me too! Bram's kiss *on my* right cheek doesn't count any more, likewise the one from Mr. Walker on my right hand.

How did I suddenly come by this kiss? Well, I will tell you.

Yesterday evening at eight o'clock I was sitting with Peter on his divan, it wasn't long before his arm went round me. "Let's move up a bit," I said, "then I don't bump my head against the cupboard." He moved up, almost into the corner, I laid my arm under his and across his back, and he just about buried me, because his arm was hanging on my shoulder.

Now we've sat like this on other occasions, but never so close together as yesterday. He held me firmly against him, my left shoulder against his chest, already my heart began to beat faster, but we had not finished yet. He didn't rest until my head was on his shoulder and his against it. When i sat upright again after about five minutes, he soon took my head in his hands and laid it against him once more. Oh, it was so lovely, I couldn't talk much, the joy was too great. He **stroked**[45] my cheek and arm a bit **awkwardly**[46], played with my curls and our heads lay touching most of the time. I can't tell you, Kitty, the feeling that ran through me all the while. I was too happy for words, and I believe he was as well.

We got up at half past eight. Peter put on his gym shoes, so that when he toured the house he wouldn't make a noise, and I stood beside him. How it came about so suddenly, I don't know, but before we went downstairs he kissed me, through my hair, half on my left cheek, half on my ear, I **tore**[47] downstairs without looking round, and am simply longing for today!

Yours, Anne

45. Stroked–rubbed  46. Awkwardly– not smooth or graceful  47. Tore–rushed

# Monday, 17 April, 1944

Dear Kitty,

Do you think that Daddy and Mummy would approve of my sitting and kissing a boy on a divan-a boy of seventeen and a half and a girl of just under fifteen? I don't really think they would, but I must rely on myself over this. It is so quiet and peaceful to lie in his arms and to dream, it is so **thrilling**[48] to feel his cheek against mine, it is so lovely to know that there is someone waiting for me.

But there is indeed a big *"but"* because will Peter be content to leave it at this? I haven't forgotten his promise already, but... he *is* a boy!

I know myself that I'm starting very soon, not even fifteen, and so independent already! It's certainly hard for other people to understand, I know almost -for certain that Margot would never kiss a boy unless there had been some talk of an engagement or marriage, but neither Peter nor I have anything like that in mind. I'm sure too that Mummy never touched a man before Daddy. What would my girl friends say about it if they knew that I lay in Peter's arms, my heart against his chest, my head on his shoulder and with his head against mine!

Oh, Anne, how **scandalous**[49]! But honestly, I don't think it is, we are shut up here, shut away from the world, in fear and anxiety, especially just lately. Why, then, should we who love each other remain apart? Why should we wait until we've reached a suitable age? Why should we bother? I have taken it upon myself to look after myself; he would never want to cause me sorrow or pain. Why shouldn't I follow the way my heart leads me, if it makes us both happy? All the same, Kitty, I believe you can sense that I'm in doubt, I think it must be my honesty which **rebels**[50] against doing anything on the sly! Do you think it's my duty to tell Daddy what I'm doing? Do you think we should share our secret with a third person? A lot of the beauty would be lost, but would my conscience feel happier? I will discuss it with "him."

---

**48.** Thrilling – exciting   **49.** Scandalous – an action regarded as morally wrong
**50.** Rebels – resists

Oh, yes, there's still so much I want to talk to him about, for I don't see the use of only just **cuddling**[51] each other. Tb exchange our thoughts, that shows confidence and faith in each other, we would both be sure to profit by it!

Yours, Anne

## Tuesday, 18 April, 1944

Dear Kitty,

Everything goes well here. Daddy's just said that he definitely expects largescale operations to take place before the twentieth of May, both in Russia and Italy, and also in the West, 1 find it more and more difficult to imagine our **liberation**[52] from here.

Yesterday Peter and I finally got down to our talk, which had already been put off for at least ten days. I explained everything about girls to him and didn't hesitate to discuss the most intimate things. The evening ended by each giving the other a kiss, just about beside my mouth, it's really a lovely feeling.

Perhaps I'll take my diary up there sometime, to go more deeply into things for once. I don't get any satisfaction out of lying in each other's arms day in, day out, and would so like to feel that he's the same.

We are having a superb spring after our long, **lingering**[53] winter, April is really **glorious**[54], not too hot and not too cold, with little showers now and then. Our chestnut tree is already quite greenish and you can even see little **blooms**[55] here and there.

Elli gave us a treat on Saturday, by bringing four bunches of flowers, three bunches of narcissus and one of grape hyacinths, the latter being for me. I must do some algebra, Kitty—goodby.

Yours, Anne

---

51. Cuddling – hugging tightly　　52. Liberation – freedom
53. Lingering – to remain feebly in thoughts　　54. Glorious – impressive
55. Blooms – produces flowers

# Wednesday, 19 April, 1944

My Darling,

Is there anything more beautiful in the world than to sit before an open window and enjoy nature, to listen to the birds singing, feel the sun on your cheeks and have a darling boy in your arms? It is so soothing and peaceful to feel his arms around me, to know that he is close by and yet to remain silent, it can't be bad, for this tranquillity is good. Oh, never to be disturbed again, not even by Mouschi.

Yours, Anne

# Friday, 21 April, 1944

Dear Kitty,

Yesterday afternoon I was lying in bed with a sore throat, but since I was already bored on the first day and did not have a temperature, I got up again today. Its the eighteenth birthday of Her Royal Highness Princess Elizabeth of York. The B.B.C. has said that she will not be **declared**[56] of age yet, though it's usually the case with royal children. We have been asking ourselves what prince this beauty is going to marry, but cannot think of anyone suitable. Perhaps her sister. Princess Margaret Rose, can have Prince Baudouin of Belgium one day.

Here we are having one misfortune after another. Scarcely had the outside doors been **strengthened**[57] than the warehouse man appeared again. In all **probability**[58] it was he who stole the potato meal and wants to put the blame on to Elli's shoulders. The whole "Secret Annexe" is understandably het up again. Elli is beside herself with anger.

I want to send in to some paper or other to see if they will take one of my stories, under a **pseudonym**[59], of course. Till next time, darling!

Yours, Anne

---

56. Declared - stated 57. Strengthened - giving solidity 58. Probability - assumption
59. Pseudonym - a fictitious name especially used by an author

# Tuesday, 25 April, 1944

Dear Kitty,

Dussel has not been on speaking terms with Van Daan for ten days and just because, ever since the burglary, a whole lot of fresh security measures have been made that don't suit him. He maintains that Van Daan has been shouting at him.

"Everything here happens upside down," he told me. "I am going to speak to your father about it." He is not supposed to sit in the office downstairs on Saturday afternoons and Sundays any more, but he goes on doing it just the same. Van Daan was furious and Father went downstairs to talk to him. Naturally, he kept on inventing excuses, but this time he could not get around even Father. Father now talks to him as little as possible, as Dussel has insulted him. None of us know in what way, but it must have been very bad.

I have written a lovely story called "Blurr, the Explorer," which pleased the three to whom I read it very much.

Yours, Anne

# Thursday, 27 April, 1944

Dear Kitty,

Mrs. Van Daan was in such a bad mood this morning, nothing but complaints! First, there's her cold, and she can't get any **lozenges**[60], and so much noseblowing is **unendurable**[61]. Next, it's that the sun's not shining, that the invasion doesn't come, that we can't look out of the windows, etc., We all had to laugh at her, and she was **sporting**[62] enough to join in. At the moment I'm reading *The Emperor Charles V*, written by a professor at Gottingen University he worked at the book for forty years. I read fifty pages in five days, it's impossible to do more. The book has 598 pages, so now you can work out how

---

60. Lozenges – small medicinal tablet       61. Unendurable – intolerable
62. Sporting – fair and generous

long it will take me—and there is a second volume to follow. But very interesting!

What doesn't a schoolgirl get to know in a single day! Take me, for example. First, I translated a piece from Dutch into English, about Nelson's last battle. After that, I went through some more of Peter the Great's war against Norway (17001721), Charles XII, Augustus the Strong, Stanislavs Leczinsky, Mazeppa, Von Gorz, Brandenburg, Pomerania and Denmark, plus the usual dates.

After that I landed up in Brazil, read about Bahia tobacco, the **abundance**[63] of coffee and the one and a half million **inhabitants**[64] of Rio de Janeiro, of Pernambuco and Sao Paulo, not forgetting the river Amazon, about Negroes, Mulattos, Mestizos, Whites, more than fifty per cent of the population being illiterate, and the malaria. As there was still some time left, I quickly ran through a family tree. Jan the Elder, Willem Lodewijk, Ernst Casimir I, Hendrik Casimir I, right up to the little Margriet Franciska (born in 1943 in Ottawa).

Twelve o'clock: In the attic, I *continued* my program with the history of the Church-Phew! Till one o'clock.

Just after two, the poor child sat working ('hm, 'hm!) again, this time studying narrow and broadnosed monkeys. Kitty, tell me quickly how many toes a hippopotamus has! ! Then followed the Bible, Noah and the Ark, Shem, Ham, and Japheth. After that Charles V. Then with Peter: *The Colonel,* in English, by Thackeray. Heard my French verbs and then compared the Mississippi with the Missouri.

I've still got a cold and have given it to Margot as well as to Mummy and Daddy. As long as Peter doesn't get it! He called me his "Eldorado" and wanted a kiss.

Of course, I couldn't! Funny boy! But still, he's a darling. Enough for today, goodby!

Yours, Anne

---

63. Abundance – sufficient          64. Inhabitants – occupants

# Friday, 28 April, 1944

Dear Kitty,

I have never forgotten my dream about Peter Wessel (see beginning of January). If I think of it, I can still feel his cheek against mine now, and recall that lovely feeling that made everything good.

Sometimes I have had the same feeling here with Peter, but never to such an extent, until yesterday, when we were, as usual, sitting on the divan, our arms around each other's waists. Then suddenly the ordinary Anne slipped away and a second Anne took her place, a second Anne who is not **reckless**[65] and **jocular**[66], but one who just wants to love and be gentle.

I sat pressed closely against him and felt a wave of emotion come over me, tears sprang into my eyes, the left one **trickled**[67] onto his **dungarees**[68], the right one ran down my nose and also fell onto his dungarees. Did he notice? He made no move or sign to show that he did. I wonder if he feels the same as I do? He hardly said a word. Does he know that he has two Annes before him? These questions must remain unanswered.

At half past eight I stood up and went to the window, where we always say goodby. I was still trembling, I was still Anne number two. He came towards me, I **flung**[69] my arms around his neck and gave him a kiss on his left cheek, and was about to kiss the other cheek, when my lips met his and we pressed them together. In a whirl we were clasped in each others arms, again and again, never to leave off. Oh, Peter does so need **tenderness**[70]. For the first time in his life he has discovered a girl, has seen for the first time that even the most irritating girls have another side to them, that they have hearts and can be different when you are alone with them. For the

---

65. Reckless – carefree          66. Jocular – humorous
67. Tickled – lightly touch in a way that causes itching or twitching
68. Dungarees – british trousers          69. Flung – throw or move forcefully
70. Tenderness – delicacy

first time in his life he has given of himself and, having never had a boy or girl friend in his life before, shown his real self. Now we have found each other. For that matter, I didn't know him either, like him having never had a trusted friend, and this is what it has come to...

Once more there is a question which gives me *no* peace: "Is it right? Is it right that I should have yielded so soon, that I am so ardent, just as ardent and eager as Peter himself? May I, a girl, let myself go to this *extent?*" There is but *one* answer: "I have longed so much and for so long-I am so lonely-and now I have found **consolation**[71]."

In the mornings we just behave in an ordinary way, in the afternoons more or less so (except just occasionally) but in the evenings the suppressed longings of the whole day, the happiness and the **blissful**[72] memories of all the previous occasions come to the surface and we only think of each other. Every evening, after the last kiss, I would like to dash away, not to look into his eyes any more—away, away, alone in the darkness.

And what do I have to face, when I reach the bottom of the staircase? Bright lights, questions, and laughter, I have to **swallow**[73] it all and not show a thing. My heart still feels too much; I can't get over a shock such as I received yesterday all at once. The Anne who is gentle shows herself too little anyway and, therefore, will not allow herself to be suddenly driven into the background. Peter has touched my *emotions more* deeply than anyone has ever done before-except in my dreams. Peter has taken possession of me and turned me inside out, surely it goes without saying that anyone would require a rest and a little while to recover from such an **upheaval**[74]?

Oh Peter, what have you done to me? What do you want of me? Where will this lead us? Oh, now I understand Elli; now, now that I am going through this myself, now I understand her doubt, if 1 were

---

71. Consolation – comfort received by someone after a loss or disappointment

72. Blissful – full of joy　　　　　　　73. Swallow – engulf

74. Upheaval – turmoil

older and he should ask me to marry him, what should I answer? Anne, be honest! You would not be able to marry him, but yet, it would be hard to let him go. Peter hasn't enough character yet, not enough will power, too little courage and strength. He is still a child in his heart of hearts, he is no older than I am, he is only searching for **tranquillity**[75] and happiness.

Am I only fourteen? Am I really still a silly little schoolgirl? Am I really so inexperienced about everything? I have more experience than most, I have been through things that hardly anyone of my age has undergone. I am afraid of myself, I am afraid that in my longing I am giving myself too quickly. How, later on, can it ever go right with other boys? Oh, it is so difficult, always **battling**[76] with one's heart and reason, in its own time, each will speak, but do I know for certain that I have chosen the right time?

Yours, Anne

---

75. Tranquillity – calm
76. Battling – fighting

## Think and Ink...

➤ Describe the tense circumstances at the Secret Annexe when the burglars plundered it?

➤ How did Anne show her devotion for her community?

➤ What tone of optimism ring in Anne's opinion?

➤ Was the 'love' between Anne and Peter mere infatuation or something real?

➤ How expressive is Anne's feeling for Peter?

➤ How divided is the personality of Anne as she reveals in her entry for 28 April 1944?

➤ What idea do you form about Peter from Anne's analysis?

## Text-Based Questions

• What changes did Anne find in her Secret Annexe?

• How had food become difficult in Secret Annexe?

• What were the food cycles the inmates have?

• What was the great attraction each week?

• How did Peter occupy Anne's mind?

• What ideas did Anne have?

• What were her writing experiences? Why did she want to be a writer?

• What were Anne's hobbies and interests?

• Narrate the incident that happened on the Sunday evening.

• Why was there a bang downstairs?

• What changes did the burglary brought in the lives of the inmates of Secret Annexe?

• How strained was the atmosphere in Secret Annexe?

- When did Anne feel sentimental?
- What difference do we find in outlook between Anne and others?
- What kept Anne from complaining?
- Why did Anne feel hopeless about her writings?
- What upset Peter?
- Why was 15th April 1944 important for Anne?
- How does Anne's tone sound in her description of the memorable moment of the 15th April?
- How according to Anne was she different from Margot in their love approach?
- What was special about 21 April 1944?
- What misfortune befell the inmates?
- What was the news about Dussel? How had he strained his relationship with Mr. Van Daan and Anne's Father?
- How had Mrs. Van Daan changed?
- What knowledge did Anne gain on a single day?
- What ultimate truth about her love for Peter and their relationship runs on Anne's mind?

# Tuesday, 2 May, 1944

Dear Kitty,

On Saturday evening I asked Peter whether he thought I ought to tell Daddy a bit about us; when we'd discussed it a little, he came to the conclusion that I should. I was glad, for it shows that he's an honest boy. As soon as I got downstairs I went off with Daddy to get some water; and while we were on the stairs I said, "Daddy, I expect you've **gathered**[1] that when we're together Peter and I don't sit miles apart. Do you think it's wrong?" Daddy didn't reply immediately, then said, "No I don't think it's wrong, but you must be careful, Anne; you're in such a **confined**[2] space here." When we went upstairs, he said something else on the same lines. On Sunday morning he called me to him and said, "Anne, I have thought more about what you said." I felt scared already. "It's not really very right-here in this house; I thought that you were just pals. Is Peter in love?"

"Oh, of course not," I replied.

"You know that I understand both of you, but you must be the one to hold back. Don't go upstairs so often, don't encourage him more than you can help. It is the man who is always the active one in these things; the woman can hold him back. It is quite different under normal circumstances, when you are free, you see other boys and girls, you can get away sometimes, play games and do all kinds of other things; but here, if you're together a lot, and you want to get away, you can't; you see each other every hour of the day—in fact, all the time. Be careful, Anne, and don't take it too seriously!"

"I don't. Daddy, but Peter is a decent boy, really a nice boy!"

"Yes, but he is not a strong character; he can be easily influenced, for good, but also for bad; I hope for his sake that his good side will remain **uppermost**[3], because, by nature, that is how he is." We talked on for a bit and agreed that Daddy should talk to him too.

---

1. Gathered – come or bring together     2. Confined – enclosed
3. Uppermost – highest in place, rank, or importance

On Sunday morning in the attic he asked, "And have you talked to your father, Anne?"

"Yes," I replied. "I'll tell you about it. Daddy doesn't think it's bad, but he says that here, where we're so close together all the time, clashes[4] may easily arise,"

"But we agreed, didn't we, never to quarrel and I'm determined to stick to it!"

"So will I, Peter, but Daddy didn't think that it was like this, he just thought we were pals; do you think that we still can be?

"I can—what about you?"

"Me too, I told Daddy that I trusted you. I do trust you. Peter, just as much as I trust Daddy, and I believe you to be worthy of it. You are, aren't you, Peter?"

"I hope so." (He was very shy and rather red in the face.)

"I believe in you. Peter," I went on, "I believe that you have good qualities, and that you'll get on in the world."

After that, we talked about other things. Later I said, "If we come out of here, I know quite well that you won't bother about me any more!"

He flared[5] right up. "That's not true, Anne, oh no, I won't let you think that of me!"

Then I was called away.

Daddy has talked to him; he told me about it today. "Your father thought that the friendship might develop into love sooner or later," he said. But I replied that we would keep a check on ourselves.

Daddy doesn't want me to go upstairs so much in the evenings now, but I don't want that. Not only because I like being with Peter; I have told him that I trust him. I do trust him and I want to show him that I do, which can't happen if I stay downstairs through lack of trust.

---

4. Clashes – meet and come into violent conflicts
5. Flared – a sudden brief burst of flame or light

No, I'm going!

In the meantime the Dussel drama has righted itself again. At supper on Saturday evening he apologized in beautiful Dutch. Van Daan was nice about it straight away, it must have taken Dussel a whole day to learn that little lesson off by heart.

Sunday, his birthday, passed peacefully. We gave him a bottle of good 1919 wine, from the Van Daans (who could give their presents now after all), a bottle of piccalilli and a packet of razor blades, a jar of lemon jam from Kraler, a book, *Little Martin,* from Miep, and a plant from Elli. He treated each one of us to an egg.

Yours, Anne

# Wednesday, 3 May, 1944

Dear Kitty,

First, just the news of the week. We're having a holiday from politics; there is nothing, absolutely nothing to announce. I too am gradually beginning to believe that the invasion will come. After all, they can't let the Russians clear up everything, for that matter, they're not doing anything either at the moment.

Mr. Koophuis comes to the office every morning again now. He's got a new spring for Peter's divan, so Peter will have to do some **upholstering**[6], about which, quite understandably, he doesn't feel a bit happy.

Have I told you that Boche has disappeared? Simply vanished-we haven't seen a sign of her since Thursday of last week. I expect she's already in the cats' heaven, while some animal lover is enjoying a **succulent**[7] meal from her. Perhaps some little girl will be given a fur cap out of her skin. Peter is very sad about it.

Since Saturday we've changed over, and have lunch at half past eleven in the mornings, so we have to last out with one cupful of porridge, this saves us a meal. Vegetables are still very difficult to

6. Upholstering – padded furniture     7. Succulent – tender and juicy

obtain; we had rotten boiled lettuce this afternoon. Ordinary lettuce, spinach and boiled lettuce, there's nothing else. With these we eat rotten potatoes, so it's a delicious combination!

As you can easily imagine we often ask ourselves here **despairingly**[8]: "What, oh, what is the use of the war? Why can't people live peacefully together? Why all this destruction?"

The question is very understandable, but no one has found a satisfactory answer to it so far. Yes, why do they make still more **gigantic**[9] planes, still heavier bombs and, at the same rime, **prefabricated**[10] houses for reconstruction? Why should millions be spent daily on the war and yet there's not a penny available for medical services, artists, or for poor people?

Why do some people have to starve, while there are **surpluses**[11] rotting in other parts of the world? Oh, why are people so crazy?

I don't believe that the big men, the politicians and the **capitalists**[12] alone, are guilty of the war. Oh no, the little man is just as guilty, otherwise the peoples of the world would have risen in revolt long ago! There's in people simply an urge to destroy, an urge to kill, to murder and rage, and until all mankind, without exception, undergoes a great change, wars will be waged, everything that has been built up, cultivated, and grown will be destroyed and disfigured, after which mankind will have to begin all over again.

I have often been **downcast**[13], but never in despair; I regard our hiding as a dangerous adventure, romantic and interesting at the same time. In my diary I treat all the **privations**[14] as amusing. I have made up my mind now to lead a different life from other girls and, later on, different from ordinary housewives. My start has been so very full of interest, and that is the sole reason why I have to laugh at the humorous side of the most dangerous moments.

---

8. Despairingly - completely disheartened     9. Gigantic - very big
10. Prefabricated - manufacture sections of a building
11. Surpluses - an amount left over     12. Capitalists - economists
13. Downcast - looking downwards
14. Privations - hardships

I am young and I possess many buried qualities; I am young and strong and am living a great adventure; I am still in the midst of it and can't **grumble**[15] the whole day long. I have been given a lot, a happy nature, a great deal of cheerfulness and strength. Every day I feel that I am developing **inwardly**[16], that the **liberation**[17] is drawing nearer and how beautiful nature is, how good the people are about me, how interesting this adventure is! Why, then, should I be in despair?

Yours, Anne

## Friday. 5 May, 1944

Dear Kitty,

Daddy is not pleased with me he thought that after our talk on Sunday I automatically wouldn't go upstairs every evening. He doesn't want any "necking" a word I can't bear. It was bad enough talking about it, why must he make it so unpleasant now? I shall talk to him today. Margot has given me some good advice, so listen; this is roughly what 1 want to say:

"I believe, Daddy, that you expect a **declaration**[18] from me, *so* I will give it you. You are disappointed in me, as you had expected more **reserve**[19] from me, and I suppose you want me to be just as a fourteen-year old should be. But that's where you're mistaken.

"Since we've been here, from July 1942 until a few weeks ago, I can assure you that 1 haven't had any easy time. If you only knew how I cried in the evenings, how unhappy I was, how lonely I felt, then you would understand that I want to go upstairs!

"I have now reached the stage that I can live entirely on my own, without Mummy's support or anyone else's for that matter. But it hasn't just happened in a night; it's been a bitter, hard struggle and I've shed many a tear, before I became as independent as I am now.

---

15. Grumble - complaint in a bad tempered way
16. Inwardly - inside　　　　　　　　17. Liberation - freedom
18. Declaration - announcement　　　　19. Reserve - retain

You can laugh at me and not believe me, but that can't harm me. I know that I'm a separate individual and I don't feel in the least bit responsible to any of you. I am only telling you this because I thought that otherwise you might think that I was under hand, but I don't have to give an account of my deeds to anyone but myself.

"When I was in difficulties you all closed your eyes and stopped up your ears and didn't help me, on the contrary, 1 received nothing but warnings not to be so **boisterous**[20], I was only boisterous so as not to be miserable all the time. I was reckless so as not to hear that **persistent**[21] voice within me continually. I played a comedy for a year and a half, day in, day out, I never grumbled, never lost my **cue**[22], nothing like that-and now, now the battle is over. I have won! I am independent both in mind and body. I don't need a mother any more, for all this conflict has made me strong.

"And now, now that I'm on top of it, now that I know that I've fought the battle, now I want to be able to go on in my own way too, the way that I think is right. You can't and mustn't regard me as fourteen, for all these troubles have made me older; I shall not be sorry for what I have done, but shall act as I think I can. You can't coax me into not going upstairs, either you forbid it, or you trust me through thick and thin, but then leave me in peace as well!"

Yours, Anne

# Saturday, 6 May, 1944

Dear Kitty,

I put a letter, in which I wrote what I explained to you yesterday, in Daddy's pocket before supper yesterday. After reading it, he was, according to Margot, very upset for the rest of the evening. (I was upstairs doing the dishes.) Poor Pim, I might have known what the effect of such an epistle would be. He is so sensitive! I immediately told Peter not to ask or say anything more. Pim hasn't said any more about it to me. Is that *yet* in store, I wonder?

---

20. Boisterous - noisy  21. Persistent - recurring, prolonged  22. Cue - signal

Here everything is going on more or less normally again. What they tell us about the prices and the people outside is almost unbelievable, half a pound of tea costs 350 florins, a pound *of coffee 80* florins, butter 35 florins per pound, an egg 1.45 florin. People pay 14 florins for an ounce of Bulgarian tobacco! Everyone deals in the black market, every errand boy has something to offer. Our bakers boy got hold of some sewing silk, 0.9 florin for a thin little skein, the milkman manages to get **clandestine**[23] ration cards, the undertaker delivers the cheese. Burglaries, murders, and theft go on daily. The police and night watchmen join in just as **strenuously**[24] as the professionals, everyone wants something in their empty stomachs and because wage increases are forbidden the people simply have to swindle. The police are continually on the go, tracing girls of fifteen, sixteen, seventeen and older, who are reported missing every day.

Yours, Anne

# Sunday Morning, 7 May, 1944

Dear Kitty,

Daddy and I had a long talk yesterday afternoon, I cried terribly and he joined in. Do you know what he said to me, Kitty? "I have received many letters in my life, but this is certainly the most unpleasant! You, Anne, who have received such love from your parents, you, who have parents who are always ready to help you, who have always **defended**[25] you whatever it might be, can you talk of feeling no responsibility towards us? You feel wronged and **deserted**[26], no, Anne, you have done us a great **injustice**[27]!" Perhaps you didn't mean it like that, but it is what you wrote, no, Anne, we haven't deserved such a reproach as this!"

Oh, I have failed miserably; this is certainly the worst thing I've ever done in my life. I was only trying to show off with my crying

---

23. Clandestine - done secretly
24. Strenuously - great exertion
25. Defended - resisted
26. Deserted - abandoned
27. Injustice - lack of justice

and my tears, just trying to appear big, so that he would respect me. Certainly, i have had a lot of unhappiness, but to accuse the good Pim, who has done and still does do everything *tor* me-no, that was too low for words.

It's right that for once I've been taken down from my **inaccessible**[28] **pedestal**[29], that my pride has been shaken a bit, for I was becoming much too taken up with myself again. What Miss Anne does is by no means always right! Anyone who can cause such unhappiness to someone else, someone he **professes**[30] to love, and on purpose, too, is low, very low!

And the way Daddy has forgiven me makes me feel more than ever ashamed of myself, he is going to throw the letter in the fire and is so sweet to me now, just as if he had done something wrong. No, Anne, you still have a **tremendous**[31] lot to learn, begin by doing that first, instead of looking down on others and accusing them!

I have had a lot of sorrow, but who hasn't at my age? I have played the clown a lot too, but I was hardly conscious of it; I felt lonely, but hardly ever in despair! I ought to be deeply ashamed of myself, and indeed I am.

What is done cannot be undone, but one can prevent it happening again. I want to start from the beginning again and it can't be difficult, now that I have Peter. With him to support me, I can and will!

I'm not alone any more; he loves me. I love him, I have my books, my storybook and my diary, I'm not so frightfully ugly, not utterly stupid, have a cheerful **temperament**[32] and want to have a good character!

Yes, Anne, you've felt deeply that your letter was too Lard and that it was untrue. To think that you were even proud of it! I will take Daddy as my example, and I *will* improve.

Yours, Anne

28. Inaccessible - unable to be reached
29. Pedestal - walking way
30. Professes - claimed openly
31. Tremendous - great intensity
32. Temperament - character

# Monday, 8 May, 1944

Dear Kitty,

Have I ever really told you anything about our family?

I don't think I have, so I will begin now. My father's parents were very rich. His father had worked himself right up and his mother came from a prominent family, who were also rich. So in his youth Daddy had a real little rich boy's upbringing, parties every week, balls, festivities, beautiful girls, dinners, a large home, etc., etc.

After Grandpa's death all the money was lost during the World War and the **inflation**[33] that followed. Daddy was therefore extremely well brought up and he laughed very much yesterday when, for the first time in his fifty-five years, he **scraped**[34] out the frying pan at table.

Mummy's parents were rich too and we often listen open-mouthed to stories of engagement parties of two hundred and fifty people, private balls and dinners. One certainly could not call us rich now, but all my hopes are pinned on after the war.

I can assure you I'm not at all keen on a narrow, **cramped**[35] existence like Mummy and Margot. I'd adore to go to Paris for a year and London for a year to learn the languages and study the history of art. Compare that with Margot, who wants to be a midwife in Palestine! I always long to see beautiful dresses and interesting people.

I want to see something of the world and do all kinds of exciting things. I have already told you this before. And a little money as well won't do any harm.

Miep told us this morning about a party she went to, to celebrate an engagement. Both the future bride and bridegroom came from rich families and everything was very grand. Miep made our mouths water telling us about the food they had: vegetable soup with minced meat balls in it, cheese, rolls, hors d'oeuvre with eggs and roast beef,

33. Inflation - general increase in prices　　34. Scraped - rub harder
35. Cramped - crowded

fancy cakes, wine and cigarettes, as much as you wanted of everything (black market). Miep had ten drinks-can that be the woman who calls herself a teetotaler? If Miep had all those, I vender however many her spouse managed to knock back? Naturally, everyone at the party was a bit tipsy. There were two policemen from the fighting squad, who took photos of the engaged couple. It seems as if we are never far from Mieps thoughts, because she took down the addresses of these men at once, in case anything should happen at some time or other, and good Dutchmen might come in useful.

She made our mouths water. We, who get nothing but two spoonfuls of porridge for our breakfast and whose tummies were so empty that they were positively **rattling**[36], we, who get nothing but half-cooked spinach (to preserve the vitamins) and rotten potatoes day after day, we, who get nothing but lettuce, cooked or raw, spinach and yet again spinach in our hollow stomachs. Perhaps we may yet grow to be as strong as Popeye, although I don't see much sign of it at present!

If Miep had taken us to the party we shouldn't have left any rolls for the other guests. I can tell you, we positively drew the words from Mieps lips, we gathered round her, as if we'd never heard about delicious food or smart people in our lives before!

And these are the granddaughters of a millionaire. The world is a queer place!

Yours, Anne

## Tuesday, 9 May, 1944

Dear Kitty,

I've finished my story of Ellen the fairy. I have copied it out on nice note paper. It certainly looks very attractive, but is it really enough for Daddy's birthday? I don't know. Margot and Mummy have both written poems for him.

---

36. Rattling - making noise

Mr. Kraler came upstairs this afternoon with the news that Mrs, B., who used *to act as* demonstrator for the business, wants to eat her box lunch in the office here at two o'clock every afternoon. Think of it! No one can come upstairs any more, the potatoes cannot be delivered, Elli can't have any lunch, we can't go to the W.C., we mustn't move, etc., etc. We thought up the wildest and most varied suggestions to **wheedle**[37] her away. Van Daan thought that a good laxative in her coffee would be sufficient. "No," replied Koophuis, "I beg of you not, then we'd never get her off the box!" Resounding laughter. "Off the box," asked Mrs. Van Daan, "what does that mean?" An explanation followed. "Can I always use it?" she then asked stupidly. "Imagine it," Elli **giggled**[38], "if one asked for the box in Bijenkorfs they wouldn't even understand what you mean!"

Oh, Kit, it's such wonderful weather, if only I could go outdoors!

Yours, Anne

# Wednesday, 10 May, 1944

Dear Kitty,

We were sitting in the attic doing some French yesterday afternoon when I suddenly heard water **pattering**[39] down behind me. I asked Peter what it could be, but he didn't even reply, simply **tore**[40] up to the loft, where the source of the **disaster**[41] was, and pushed Mouschi, who, because of the wet earth box, had sat down beside it, **harshly**[42] back to the right place. A great din and disturbance followed, and Mouschi, who had finished by that time, **dashed**[43] downstairs.

Mouschi, seeking the convenience of something similar to his box, had chosen some wood shavings. The pool had **trickled**[44] down from the loft into the attic immediately and, unfortunately, landed

---

| | |
|---|---|
| 37. Wheedle - flattery | 38. Giggled - laughed |
| 39. Pattering - light sound | 40. Tore - put in pieces |
| 41. Disaster - a sudden accident or a natural catastrophe | |
| 42. Harshly - roughly | 43. Dashed - rushed |
| 44. Trickled - a small flow of liquid | |

just beside and in the barrel of potatoes. The ceiling was **dripping**[45], and as the attic floor is not free from holes either, several yellow drips came through the ceiling into the dining room between a pile of stockings and some books, which were lying on the table. I was doubled up with laughter, it really was a scream. There was Mouschi **crouching**[46] under a chair, Peter with water, bleaching powder, and floor cloth, and Van Daan trying to soothe everyone. The **calamity**[47] was soon over, but it's a well-known fact that cats' **puddles**[48] positively **stink**[49]. The potatoes proved this only too clearly and also the wood shavings, that Daddy collected in a bucket to be burned. Poor Mouschi! How were **you to** know that **peat**[50] is unobtainable?

PS: Our beloved Queen spoke to us yesterday and this evening. She is taking a holiday in order fo be strong for her return fo Holland. She used words like "soon, when I am back, speedy liberation, heroism, and heavy burdens."

A speech by Gerbrandy followed. A clergyman concluded with a prayer to God to take care of the Jews, the people in concentration camps, in prisons, and in Germany.

Yours, Anne

## Thursday, 11 May, 1944

Dear Kitty,

I'm frightfully busy at the moment, and although it sounds mad, I haven't time fo *get* through my pile of work. Shall I tell you briefly what I have got to do? Well, then, by tomorrow I must finish reading the first part of *Galileo Galilei,* as it has to be returned to the library. I only started it yesterday, but I shall manage it.

Next week I have got to read *Palestine at the Crossroads* and the second part of *Galilei.* Next I finished reading the first part of the

---

| | |
|---|---|
| 45. Dripping - extremely wet | 46. Crouching - stance |
| 47. Calamity - disaster | 48. Puddles - a small pool of liquid |
| 49. Stink - unpleasant smell | 50. Peat - a coal variety |

biography of *The Emperor Charles* V yesterday, and it's essential that I work out all the diagrams and family trees that I have collected from it. After that I have three pages of foreign words gathered from various books, which have all got to be recited, written down, and learned. Number four is that my film stars are all mixed up together and are simply **gasping**[51] to be tidied up; however, as such a **clearance**[52] would take several days, and since Professor Anne, as she's already said, is **choked**[53] with work, the **chaos**[54] will have to remain a chaos.

Next Theseus, Oedipus, Peleus, Orpheus, Jason, and Hercules are awaiting their turn to be arranged, as their different deeds lie **crisscross**[55] in my mind like fancy threads in a dress; it's also high time Myron and Phidias had some treatment, if they wish to remain at all **coherent**[56]. Likewise it's the same with the *seven* and nine years' war, I'm mixing everything up together at this rate. Yes, but what can one do with such a memory! Think how forgetful I shall be when I'm eighty!

Oh, something else, the Bible; how long is it still going to take before I meet the bathing Suzanna? And what do they mean by the guilt of Sodom and Gomorrah? Oh, there is still such a terrible lot to find out and to learn. And in the meantime I've left Lisolette of the Pfalz completely in the **lurch**[57].

Kitty, can you see that I'm just about bursting?

Now, about something e.lse: you've known for a long time that my greatest wish is fo become a journalist someday and later on a famous writer. Whether these **leanings**[58] towards greatness (or **insanity**[59]?) will ever **materialize**[60] remains to be seen, but I certainly have the subjects in my mind. In any case.

---

51. Gasping - desperate            52. Clearance - process of being dispersed
53. Choked - extremely engulfed in work     54. Chaos - complete confusion
55. Crisscross - a pattern of intersecting straight line or paths
56. Coherent - together            57. Lurch - a sudden unsteady movement
58. Leanings - tendency            59. Insanity - crazy
60. Materialize - come true

I want to publish a book entitled *Het Achterbuis* after the war. Whether I shall succeed or not, I cannot say, but my diary will be a great help. 1 have other ideas as well, besides *Het Achterbuis*. But I will write more fully about them some other time, when they have taken a clearer form in my mind.

Yours, Anne

## Saturday, 13 May, 1944

Dearest Kitty,

It was Daddy's birthday yesterday. Mummy and Daddy have been married *nineteen* years. The charwoman wasn't below and the sun shone as it has never shone before in 1944. Our horse **chestnut**[61] is in full bloom, thickly covered with leaves and much more beautiful than last year.

Daddy received a biography of the life of Linnaeus from Koophuis, a book on nature from Kraler, *Amsterdam* fay *the Water* from Dussel, a gigantic box from Van Daan, beautifully done up and almost professionally decorated, containing three eggs, a bottle of beer, a bottle of yoghourt, and a green tie. It made our pot of syrup seem rather small. My roses smelled lovely compared with Miep's and Ellis carnations, which had no smell, but were very pretty too. He was certainly spoiled. Fifty fancy pastries have arrived, heavenly. Daddy himself treated us to spiced gingerbread, beer for the gentlemen, and yoghourt for the ladies. Enjoyment all around!

Yours, Anne

## Tuesday, 16 May, 1944

Dearest Kitty,

Just for a change, as we haven't talked about them jpr so long, I want to tell you a little discussion that went on between Mr and Mrs. Van Daan yesterday.

---

61.　Chestnut - tree

Mrs. Van Daan: "The Germans are sure to have made the Atlantic Wall very strong indeed, they will certainly do all in their power to hold back the English. It's amazing how strong the Germans are!"

Mr. Van Daan: "Oh yes, incredibly."

Mrs. Van Daan: "Ye-es."

Mr. Van Daan: "The Germans are so strong they're sure to win the war in the end, in spite of everything!"

Mrs. Van Daan: "It's quite possible, I'm not convinced of the opposite yet."

Mr. Van Daan: "I won't bother to reply any more."

Mrs. Van Daan: "Still you always do answer me, you can't resist capping me every time."

Mr. Van Daan: "Of course not, but my replies are the bare minimum."

Mrs. Van Daan: "But still you do reply, and you always have to be in the right! Your prophecies don't always come true by a long shot."

Mr. Van Daan: "They have up till now."

Mrs. Van Daan: "That's not true. The invasion was to have come last year, and the Finns were to have been out of the war by now. Italy was finished in the winter, but the Russians would already have Lemberg, oh, no, I don't think much of your **prophecies**[62]."

Mr. Van Daan (standing up): "It's about time you shut your mouth. One day I'll show you that I'm right; sooner or later you'll get enough of it. I can't bear any more of your grousing. You're so infuriating but you'll stew in your own juice one day."

I really couldn't help laughing. Mummy too, while Peter sat biting his lip. Oh, those stupid grownups, they'd do better to start learning themselves, before they have so much to say to the younger generation!

Yours, Anne

---

62. Prophecies - predictions

# Friday, 19 May, 1944

Dear Kitty,

1 felt **rotten**[63] yesterday, really out of **sorts**[64] (unusual for Anne!), with tummy-ache and every other imaginable misery. I'm much better again today, feel very hungry, but I'd better not touch the kidney beans we're having today.

All goes well with Peter and me. The poor boy seems to need a little love even more than I do. He blushes every evening when he gets his goodnight kiss and simply begs for another. I wonder if I'm a good substitute for Boche? I don't mind, he is so happy now that he knows that someone loves him.

After my **laborious**[65] conquest I've got the situation a bit more in hand now, but I don't think my love has cooled off—He's a darling, but I soon closed up my inner self from him. If he wants to force the lock again he'll have to work a good deal harder than before!

Yours, Anne

# Saturday, 20 May, 1944

Dear Kitty,

Last evening I came downstairs from the attic and as I entered the room saw at once the lovely vase of **carnations**[66] lying on the floor. Mummy down on hands and knees **mopping**[67] up and Margot fishing up some papers from the floor.

"What's happened here?" I asked, full of **misgivings**[68] and, not even waiting for their answer, tried to sum up the damage from a distance. My whole portfolio of family trees, writing books, textbooks, everything was **soaked**[69]. I nearly wept and was so worked up that

---

63. Rotten - unpleasant
64. Sorts - categories
65. Laborious - hard efforts
66. Carnations - a variety of flower
67. Mopping - cleaning
68. Misgivings - doubts
69. Soaked - extremely wet

I can hardly remember what I said, but Margot said that I let fly something about "**incalculable**[70] loss, frightful, terrible, can never be repaired," and still more. Daddy burst out laughing. Mummy and Margot joined in, but I could have cried over all the toil that was wasted, and the diagrams I'd so carefully worked out.

On closer inspection the "incalculable loss" didn't turn out to be as bad as I'd thought. I carefully sorted out all the papers that were stuck together and separated them in the attic. After that I hung them all up on the clothes lines to dry. It was a funny sight and 1 couldn't help laughing myself. Maria de Medici beside Charles V, William of Orange and Marie Antoinette; it's a "racial **outrage**[71]," was Mr. Van Daan's joke on the subject. After I'd entrusted my papers into Peter's care I went downstairs again.

"Which books are spoiled?" I asked Margot, who was checking up on them. "Algebra," she said. 1 hurried to her side, but unfortunately not even the algebra book was spoiled. I wish it had fallen right in the vase, I've never **loathed**[72] any other book so much as that one. There are the names of at least twenty girls in the front, all previous owners, it is old, yellow, full of **scribbles**[73] and improvements. If I'm ever in a really very **wicked**[74] mood, I'll tear the **blasted**[75] thing to pieces!

Yours, Anne

# Monday, 22 May, 1944

Dear Kitty,

On May 20th Daddy lost five bottles of yoghourt on a bet with Mrs. Van Daan. The **invasion**[76] still hasn't come yet, it's no exaggeration to say that all Amsterdam, all Holland, yes, the whole

---

70. Incalculable - not able to be calculated
71. Outrage - strong reaction of indignation
72. Loathed - disgusted                    73. Scribbles - careless drawings
74. Wicked - evil or morally wrong         75. Blasted - annoyed
76. Invasion - attack

west coast of Europe, right down to Spain, talks about the invasion day and night, **debates**[77] about it, and makes bets on it and ... hopes.

The suspense is rising to a **climax**[78]. By no means everyone we had regarded as "good" Dutch have stuck to their faith in the English; by no means everyone thinks the English bluff a masterly piece of **strategy**[79], oh no, the people want to see deeds at last, great, heroic deeds. Nobody sees beyond his own nose, no one thinks that the English are fighting for their own land and their own people, everyone thinks that it's their duty to save Holland, as quickly and as well as they can.

What **obligations**[80] have the English towards us? How have the Dutch earned the generous help that they seem so explicitly to expect? Oh no, the Dutch will have made a big mistake, the English, in spite of all their **bluff**[81], are certainly no more to blame than all the other countries, great and small, which are not under occupation. The English really won't offer us their apologies, for even if we do **reproach**[82] them for being asleep during the years when Germany was **rearming**[83], we cannot deny that all the other countries, especially those bordering Germany, also slept. We shan't get anywhere by following an **ostrich**[84] policy. England and the whole world have seen that only too well now, and that is why, one by one, England, no less than the rest, will have to make heavy sacrifices.

No country is going to sacrifice its men for nothing and certainly not in the interests of another. England is not going to do that either. The invasion, with liberation and freedom, will come sometime, but England and America will appoint the day, not all the occupied countries put together.

To our great horror and **regret**[85] we hear that the attitude of a great many people towards us Jews has changed. We hear that there is

---

77. Debates - formal discussion  78. Climax - high point, most important point
79. Strategy - planning          80. Obligations - a debt of gratitude
81. Bluff - lies                 82. Reproach - disapproval
83. Rearming - provide with a new supply of weapons
84. Ostrich - an African bird    85. Regret - feel sorry

anti-Semitism now in circles that never thought of it before. This news has affected us all very, very deeply. The cause of this hatred of the Jews is understandable, even human sometimes, but not good. The Christians blame the Jews for giving secrets away to the Germans, for **betraying**[86] their helpers and for the fact that, through the Jews, a great many Christians have gone the way of so many others before them, and suffered terrible punishments and a **dreadful**[87] fate.

This is all true, but one must always look at these things from both sides. Would Christians behave differently in our place? The Germans have a means of making people talk. Can a person, entirely at their mercy, whether Jew or Christian, always remain silent? Everyone knows that is practically impossible. Why, then, should people demand the impossible of the Jews?

It's being murmured in underground circles that the German Jews who emigrated to Holland and who are now in Poland may not be allowed to return here; they once had the right of asylum in Holland, but when Hitler has gone they will have to go back to Germany again.

When one hears this one naturally wonders why we are carrying on with this long and difficult war. We always hear that we're all fighting together for freedom, truth, and right! Is **discord**[88] going to show itself while we are still fighting, is the Jew once again worth less than another?

Oh, it is sad, very sad, that once more, for the **umpteenth**[89] time, the old truth is **confirmed**[90]: "What one Christian does is his own responsibility, what *one Jew does* is thrown back at all Jews."

Quite honestly, I can't understand that the Dutch, who are such a good, honest, **upright**[91] people, should judge us like this, we, the most oppressed, the unhappiest, perhaps the most **pitiful**[92] of all peoples of the whole world.

---

86. Betraying - act treacherously
87. Dreadful - extremely bad or serious
88. Discord - lack of harmony
89. Umpteenth - indefinitely many
90. Confirmed - made definite
91. Upright - honorable
92. Pitiful - deserve pity

I hope one thing only, and that is that this hatred of the Jews will be a passing thing, that the Dutch will show what they are after all, and that they will never **totter**[93] and lose their sense of right. For **anti-Semitism**[94] is unjust!

And if this terrible threat should actually come true, then the pitiful little collection of Jews that remain will have to leave Holland. We, too, shall have to move on again with our little bundles, and leave this beautiful country, which offered us such a warm welcome and which now turns its back on us.

I love Holland. I who, having no native country, had hoped that it might become my fatherland, and I still hope it will!

Yours, Anne

# Thursday, 25 May, 1944

Dear Kitty,

There's something fresh every day. This morning our vegetable man was picked up for having two Jews in his house. It's a great blow to us, *not* only that those poor Jews are balancing on the edge of an **abyss**[95], but it's terrible for the man himself.

The world has turned **topsy-turvy**[96], respectable people are being sent off to concentration camps, prisons, and lonely cells, and the dregs that remain govern young and old, rich and poor. One person walks into the trap through the black market, a second through helping the Jews or other people who've had to go "underground"; anyone who isn't a member of the N.S.B. doesn't know what may happen to him from one day to another.

This man is a great loss to us too. The girls can't and aren't allowed to haul along our share of potatoes, so the only thing to do is to eat less. I will tell you how we shall do that; its certainly not going to make things any pleasanter. Mummy says we shall cut out breakfast altogether, have porridge and bread for lunch, and for supper fried

93. Totter – feel insecure   94. Anti-semitism – hostility to prejudice against Jews
95. Abyss – a very deep chasm   96. Topsy-turvy – upside down

potatoes and possibly once or twice per week vegetables or lettuce, nothing more. We're going to be hungry, but anything is better than being discovered.

Yours, Anne

# Friday, 26 May, 1944

Dear Kitty,

At last, at last I can sit quietly at my table in froftt of a **crack**[97] of window and write you everything. I feel so miserable, I haven't felt like this for months; even after the burglary i didn't feel so utterly broken. On the one hand, the vegetable man, the Jewish question, which is being discussed minutely over the whole house, the invasion delay, the bad food, the strain, the miserable atmosphere, my disappointment in Peter, and on the other hand. Bill's engagement, Whitsun reception, flowers, Kraler's birthday, fancy cakes, and stories about cabarets, films, and concerts. That difference, that huge difference, it's always there, one day we laugh and see the funny side of the situation, but the next we are afraid, fear, suspense, and despair staring from our faces. Miep and Kraler carry the heaviest burden of the eight in hiding, Miep in all she does, and Kraler through the **enormous**[98] responsibility, which is sometimes so much for him that he can hardly talk from **pentup**[99] nerves and strain. Koophuis and Elli look after us well too, but they can forget us at times, even if it's only for a few hours, or a day, or even two days. They have their own worries, Koophuis over his health, Elli over her engagement, which is not altogether rosy, but they also have their little **outings**[100], visits to friends, and the whole life of ordinary people. For them the suspense is sometimes lifted, even if it is only for a short time, but for us it never lifts for a moment. We've been here for two years now, how long have we still to put up with this almost **unbearable**[101], ever increasing pressure?

---

97. Crack - a narrow opening between two parts     98. Enormous - huge
99. Pentup - closely confined          100. Outings - a short journey from home
101. Unbearable - intolerable

The sewer is blocked, so we mustn't run water, or rather only a trickle, when we go to the W.C we have to take a lavatory brush with us, and we keep dirty water in a large Cologne pot. We can manage for today, but what do we do if the plumber can't do the job alone? The municipal scavenging service doesn't come until Tuesday.

Miep sent us a currant cake, made up in the shape ot a doll with the words "Happy Whitsun" on the note attached to it. It's almost as if she's **ridiculing**[102] us; .our present frame of mind and our uneasiness could hardly be called "happy." The affair of the vegetable man has made us more nervous, you hear "shh, shh" from all sides again, and we're being quieter over everything. The police forced the door there, so they could do it to us too! If one day we too should ... no, I mustn't write it. but I can't put the question out of my mind today. On the contrary, all the fear I've already been through seems to face me again in all its irightfulness.

This evening at eight o'clock I had to go to the downstairs lavatory all alone; there was no one down there, as everyone was listening to the radio; I wanted to be brave, but it was difficult. I always feel much safer here upstairs than alone downstairs in that large, silent house; alone with the mysterious **muffled**[103] noises from upstairs and the tooting of motor horns in the street. I have to hurry for I start to **quiver**[104] if I begin thinking about the situation.

Again and again I ask myself, would it not have been better for us all if we had not gone into hiding, and if we were dead now and not going through all this misery, especially as we shouldn't be running our **protectors**[105] into danger any more. But we all recoil from these thoughts too, for we still love life, we haven't yet forgotten the voice of nature, we still hope, hope about everything. I hope something will happen soon now, shooting if need be-nothing can crush us more than this restlessness. Let the end come, even if it is hard, then at least we shall know whether we are finally going to win through or go under.

Yours, Anne

---

102. Ridiculing - making fun
104. Quiver - tremble, shake

103. Muffled - wrapped
105. Protectors - those who protect

# Wednesday, 31 May, 1944

Dear Kitty,

It was so frightfully hot on Saturday, Sunday, Monday, and Tuesday that I simply couldn't hold a fountain pen in my hand. That's why it was impossible to write to you. The drains went **phut**[106] again on Friday, were **mended**[107] again on Saturday, Mr. Koophuis came to see us in the afternoon and told us masses about Corry and her being in the same hockey club as Jopie.

On Sunday Elli came to make sure no one had broken in and stayed for breakfast, on Whit Monday Mr. Van Santen acted as the hideout watchman, and finally, on Tuesday the windows could be opened again at last.

There's **seldom**[108] been such a beautiful, warm, one can even say hot, Whitsun. The heat here in the "Secret Annexe" is terrible; I will briefly describe these warm days by giving you a sample of the sort of complaints that arise:

Saturday: "Lovely, what perfect weather," we all said in the morning. "If only it wasn't quite so warm," in the afternoon when the windows had to be closed.

Sunday: "It's positively unbearable, this heat. The butters melting, there's not a cool spot anywhere in the house, the breads getting so dry, the milk's going sour, windows can't be opened, and we, wretched outcasts, sit here suffocating while other people enjoy "their Whitsun holiday."

Monday: "My feet hurt me, I haven't got any thin clothes. I can't wash the dishes in this heat," all this from Mrs. Van Daan. It was extremely unpleasant.

I still can't put up with heat and am glad that there's a stiff breeze today, and yet the sun still shines.

Yours, Anne

---

106. Phut - blocked          107. Mended - repaired
108. Seldom - rare

## Think and Ink...

➢ Do you think Anne has the maturity to distinguish between love and friendship? Justify your claim.

➢ How does Anne analyse war? Do you agree with her?

➢ Why does Anne call her hiding itself as an adventure?

➢ In what ways, according to you, had Anne achieved her independence in mind and body?

➢ Analyse Anne's letter to her father?

➢ Why did Anne feel that her pride had been shaken up? Write your own opinion about the situation she had been in?

➢ Comment on Anne's self-analysis and her transformation.

➢ What contrast do we find in the way of life of the 'millionaire' and his grand daughters? What brought them their downfall?

➢ Why did Anne call the understand from Anne's remark, 'I soon closed up my inner self from him'?

➢ From Anne's description of the political situation do you understand the significance of the old truth "What one Christian does is his own responsibility what one Jew does is thrown back at all Jews"?

## Text-Based Questions

• How did Anne's father view the relationship between her and Peter? What was his advice to Anne?

• How was Dussel's birthday celebrated?

• What happened to Boche?

• What changes had been brought in their food habit?

• How does Anne regard her life style in the hiding now after two years of war?

• What advice had Margot given to Anne?

- Why did Anne feel herself independent now?
- How did Anne's father react to her letter?
- What was the economic situation as Anne found it?
- What did Anne's father confide in her?
- Why did Anne feel that she had failed miserably?
- Why did, and in what way did Anne feel guilty?
- What resolution did Anne take finally?
- What change is apparent in the presentation of Anne's diary entry?
- How positive is Anne's tone after her self analysis?
- How was the upbringing of Anne's father?
- What sort of family did Anne's mummy belong to?
- Compare Anne's aims with those of Margot's.
- What did Miep told them about?
- How was the condition of the inmates of Secret Annexe with that of one at the party described by Miep?
- What things did the inmates miss in their hide out?
- What was the condition of "the grand daughters of a millionaire"?
- What news did Mr. Kraler bring?
- What way were the inmates movements restricted?
- What calamity did Mouschi bring?
- What did the Queen tell the people?
- What assignments did Anne have for the week?
- Why did Anne feel that she could not read the Bible yet?
- How was the birthday of Anne's father celebrated?
- Briefly summarise the discussion between Mr. and Mrs. Van Daan.
- What seen did Anne encounter evening previous to 20th May 1944?

- Which book did Anne hate? Why?
- Why did Anne's father lose his bet with Mrs. Van Daan?
- What was the strategy of the English? Why should it make heavy scarifies?
- How had the attitude toward the Jews changed?
- What was the confute between the christens and the Germans?
- Do you agree that the Jews were the most pitiful of all peoples of the world? Why?
- Why should the Jews leave Holland?
- How were the poor Jews balancing on the edge of an abyss?
- Why did Anne feel miserable?
- How worried were the people around?
- What was the present frame of mind of the inmates and why were they nervous?
- Why was Anne Afraid to go downstairs?
- Why did Anne feel that they should not have gone into hiding?
- How was the weather for the week?

# Monday, 5 June, 1944

Dear Kitty,

Fresh "Secret Annexe" troubles, a quarrel between Dussel and the Franks over something very trivial: the sharing out of the butter. Dussel's **capitulation**[1]. Mrs. Van Daan and the latter very thick, **flirtations**[2], kisses and friendly little laughs. Dussel is beginning to get longings for women. The Fifth Army has taken Rome. The city has been **spared**[3] **devastation**[4] by both armies and air forces, and is undamaged. Very few vegetables and potatoes. Bad weather. Heavy **bombardments**[5] against the French coast and Pas de Calais continue.

Yours, Anne

# Tuesday, 6 June, 1944

Dear Kitty,

"This is D-day" came the announcement over the English news and quite rightly, "this is *the* day." The invasion has begun!

The English gave the news at eight o'clock this morning: Calais, Boulogne, Le Havre, and Cherbourg, also the Pas de Calais (as usual), were heavily bombarded. Moreover, as a safety measure for all occupied territories, all people who live within a **radius**[6] of thirty-five kilometers from the coast are warned to be prepared for bombardments. If possible, the English will drop **pamphlets**[7] one hour beforehand.

According to German news, English parachute troops have landed on the French coast, English landing craft are in battle with the German Navy, says the B.B.C.

We discussed it over the "Annexe" breakfast at nine o'clock: Is this just a trial landing like Dieppe two years ago?

---

1.  Capitulation - the action of capitulating
2.  Flirtations - casual interest
3.  Spared - excepted
4.  Devastation - destroy, ruin
5.  Bombardment - continuous bombing
6.  Radius - surrounding
7.  Pamphlets - small leaflets

English broadcast in German, Dutch, French, and other languages at ten o'clock: "The invasion has begun!" that means the "real" invasion. English broadcast in German at eleven o'clock, speech by the Supreme Commander, General Dwight Eisenhower.

The English news at twelve o'clock in English: "This is D-day." General Eisenhower said to the French people: "Stiff fighting will come now, but after this the victory. The year 1944 is the, year of complete victory, good luck."

English news in English at one o'clock (translated): 11,000 planes stand ready, and are flying to and fro non stop, landing troops and attacking behind the lines; 4000 landing boats, plus small craft, *are* landing troops and materiel between Cherbourg and Le Havre incessantly[8]. English and American troops are already engaged in hard fighting. Speeches by Gerbrandy, by the Prime Minister of Belgium, King Haakon of Norway, De Gaulle of France, the King of England, and last, but not least, Churchill.

Great commotion[9] in the "Secret Annexe"! Would the long-awaited liberation that has been talked of so much, but which still seems too wonderful, too much like a fairy tale, ever come true? Could we be granted victory this year, 1944? We don't know yet, but hope is revived[10] within us; it gives us fresh courage, and makes us strong again. Since we must put up bravely with all the fears, privations[11], and sufferings, the great thing now is to remain calm and steadfast[12]. Now more than ever we must clench[13] our teeth and not cry out. France, Russia, Italy, and Germany, too, can all cry out and give vent to their misery, but we haven't the right to do that yet!

---

8. Incessantly - difficult to reach
9. Commotion - a state of confuse and noisy disturbance
10. Revived - restore to life
11. Privations - lack of food
12. Steadfast - resolutely or dutifully firm and unwavering
13. Clench - press together tightly

Oh, Kitty, the best part of the invasion is that I have the feeling that friends are approaching. We have been oppressed by those terrible Germans for so long, they have had their knives so at our throats, that the thought of friends and delivery fills us with confidence!

Now it doesn't concern the Jews any more, no, it concerns Holland and all occupied Europe. Perhaps, Margot says, I may yet be able to go back to school in September or October.

PS: I'll keep you up to date with all the latest news!

Yours, Anne

## Friday, 9 June, 1944

Dear Kitty,

Super news of the invasion. The Allies have taken Bayeux, a small village on the French coast, and are now fighting for Caen. It's obvious that they intend to cut off the **peninsular**[14] where Cherbourg lies. Every evening war correspondents give news from the battle front, telling us of the difficulties, courage, and **enthusiasm**[15] of the army; they manage to get hold of the most **incredible**[16] stories. Also some of the wounded who are already back in England again came to the microphone. The air force are up all the time in spite of the miserable weather. We heard over the B.B.C. that Churchill wanted to land with the troops on D-day, however, Eisenhower and the other generals managed to get him out of the idea. Just think of it, what pluck he has for such an old man-he must be seventy at least.

The excitement here has worn off a bit; still, we're hoping that the war will be over at the end of this year. It'll be about time too! Mrs. Van Daan's grizzling is absolutely unbearable, now she can't any longer drive us crazy over the invasion, she **nags**[17] us the whole day long about the bad weather? It really would be nice to dump her in a bucket of cold water and put her up in the loft.

---

14. Peninsular - a long narrow piece of land
15. Enthusiasm - intense enjoyment
16. Incredible - unbelievable
17. Nags - constantly asks

The whole of the "Secret Annexe" except Van Daan and Peter have read the trilogy Hungarian *Rhapsody*. This book deals with the life history of the composer, virtuoso, and child prodigy, Franz Liszt. It is a very interesting book, but in my opinion there is a bit too much about women in it. In his time Liszt was not only the greatest and most famous pianist, but also the greatest ladies' man—right up to the age of seventy. He lived with the Duchess Marie d'Agould, Princess Caroline Sayn-Wittgenstein, the dancer Lola Montez, the pianist Agnes Kingworth, the pianist Sophie Menter, Princess Olga Janina, Baroness Olga Meyendorff, the actress Lilla what's-her-name, etc., etc. it is just endless. The parts of the book that deal with music and art are much more interesting. Among those mentioned are Schumann, Clara Wieck, Hector

Berlioz, Johannes Brahms, Beethoven, Joachim, Richard Wagner,- Hans von Bulow, Anton Rubinstein, Frederic Chopin, Victor Hugo, Honore de Balzac, Hiller, Hummel, Czerny, Rossini, Cherubini, Paganini, Mendelssohn, etc., etc.

Liszt was personally a fine man, very generous, and modest about himself though exceptionally vain. He helped everyone, his art was everything to him, he was mad about cognac[18] and about women, could not bear to see tears, was a gentleman, would never refuse to do anyone a favor, didn't care about money, loved religious liberty and world freedom.

Yours, Anne

# Tuesday, 13 June, 1944

Dear Kitty,

Another birthday has gone by, so now I'm fifteen. I received quite a lot of presents.

All five parts of Sprenger's *History of Art*, a set of underwear, a handkerchief, two bottles of yoghourt, a pot of jam, a spiced gingerbread cake, and a book on botany from Mummy and Daddy,

18.   Cognac - a high quality brandy

a double bracelet from Margot, a book from the Van Daans, sweet peas from Dussel, sweets and exercise books from Miep and Elli and, the high spot of all, the book Maria *Theresa* and three slices of full-cream cheese from Kraler. A lovely bunch of peonies from Peter, the poor boy took a lot of trouble to try and find something, but didn't have any luck.

There's still excellent news of the invasion, in spite of the wretched weather, countless gales, heavy rains, and high seas.

Yesterday Churchill, Smuts, Eisenhower, and Arnold visited French villages which have been conquered and liberated. The **torpedo**[19] boat that Churchill was in shelled the coast. He appears, like so many men, not to know what fear is-makes me **envious**[20]!

It's difficult for us to judge from our secret **redoubt**[21] how people outside have reacted to the news. Undoubtedly people are pleased that the idle English have rolled up their sleeves and are doing something at last. Any Dutch people who still look down on the English, **scoff**[22] at England and her government of old gentlemen, call the English cowards, and yet hate the Germans deserve a good shaking. Perhaps it would put some sense into their **woolly**[23] brains.

I hadn't had a period for over two months, but it finally started again on Saturday. Still, in spite of all the unpleasantness and bother, I'm glad it hasn't failed me any longer.

Yours, Anne

---

19. Torpedo - a kind of a missile
20. Envious - a resentful longing aroused by another's possessions
21. Redoubt - secret place
22. Scoff - speak about something in a scornfully derisive way
23. Woolly - distorted

# Wednesday, 14 June, 1944

Dear Kitty,

My head is haunted by so many wishes and thoughts, **accusations**[24] and **reproaches**[25]. I'm really not as **conceited**[26] as so many people seem to think, I know my own faults and shortcomings better than anyone, but the difference is that 1 also know that I want to improve, shall improve, and have already improved a great deal.

Why is it then, I so often ask myself, that everyone still thinks I'm so terribly knowing and forward? Am I so knowing? Is it that I really am, or that maybe the others aren't? That sounds queer, I realize now, but I shan't cross out the last sentence, because it really isn't so crazy. Everyone knows that Mrs. Van Daan, one of my chief accusers, is unintelligent. I might as well put it plainly and say "stupid." Stupid people usually can't take it if others do better than they do.

Mrs. Van Daan thinks I'm stupid because I'm not quite so lacking in intelligence as she is, she thinks I'm forward because she's even more so; she thinks my dresses are too short, because hers are even shorter. And that's also the reason that she thinks I'm knowing, because she's twice as bad about joining in over subjects she knows absolutely nothing about. But one of my favorite sayings is "There's no smoke without fire," and I readily admit that I'm knowing.

Now the trying part about me is that I **criticize**[27] and scold myself far more than anyone else does. Then if Mummy adds her bit of advice the pile of **sermons**[28] becomes so **insurmountable**[29] that in my despair I become rude and start **contradicting**[30] and then, of course, the old wellknown Anne watchword comes back: "No one understands me!" This phrase sticks in my mind; I know it sounds silly, yet there is some truth in it. I oiten accuse myself to such an

---

24. Accusations - a charge or claim
25. Reproaches - accuse someone of
26. Conceited - excessively proud
27. Criticize - indicate faults
28. Sermons - a talk on a religious or moral subject
29. Insurmountable - too great to overcome
30. Contradicting - opposite statements

extent that I simply long for a word of comfort, for someone who could give me sound advice and also draw out some of my real self, but, alas, I keep on looking, but I haven't found anyone yet.

I know that you'll immediately think of Peter, won't you. Kit? It's like this: Peter loves me not as a lover but as a friend and grows more affectionate every day. But what is the mysterious something that holds us both back? I don't understand it myself. Sometimes 1 think that my terrible longing for him was exaggerated, yet that's really not it, because if I don't go up to see him for two days, then I long for him more desperately than ever before. Peter is good and he's a darling, but still there's no denying that there's a lot about him that disappoints me. Especially his dislike of religion and all his talk about food and various other things don't appeal to me. Yet I feel quite convinced that we shall never quarrel now that we've made that straightforward agreement together. Peter is a peace loving person, he's tolerant and gives in very easily. He lets me say a lot of things to him that he would never accept from his mother, he tries most **persistently**[31] to keep his things in order. And yet why should he keep his **innermost**[32] self to himself and why am I never allowed there? By nature he is more closed-up than I am, I agree, but I know—and from my own experience—that at some time or other even the most uncommunicative people long just as much, if not more, to find someone in whom they can **confide**[33].

Both Peter and I have spent our most **meditative**[34] years in the "Secret Annexe." We often discuss the future, the past, and the present, but as I've already said, I still seem to miss the real thing and yet I know that it's there.

Yours, Anne

---

31. Persistently - continuous persistent
32. Innermost - most private
33. Confide - disclose
34. Meditative - a discourse expressing thoughts on a subject

# Thursday, 15 June, 1944

Dear Kitty,

I wonder if it's because I haven't been able to poke my nose outdoors for so long that I've grown so crazy about everything to do with nature? I can perfectly well remember that there was a time when a deep blue sky, the song of the birds, moonlight and flowers could never have kept me **spellbound**[35]. That's changed since I've been here.

At Whitsun, for instance, when it was so warm, I stayed awake on purpose until half past eleven one evening in order to have a good look at the moon for once by myself. Alas, the sacrifice was all in vain, as the moon gave far too much light and I didn't dare risk opening a window. Another time, some months ago now, I happened to be upstairs one evening when the window was open. I didn't go downstairs until the window had to be shut. The dark, rainy evening, the gale, the **scudding**[36] clouds held me **entirely**[37] in their power, it was the first time in a year and a half that I'd seen the night face to face. After that evening my longing to see it again was greater than my fear of burglars, rate, and raids on the house. I was downstairs all by myself and looked outside through the windows int he kitchen and the private office. Lot of people are fond of nature, many sleep outdoors occasionally, and people in prisons and hospitals long for the day when they will be tree to enjoy the beauties of nature, but few are so shut away and isolated from that which can be shared alike by rich and poor. It's not imagination on my part when I say that to look up at the sky, the clouds, the moon, and the stars makes me calm and patient. It's a better medicine than either valerian or bromine. Mother Nature makes me humble and prepared to face every blow courageously.

---

35. Spellbound – complete attention
36. Scudding – moving fast in a straight line
37. Entirely – completely

Alas, it has had to be that I am only able-except on a few rare occasions—to look at nature through dirty net curtains hanging before very dusty windows. And it's no pleasure looking through these any longer, because nature is just the one thing that really must be **unadulterated**[38].

Yours, Anne

# Friday, 16 June, 1944

Dear Kitty,

New problems: Mrs. Van Daan is desperate, talks about a bullet through her head, prison, hanging, and suicide. She's jealous that Peter **confides**[39] in me and not her. She's offended that Dussel doesn't enter into her flirtations with him, as she'd hoped, afraid that her husband is smoking all the furcoat money away, she quarrels, uses abusive language, cries, pities herself, laughs, and then starts a fresh quarrel again. What on earth can one do with such a foolish, blubbering specimen? No one takes her seriously, she hasn't any character, and she grumbles to everyone. The worst of it is that it makes Peter rude, Mr. Van Daan irritable, and Mummy **cynical**[40]. Yes, it's a frightful situation! There's one golden rule to keep before you: laugh about everything and don't bother yourself about the others! It sounds selfish, but it's honestly the only cure for anyone who has to seek consolation in himself.

Kraler has received another call-up to go digging for four weeks. He's trying to get out of it with a doctor's certificate and a letter from the business. Koophuis wants to have an operation on his stomach. All private telephones were cut off at eleven o'clock yesterday.

Yours, Anne

---

38. Unadulterated – pure                    39. Confides – discloses
40. Cynical – contemtous

# Friday, 23 June, 1944

Dear Kitty,

Nothing special going on here. The English have begun their big attack on Cherbourg; according to Pim and Van Daan, we're sure to be free by October 10. The Russians are taking part in the campaign, and yesterday began their offensive near Vitebsk, it's exactly three years to a day since the Germans attacked. We've hardly got any potatoes; from now on *we're* going to count them out lor each person, then everyone knows what he's getting.

Yours, Anne

# Tuesday, 27 June, 1944

Dearest Kitty,

The mood has changed, everything's going wonderfully. Cherbourg, Vitebsk, and Sloben fell today. Lots of prisoners and booty. Now the English can land what they want now they've got a harbor, the whole Cotentin Peninsular three weeks after the English invasion! A tremendous achievement! In the three weeks since D-day not a day has gone by without rain and gales, both here and in France, but a bit of bad luck didn't prevent the English and Americans from showing their **enormous**[41] strength, and how! Certainly the "wonder weapon" is in full swing, but of what consequence are a few squibs apart from a bit of damage in England and pages full of it in the Boche newspapers? For that matter, when they really realize in "Bocheland" that the Bolshevists really are on the way, they'll get even more jittery.

All German women not in military service are being **evacuated**[42] to Groningen, Friesland, and Gelderland with their children. Mussert[1] has announced that if they get as far as here with the invasion hell put on a uniform. Does that old fatty want to do some fighting?

Mussert was the Dutch National Socialist leader.

---

41. Enormous – huge
42. Evacuated – removed from a place of danger to a safer place

He could have done so in Russia before now. Some time ago Finland turned down a peace offer, now the **negotiations**[43] have just been broken off again, they'll be sorry for it later, the silly fools!

How far do you think we'll be on July 27?

Yours, Anne

# Friday, 30 June, 1944

Dear Kitty,

**Bad weather, or bad weather at a stretch to the thirtieth** *of June.*[2] Isn't that well said! Oh yes, I have a **smattering**[44] of English already, just to show that I can. I'm reading *An Ideal Husband* with the aid of a dictionary. War going wonderfully! Bobroisk, Mogilef, and Orsa have fallen, lots of prisoners.

Everything's all right here and tempers are improving. The super optimists are triumphing. Elli has changed her hair style, Miep has the week off. That's the latest news.

Yours, Anne

---

43. Negotiations – discussion
44. Smattering – (here) little

## Think and Ink...

➢ In what ways does Anne's analysis of her own self and Peter? Justify her statement that her 'terrible longing' for peter was 'exaggerated'.

➢ Do you think that because she could not live in the outside reality Anne had been critical and analytical about everything? Why/Why not?

➢ Comment on the significance of Anne's remark – 'Nature is just the one thing that really must be unadulterated'.

## Text-Based Questions

• What was the situation at home and at the political level outside?

• What was the D-day ? What things were happening outside?

• How was hope revived within the people of the 'Secret Annexe'?

• What news does the evening war correspondent give?

• How did Anne analyse the trilogy 'Hungarian Rhapsody"?

• How was Anne's fifteenth birthday celebrated?

• What was Mrs. Van Daan's opinion about Anne?

• Why was Mrs. Van Daan desperate?

• How were things going on a cross the country?

• What circumstance prove that the super optimists are triumphing?

• What circumstances had changed for Anne since she had come to the Secret Annexe?

# Thursday, 6 July, 1944

Dear Kitty,

It strikes fear to my heart when Peter talks of later being a criminal, or of gambling; although it's meant as a joke, of course, it gives me the feeling that he's afraid of his own weakness. Again and again I hear from both Margot and Peter: "Yes, if I was as strong and **plucky**[1] as you are, if I always stuck to what I wanted, if I had such persistent energy- yes then ...!" I wonder if it's really a good quality not to let myself be **influenced**[2]. Is it really good to follow almost entirely my own conscience?

Quite honestly, I can't imagine how anyone can say: "I'm weak," and then remain so. After all, if you know it, why not fight against it, why not try to train your character? The answer was: "Because it's so much easier not to!" This reply rather discouraged me. Easy? Does that mean that a lazy, **deceitful**[3] life is an easy life? Oh no, that can't be true, it mustn't be true, people can so easily be tempted by **slackness**[4]... and by money. I thought for a long time about the best answer to give Peter, how to get him to believe in himself and, above all, to try and improve himself, I don't know whether my line of thought is right though, or not.

I've so often thought how lovely it would be to have someone's complete confidence, but now, now that I'm that far, I realize how difficult it is to think what the other person is thinking and then to find the right answer. More especially because the very ideas of "easy" and "money" are something entirely foreign and new to me. Peter's beginning to lean on me a bit and that mustn't happen under any circumstances. A type like Peter finds it difficult to stand on his own feet, but it's even harder to stand on your own feet as a conscious, living being. Because if you do, then it's twice as difficult to **steer**[5] a right path through the sea of problems and still remain constant through it all. I'm just **drifting**[6] around, have been searching for

---

1. Plucky - courageous   2. Influenced - effect   3. Deceitful - cheating
4. Slackness - laxness   5. Steer - guide   6. Drifting - moving slowly away

days, searching for a good argument against that terrible word "easy," something to settle it once and for all.

How can 1 make it clear to him that what appears easy and attractive will drag him down into the depths, depths where there is no comfort to be found, no friends and no beauty, depths from which it is almost impossible to raise oneself?

We all live, but we don't know the why or the wherefore. We all live with the object of being happy, our lives are all different and yet the same. We three have been brought up in good circles, we have the chance to learn, the possibility of attaining something, we have all reason to hope for much happiness, but... we must earn it for ourselves. And that is never easy. You must work and do good, not be lazy and gamble, if you wish to earn happiness. Laziness may *appear* attractive, but work gives satisfaction.

I can't understand people who don't like work, yet that isn't the case with Peter, he just hasn't got a fixed goal to ainr at, and he thinks he's too stupid and too inferior to achieve anything. Poor boy, he's never known what it feels like to make other people happy, and I can't teach him that either. He has no religion, scoffs at Jesus Christ, and swears, using the name of God, although I'm not orthodox either, it hurts me every time I see how **deserted**[7], how **scornful**[8], and how poor he really is.

People who have a religion should be glad, for not everyone has the gift of believing in heavenly things. You don't necessarily even have to be afraid of punishment after death, **purgatory**[9], hell, and heaven are things that a lot of people can't accept, but still a religion, it doesn't matter which, keeps a person on the right path. It isn't the fear of God but the upholding of one's own honor and conscience. How noble and good everyone could be if, every evening before falling asleep, they were to recall to their minds the events of the

7. Deserted - abandoned    8. Scornful - disdainful
9. Purgatory - in Roman Catholic theology the place where those who have died in a state of grace undergo limited torment to expiate their sins

whole day and consider exactly what has been good and bad. Then, without realizing it, you try to improve yourself at the start of each new day, of course, you achieve quite a lot in the course of time. Anyone can do this, it costs nothing and is certainly very helpful. Whoever doesn't know it must learn and find by experience that: "A quiet conscience makes one strong!"

Yours, Anne

## Saturday, 8 July, 1944

Dear Kitty,

The chief representative of the business, Mr. B., has been in Beverwijk and managed, just like that, to get strawberries at the auction sale.* They arrived here dusty, covered with sand, but in large quantities. No less than twenty-four trays for the office people and us. That very same evening we bottled six jars and made eight pots of jam. The next morning Miep wanted to make jam for the office people.

At half past twelve, no strangers in the house, front door bolted, trays fetched. Peter, Daddy, Van Daan **clattering**[10] on the stairs: Anne, get hot water; Margot, bring a bucket; all hands on **deck**[11]! I went into the kitchen, which was **chockfull**[12], with a queer feeling in my tummy, Miep, Elli, Koophuis, Henk, Daddy, Peter: the families in hiding and their supply **column**[13], all **mingling**[14] together, and in the middle of the day too!

People can't see in from outside because of the net curtains, but, even so, the loud voices and banging doors positively gave me the **jitters**[15]. Are we really supposed to be in hiding? That's what **flashed**[16] through my mind, and it gives one a very queer feeling to be able to

---

* It is compulsory in Holland for all growers to sell their produce at public auction.

| | |
|---|---|
| 10. Clattering - rattling sound | 11. Deck - the ground |
| 12. Chockfull - packed full to capacity | 13. Column - partition |
| 14. Mingling - mixing | 15. Jitters - extreme nervousness |
| 16. Flashed - shine in a bright way | |

appear in the world again. The pan was full, and I dashed upstairs again. The rest of the family was seated round our table in the kitchen busy **stalk-picking**[17]-at least that's what they were supposed to be doing; more went into mouths than into buckets. Another bucket would soon be required. Peter went to the downstairs kitchen again— the bell rang twice; the bucket stayed where it was. Peter tore upstairs, locked the cupboard door! We were kicking our heels **impatiently**[18], couldn't turn on a tap, even though the strawberries were only half washed, the rule is: "If anyone in the house, use no water, because of the noise," was strictly maintained.

At one o'clock Henk came and told us that it was the postman. Peter hurried downstairs again. Ting-a- ling... the bell, right about turn. I go and listen to see if I can hear anyone coming, first at our cupboard door and then creep to the top of the stairs. Finally Peter and I both lean over the **banisters**[19] like a couple of thieves, listening to the **din**[20] downstairs. No strange voices. Peter sneaks down, stops halfway, and calls out: "Elli!" No answer, one more: "Elli!" Peter's voice is drowned by the din in the kitchen. He goes right down and into the kitchen. I stand looking down **tensely**[21]. "Get upstairs at once. Peter, the accountant is here, clear out!" It was Koophuis speaking. Peter comes upstairs sighing, the cupboard door closes. Finally Kraler arrives at half past one. "Oh, dearie me I see nothing but strawberries, strawberries at breakfast, strawberries stewed by Miep, I smell strawberries, must have a rest from them and go upstairs—what is being washed up here... strawberries."

The remainder are being bottled. In the evening: two jars unsealed. Paddy quickly makes them into jam. The next morning: two more unsealed and four in the afternoon. Van Daan hadn't brought them to the right temperature for **sterilizing**[22]. Now Daddy makes jam every evening.

---

| | |
|---|---|
| 17. Stalk-picking - a vegetable | 18. Impatiently - restlessly |
| 19. Banisters - railing | 20. Din - a loud noise |
| 21. Tensely - in a tense manner | 22. Sterilizing - disinfecting |

We eat strawberries with our porridge, skimmed milk with strawberries, bread and butter with strawberries, strawberries for dessert, strawberries with sugar, strawberries with sand. For two whole days strawberries and nothing but strawberries, then the supply was finished or in bottles and under lock and key.

"I say, Anne," Margot calls out, "the greengrocer on the corner has let us have some green peas, nineteen pounds." "That's nice of him," I replied. And it certainly is, but oh, the work . . . ugh!

"You've all got to help shelling peas on Saturday morning," Mummy announced when we were at table. And, sure enough, the big enamel pan duly appeared this morning, filled to the brim. Shelling peas is a boring job, but you ought to try "skinning" the pods. I don't think many people realize how soft and tasty the pod is when the skin on the inside has been removed. However, an even greater advantage is that the quantity which can be eaten is about triple the amount of when one only eats the peas. It's an exceptionally precise, **finicky**[23] job, pulling out this skin; perhaps it's all right for pedantic dentists or precise office workers, but for an impatient teenager like me, it's frightful. We began at half past nine, I got up at half past ten, at half past eleven I sat down again. This **refrain**[24] hummed in my ears: bend the top, pull the skin, remove the string, throw out the pod, etc., etc., they dance before my eyes, green, green, green maggots, strings, rotten pods, green, green, green. Just for the sake of doing something, I chatter the whole morning, any nonsense that comes into my head, make everyone laugh, and bore them stiff. But every string that I pull makes me feel more certain that I never, never want to be just a housewife only!

We finally have breakfast at twelve o'clock, but from half past twelve until quarter past one we've got to go skinning pods again. I'm just about seasick when I stop, the others a bit too. I go and sleep till four o'clock, but I'm still upset by those wretched peas.

Yours, Anne

---

**23.** Finicky - fussy                    **24.** Refrain - restrict

# Saturday, 15 July, 1944

Dear Kitty,

We have had a book from the library with the challeng title of: *What Do You Think of the Modern Young Girl?* I want to talk about this subject today.

The author of this book criticizes "the youth of today" from top to toe, without; however, **condemning**[25] the whole the young **brigade**[26] as "incapable of anything good." On the contrary, she is rather of the opinion that if young people wished, they have it in their hands to make a bigger, more beautiful and better world, but that they occupy themselves with **superficial**[27] things, without giving a thought to real beauty.

In some passages the writer gave me very much the feeling she was directing her criticisms at me, and that's why I want to lay myself completely bare to you for once and defend myself against this attack.

I have one outstanding trait in my character, which must strike anyone who knows me for any length of time, and that is my knowledge of myself. I can watch myself and my actions, just like an outsider. The Anne of every day I can face entirely without prejudice, without making excuses for her, and watch what's good what's bad about her. This "self-consciousness" **haunts**[28] me, and every time I open my mouth I know as soon as I've spoken whether "that ought to have been different" or "that was right as it was." There are so many things about myself that I condemn, I couldn't begin, to name them all. I understand more and more how true Daddy's words were when he said: "All children must look after their own upbringing." Parents can only give good advice or put them on the right paths, but the final forming of a person's character lies in their own hands.

In addition to this, I have lots of courage, I always feel so strong and as if I can bear a great deal, I feel so free and so' young! I was glad

---

25. Condemning - disapproving          26. Brigade- a subdivision of an army
27. Superficial - apparent rather than actual **28.** Haunts - obsess

when I first realized it, because I don't think I shall easily bow down before the blows that **inevitably**[29] come to everyone.

But I've talked about these things so often before. Now I want to come to the chapter of "Daddy and Mummy don't understand me." Daddy and Mummy have always thoroughly spoiled me, were sweet to me, **defended**[30] me, and have done all that parents could do. And yet I've felt so terribly lonely for a long time, so left out, neglected, and misunderstood. Daddy tried all he could to check my **rebellious**[31] spirit, but it was no use, I have cured myself, by seeing for myself what was wrong in my behavior and keeping it before my eyes.

How is it that Daddy was never any support to me in my struggle, why did he completely miss the mark when he wanted to offer me a helping hand? Daddy tried the wrong methods, he always talked to me as a child wha was going through difficult phases. It sounds crazy, because Daddy's the only one who has always taken me into his confidence, and no one but Daddy has given me the feeling that I'm sensible. But there's one thing he's omitted: you see, he hasn't realized that for me the fight to get on top was more important than all else. I didn't want to hear about "symptoms of your age" or "other girls," or "it wears off by itself." I didn't want to be treated as a girl-like-all-others, but as Anne-on-her-own-merits. Pim didn't understand that. For that matter, I can't **confide**[32] in anyone, unless they tell me a lot about themselves, and as 1 know very little about Pim, I don't feel that I can tread upon more intimate ground with him. Pim always takes up the older, fatherly attitude, tells me that he too has had similar passing tendencies. But still he's not able to feel with me like a friend, however hard he tries. These things have made me never mention my views on life nor my well-considered theories to anyone but my diary and, occasionally, to Margot. I **concealed**[33] from Daddy everything that **perturbed**[34] me; I never shared my ideals with him. I was aware of the fact that I was pushing him away from me.

---

| | |
|---|---|
| 29. Inevitably - unavoidable | 30. Defended - resisted |
| 31. Rebellious - revolting | 32. Confide - disclose |
| 33. Concealed - hidden | 34. Perturbed - disturbed |

I couldn't do anything else. I have acted entirely according to my feelings, but I have acted in the way that was best for my peace of mind. Because I should completely lose my **repose**[35] and self-confidence, which I have built up so **shakily**[36], if, at this stage, I were to accept criticisms of my half-completed task. And I can't do that even from Pim, although it sounds very hard, for not only have I not shared my secret thoughts with Pim but I have often pushed him even further from me, by my **irritability**[37].

This is a point that I think a lot about: why is it that Pim annoys me? So much so that I can hardly beai him teaching me, that his affectionate ways strike me as being put on, that I want to be left in peace and would really prefer it if he dropped me a bit, until I felt more certain in my attitude towards him? Because I still have a **gnawing**[38] feeling of guilt over that horrible letter that I dared to write him when I was so wound up. Oh, how hard it is to be really strong and brave in every way!

Yet this was not my greatest disappointment; no, I **ponder**[39] far more over Peter than Daddy. I know very well that I conquered him instead of he conquering me. I created an image of him in my mind, pictured him as a quiet, **sensitive**[40], lovable boy, who needed affection and friendship. I needed a living person to whom I could pour out my heart, I wanted a friend who'd help to put me on the right road. I achieved what I wanted, and, slowly but surely, I drew him towards me. Finally, when I had made him feel friendly, it automatically developed into an **intimacy**[41] which, on second thought, I don't think I ought to have allowed.

We talked about the most private things, and yet up till now we have never touched on those things that filled, and still fill, my heart and soul. I still don't know quite what to make of Peter, is he **superficial**[42], or does he still feel shy, even of me? But dropping

---

35. Repose - calmness    36. Shakily - trembling    37. Irritability - fretfulness
38. Gnawing - continuous, constant worry    39. Ponder - meditate
40. Sensitive - capable or perceiving with a sense or senses
41. Intimacy - closeness    42. Superficial - careless

that, I committed one error in my desire to make a real friendship: I switched over and tried to get at him by developing it into a more intimate relation, whereas I should have **explored**[43] all other possibilities. He longs to be loved and I can see that he's beginning to be more and more in love with me. He gets satisfaction out of our meetings, whereas they just have the effect of making me want to try it out with him again. And yet I don't seem able to touch on the subjects that I'm so longing to bring out into the daylight. I drew Peter towards me, far more than he realizes. Now he clings to me, and for the time being, I don't see any way of shaking him off and putting him on his own feet. When I realized that he could not be a friend for my understanding, I thought I would at least try to lift him up out of his narrow-mindedness and make him do something with his youth.

"For in its **innermost**[44] depths youth is lonelier than old age." I read this saying in some book and I've always remembered it, and found it to be true. Is it true then that grownups have a more difficult time here than we do? No. I know it isn't. Older people have formed their opinions about everything, and don't waver before they act. It's twice as hard for us young ones to hold our ground, and maintain our opinions, in a time when all ideals are being shattered and destroyed, when people are showing their worst side, and do not know whether to believe in truth and right and God.

Anyone who claims that the older ones have a more difficult time here certainly doesn't realize to what extent our problems weigh down on us, problems for which we are probably much too young, but which thrust themselves upon us continually, until, after a long time, we think we've found a solution, but the solution doesn't seem able to resist the facts which reduce it to nothing again. That's the difficulty in these times: ideals, dreams, and cherished hopes rise within us, only to meet the horrible truth and be shattered.

---

43. Explored - discovered　　　　　　　　44. Innermost - inmost

It's really a wonder that I haven't dropped all my ideals, because they seem so absurd and impossible to carry out. Yet I keep them, because in spite of everything I still believe that people are really good at heart. I simply can't build up my hopes on a foundation consisting of confusion, misery, and death. I see the world gradually being turned into a **wilderness**[45], I hear the ever approaching thunder, which will destroy us too, I can feel the sufferings of millions and yet, if I look up into the heavens, I think that it will all come right, that this cruelty too will end, and that peace and tranquillity will return again. I, in the meantime, I must **uphold**[46] my ideals, for perhaps the time will come when I shall be able to carry them out.

Yours Anne

# Friday, 21 July. 1944

Dear Kitty,

Now I am getting really hopeful, now things are going well at last. Yes, really, they're going well! Super news! An attempt has been made on Hitler's life and not even by Jewish communists or English capitalists this time, but by a proud German general, and what's more, he's a Count, and still quite young. The Fuhrer's life was saved by Divine Providence and, unfortunately, he managed to get off with just a few scratches and burns. A few officers and generals who were with him have been killed and wounded. The chief culprit was shot.

Anyway, it certainly shows that there are lots of officers and generals who are sick of the war and would like to see Hitler **descend**[47] into a bottomless pit. When they've disposed of Hitler, their aim is to establish a military **dictator**[48], who will make peace with the Allies, then they intend to **rearm**[49] and tart another war in about twenty years' time. Perhaps the Divine Power **tarried**[50] on purpose in getting him out of the way, because it would be much easier and more

---

45. Wilderness - jungle      46. Uphold - preserve
47. Descend - go down      48. Dictator - speaker
49. Rearm - fortify      50. Tarried - to wait

advantageous to the Allies if the **impeccable**[51] Germans kill each other off; it'll lake less work for the Russians and the English and they'll be able to begin **rebuilding**[52] their own towns all the sooner.

But still, we're not that far yet, and I don't want to **anticipate**[53] the glorious events too soon. Still, you must have noticed, this is all sober reality and that I'm in quite a matter-of-fact mood today for once, I'm not **jabbering**[54] about high ideals. And what's more. Hitler has even been so kind as to announce to his faithful, devoted people that from now on everyone in the armed forces must obey the Gestapo, and that any soldier who knows that one of his superiors was involved in this low, cowardly attempt upon his life may shoot the same on the spot, without **courtmartial**[55].

What a perfect **shambles**[56] it's going to be. little Johnnies feet begin hurting him during a long march, he's snapped at by his boss, the officer, Johnnie grabs his rifle and cries out: "You wanted to murder the Fuhrer, so there's your reward." One bang and the proud chief who dared to tick off little Johnnie has passed into **eternal**[57] life (or is it eternal death?). In the end, whenever an officer finds himself up against a soldier, or having to take the lead, he'll be wetting his pants from anxiety, because the soldiers will dare to say more than they do. Do you gather a bit what 1 mean, or have 1 been **skipping**[58] too much from one subject to another? I can't help it; the **prospect**[59] that 1 may be sitting on school benches next October makes me feel far too cheerful to be logical! Oh, dearie me, hadn't 1 just told you that 1 didn't want to be too hopeful? Forgive me, they haven't given me the name "little bundle of **contradictions**[60]" all for nothing!

Yours, Anne

---

51. Impeccable - perfect

52. Rebuilding - reconstruction

53. Anticipate - expect

54. Jabbering - babble, chatter

55. Courtmartial - removal from army services

56. Shambles - disorder

57. Eternal - everlasting

58. Skipping - jumping

59. Prospect - chance

60. Contradictions - oppositeness

# Tuesday, 1 August, 1944

Dear Kitty,

"Little bundle of contradictions." That's how I ended my last letter and that's how I'm goingio begin this one. "A little bundle of contradictions", can you tell me exactly what it is? What does contradiction mean? Like so many words, it can mean two things, contradiction from without and contradiction from within.

The first is the ordinary "not giving in easily, always knowing best, getting in the last word," *enfin,* all the unpleasant qualities for which I'm **renowned**[61]. The second nobody knows about, that's my own secret.

I've already told you before that I have, as it were, a dual personality. One half embodies my **exuberant**[62] cheerfulness, making fun of everything, *my* high spiritedness, and above all, the way I take everything lightly. This includes not taking **offense**[63] at a **flirtation**[64], a kiss, an **embrace**[65], a dirty joke. This side is usually lying in wait and pushes away the other, which is *much* better, deeper and purer. You must realize that no one knows Anne's better side and that's why most people find me so **insufferable**[66].

Certainly I'm a **giddy**[67] clown for one afternoon, but then everyone's had enough *of me* for another month. Really, it's just the same as a love film is for deep thinking people, simply a diversion, amusing just for once, something which is soon forgotten, not bad, but certainly not good. I loathe having to tell you this, but why shouldn't I, if I know it's true anyway? My lighter superficial side will always be too quick for the deeper side of me and that's why it will always win. You can't imagine how often I've already tried to push this Anne away, to cripple her, to hide her, because after all,

---

61. Renowned - famous
62. Exuberant - high spirited
63. Offense - crime
64. Flirtation - temporary romance
65. Embrace - hug
66. Insufferable - intolerable
67. Giddy - dizzy

she's only half of what's called Anne: but it doesn't work and I know, too, why it doesn't work.

I'm awfully scared that everyone who knows me as I always am will discover that I have another side, a finer and better side. I'm afraid they'll laugh at me, think I'm ridiculous and sentimental, not take me seriously. I'm used to not being taken seriously but it's only the "lighthearted" Anne that's used to it and can bear it; the "deeper" Anne is too frail for it. Sometimes, if I really compel the good Anne to take the stage for a quarter of an hour, she simply **shrivels**[68] up as soon as she has to speak, and lets Anne number one take over, and before I realize it, she has disappeared.

Therefore, the nice Anne is never present in company, has not appeared one single time so far, but almost always predominates when we're alone. I know exactly how I'd like to be, how I am too ... inside. But, alas, I'm only like that for myself. And perhaps that's why, no, I'm sure it's the reason why I say I've got a happy nature within and why other people think I've got a happy nature without. I am guided by the pure Anne within, but outside I'm nothing but a frolicsome little goat who's broken loose.

As I've already said, I never utter my real feelings about anything and that's how I've acquired the name of chaser-after-boys, flirt, know-all, reader of love stories/The cheerful Anne laughs about it, gives cheeky answers, shrugs her shoulders indifferently, behaves as if she doesn't care, but, oh dearie me, the quiet Anne's reactions are just the opposite. If I'm to be quite honest, then I must admit that it does hurt me, that I try terribly hard to change myself, but that I'm always fighting against a more powerful enemy.

A voice sobs within me; "There you are, that's what's become of you: you're **uncharitable**[69], you look **supercilious**[70] and **peevish**[71], people dislike you and all because you *won't listen to the* advice given

---

68.  Shrivels – shrinks
69.  Uncharitable – ungenerous, stingy
70.  Supercilious – haughty
71.  Peevish – pettish

you by your own better half." Oh, I would like to listen, but it doesn't work; if I'm quiet and serious, everyone thinks it's a new comedy and then I have to get out of it by turning"it into a joke, not to mention my own family, who are sure to think I'm ill, make me swallow pills for headaches and nerves, feel my neck and my head *to see* whether I'm running a temperature, ask if I'm **constipated**[72] and criticize me for being in a bad mood. I can't keep that up: if I'm watched to that extent, I start by getting **snappy**[73], then unhappy, and finally I twist my heart round again, so that the bad is on the outside and the good is on the inside and keep on trying to find a way of becoming what I would so like to be and what I could be, if... there weren't any other people living in the world.

Yours, Anne

---

72. Constipated – stiff
73. Snappy – lively, energetic.

## Think and Ink...

➤ What sort of a boy is Peter?

➤ According to Anne, though her father had defended her, he had not been friendly towards her? What arguments does Anne place to strength this view point?

➤ Anne says that she had been a self made girl. What truth in her prove this?

➤ Do you think Anne has come out of her infatuation towards Peter? What thoughts of Anne exhibit this?

➤ Anne is a representative of an ideal youth, cherishing hopes and dreams – Elucidate this idea.

➤ Anne says she has a dual personality. Of the two, who do you think is lovable? Why?

➤ The diary of Anne presents her mental growth, from being an innocent, fun loving girl, to a thoughtful, matured girl. Analyse the turning points in her life that led to this transformation in her.

## Text-Based Questions

• Why was Peter showing desperation? Why could not Anne influence him?

• What arguments does Anne place for hark work and happiness?

• How did Peter show himself to be a deserted, scornful, spoilt boy?

• How do people who have a religion are advantageous than those who don't have?

• How were the family occupied with strawberries and greenpear?

• What outstanding trait in her character does Anne boast about?

• How had Anne's self analysis alien improved her character?

• What thing had Anne's father failed to realize about her?

• What happened to Hitler?

• Why according to Anne, did the divine power save Hitler?

• Was Anne ready to go to school? Why?